THE
STOLEN
KINGDOM

ALSO BY JILLIAN BOEHME

Stormrise

THE
STOLEN
KINGDOM

JILLIAN BOEHME

A TOM DOHERTY ASSOCIATES BOOK   TOR TEEN   NEW YORK

THE STOLEN KINGDOM

Copyright © 2021 by Jill Schafer Boehme

A Tor Teen Book
Published by Tom Doherty Associates
120 Broadway
New York, NY 10271

www.tor-forge.com

Tor® is a registered trademark of Macmillan Publishing Group, LLC.

The Library of Congress Cataloging-in-Publication Data
is available upon request.

ISBN 978-1-250-29882-9 (hardcover)
ISBN 978-1-250-29883-6 (ebook)

Our books may be purchased in bulk for promotional, educational,
or business use. Please contact your local bookseller or the Macmillan Corporate
and Premium Sales Department at 1-800-221-7945, extension 5442,
or by email at MacmillanSpecialMarkets@macmillan.com.

First Edition: March 2021

Printed in the United States of America

0 9 8 7 6 5 4 3 2 1

For Eric.
Forever.

THE
STOLEN
KINGDOM

1

MARALYTH

I crushed the dried sage between my fingertips and added it to the bubbling stew, breathing deeply of my favorite herb. Everything green and growing sang music to my soul. Music I knew, by now, nobody else could hear. It was the only thing that made long hours in the kitchen bearable. Barely.

"Is that stewed quail?" My brother Nestar sidled past me to grab the tray of plates and utensils that sat waiting on the counter behind me, his dark curls tumbling across his face as always.

"More stew than quail." I lifted my chin toward the tray. "I can bring those."

"I've got them. Plates on the table will tell the men the food isn't far behind."

"It's nearly ready," I said, the words tiresome and familiar on my lips.

"You're fine, Mara." Nestar flashed me an understanding look as he left, though his words held the harder edge that had been growing lately.

I gave the stew a final stir and started to spoon it into the large tureen that would empty quickly at the hands of the vineyard workers I fed every day. Graylaern Vineyards, run by my father and all the Graylaerns before him, was the most famous winery in Perin Faye. I'd grown up running up and down the rows of vines, and sun-warmed grapes had been sweet on my tongue since I'd first eaten solid food. I wished I could spend most of my time tending the vines instead of behind pots of stew.

Mother had been so graceful in the kitchen, never flustered and seldom showing signs of wear, unlike the splattered apron around my own waist. She'd taught me as much as my meandering mind had allowed her—how to slice carrots thin, to stretch them; how to season a soup so no one would notice how scant the meat was. The workers would smile at me when I brought napkins or knives or wooden bowls of roasted corn to the table—little Mara, her mother's shadow.

I never wanted to be her shadow, though. Her own was long and dark, and she wanted me to hide in it. "The world beyond our vineyards can swallow you before you catch your next breath," she would say. "Your life is here, where you are safe and needed."

I didn't mind feeling safe, but being "needed" in the kitchen didn't make my heart dance when I lifted my head from the pillow each morning. I knew our vineyards as well as Poppa did, and better than Nestar. More than anything, I wanted to be out there with the workers. When Poppa wasn't there, they listened to me. Asked my advice and came to me to settle their petty disputes. They didn't know I whispered to the grapes to make them ripen plump and juicy. They never saw my hands banishing rot from vines before death took hold.

Mother had warned me long ago never to speak of the dark magic that came unbidden, and especially never to entertain it.

"No good comes from dark thoughts, Mara," she'd said whenever she sensed my mind was wandering places she didn't want it to go. And then she would hand me a ball of dough to pinch into biscuits.

It had been almost two years since she had breathed her last, and I was more convinced than ever that I could never take her place. And that I didn't want to.

Gravy splashed my hands as I bumped the door open with my hip, and I flinched. An appreciative murmur arose from the men seated at the long table near our house; I set the tureen on the table before turning back toward the kitchen.

"Smells like heaven, Maralyth!" Kenton, Poppa's assistant, was always quick to compliment me. His gray-whiskered face crinkled in a smile.

I smiled back. "The credit's yours, for bringing the quail." Meat and fowl were hardest to come by.

I went to fetch the roasted root vegetables and fresh-baked bread, Nestar close behind me.

"Honestly, I don't need your help," I said, cutting him off as he reached for the steaming vegetables.

"It's almost half an hour past noon. I'm just trying to help."

"Has anyone complained?" I gave up on the vegetables and grabbed the bread instead.

"Of course not. They're grateful."

"And impatient."

"Hungry," Nestar said. "They're hungry, that's all."

"Well, I'm feeding them." I hooked the butter crock with one finger and slid it onto the top loaf of bread, steadying it with my chin.

"Mara." Nestar slid in front of me, blocking the door. "It doesn't have to be this lavish every day. Bread and cheese fills bellies just as well."

My insides tightened, ready to snap. "Mother never would have served that."

"You're not Mother."

"Thanks for the reminder." I nudged him out of my way and waited for him to open the door so I wouldn't drop something.

He sighed. "Maybe start a little earlier, then?"

"When I start telling you what to do in the vineyards, you can tell me what to do in the kitchen."

"You *do* tell me what to do in the vineyards."

But I ignored him and presented the bread at the table as though it were grand prize. Poppa appeared around the corner of the house just then; I caught his eye, but his smile lacked its usual brightness.

Not that it had been all that bright since Mother died.

"Join us, Doreck!" several of the workers called.

But Poppa raised his hand and kept walking. "In a minute! I'm looking for these two." He motioned for Nestar and me to follow him to the front of the house.

I checked to see that I'd remembered to lay out knives for spreading the butter, then followed Nestar and Poppa. The glorious rows of grapes spread before us on either side of the pathway leading to the main road, their canopies rustling faintly in the breeze. Always my heart sang when I beheld the beauty of our vineyards; I wondered if Poppa merely wanted us to drink in their bounty the way I often caught him doing as the sun set.

But no. He drew us to his sides, his arm encircling my shoulders.

"What do you make of that?" he asked, dipping his head toward the north.

I followed his gaze along the length of the road. Two riders on white horses made their way toward our gate, decked in the azure blue of the House of Nelgareth.

My stomach dropped. Ogden Nelgareth ruled the lordland of Delthe as though he were king. He kept our roads in good condition and an army known for its fierce loyalty, but stories of his dark temper had graced the ears of many a fireside listener.

He wasn't too pleased with the crown's control of our vineyards, either. Generations ago, the king of Perin Faye had subsidized Graylaern Vineyards after the Great Blight had decimated over half the vines. The subsidy saved the vineyard—and satisfied the thirst of the nobility for Graylaern reds and whites.

But then the first Thungrave king seized the throne, and soon after, he limited wine production to ensure a high price, except for fifteen percent of the yield from every acre—wine for his own cellars. The Law of Firstfruits, it was called, and it was applied to anything produced in the fields—linen, barley, oats. By law, Lord Nelgareth was allowed to require his own ten percent, bringing our yearly offering to twenty-five percent.

A famous vintner who provided drinks for the tables of a king ought to have been well off. We were left each year with barely enough to live on.

"Do you think they're coming here?" I asked.

"Perhaps."

Nestar made a bitter sound in the back of his throat. "What business would they have with us right now? Fermentation has another two months at least for the Clarion red, and harvest is a few weeks out as well."

"We'll know shortly," Poppa said. "If they turn in at the gate, I'll go meet them."

"I'll come with you." Nestar was Poppa's only son—my half brother—and stood to inherit the vineyards someday. At nineteen, he was already more than capable of handling the daily demands of grape-growing and winemaking, though I often felt like I could do it better.

He didn't love the vines the way I did. The way Poppa did. His eyes didn't shine when he saw the first, hard-green grapes, tiny and new, emerge from beneath the blooms each spring. He only stood at sunset to gaze across the rows of vines because Poppa was doing the same—and he valued his place by Poppa's side perhaps better than anything. Which is why I knew he wouldn't shrink from meeting Nelgareth's men and defending Poppa any way he could.

Neither would I—in my thoughts, where sharp words took shape and humbled Nelgareth's faceless riders. In reality, I'd stay silent, Mother's "be seen and not heard" still reminding me how to behave to strangers, even though I'd much rather be seen *and* heard.

And I *would* be—soon. I had a plan that could benefit small, family vineyards in nearby Windsbreath and across Delthe, and tomorrow I'd take my first step toward implementing it. It was my greatest excitement—and biggest secret.

My hope that the men would pass us by fizzled as they turned their horses into our entry, and I sighed.

"Gracing Graylaern Vineyards after all." Poppa's pride for his winery was evident in each syllable. "For all I know, it may simply be a request to purchase any barrels I might've laid by," Poppa said.

"That would take a simple written message," Nestar said. "Not a special visit."

Poppa gave me a squeeze, then released me. "Come, Nestar. We'll treat them as guests."

"Will they want some food?" I asked.

"We'll offer wine, I think," Poppa said. "Will you go fill a flagon awhile?"

"I'd rather come with you."

Poppa nodded. Slowly, he was learning how important it was to me to be included in his work. "Of course you would. But look." He lifted his chin in the direction of the house.

I turned to see several workers hanging just behind the corner of the house, curious. Watching.

"Poppa, no." I wasn't in the mood to manage nosy workers.

"Please, Mara."

My sigh had a hard edge. "Fine. I'll take care of them."

"You always do," Poppa said.

I was glad Poppa could count on me, but I wished I didn't have to miss whatever was about to happen. I had done more for the well-being of these vineyards than anyone knew.

My heart pattered as I hastened toward the house, determined not to let myself become unraveled by these unwanted visitors. Five of Poppa's workers stood with their hands in their pockets, shuffling under my scrutiny but not trying to hide the fact that they'd come to see what was going on.

"You've eaten your stew already?" I asked, raising an eyebrow.

Swish, one of Poppa's more recent hires, stepped forward. "Helps to know what's going on."

Indignation flared inside me. "You've been here for two months. Why do you think it's your business to know what's going on?"

"It's not just him." Waylen, who'd worked for Poppa since I was seven or eight, crossed his arms. "If there's trouble for Doreck, there's trouble for all of us."

I frowned. "Who said anything about trouble?"

"We all know the color blue." Swish—he hadn't offered any other name—gestured toward the riders with his chin, his sandy hair going every which way, as usual. He couldn't have been much older than Nestar, though he acted like he knew things beyond his years, irritating me at every turn. "Why would Nelgareth send his men unless there was a problem?"

I stepped as close to him as I dared. "My father wants you to finish your meal." I swept the others with my gaze. "All of you."

"We just wanted to make sure we hadn't caused any trouble," Waylen said.

I knew what he was referring to—several of the workers had fallen into the habit of grumbling against our king, Selmar II, whenever Poppa wasn't nearby. "If you're worried about causing trouble, stop planning a revolt we all know none of you would actually fight for."

"They're just words," Rake, another of the younger workers, said.

"Words that could land you in prison." I gestured with both hands toward the back of the house. "Go on. Finish your meal—there's dessert today."

They turned, listening to me as they always did, despite the way my heart pounded in my throat. All but Swish.

Poppa's quiet voice and sounds of horses drew nearer. Torn between ignoring Swish and insisting that he return to his meal, I stood rooted like a tree, watching Nelgareth's men approach and trying to read the expression on Poppa's face.

The two men dismounted, and Poppa said something about Nestar attending the horses.

Swish stepped forward. "I'll tether them, Doreck, sir. I've had enough to eat."

I wrinkled my nose and didn't care if he'd seen me. Always he attempted to be helpful, but I didn't like the way he skulked about.

"That's very kind, Swish," Poppa said.

I caught Poppa's eye as Swish took the reins from Nestar. He cleared his throat the way he always did when he was uncomfortable.

"This is my daughter," he said. "Maralyth, this is Jamery Devon, Lord Nelgareth's Secretary of Accounts. And this is Jamery's personal secretary."

I made myself look directly at Jamery Devon, taking in his broad shoulders, hooked nose, and haughty expression. Then, legs trembling beneath my dress, I offered a small curtsy.

His only acknowledgement of my presence was a barely perceptible nod.

Cheeks burning, I cut a wide circle around Swish and made my way to the table where the rest of the workers were still gathered, grabbing an empty pitcher before slipping through the back door to the kitchen. Poppa called for Kenton, who rose as I hastened back inside to prepare the wine.

I'd just finished filling the stoneware flagon when the front door opened and the clatter of boots filled the house. Quickly, I placed two goblets and the flagon on a wooden tray. I walked light-footed into the sitting room, its stone hearth dark in the heat of summer and Mother's seat beside it still draped with the knit lap blanket she always used in wintertime. Somehow, none of us wanted to be the one to finally fold it away into the small trunk that held several other of her belongings.

Poppa, Kenton, and the two men stood assembled by the doorway in an awkward formation for a few seconds before Poppa gestured for everyone to sit. He raised his eyebrows at me.

"Ah, thank you, Mara. Will you set it down over here?"

I nodded, my gaze lingering for a breath or two on Poppa's eyes, which were tender and spoke to me of his desire to draw me in, where he knew I wanted to be.

The only good thing that had come of Mother's death, he'd said recently, was that he saw me more clearly, freed from the veil of protection Mother had always draped over me. He couldn't give me what I really wanted, though. Nestar would take over Graylaern Vineyards someday, not me. And even if there were no Nestar, I could never do more than fix the meals and tend the house—and possibly continue to boss the workers.

Because I was a girl.

"I'll come right to the point," Jamery said.

"May I offer you some wine?" Poppa asked as he poured.

The secretary glanced at the wine as though he very much wanted some. Jamery offered a tight-lipped smile. "Very well, then. Thank you."

He made his way toward the couch and his secretary followed. I stepped back, intending to stay as long as Poppa allowed me.

Jamery reached for a goblet. "Lord Nelgareth has expressed concern that your Firstfruits have fallen short over the past six months. I offered to come in person to sort out any miscommunication."

My bones went rigid. There was no way Poppa had made a mistake.

Determined to show his always-present hospitality, Poppa smiled at Jamery's secretary and gestured to the remaining goblet. "Please—have some wine. I'll be happy to listen to your concerns." He turned his attention to me. "Will you bring some goblets for Kenton and me, please?"

I nodded—too curtly, probably—and glanced once more at the men. Jamery rolled his cup between his hands, his mouth twisted like a thirsty leaf. I shuddered and returned to the kitchen to fetch more goblets, fighting a sudden urge to stay there, hidden among the pots and pans and cooking mess. Invisible, the way Mother had kept me. Safe.

But I didn't want to be invisible. So I grabbed two goblets and turned to face the sitting room. Safety be damned.

2

ALAC

I pulled the pen from the wall where it had lodged itself after a particularly well-aimed throw. A trail of thick ink snaked its way toward the floor, eliciting barely veiled giggles from my three charges.

It would have felt good to knock their heads together, just once.

"I take no pleasure in sending negative reports to your parents," I said, laying the pen pointedly in front of the offender—ten-year-old Rupert, youngest son of Lord Gryndock of Sailings Port.

"It was an accident, my prince." But the gleam in Rupert's eye said something different.

"In any case, you'll not be excused until you've scrubbed the ink from the wall." I reached for the brass bell next to my pile of books and maps.

Rupert's mouth dropped. "I don't know how to scrub ink from a wall."

"Then it's time for you to learn." I rang the bell. "Nathan, Figg, you're excused."

My two exonerated pupils hastily gathered their things—probably because they feared I'd change my mind. A servant entered as the boys made their way to the door, my brother Cannon close on his heels.

I ignored him and addressed the servant. "Please bring Master Rupert something to clean the wall." I gestured to the ink stain, which had spread almost to the baseboard.

"Enjoying your stint as a stand-in tutor?" Cannon had a way of saying things that made me wish he'd swallow all his teeth and choke on them.

"Is there something you wanted?" I straightened my maps and stacked them on the books, one eye on Rupert, who had slid down in his chair with a dark expression.

"Just to let you know that Father wants to see you," Cannon said. "I figured I'd catch you in here boring young boys to death."

His disdain for me was palpable as always, but my dread at having to speak to my father outweighed any feelings of irritation toward my brother. I was nothing more than a spare, and neither of them let me forget it. When I was younger, I once tried to remind Cannon how he'd almost died of the Black Death when he was small. He'd grabbed my collar and pulled my face so close to his own that my eyes crossed.

"As long as Father lives, I will *never* die," he'd hissed.

I was nine. It terrified me. I knew of the dark magic that Cannon stood to inherit along with the throne, and I believed what he said.

"Where is he?" I asked.

"In his study, making last minute plans for his journey. Don't keep him waiting."

I swallowed the indignant reply that buzzed behind my lips. "I'll see him as soon as Rupert has finished cleaning the wall."

"Don't be ridiculous." Cannon walked over to Rupert and clapped him on his shoulder. "Off you go, lad. Leave the cleaning to those whose station demands it."

Rupert looked at Cannon, wide-eyed, and then at me. I stood frozen by the cold rage that shot through me, balling my hands into fists and setting my jaw against words that, if spewed, would've been inappropriate in front of a ten-year-old.

"Thank you, Your Grace," Rupert offered as he hastily grabbed his things and left, almost running headlong into the servant who had returned with a bucket of soapy water.

"Take care of that," Cannon said, gesturing to the wall.

"You have no right to undermine my authority." My words were tight, teeth clenched.

Cannon rolled his eyes. "Teaching Elred's pupils while he attends his niece's wedding isn't *authority*."

"Bastard."

"Hardly. But your life would be more interesting if that were true." He started walking toward the door. "At any rate, you're free to see Father now. You're welcome."

I picked up an inkwell to lob at the back of his head, but thought better of it. After the door had closed behind him, I placed the inkwell on the table and let out a long stream of air—softly, so the servant wouldn't hear. Then I straightened my tunic with a sharp pull and made my way to Father's study.

⁓

I stood for long seconds before the closed door, flanked on either side by a guard standing at full attention.

"My prince," they both said, their eyes never meeting mine.

Not even the palace guards took me seriously.

I wiped my palms on my breeches, then knocked three times, as Father required.

"Come."

Even through the heavily paneled doors, his voice had the power to make my bones wilt. I turned the brass knob and pulled the door open. King Selmar II of Perin Faye—my father—sat in his usual splendor at a desk three times the size it needed to be, as though the vast space at his elbows made him feel the reach of his power with every stroke of the pen. I'd caught Cannon more than once running his fingers along its surface, coveting.

To me, it was just a desk.

"Your Grace," I said, bowing.

"Close the door, Alac."

I pushed my back against the door until it latched behind me, facing my father at all times—another royal requirement. He regarded me with mild interest—the best I could hope for—as I approached him. His silk robe was encrusted with a ridiculous number of gemstones that winked in the light of the candelabras sitting at either end of the desk. The crown resting on his pale blond head was a mute reminder of his station. I swore he slept in it.

He rested his quill in its holder and folded his hands before him. "I'm leaving at first light."

I nodded. For a brief moment, I thought perhaps he was going to invite me to join him, the way Cannon had joined him on his late-summer progresses in the past. But that was less likely than his telling me I had an ounce of worth in the royal household, and I didn't want to go, anyway.

"I'll be cutting my journey short, of course, considering Cannon's upcoming wedding." As if I didn't know that. "You'll need to offer him your support while I'm away."

"I'm sure Cannon doesn't need anything from me."

Father's eyes blazed silently. "I don't need to remind you that, until he has a son, you're second in line for the throne."

I shrank smaller in my skin. The throne—and the dark secrets that came with it—was never something I'd aspired to.

"Yes, Your Grace." Holy God, I hated calling him that.

"There's something else." Father reached into his top desk drawer and pulled out a plate and a small dagger.

I quailed. I'd seen the dagger before, glowing with an unearthly light as he cut the flesh of his own hand and spilled the blood into a crystal goblet. He hadn't cried out or even flinched—just cut his flesh as though it were a sack of grain. I was six, hiding beneath a table-cloth in my father's private chapel, where I knew I wasn't allowed. And I remembered it like it was yesterday.

Father took the plate and moved it beneath his hand. As I watched, thirteen-year-old terror clenching my heart, he made a small cut in his palm, deep enough to draw a steady stream of blood droplets onto the pristine, white plate.

"I trust there will never be a need for the magic to pass to you," he said, his eyes on the blood. "But I can't leave anything to chance."

Before I could react, he grabbed my hand and slashed it with the dagger. I sucked in a hot breath, more from shock than pain. As I watched, horrified, he pulled my hand over the plate and allowed my blood to mingle with his own.

By the time he released my hand, I was too mesmerized by what was happening on the plate to pay the pain much heed. As my father uttered words I could barely hear and couldn't understand, the blood sizzled and smoked, swirling slowly on the plate until it formed a per-fect circle. Instead of crimson, it was black.

Wordlessly, he tipped the plate so that the darkened blood spilled into a metal box the size of a shoe buckle. He flipped its hinged lid closed, and I swore I saw, for a moment, a thin, black mist swirl around the box before quickly dissipating.

"Take this." He held out the box, which was attached to a chain. "Wear it."

I didn't want to touch it, but refusing the king wasn't something even a son could do. Especially a second-born.

"Why?" I whispered.

"For protection."

No way in damnation did I want that. "From what?"

"From harm." I must've had a stupid expression on my face, because his grew impatient. "I wouldn't go on this progress if I didn't need to waste time convincing people of the merits of my war effort. If something were to happen to me, the transferal of the power to Cannon could be delayed. You know how dangerous that would be."

It was what the Thungrave kings had prided themselves on—a glorious history I'd been forced to memorize. A century ago, a dark magic had appeared that roamed free, destroying anything in its path. The Thungrave ritual, passed from father to son, ensured that the magic would stay contained.

My father refused to acknowledge the truth—that the roaming magic was never meant for the Thungraves, and that using a ritual to harness its power didn't make it rightfully ours.

But I couldn't say that.

Reluctantly, I took the locket and held it in my palm. "That's it? I wear it and nothing can hurt me?"

"Correct."

"And when you return, I can take it off?"

His smile was slow and unnerving. "You won't want to take it off. But, no." He pressed his fingers together, tip to tip. "Wear it until Cannon produces an heir."

"That could take years."

"Then you'll wear it for years," he said.

"Why now?" I asked. "You've gone on progresses every year without making me wear a locket." Or whatever it was.

An odd expression passed Father's face. Sorrow? Fear? "Because

I've decided it's necessary. You may not be the crown prince, but you still have a duty to the throne."

"A throne kept with stolen magic."

I knew I shouldn't have said it as soon as the words left my mouth. Father's eyes went cold, his face hard.

"I *am* the magic," he said, "as will Cannon be after me. Only we can contain this magic. Only we can control it."

My chest tightened. "Do you control it, Father? Or does it control you?"

He fisted his hands on the desk, a sign that I was bordering on angering him beyond his ability to contain it. "The kingdom was almost destroyed by dark magic over a century ago. If my great-grandfather hadn't received the gift of the magic, Perin Faye would be. No. More." He pounded a fist on the table with each word.

I swallowed, wanting to tell him once and for all that I hated the magic—and that I didn't want the throne, anyway. But I'd angered him enough; one more ill-spoken word would see me on the receiving end of wrath that seemed beyond human.

I'd been there before and never wanted to see it again.

"Yes, Your Grace." It's what I always said, because what else was there to say?

"Tell me what is required."

I sighed. "The breath. The blood. The words."

"And where will you find what you need?"

"In your chapel."

He nodded. "And the missing element?"

"Cannon has the scroll, which he will give to me as soon as he becomes king." In other words, as soon as Father was dead.

Father regarded me with eyes that were still smoldering. "Wear the locket beneath your tunic. Let no one see it. And don't open it."

Reluctantly, I slipped the chain over my head and tucked the blood-filled box beneath my tunic, where it left a strange bump.

He nodded once. "That will be all."

No fatherly smile, no warm expression that perhaps I meant something to him. He wasn't the father I remembered from childhood—the one who would sit me upon his knee and give me "horse rides," the one who held my hand and Cannon's at court functions. That father had left the day my grandfather died, leaving him the throne and the legacy of magic that forever changed him.

I'd be damned if I ever let that happen to me.

⚛︎

At first light, the royal entourage gathered in the courtyard, preparing to leave. I stood dutifully at the base of the stairs, the blood locket pressing uncomfortably against my chest beneath my tunic.

When Father finally swept onto the patio, the light seemed to dim, as it often did when he first appeared. Either most people chose to ignore it, though, or else they were so used to the effect that it didn't bother them.

It would never stop bothering me.

He clasped Cannon's shoulder before climbing into the carriage. Cannon stepped back, hand on his hip as though the universe would be his as soon as Father rolled out of sight.

After a few last-minute adjustments and orders, the entourage started off—Father's carriage, a supply wagon, and twenty men-at-arms, bearing the king away to the north. Already, I tasted freedom. Not only would my father's heavy presence be gone for four weeks, but also I was paid so little mind to begin with that I was sure I'd be nigh invisible.

I turned and entered the palace, my steps light. The first thing I'd do was to take off the annoying blood locket. I wouldn't let the magic rule me the way it ruled my father.

Not today. Not ever.

3

MARALYTH

"Lord Nelgareth has determined that your last shipment was seven barrels short," Jamery was saying, his goblet balanced carefully between his hands. "I'm prepared to go over the paperwork with you."

"We keep impeccable paperwork ourselves." Kenton's words sounded stretched, as though he were pulling them through his teeth.

"Our good lord would beg to differ." Jamery handed his goblet to his secretary and reached inside his riding cloak. "I carry documents signed by Lord Nelgareth himself."

I handed the fresh goblets to Poppa, trying unsuccessfully to catch his eye. His face was placid and purposefully unreadable.

I knew that face. It was long worn by a man accustomed to grief and hardship. Losing Mother had been the second such blow in his forty-odd years; his first wife, Nestar's mother, had died in childbirth. Poppa carried grief and worry deep inside, though, where others wouldn't see. He would never let these men guess that he was in any way concerned.

He poured wine into a goblet and handed it to Kenton while he waited for Jamery to unfold a crisp sheet of paper. The door opened and Nestar came softly in, standing behind Poppa with an expression much less studied.

Poppa turned his head toward me, his mouth curved up at the corners in an approximation of a smile. When he spoke, his voice was low and steady. "Maralyth, will you see to the workers, please?"

I opened my mouth to protest. But then I thought better of it.

"Of course," I said.

I left the room without acknowledging anyone else, my face burning from Poppa's dismissal. I was certain he still saw me as a child, despite his recent efforts to make me feel included.

Some girls married at seventeen and started having babies. Some pursued positions with noble families, serving as governess or nursemaid to children with full bellies and fine clothing.

I wanted more.

My connection to the vines, the fruit, the barrels of fermenting wine, was undeniable and deep. No one knew that I could ripen grapes with a few whispered words. Or that I spoke health to leaves spotted with blight.

For as much as I did for Poppa's vineyards, though, my place would always be beneath Nestar's. And if he married one day, where would that leave me? No wife would want to share space with her husband's half sister.

I had a plan, though. And tomorrow I would implement it.

I dished gobs of peach cobbler into a large serving bowl, the spoon clattering more noisily than it needed to. When the bowl would hold no more, I took it outside and placed it in the center of the table.

"That's what I've been waiting for!" Tibel had worked the vineyards since before I was born, and had always made me feel like a special favorite. Sometimes he even let me braid his long, white hair.

I tried to smile, though my heart still beat an irritated rhythm. "Sorry it's late."

"It's right on time." Tibel patted his stomach with exaggerated care. "It'll keep me from gorging on more of that delicious stew." Not that there was any left.

"Mara's never late," someone else called out. "She just likes to keep us in suspense."

Laughter trickled down the table. Not unkind, surely, but defensiveness coiled inside me, hot and ready to strike.

I clenched my teeth and spoke through them. "I actually hate cooking."

Once the words had flown free, I felt strangely giddy, despite the heat rising to my cheeks. The sound of my breathing filled my ears, and I realized everyone had gone quiet. A single clink of the serving spoon seemed unnaturally loud.

"You're awfully good at it, though," Tibel said.

I looked at his time-worn face, at the faces of all the workers around the table. Rake averted his gaze. Round-faced Severn offered what was probably supposed to be an encouraging smile. Swish appeared around the corner of the house, fresh from tethering the horses.

"I thought you'd had enough to eat," I said, desperate to break the silence.

Swish shrugged. "It's not like we have dessert every day."

I wiped my hands self-consciously on my apron. "Leave everything on the table when you're done."

Then I turned and headed for the vines.

The ground was soft beneath my feet, still saturated from the rain that fell two days ago. When I was certain I was out of the workers' sight, I ran, heading for my favorite grapes—the almost-black Chansons with skins so thick the grape's meat popped out if you squeezed it. The skin meant high tannins and a more robust flavor, but to me they had always meant exploding treats that I'd mastered squeezing into my mouth from a greater distance than Nestar ever could.

The Chansons weren't ripe. When it came to harvesting, timing was critical, and I knew better than anyone exactly when the grapes were at their peak. I was careful, though, to not always say so. Mostly, Poppa and the workers knew, too. Winemaking was an art, a dance between nature and a master's skill.

But my secret gift offered more.

That was why I'd made my plan. Not to hurt Poppa or to make things hard for him, but to find a place for myself that was more than cooking and filling in tiny gaps.

Glean the grapes, Mara.

You can help Tibel tie the vines today; he's not feeling well.

These barrels need washing.

I could do all those things, and I was glad to be even a small part of what went on every day. But with Mother gone, there was no one but me to take her place instead of tending the grapes and processing the wine. And I didn't want that anymore.

The workers' wives could pack their lunches, couldn't they?

It was Lia, Severn's wife, who'd planted the idea. Her middle swollen with their first child, she'd ridden to the vineyards to bring her husband a repaired pair of shoes.

"After the Great Blight, none of the other vineyards in Delthe were subsidized by the crown the way Graylaern was, and they didn't survive," she'd said. "The small vineyards that some families have today do no more than provide wine for themselves. If there were some way to band together, to help each other . . . it could make a difference. A local wine market for those of us who can't drink the king's wine."

I'd pondered it for days. Finally I'd come up with a plan, and several letters back and forth between Lia and me settled it. Nine families in Windsbreath had agreed to meet with me, to listen to my ideas on how I could help them form a cooperative.

Our first meeting was in the morning.

I turned into a pathway between rows of still-green Chansons, stopping by the first, low-hanging cluster. I cupped the grapes in my hands, feeling their weight and the promise of sweetness hidden deep within. Closing my eyes, I brushed my lips against them and spoke words only they could hear.

"Swell," I whispered. "Be sweet."

The magic awoke as it always did, warming first my hands, and then the grapes. A gentle wind wove between and around my fingers, encircling the grapes and bleeding into them as though it were being drunk. The grapes swelled and darkened, the ripening of several weeks happening in mere seconds. My seasoned eye knew exactly when their color was perfect—but I didn't pay attention to that. I knew the grapes were ready because I sensed it, as though the fruit were an extension of myself.

I plucked a single grape. It was still warm as I squeezed it between my fingers, the skin relinquishing its sweet prize into my waiting mouth. I swallowed the ill-gotten goodness, knowing I should have left the grapes alone. It was one thing to gently coax blossoms to life during a too-cool spring or to whisper away a touch of frost—that, at least, was a contribution to the vineyards. But there was no way to justify ripening the grapes for my own pleasure.

I ate them anyway, one succulent globe at a time, until my fingers were stained and the cluster of stems was empty.

Mother had caught me once. I was eleven and had recently discovered what I was capable of. Her face had gone white, then red, when she discovered me behind a storage shed, my lap laden with grapes that shouldn't have been ripe.

"Where did you get those?" I'd never heard her voice hiss like that.

But even as she spoke the words, I saw it in her eyes—she knew I'd used magic I'd never spoken of. For one frozen moment, I thought she was afraid of me.

Then, wordlessly, she laid her hands over the grapes, fingers spread and trembling. I felt the warmth and the shifting of the grapes as they reverted to their green, unripe selves. I wasn't looking at the grapes, though—I was staring at Mother, her eyes hooded, her lower lip tucked behind her upper teeth.

When she was finished, she'd covered her face with her hands and sat for what felt like an eternity. I glanced at the grapes, now inedible, and suddenly wanted them far away. I tossed them to the ground.

Mother grabbed my wrist. "How long? *How long have you known?*"

I guessed she meant the magic, the stirrings of which I'd first felt when I was six. But I shrugged and said nothing.

She tightened her grip. "Listen to me, Maralyth. There is nothing good that comes of magic. *Nothing.* I forbid you to ever do anything like this again."

"But . . ." Hadn't I just watched her wield the same magic, undoing what I'd done? A strange, crawling sensation twisted its way through me. What else didn't I know about her? "But you—"

"Never use it. It's a curse, and nothing more." She released my wrist. "You've heard the stories, haven't you? People with magic stones or other means of creating magic they shouldn't be dabbling in? The Holy God never intended for commoners to touch the magic of their realm."

"I don't have a magic stone." My voice felt tiny, as though it were squeezing itself through a pinprick.

For a breath or two, Mother looked like she was going to cry. Then she gathered her wits and hardened her face into something closer to anger. "That's even worse. I want you to promise me on your own grave that you will never use this magic again. Do you hear me?"

I nodded. I heard.

"And do not speak of it—ever. It carries more danger than you know."

My heart felt like it was beating inside my mouth. "What danger?"

"Danger too great to explain to a small girl."

She'd kissed my forehead then, but my skin and all the rest of me felt numb. The shock of learning that Mother had the same magic was worse than her rebukes and warnings. Worse than the thought that I had being doing something terribly wrong. Dangerous.

For weeks, I thought I'd never feel happy again.

But then, in the quiet dark of my room, the magic nudged me, and I breathed life into a bloom that had begun to sag in a vase by my bed. A small thing, barely noticeable—but the heaviness within me lifted, as though the magic itself were capable of raising my spirits. Affirming me.

Mother and I never again spoke of it, though I had more questions than I could count. Why did we have magic in our blood, and how could it be bad if it wasn't our fault in the first place? Quietly, without ever drawing attention to myself, I used the magic whenever I could—larvae on the underside of leaves, a canopy grown too thin during a dry spell. By the time I was fourteen, I'd learned to command the magic with barely a thought, a brush of my fingertips. It was the secret part of me that gave me a purpose beyond learning how to stretch one chicken into two meals or whipping turnips into a yellowy-white bowl of fluff.

Almost, I'd summoned the courage to bring the subject up again with Mother, holding out a wild and feeble hope that, if I showed her the good I'd been doing, she would see things differently. She'd change her mind about my magic—and her own.

And then the Black Death took her, a tortuous, six-day journey that

Nestar and I spent at Kenton's home, away from the illness that was so catching. Poppa alone stayed with her, since he had contracted the Black Death in his early twenties and survived.

"I lived, and so will she" were his parting words to me.

But she didn't. And at fifteen, I was thrust into Mother's role in the kitchen while I was still reeling from her loss.

"Mara?" Nestar peered at me with a dubious expression I'd seen before. "What are you doing? Swish and Tibel are down there clearing the table."

"I told them to leave everything." I frowned. "How did you find me?"

"I always find you."

That was true enough. "What did the men say? Is Poppa in trouble?"

Nestar blew out a puff of air. "Kenton was very convincing in his presentation of our books, but it comes down to Nelgareth's word against ours. We had to sign a paper stating that the missing barrels would be added to the next Firstfruits."

Anger curled inside me, an impotent snake. "That's not fair."

"Since when has anything been fair?" He gestured with his chin. "You'd better get down there."

"I know." I tried to sidle past him, but he caught me by the shoulders and turned me to face him.

"Tibel told me the men were teasing you," he said. "You know they're fond of you; there's no need to cry."

Every inch of me bristled. "You think I came here to *cry*?"

"No, I just . . . well, maybe."

"I was thinking. Not crying."

"You've been in the kitchen too long today."

Like every other day. "Have you been talking with Swish and the others again?"

It was Nestar's turn to frown. "I talk to everyone."

"You know what I mean."

"Mara, it's no secret that no one outside of the nobility can rub two coins together."

I poked him in the chest. "You remember what the king did the last time there was an uprising?"

"That wasn't an uprising. They were spreading unrest."

"Exactly," I said. "And thirty-six men were put to death, anyway, right in the king's hall."

"Sixteen."

"Does it matter?"

"There's nothing wrong with expressing our views on Selmar's war effort," Nestar said. "He's already taxing us dry, and if he declares war on Northland next spring, we won't be able to export our wine there on top of it."

"The men who were put to death were grumbling against the king, too."

"It's just talk. It's better than pretending life's easy."

"I'm not asking you to pretend." I gentled my voice. "I'm asking you to be careful."

"I'll be careful."

He was appeasing me, I knew. But I let it go.

"I think I'll make porridge tomorrow. Give myself a break."

"Good thing, because Severn just got word that his wife has finally gone into labor. You can take his place."

My heart sank—normally I'd have been thrilled. "Do I have to?"

Nestar raised an eyebrow. "That's not like you."

"I mean . . ." I couldn't tell him I wouldn't be home until well after lunch. "The men might be glad not to have me."

"You work faster than any of them. Except when you're in the kitchen."

I tossed a twist of dead tendril at Nestar's face; he reached quickly and caught it before it hit him. "I'll be there."

I hated the way he nodded, believing my lie.

❧

The mirror in the washroom reflected a lifetime of Mother's presence displayed on the shelves behind me—small, amber bottles of healing oils; a nail file; a beautifully carved hairbrush with strands of her silver-white hair still threaded in its bristles. Sometimes when I looked in the mirror, I felt like Mother was standing behind me. I could never tell if she was smiling or frowning.

I pulled my belt a notch tighter; my ample hips filled Nestar's old breeches respectably, but the waistline far exceeded my own. After checking to make sure I wouldn't end up losing my bottoms, I braided my hair and slipped quietly out.

"You're up early." Poppa's voice was hushed in the nearly-dark sitting room.

My stomach tightened. "So are you."

"Well"—he grunted as he pulled his second boot on—"Nestar almost finished repairs on the press last night, so I thought I'd get a leg up this morning and finish it before the men arrive." He eyed my too-big breeches. "Filling in for Severn today?"

"Yes." I kissed his head, ashamed of my duplicitousness.

I'll tell you later, Poppa. After everything's in place.

"You do know what the men call you, don't you?" he said.

"Mara."

He laughed. "Besides that." He waited while I raised an eyebrow. "Little Doreck."

Warmth spread through me like a hug. "Do they?"

"Apparently they'd rather follow your instructions than mine."

"You know that's not true." But I couldn't help smiling. "Love you, Poppa."

He blew me a kiss, and I slipped through the door into the cool, predawn air. It was barely light enough to see; by the time the sun nipped its way past the horizon, the vineyards would be bustling. I wondered how long it would take them to miss me.

Early birdsong broke forth first from trees dividing our northern fields and then from the dense copse across the road. I waved my fingers in a wide arc that spanned the vines to my left.

"Reject them."

It was a reminder to the vines to refuse the birds, who for reasons of their own liked to eat the grapes slightly before they were ripe enough for harvest. For several years, Poppa and the others had marveled at how little loss they'd suffered from the beaks of hungry birds.

If only they knew.

I reached the road and stopped, my heart suddenly in my throat.

During childhood, Nestar and I had sometimes played in the thick stand of trees, climbing and hiding and even building a tree house of sorts, the weathered remnants of which could still be spied in the branches of a venerable corn oak.

I hesitated, torn between guilt and memories. A brief movement to the left, where the trees grew thinner, caught my attention—a deer, perhaps. Beyond the trees lay an open field where deer often roamed. Our "field of battle," Nestar called it, though neither of us had ever seen one. We'd pretend our tree house was the castle and we were a king and queen of old—kind and beloved, unlike Selmar Thungrave, our current king. The stories of life in Perin Faye during the reign of the Dallowyn kings and queens had always seemed too good to be true.

I squared my shoulders, determined to start out, but what sounded like the soft whuffle of a horse arrested me. Strange, because our men all walked to work. I scanned the area and thought I detected movement where the deer—or whatever it was—had been moments ago. Who would be on a horse off the main road at this hour?

Too curious to ignore it, I crossed the road and headed toward the trees, where I stood still, senses heightened. All I heard was the continued song of a bird somewhere above me and my own breathing, suddenly harsh in my ears.

Nerves. That's what this was.

I glanced through the trees, where the field lay wide and beckoning, as it had in childhood. I felt a rush of glorious freedom—today I was taking a step toward something bigger than the kitchen that kept me caged.

Bigger than myself.

An arm came around the back of my head and pressed a rough hand to my mouth. Instinctively, I tried to scream, but the hand muffled both sound and breath. I raised my arm and tried to swing, but a wiry boy with huge teeth stepped from behind and grabbed me by the forearm, pushing me into whoever was holding me.

My head was pressed against his unseen chest so that I couldn't move. The wiry boy moved toward me with a sack in his fist while a third person stepped into my line of vision. Recognition stabbed me like a blade of ice.

Swish's satisfied smile was the last thing I saw before the rough sack was pulled over my head.

4

ALAC

Your charges, my prince."

Nella, Mistress of the Wardrobe, wasn't hiding her irritation well. She herded the three boys into the library, urging them forward with her substantial arms and blocking their retreat with her round, unmoving form.

"Thank you, Mistress Nella." I closed the book on winemaking I'd been reading for the past hour and tried to smile at the boys, but they looked particularly sullen this morning, and the best I could muster was closer to a smirk.

Thank the Holy God this was my last day with these monsters. Especially Rupert.

"They claim they've lost their books." Nella placed fisted hands on her hips and lifted a skeptical, bushy-gray eyebrow.

"Have they?" I tried to sound stern, but this was admittedly better than flying ink pens. I probably hated teaching history and geography as much as they hated learning it.

"We can go look for them, if you'd like," Rupert said, his feigned innocence making him sound ridiculous. "We think we may have left them in the stables."

Nella rolled her eyes, and I suppressed a laugh. "What do you think, mistress? Shall I tell their fathers?"

The glint in her eye told me she'd play along. "If you'd like, I can send a message to Zeth directly."

"No!" Rupert and Nathan said. Figg looked like he was going to be sick.

"I think we'll take this opportunity to study something new," I said. "But thank you, Mistress Nella."

She gave the boys another collective shove, but her expression had softened. "Let me know if you change your mind."

Her parting curtsy felt more like a hug than an expression of deference. After my mother's death, Nella had stepped in when no one else had, reaching out to me when I was small and brokenhearted without ever trying to replace the parent I'd lost. I might be invisible to a lot of people, but never to Nella.

"Come sit," I said to the boys.

They gathered around me at the table, looking only slightly apprehensive. I glanced at my piles of maps and drawing paper—I'd planned to have the boys create their own maps of Perin Faye and label the seven lordlands and the most historically important locations in each. Without their books, though, the task would be insurmountably harder.

"What are we going to study?" Nathan asked.

I tapped my fingers on my book, thinking. And then it hit me.

"Winemaking," I said.

Their incredulous expressions told me I'd made the right choice. And why not? Wine was Delthe's most profitable commodity, though the wines of Fanley and Tell Doral were excellent, too. The crown's subsidy of Graylaern Vineyards afforded my father control of everything from pricing to exports to the quantity in the royal cellars of the best wine in Perin Faye. A cask of Graylaern Clarion or Fionna was synonymous with status; any noble boasting one gladly suffered the envy of his peers.

Since I'd first had a sip of diluted wine at the age of nine, I'd wanted to learn how to make it. I'd read everything I could get my hands on, teaching myself the entire process, from planting to harvesting to fermentation. And I could discern the subtle differences in vintages, having learned from Graem Eldar, the palace wine steward, how to choose the best wines for everything from private suppers to affairs of state. He'd dubbed me an expert when I was just sixteen.

It was easy to identify a Graylaern red from a Bothshed or a Lilyport—Graylaern was by far the finest. But I prided myself on being able to tell whether a Clarion was from 896 or 897, or whether it had been a dry or a wet season for the Fionna white.

Not a skill set prized in a second-born prince. But I had plans my father knew nothing about that I hoped to set in motion soon.

I opened the book, but then thought better of it and closed it again. "Who can tell me where the nearest vineyard lies?"

"Just to the northeast," Figg said.

"Right!" It was a small family vineyard; I'd spent hours of my youth skulking among its vines, tasting grapes and asking the workers questions. "So let's head to the stables and saddle up. It's a short ride."

Rupert's eyes were biggest. "You mean . . . we're going to have our lesson outside?"

"That's exactly what I mean." I rose and gestured to the door. "Who knows—maybe we'll come across your books in the stables."

✑

I pulled off my boots and sweaty socks and plopped onto the tufted lounge chair in my quarters. My morning at the vineyard had stretched well past midday, and I'd brought my students back eager to plant their own vines and taste their fathers' wine stores—which I was sure I'd hear about later.

Our long trip meant I was late to my afternoon sparring. It didn't matter, though; I enjoyed the freedom of not having to appear for supper at the preappointed seven o'clock, opting instead to order food be brought to my rooms. I could definitely get used to this no-father-at-home routine.

The servants knocked as I was pouring my first goblet of wine. They entered, bearing a folding table and a large tray covered with a silver dome. The last time I'd been served food in my own quarters was when I'd been sick with a lingering cough, and then it had only been diluted quail broth and soft custard. This evening, my mouth watered as the dome was raised, releasing the heavy scent of roasted pork with peppered peaches and turnip mash. It was Cannon's least favorite, so naturally it was almost never served when Father presided.

"This smells amazing," I said, reaching for my fork.

The servants looked a bit startled, as usual, by my words. I didn't see a problem with acknowledging their work, though I stayed silent when Father was around.

Halfway through the meal, someone knocked again. I frowned and called through a mouthful of peaches, "Enter!"

"Begging your pardon, my prince." Zeth, High Minister to my father and grandfather, was one of the few people at court, besides Nella, who took an interest in me. It was no secret that he was proud of his long-standing position of trust, though I'd never seen him take advantage of it. I gave him credit for his fierce loyalty, even if I didn't understand it.

"Is something wrong?"

"Not at all," he said. "I apologize for the interruption."

I waited for him to continue, fork poised.

He straightened his shoulders, which made him look taller than his already impressive height. His long, black-and-silver hair lay plaited over one shoulder—an odd fashion statement I'd never understood. "Naturally, your father left me with a list of things to keep in order during his absence."

Naturally. I stuffed pork into my mouth and waited for him to continue.

He cleared his throat. "He bade me remind you to abide by his wishes concerning a certain locket."

My stomach tightened. "He told you about that?"

"Not with any amount of detail." Zeth's gaze dropped briefly to my chest, then back again.

"I'll wear it as I see fit," I said. I wasn't going to let Father bully me through his counselor-puppet.

"As you wish." He offered a thin scroll. "Also, here's the schedule for Cannon's wedding week."

I frowned and took the scroll, its contents sure to be the bane of my existence. "Is there anything else?"

"No, my prince." He hesitated. "Can I serve you in any way . . . ?"

"Not at the moment," I said through another mouthful of peppered peaches.

"I'm at your disposal, should you need me."

I chewed and swallowed the peaches. "You're at my disposal? Since when?"

Zeth looked positively mortified. "My prince, I serve you to the same extent I serve your father and brother."

"I was joking." Sort of. "You have to admit Cannon commands all the attention around here."

Something in him softened. "True enough. You've had precious little attention over the years."

I nodded, not sure how to respond. Fortunately, he chose that moment to bow and excuse himself. When he reached the door, I called out to him, and he turned, his expression expectant.

"Thank you," I said.

He bowed again and left. I dug into another mouthful of pork and hoped Zeth would forget about the locket.

༄

I should've been asleep, but I lay in bed and stared wide-eyed at the latticework of my window, which cast dark shadows in the moonlight that spilled across the window seat and onto the floor. The unease had begun shortly after Zeth left, and at first I thought I'd eaten too fast. It wasn't that I was anxious, exactly. The feeling was like a tickle inside my head, scratching at me.

It was vaguely familiar, but I'd pushed it away all evening and into the night, not wanting to admit what I was certain to be true. I rolled over, away from the moonlight, and closed my eyes, determined to ignore it.

My eyes popped open. I sat up and reached for the narrow drawer in the table beside my bed. The blood locket sat inside, ever since I'd tossed it there. I withdrew it, and it was warm, as though I'd been wearing it against my skin. The creeping dread that always accosted me when I encountered Father's dark magic rose within me, and I almost threw the thing back into the drawer.

Instead, I held it between thumb and forefinger, gazing at what I could make of the scrollwork design in my moonlit chambers and feeling the almost-imperceptible buzz of the magic contained within. I'd tried to tell myself it was all smoke and mirrors, nothing beyond the commoner's grasping for the magic of the Holy God that they were never meant to have. But always the memory of Father plunging the dagger into his hand returned, and the palpable darkness that had permeated his private chapel. I knew he'd tapped into something powerful—deadly—that had been passed down from my grandfather, and from his father and father's father before him.

I knew it was real. I'd seen storm clouds swell from nothing and erupt over the castle—and nowhere else. I'd seen a man drop dead in Father's presence—from fear, others said. I might've believed that if I hadn't seen the ritual with the dagger. But I knew better.

I closed my fingers around the locket, feeling the vague thrum of the power within it. Would it really protect me? I wasn't worried about something happening to Father—nothing ever did—but if I were wrong, and the dark magic wasn't contained quickly enough, would I be immune to it?

And if the power of the locket would protect me from such dark magic, would it protect me from other harm as well? Save my life if I were impaled or struck down? If I jumped from the roof, would I land like a feather without a single broken bone?

It seemed ludicrous. But it also felt tempting. And that was the part I didn't like.

I opened my fingers and stared at the locket. An urge to draw near to the magic swelled suddenly inside me, as though I were burning with thirst that only it could quench.

Don't open it, Father had said.

If the magic was there to protect me, why couldn't I open it?

I fingered the locket, tracing the seam between its two halves with my thumb. The room seemed to dim around me, until all I could see was the locket.

Holy God, I had to open it.

I took a slow breath. And another.

Then I unclasped the lid and pushed it open with my thumb. A swirl of black, finer than dust, rose from within and began to curl toward my fingertips.

Clear as daybreak, cold as winter, a single word echoed inside my head like a living thought.

Alac.

I slammed the locket closed and tossed it back into the drawer, chest heaving.

Fear clawed its way into my heart—not because of the black swirl or even the hollow sound of my own name, but because I found myself wanting more.

More knowledge of the magic.

More power.

More of everything I'd hated my whole life.

"I'm not interested," I whispered through clenched teeth.

I was lying.

5

MARALYTH

Day and night melted together. A bitter edge to the first drink of water they gave me told me they'd drugged me. I couldn't tell waking from sleeping; only the constant jostling in the saddle reminded me vaguely that I was traveling somewhere. Voices blended, faces blurred. I existed outside of time, unable to grasp lucid moments long enough to ask questions, incapable of turning my head away when more tainted water was forced into my mouth and down my throat.

Sometimes I awakened in what felt like a bed, darkness pressing against my eyes like a gloved hand. Magic thrummed in my temples and fingertips, as though it sought to comfort or free me. But I couldn't make sense of anything, couldn't sort my thoughts into words, couldn't fight.

At a time that seemed near dusk on what might've been three or four or a hundred days later, we rode alongside a white, stone wall that was lit at even intervals by fat lanterns hanging from iron hooks. A faint breeze lifted the unruly strands of hair around my face, tickling my skin. My head felt clearer; perhaps they'd stopped adding a sedative to my water. I ran my tongue along my teeth, silently assessing my ability to speak.

"He lives behind that, like a king in a castle." Was Swish talking to me?

I didn't answer. Didn't care. My thighs ached from riding and my stomach was hollow. Had they fed me at all? I couldn't remember.

A slow-moving dozen or so cowled Brothers of the Holy God, hands folded, walked in an orderly group in the opposite direction. It crossed my mind, briefly, to call out to them for help, but my mouth and my brain still weren't properly connected. My eyes grew heavy again as we approached armed guards at a gate in the wall.

Vaguely, I was aware of someone helping me dismount, and strong arms guiding me along a cobbled path. I blinked and looked up; a sprawling edifice lay before me, looking every bit the way I imagined a castle would look, including battlements and turrets. The roof was many-gabled, the windows diamond-latticed.

I shook my head, trying to further clear it. The strong grasp on my arms grew tighter.

"Almost there." It was a girl's voice, deep and gravely. Was this the mountain of muscle that had held me fast in the saddle day after day? It was hardly possible.

We skirted the side of the fortresslike home until we came to a stone stairway that led down to an arch-shaped wooden door. I stumbled my way down, the girl's grip never loosening. Through a large larder containing wheels of cheese, baskets of root vegetables, and crocks of cream, I hobbled until I thought I'd collapse. We entered a small room that smelled like yeast, and I collapsed onto the nearest wooden chair.

Someone pressed a cold, wet cloth to my face, and I gasped and drew back. Swish's face moved in and out of focus as he continued to dab my face. I heard the door open, and the scent of peppery broth made my stomach curl eagerly in on itself.

"Drink this," Swish said, taking an earthenware mug from a tray someone had brought. "It'll help you wake up."

I sipped the broth while the beefy girl brushed my hair until my scalp ached. It didn't do much to fill my belly, but with each swallow I felt better than I had since the abduction.

"Why are you brushing my hair?" I asked, my words still feeling a bit slurry.

The girl didn't answer.

Swish reappeared—when had he left?—as I swallowed the last of the broth. He assessed me for a moment, frowning slightly. Then he leaned over the table and took me by the shoulders.

"Is your head clear?"

I slapped him.

He looked surprised, but not angry. "Clear enough."

"Clear enough for what?" I asked through clenched teeth.

Swish leaned closer. "To tell the truth about your little secret."

The fear that had lived inside me since I was eleven wrapped itself around my heart. "What secret?"

"Magic, love. Whispering to the vines, sending the grape-hungry birds away. No one else may have seen you, but I did."

My mouth was dust, words crumbling behind my teeth. Knowing that he'd seen me working magic made me feel like I was falling and falling with no landing in sight.

"You're mad." It was all I could muster.

"The magic is your greatest asset," Swish continued. "Don't hide it."

Before I could reply, he and the girl had pulled me to my feet. I felt steadier and more alert, but not recovered enough to make any kind of sensible escape.

"Where are you taking me?" I asked.

But Swish shushed me, and the girl tightened her grip on my arm. They led me through a kitchen filled with tantalizing smells and into a well-lit foyer leading to several rooms, each closed behind an arched wooden door, except the dining room, which was visible through a wide archway, its table gleaming in the reflected light from the foyer. Swish stopped by one of the closed doors, knocked four times, and then opened the door. He and the girl loosened their hold on me, and Swish gave me a gentle shove in the small of my back.

I took a few halting steps into the most luxurious room I'd ever seen. The walls were the color of red wine, with rich tapestries hung to either side of a broad, stone hearth. A highly polished desk sat in the center of the room, facing the door; behind it, several oversized chairs upholstered in rich damask sat around the fireplace, in which fat candles had been set, their glow taking the place of a too-warm fire.

It wasn't the room that commanded the most attention, though. At the desk, a well-dressed, middle-aged man sat perfectly straight, as though he were posing for a portrait. His hair, though thinning, showed no sign of gray, and his face was strikingly handsome for a man his age.

"Lord Nelgareth," Swish said. "Here she is."

Lord Nelgareth?

My bones shrank within me. Here sat the man who had wrongfully accused Poppa of underpaying his Firstfruits—who lived in luxury while we struggled to stretch our money from month to month, year to year.

What in the name of the Holy God did he want with me?

Nelgareth rose slowly, his gaze direct and unwavering. "Thank you, Swish," he said in a rich voice, continuing to gaze at me as the door closed behind Swish and the girl. The next time Nelgareth spoke, his voice dropped to an almost-whisper. "Maralyth Graylaern, is it?"

I swallowed. "Yes."

"Doreck Graylaern's daughter." He continued to stare at me, his hand coming slowly to his mouth.

Perhaps captivity had frayed the edges of my nerves, because I suddenly raised my chin and said, "I was kidnapped, my lord. In case you weren't aware."

He lowered his hand and his expression shifted to mild surprise. Or perhaps amusement.

"Come and sit." He gestured to the seats behind him.

I hesitated a moment, then made my way around the desk toward the seat on the left, which was wide and deep and scattered with pillows. I perched on the edge, shoulders stiff, hands on my lap.

"Some wine?"

"No."

"A Northland ale, perhaps? Or some brandy from the lower regions."

"Nothing."

"Hmm." He poured himself a full goblet of red wine, then sat across from me, his bearing still erect. "I suppose you're expecting an apology, or at the very least an explanation."

Nothing felt real. Even my voice sounded strange and foreign. "I want to go home."

"Of course you do." He smiled, but I felt his condescension. "I'm sorry for the inconvenience, Maralyth Graylaern. Truly."

Inconvenience? The word boiled inside me, but I pressed my teeth together and willed myself to stay calm. I would learn more—

and sooner—if I didn't antagonize him. I inclined my head and said nothing.

"So. Tell me about yourself." He crossed his ankle over his knee, appearing as casual as though we had decided to spend a friendly evening together.

"Tell you what?"

He shrugged. "How old you are? Where your mother is from?"

My mother? "She died almost two years ago."

"I see." An expression crossed his face that I couldn't read. "May I ask how she . . . ?"

"The Black Death."

I'd hoped he'd at least have the decency to shudder or lower his eyes, but he did neither. "My condolences." He lifted his goblet and drank another liberal mouthful. "Did you know that there was no Black Death until after the Thungraves took the throne?"

My throat tightened. "Is that supposed to make me feel better?"

Nelgareth had the decency to look abashed. "Of course not. Forgive me." When I didn't respond, he continued, "It must be a comfort to your father to have a daughter that bears her mother's likeness. That is, assuming she had the same fair face and auburn hair as you."

I frowned. "Her hair was silver."

"Some people gray early."

"She didn't *gray*. Her hair was always silver."

"Was it, indeed?" More to himself than to me. He poured more wine into his goblet, which he raised. "To your future, Maralyth Graylaern."

He took another drink of his wine while I forced myself to look at him.

Forced myself not to feel smaller, even though I felt as though I were shrinking.

"So," Nelgareth said, rolling his goblet between his palms. "Tell me about your family."

"I'm sure they're worried ill about me."

"They'll learn of your safety soon enough." He smiled again; this time it was the smile of a benefactor.

"And will you tell them why I'm here?"

"I'm sure you're wondering the same thing."

"I am. My lord."

"Very well. I've asked you here to do me a small favor. Will you oblige me?"

I nodded warily. Nelgareth swallowed some wine, put down his goblet, and rose. He crossed the room to fetch something from the mantel and then returned to the table and placed a pressed flower on it. It was a soft, dusky pink edged in brown, not well preserved.

"This flower was given to me by someone very dear," he said softly. "I'd like to see it restored to its former beauty. Can you help?"

Fear hollowed out my heart even as the magic buzzed in my fingertips, eager and insistent. I curled my hands into my lap.

"I don't know what you mean."

Nelgareth sat and folded his hands on the table. "You're safe here. If you can help me, I assure you your secret will not reach beyond these walls."

"And if I can't?"

"Can't? Or won't?"

My heart thrummed and I tightened my fists. Swish had likely told Nelgareth he'd seen my magic. And Nelgareth obviously believed him.

The magic is your greatest asset, Swish had said. *Don't hide it.*

I met Nelgareth's gaze, determined not to let him see my anxiety— though each breath was harder to draw than the last.

"I'm . . . not sure—"

"You have an older brother, don't you?" Nelgareth's tone was light, as though his question were inconsequential.

But I sensed the danger in his words, and my answer came out like a squeak. "Yes."

"I hear he's a fine, young man," Nelgareth went on. "If anything were to happen to your father, I'm sure your brother would have no trouble keeping the vineyards running."

It was a perfectly crafted threat, and he knew I'd comprehended it. I watched him smile, vowing I'd never let him hurt Poppa or anyone else. Then, through the weight of fear so palpable I could taste it like blood on my tongue, I unfurled one hand and laid it on the table near the desiccated flower. Magic hummed in me, through me, a joy-ous tumult longing to escape.

"Refresh," I said to the flower. "Be restored."

My eyes were on the flower as it softened and unfurled, its color returning in a vibrant swirl and its fragrance rising like breath itself—but I heard Nelgareth's sharp intake of air, and I could feel the intensity of his gaze. When the flower had fully awakened, I picked it up and handed it to him.

He stared at it, mouth slightly open. Instead of fear, though, there was wonder on his face. And something that looked vaguely like triumph.

"I've been looking for you for a long time," he said, and at first he seemed to be speaking to the flower. But then he looked at me. "Quite a long time."

"You don't even know me."

"That's true." He twirled the stem of the flower between his fingers, then drew it to his nose, breathing deeply. "*Cruce,*" he swore. It seemed a long time before he finally placed the flower on the table, though he continued to stare at it.

"Why did you want to see my magic?" Each word trembled on its way out.

He looked up. "Because I have great need of it. Or, specifically, of you."

"Why?"

"You're not afraid to ask questions. Good." Nelgareth sat and crossed his leg again. "I need to ask you a few first, though. Then you may ask yours. Is that fair?"

It wasn't fair at all. "Yes."

"Tell me about your mother."

I didn't like how he kept asking about her. "I told you, she's dead."

"What was her name?"

"Tessa Graylaern. Most people know that."

He picked up his goblet and swirled the wine around inside. "Do you happen to know where she was born?"

Mother never spoke of her childhood or any of her family. Always,

I'd had a dark sense that there was pain in her past that she wished not to speak of. Nelgareth's interest in her set my nerves on edge.

"She wasn't from Perin Faye," I said, unwilling to impart even the small bit of knowledge I possessed.

Nelgareth leaned forward. "Was she, perhaps, from Northland?"

My breath caught in my throat. "Yes, but—"

"Tell me," Nelgareth continued. "How much do you know of your mother's bloodline?"

He made her sound like a warhorse. Or a kingdom. "She had no family to speak of."

"But that doesn't mean she had no family," Nelgareth said. "Weren't you ever curious, Maralyth? Did you never ask her who her parents were? Your grandparents?"

"Yes. She never answered."

"And that didn't bother you?"

I was beginning to feel more angry than afraid. "Why is this so important?"

"Because I knew her."

If my heart had been able to stop beating, it would have. Torn between disbelieving him and wanting him to say more, I sat with my mouth open, unable to pretend I wasn't drawn in by his tale.

My response was clearly what Nelgareth had desired, because he looked rather pleased with himself as he continued. "When you walked in, I couldn't believe the likeness. Years ago, I'd stopped believing that you might exist, and then—in you came. Straight from Perin Faye's famous winery."

I finally found my voice. "I may look like someone you once knew, but that doesn't mean she was my mother."

"Let me tell you a story, Maralyth Graylaern." He took another large swallow of wine; I wondered how he could manage so much. "I was once in love with a beautiful woman of Northland, but she was promised to my older brother Leon instead, so I married someone else. That's the short story."

I waited for the long story while he worried a loose thread from his cuff.

"Shortly after their marriage, my ambitious brother decided to attempt a coup against King Selmar. It was poorly planned and even more poorly funded, and he was tried and executed for treason. Prior to his trial, his wife fled and was never seen again, though the king's men searched until the winter snows stopped them. Of course, the assumption was that she would have returned to her Northland home, for she would certainly have been friendless elsewhere. But several years after they'd given up, I had another idea." He lowered his voice dramatically. "Can you think why she ran away?"

"Her husband committed treason."

"Yes, but it was his plot, not hers. What do you think terrified her so?"

I twisted my fingers together. "I don't know."

"Because she was the reason Leon attempted the coup." His eyes grew more intense. "She shared a secret with him that she probably shouldn't have. It seems she wasn't a natural daughter of her parents after all, but had been adopted from a convent orphanage when she was only seven. Her real father was a Dallowyn descendent. Do you understand now?"

I understood. Selmar Thungrave I had murdered a young Dallowyn king who'd stolen the throne from his own father and half brothers. To secure his throne, Selmar had called for the murder of every Dallowyn that could be found. The hunt had eventually died down, but every once in a while throughout the past century, a pretender had arisen here or there, claiming Dallowyn blood and asserting a right to the throne. Each time, the rebellion had been quelled. The Thungrave kings were historically powerful and merciless; it seemed a fool's game to attempt anything against any of them.

"Your story has nothing to do with me," I said.

"My sister-in-law didn't flee to Northland," Nelgareth said, "which is why she was never found. She was presumed dead and that was the end of it—until our friend Swish responded to my hunch about Doreck Graylaern's reclusive wife. And now here you are—a Dallowyn whose resemblance to Constance Nelgareth is remarkable."

My pulse beat against my temples. "You can't prove that."

Without a word, he rose and crossed to his desk, where he retrieved something flat wrapped in green velvet. I dug my fingernails into my palms as he returned to his seat, holding the covered thing on his knees.

"When Connie disappeared, I spent much of my own money on recovery efforts. This"—Nelgareth gestured to the velvet-wrapped thing—"was my only consolation when she wasn't found."

With dark curiosity, I watched him unwrap the velvet and drape it over his forearm, revealing a framed canvas. He turned it around and held it up for me to see.

My world tilted and swam. In lifelike detail, the beautiful face of a young woman graced the canvas, so familiar that my heart ached. The turn of her nose, the fullness of her lips, the shape of her eyes. It was a younger version of Mother, the hair auburn instead of silver— the only noticeable difference.

It might as well have been a painting of me.

6

MARALYTH

I stared, unable to speak.

"She was eighteen when this was painted. I had it taken down and hidden away once she went missing." Nelgareth studied my face, eyes swimming with unnamed emotion. "The likeness is astounding."

My silence confirmed what he already knew—that my recognition of Mother's face was undeniable, and I'd been shaken by it.

"You must be overwhelmed," Nelgareth said softly. "Perhaps you'd like to ask some questions?"

I wanted to shrink into my own bones and disappear. Or to lash out at him, clawing his face until he was blinded by his own blood. And in my indecision, I became numb. Unresponsive.

I thought of Mother, tucked away in the kitchen and raising me behind her skirts. Had she hidden me for reasons I'd never dreamed? I couldn't believe she'd kept so much from me. From all of us.

Or did Poppa know? And if he did, would he guess what had happened to me? A flicker of hope nestled its way into my heart.

"Her hair was silver." I'd already said that, and the words felt flimsy.

"It may be you have no memory of her hair before it lost its color. Or perhaps . . . she took care of it herself."

My stomach sank lower as I caught his meaning.

Magic.

I couldn't let myself believe it.

Nelgareth cleared his throat. "Your mother knew what she was. If she never told you, I'm sure it was because she wanted to protect you."

"What do you want from me?"

"Ah." He rewrapped the painting and placed it gently—almost

lovingly—on the floor beside him. "I'm convinced you are a Dallowyn, not only because of your likeness to your mother, but because of the strength of your magic. Over the years, the truth that only a *true Dallowyn* has access to the fullness of the magic has been lost. *All* magic has been declared stolen—except the king's. When actually, the opposite is true."

I'd grown up believing my magic was wrong. A mistake to be hidden. How could the opposite be true?

"Selmar I stole the throne from the Dallowyns a century ago," Nelgareth continued. "But it wasn't the true line he stole it from. Do you know the story?"

"King Wexen's son killed his father and brothers so he could have the throne, and then Selmar killed him and took it."

"Quite right," Nelgareth said. "Tommas Dallowyn was a bastard son, and he didn't like the idea that he would never have a chance to rule. He apparently delved into forbidden blood magic to learn how to bestow the magic on whomever he pleased. His politically powerful friend, Selmar Thungrave, agreed to champion him as the new king in exchange for some magic. Shortly after Tommas killed his family, though, Selmar had him murdered—not only for the throne, but also because Tommas's death meant that he could never take the magic back; it could now be passed down through the Thungrave bloodline. Selmar Thungrave had stolen both the magic and the crown."

"Thrones are won and lost. Ours belongs to the Thungraves now."

"It's yours by right, and I'm going to place you on it."

I swallowed. "That's treason."

Nelgareth kept his voice soft, almost calming. "The Dallowyns are the rightful rulers of Perin Faye, and always have been. History has shown us that we are far worse off under Thungrave rule than ever we were before."

I might've pointed out that Nelgareth seemed very well off, indeed.

"If you're planning treachery against our king, I want no part of it," I said.

"You're already part of it," Nelgareth said. "Heirs to thrones don't have the luxury of saying no."

"You'll *force* me to do this?"

"You wouldn't be the first reluctant ruler." There was a finality in Nelgareth's words that I couldn't deny. "My desire, though, is for you to embrace this. To see it for the gift it truly is."

"This is no gift," I hissed.

"I do have something for you to consider." His pause felt dramatic, as though he were weighing the effect of his words. "I believe we've found a discrepancy in your father's Firstfruits records."

Ice formed in my stomach. "A false accusation."

"Everyone says that," Nelgareth said. "But I'm willing to forgive the underpayment and clear him of the debt." He waited, but I said nothing, not trusting where this was going. "I'm also willing to make restitution for the loss of his daughter. Three hundred silvers should cover it."

I couldn't keep my jaw from dropping. Three hundred silver coins was enough to live on for years. I couldn't fathom having that much money at my elbow. Or being the means of Poppa's receiving it.

"You'll do that if I cooperate?" I said.

"Yes," Nelgareth said.

Suddenly I held Poppa's world in my hands. Tears came unbidden, and I hastily swept them away.

Nelgareth rang a small bell. "Your room has been prepared. I think you'll find everything you need there, but if you don't, you can let Hesta know."

A room? Hesta? I was no Dallowyn queen—I was a prisoner.

Hesta arrived—a bony, broad-shouldered woman who looked old enough to be my grandmother, though there was only a little gray in her hair.

"Take our lady to her room," he said. "And have some food brought up, in case she's hungry later."

"Yes, my lord." Hesta eyed my clothing with a tight-lipped expression I couldn't read. "This way, my lady."

"I'm not a lady," I said.

"Pay her no mind, Hesta," Nelgareth said lightly. "She's had a wearisome journey."

I rose woodenly, grateful only that I would soon be out of his presence. Without further acknowledging him, I followed Hesta to the door. She opened it and motioned for me to walk through. Then she joined me in the foyer.

"If you'll come with me." She spoke with deference, as though I *were* a lady.

Trembling, empty of stomach and spirit, I followed Hesta across the foyer and up a wide, marble staircase.

When we reached the top landing, I froze. Two large, black dogs lay sprawled on the carpet. They rose, and one of them growled low in his throat. Terror shot through me.

When I was six or seven, one of Poppa's workers was set upon by a wild dog near the edge of the vineyards. I remembered the blood on the table where they laid him so Mother could stitch up the deep gashes in his forearms and on his face. There was so much blood that I didn't know how she could see what she was doing.

Holy God, I hated wild dogs. I hadn't seen many domesticated ones.

"Quiet, Sticks," Hesta said. "Both of you, stay."

She walked past them, but I couldn't make my feet move. When Hesta realized I wasn't right behind her, she stopped and turned around.

"It's safe, my lady. They're trained to attack intruders, not guests."

I wanted to ask her how they would know the difference. Instead, I gathered my courage into a knot and sidled past the dogs, who regarded me with mild curiosity.

Oh, Poppa. I want to go home.

We stopped at the last door down a hallway to the left. "There's a steaming bath waiting for you," she said. "Unless you require my assistance, I'll wait out here."

"I don't require assistance," I said.

The washroom was long and narrow with a tiled floor and shelves upon shelves holding linens and soaps and all shapes and sizes of bottles and jars. Candles were scattered throughout the room, giving it a warm glow. A round, copper tub stood in the center, with soap, a towel, and a folded dressing gown sitting on a small table beside it. The water steamed in the candlelight.

It was nothing like our washroom at home.

When I'd finishing bathing, I leaned back and closed my eyes. The warm water eased the ache in my thighs, and the lavender-scented soap was lovely—but I couldn't relax. I'd been catapulted into a plot for the throne, and there didn't seem to be any way out.

I dried myself and shrugged into the dressing gown, which was too long. Then, hesitating only a moment when I remembered the dogs, I opened the door to find Hesta waiting, as she'd said.

"Would you like me to send someone to brush your hair?" she asked.

Why would I want her to do that? "No, thank you."

"Very well, my lady. You'll find a brush in your room."

I followed her back up the hallway; she stopped at a door on the right. She unlocked it and stepped back, allowing me to enter first.

The room was modestly sized, with a large bed, tufted chair, and thickly draped window. As in the washroom, candles were clustered here and there, casting a warm light. Beneath the window stood an ornately carved dressing table.

"I'll be back with your supper," Hesta said. She curtsied before closing the door behind her.

Wobbly-legged, I sat in the chair, which yielded to my weight and cushioned me so delightfully I felt I could sleep there. My own bedroom held only simple wooden furniture and a hand-knotted rug. Never had I experienced such luxury.

I didn't belong here.

Surely Nelgareth didn't believe he could make me queen of Perin Faye. He'd spoken of it as though it were a matter of course, like choosing a horse or changing the date of a supper party.

Would he really send Poppa three hundred pieces of silver if I cooperated?

And if I didn't, would he hold Poppa's life over my head?

Remembering my wet, tangled hair, I got up and took the brush from the dressing table, working through the snarls until my eyes stung with tears. I'd just finished when someone knocked. Remembering the promise of food, I rose and opened the door. Hesta stood with a domed platter in her hands.

"Thank you," I said as I took it, grateful for a hot supper.

"And here's something for you to wear in the morning," Hesta said, placing a folded garment on the bed. "Rest well, my lady." I barely had time to discern the odd expression on her face before she was gone.

I placed the dome on the table beside the bed, which was larger than any I'd slept in. It sat against the wall to my left, draped with rich linens and a quilted coverlet. Lying next to the brown, embroidered dress Hesta had brought was a simple, white nightdress, spread carefully with its sleeves folded as though in prayer. I ran my fingertips over the soft fabric.

Silk.

I knew what silk felt like. Mother had one silken dress that she wore for special occasions. Once I'd overheard Poppa telling her he loved the way she felt beneath his hands when she wore it. My face had burned at having witnessed such a private moment. It burned now at the thought of sleeping in fine nightclothes provided by Lord Nelgareth.

I lifted the dome from the plate; a tiny fowl, roasted and stuffed with greens and cheese, sat glistening beside thin spears of candied carrots and a large roll dotted with currants. It was exquisite—a presentation of food unlike any I'd seen.

I ate my fill and drank water until my parched mouth felt quenched. When I'd finished, I slipped out of the dressing gown and pulled the silken nightdress over my head. It felt like a cloud against my skin. For a while, I sat in the silence, feeling every bit the trapped bird I was. When I could stand it no longer, I blew out all the candles but one, which I left lit on the bedside table.

The bed was luxurious—a nest of comfort in the midst of a nightmare. In the silence, my heartbeat was a drum, banging time to the passage of seconds that seemed they'd never weave together to make an entire night pass. The single candle I'd left burning kept a steady light, piercing the darkness and dispelling the shadows that tried to encroach upon my heart.

Sleep wouldn't come. It wasn't fear that kept my eyes from shutting—it was a sense of powerlessness. I sat up, railing wordlessly against it.

Then I took the knife from my tray, wiped it carefully with the napkin, and slipped it beneath my pillow.

I fell asleep with my fingers curled around it.

7

ALAC

For three days, I didn't touch the blood locket—didn't even open the drawer to look at it.

I wanted to, though. And that's what bothered me.

I didn't fear the thing; not exactly. The magic had never held me in its thrall, and I was certain I could master this inexplicable temptation.

Almost certain.

Cannon was different. He seemed to crave the magic the way Father did. I used to tell myself that was why Father favored him. It was easier to blame the magic than to believe I was inconsequential. A second son, not overly necessary.

Which was presumptuous, since anything might've happened to Cannon before he had a chance to procreate. Might *still* happen. I didn't want that, though. I'd never wanted the throne.

On my third full day alone, I dodged an unnecessary fitting for Cannon's upcoming wedding—honestly, I hadn't grown or shrunk since the tunic had been pieced, so what was the point?—and found myself in the library poring over one of my favorite volumes: *From Grape to Goblet: Winemaking in the Northern Lordlands of Perin Faye.*

"Still spending your afternoons with books?"

I looked up to see my best friend—and a member of my personal guard—leaning in the doorway, his face in a wide grin.

"Tucker! When did you get back?"

"This morning. My mother's doing much better."

"Glad to hear it." I closed the book. "Does Derek know you're back?"

Tucker made a sour face. "He does. I swear he only granted me leave because he still owes me three bronzes from a card game two weeks ago."

I laughed. Captain Derek Towe was a good soldier but not an easy man to please. None of the members of my personal guard were particularly thrilled to be under his command.

"What boring things have you been reading about?" Tucker asked.

I grinned. "Wine. Not boring at all."

"It is if you're reading about it instead of drinking it."

"When I own my own winery, you'll think differently." I'd shared my winemaking dreams with Tucker years ago.

"You really think this is the best time to pursue that?"

"Once this wedding's over with," I said, "Father will be too busy congratulating himself on marrying off his beloved heir to worry about me."

"And you'll just . . . head out the door and promise to send samples?"

"Something like that." I closed my book. "Supper? Or are you on duty?"

"Supper before duty, always."

Tucker was the only person I could talk to about the magic. After I'd ordered that two meals be brought to my quarters instead of one, we walked there and waited until the servants brought trays of food. Then I poured two large tankards of beer as Tucker pulled off his boots and stretched his legs onto the chair beside him. He took one of the tankards and raised it.

"To your new sister-in-law."

"That's hardly worth toasting," I said.

"She's going to need someone sane to rely on if she's marrying your brother."

"True." I took a long draw of some of the best beer in our storehouse—another advantage of Father's absence.

"When is she arriving?" Tucker asked.

"In a few days, along with seven hundred family members and other people."

"You're exaggerating, of course."

"Of course." I took another pull from my tankard. "At least Father seems to like her. That's no small thing."

"What about you?" Tucker reached for a knife to carve the peppered roast on his plate.

"Other than not knowing how she can stand to be with Cannon, I think she's fine."

"He seems awfully taken with her," Tucker said through a mouthful.

"Lust," I said. "All he talks about is how he bedded her when he visited her family's keep two months ago. I doubt he even knows what her favorite color is."

"Guess it doesn't matter in the dark."

That's what I liked about Tucker—I could say things about my royal sibling that would normally be frowned upon at best, and he didn't miss a beat. I chewed a mouthful of pickled beets, thinking of how I could bring up the blood locket without sounding crazy.

"So, this magic thing."

Tucker frowned over the rim of his tankard. "What magic thing?"

"The thing everyone whispers about," I said.

"You mean your weird family secrets?"

"Yeah. Those." That was one way to put it.

"You know I'm not superstitious," Tucker said. "Any strangeness your father dabbles in doesn't concern me much."

Possibly because I'd never told him about the dagger and the blood. And I was fairly sure he wasn't fazed by my complaints of Father's insisting I memorize a ritual that, should the need arise, would transfer the magic to me.

"People do talk, though," I said. "They fear him because of it."

"They fear him because he's . . . well, fearsome."

"He didn't used to be." I plucked a grape from the plate of fruit on the table.

Tucker cut another mouthful of meat. "So you've said."

"What if I told you he gave me an amulet before he left?"

"I'd say he was no better than the one-eyed hag who sells charmed rabbit's feet just outside the city gate."

Unsaid, but heavily implied, was the fact that the hag, and anyone else who dipped their fingers into the realm of magic, was breaking an unspoken law. Mostly, people didn't remember the why behind it—but I knew my history. Long ago, the Holy God had bestowed magic on Daxion Dallowyn, the first king of Perin Faye, and all his offspring, to wield for the benefit of the kingdom. Magic, it was told, existed in time itself, woven into every grass blade, every tree, every squirrel or horse or murder of crows. Only the kings of Perin Faye were gifted with the ability to bend the magic to their will. Anything else was considered thievery.

That included my father. His great-grandfather took the throne from the last Dallowyn's bastard son Tommas, who had agreed to share magic with Selmar Thungrave in exchange for support in a coup against his father and brothers, so that he could take the throne. Selmar I was treacherous, though, and had Tommas murdered so he could claim the throne—and the magic. It didn't seem like a coincidence that, after the Thungraves took the throne, Perin Faye's history took a dark turn.

Wars with kingdoms with whom we'd never had a quarrel. The Black Death, a highly contagious illness that had never existed before. And not a single queen had outlived her husband, including my mother, who died when I was eleven.

"He says it's to protect me," I said.

"From what?"

"Death." No use pretending I didn't know what Father was talking about. "If he dies and there's a lapse of time before Cannon can perform the ritual to take the magic, it will be dangerous for everyone. The locket is supposed to protect me."

"And good luck to the rest of us?"

"The rest of you aren't in line for the throne."

"Thank the Holy God." He drank deeply. "Why are you so uneasy about this amulet?"

"Because something strange happened the other night."

Tucker waggled his eyebrows. "Matilda finally said yes?"

"I'm serious."

"Sorry." He wiped his mouth on the edge of the tablecloth. "What happened?"

"My father told me I have to wear the amulet until Cannon produces an heir," I said. "As soon as he left, I took it off. But that night, when I was in bed, I couldn't stop thinking about it, so I took it out of the drawer and opened it."

"What's inside?"

"Blood."

"Cruce."

"I already knew about the blood—some of it was my own," I said. "But as I was looking at it, I heard someone say my name."

"Heard someone . . . where?"

"I don't know. Maybe it was inside my head."

"You may have imagined it."

"I thought of that." Suddenly, talking about this over supper with Tucker made it seem less than believable. "I've never touched the magic before. I've never wanted any part of it. He was very insistent about the locket, though."

"I guess I didn't realize the king was so serious about his superstitions."

"For the past three days I haven't been able to stop thinking about it," I said. "I thought I'd mastered it by putting it in the drawer, but . . ."

Tucker emptied his tankard. "May I see it?"

I hesitated, repelled by the locket, even while a part of me whispered that perhaps power of protection wasn't a bad thing. I shook off that thought and rose. "I'll get it."

I retrieved the blood locket from my drawer. As soon as I touched it, I felt its warmth, as though it had been held within someone's palm.

Unnatural thing.

I brought it to the table and laid it beside Tucker's plate. He put his fork down and picked it up, rolling it into his palm and holding it at eye level.

"Doesn't seem like anything out of the ordinary when you look at it," he said.

"Don't you feel the warmth?"

He gave me an odd look. "No?"

I reached for the locket and he tipped it into my hand. Now that I was holding it, it didn't seem as dreadful as it had for the past three days, hiding in the drawer. Without giving myself too much time to think about it, I flipped it open. Tucker leaned across the table, his head near mine, to see.

As before, a pale black mist rose lazily from within the locket, caressing the tips of my fingers and fanning beyond them, so thin it was almost invisible. I hazarded a glance at Tucker, who was staring, eyes narrowed.

"What do you think?" I said softly.

He sat back down. "I think you should close that thing and put it away."

I gazed at the mist, simultaneously drawn to and repelled by it. Something about it seemed insistent, as though it desired nothing more than to be free of the locket. I slapped the lid shut, certain I'd heard my name again, whispered in the farthest corners of my mind.

"*Cruce.*" Tucker's gaze was resting on the plate of fruit, his mouth slack.

I looked at the fruit, at first not seeing anything. Then a strange movement caught my eye—a film of the pale mist clinging to a single grape, barely visible yet clearly moving. As I watched in horror, the grape beneath it shriveled and darkened until it was rotten. A sickly layer of mold grew upon its remains, and even then it continued to disintegrate. When, moments later, the mist rose, it left behind a grape that looked as though it had been sitting there for a month.

Tucker's whisper was so soft I almost missed it. "What in damnation was that?"

The mist, like a twisting claw, fanned out and came together again in a small cloud, almost invisible unless you knew where to look. I reached out and batted it with my hand as though it were an insect, a mild tingle brushing my skin as my hand passed through it. As Tucker and I watched, spellbound, it stretched thin and flew toward the window, where it seemed to vanish.

I looked at the rotten grape, and a sick, hollow feeling twisted through my stomach. The blood locket was heavy in my palm. Without a word, I walked to my bedside table and put it in the drawer. When I returned to the table, Tucker was still staring at the grape.

"It . . . killed the grape."

"Not exactly." But it seemed a fitting way to describe it.

Tucker finally looked at me. "You're not actually going to keep that thing?"

"And how would I go about getting rid of it? Aside from melting it down, there's no way to do it."

"Melt it down, then."

"And then what will contain whatever's inside it? You saw what just happened."

Tucker shook his head. "I have no idea what I just saw."

Part of me felt like I should be able to explain this. But I couldn't do it. I didn't understand.

"I shouldn't have opened it," I said.

"I think I've just grown more respect for that one-eyed hag."

I tried to smile, to support Tucker's attempt to lighten the mood, but it felt more like a grimace. "Let's keep this between you and me."

He didn't answer at first. "No one needs to know about this. There's enough displeasure against your father out there—the last thing I need to do is to feed that by painting him as some sort of sorcerer."

I nodded. For years, I'd been convinced my father had become just that, but I didn't say so.

"And for the love of the Sacred Church, keep that thing in your drawer."

I reached for my tankard, suddenly desperate for more beer. "I will."

But somewhere in the depths of my mind, a cold whisper answered, *No, you won't.*

8

MARALYTH

I awoke in utter darkness, the candle by my bedside having long since burned out. I lay in the silence for what seemed an eternity, until I heard the lone call of a morning bird, which meant dawn wasn't too far off.

I fumbled in the dark for the tinderbox and lit another candle, its flame piercing my sleep-blinded eyes. Then I dressed in the slightly too-big dress Hesta had left for me and slipped into my shoes. Softly, I walked to the window and pulled aside the curtain. It was too dark to get a clear idea if there was any way out of this walled fortress.

Nelgareth had threatened Poppa's life—there was no denying it. But if I escaped, wouldn't he be more interested in finding me than carrying out his threat? And if I made his plan known, he would be arrested for treason, like his brother before him.

Still, I was torn. Did I dare risk Poppa's life by running away? Would even *trying* to escape cause Nelgareth to carry out his threat?

Perhaps it was all words, to make me do his bidding. Didn't powerful people do that sometimes? Make threats they didn't intend to carry out, so others would bow to their will?

I couldn't stay in this room and do nothing. I had to at least find out if there was a way to slip out unnoticed. The door we'd come through last night had been some sort of servants' entrance. Surely I could find it.

It was no great comfort that my door had been left unlocked. The huge dogs roaming the hallways would be an obstacle to my attempting to leave; the unlocked door was a false show of freedom. Facing one of those dogs alone was more terrifying than Nelgareth's threats.

I waited for an extra breath before opening the door and slipping into the hallway. The light from my candle danced along the walls, announcing my presence to anyone who might be up and about. I blew it out and placed it outside my door instead of risking the noise of opening my door a second time.

Heart in my teeth, I approached the landing where the dogs had been lying. It was empty. I tiptoed down the long staircase, listening for the slightest sound of claws on marble. I'd just made it safely to the main foyer when I heard a growl.

Terror stabbed into me like talons; I backed against the wall while frantically searching the dimly lit space for the dog. There it stood, not ten paces from me, its fangs catching the faint light from a single sconce.

The worker's cries. Mother's needle and thread. Blood everywhere.

I couldn't think. Couldn't move.

Couldn't move.

Couldn't move.

A long wail, echoing and mournful, cut through my fear. The dog's ears perked up, too, and it seemed momentarily distracted. There it was again—a cry of anguish that seemed, in the wee hours, to come from another world.

The dog barked once, and a narrow door to the left of the kitchen entrance swung open. Hesta bustled through, arms laden with darkly stained linens.

Bloodstained.

She stopped with a start when she saw me. "Holy God, my lady. What are you about?"

"I—" *Think!* "I was hungry."

Hesta noticed the dog. "Pinion! Go on!"

The dog whined and turned to leave as another wail, clearer this time, snaked through the foyer from the doorway Hesta had left open. "You'd best go back to your room."

I wasn't going to let her send me away. "Let me help you."

She hesitated for just a moment, something like relief softening her face. "Wait here."

I sank farther into the shadows as she disappeared through the kitchen door. A minute later, she returned with a fresh pile of towels.

"Can you handle the sight of blood?"

I nodded, dread crushing against my heart. Immediately she turned toward the narrow door, and I followed her down a steep set of steps as another wail broke forth. At the bottom, Hesta turned to face me.

"Her tongue's been cut out," she said, "and she won't let us cauterize it. I could use a second person to hold her down before she bleeds to death."

Horror squeezed through me. "Why? Who . . . ?"

"Lord Nelgareth brooks no gossiping about household secrets. Come."

I forced my wooden legs to move quickly down the dimly lit hallway, unable to comprehend her words. Nelgareth ordered *tongues to be cut out?*

I braced myself and entered the small room behind Hesta. On a slender bed against the wall, a dark-haired girl lay curled on her side, a blood-sodden cloth pressed to her mouth. Beside her sat a grim-faced man with messy, gray whiskers, who looked at me with questioning eyes.

"She's come to help hold her down," Hesta said.

The girl's eyes popped open and a look of terror darkened her features. She moaned and pressed the bloody cloth more tightly to her mouth.

"Best be quick about it," the man said.

Hesta touched my shoulder. "You're smaller than me. Climb to her other side."

There was no time to feel awkward. I climbed over the wretched girl, who writhed and bucked while the man tried to keep her still. The pillow was soaked with blood, and her hair was matted with it. I steeled myself against the gore while Hesta took her place on the other side and the man reached for a poker that sat with its end resting inside a lantern.

In her terror, the girl was stronger than I'd imagined. She fought while Hesta wrenched the cloth from her fists; she heaved and twisted while we attempted to lay her flat on her back and hold her still. I felt helpless. Cruel.

The magic itched at my fingertips, buzzed in my ears. If I could clear blight from leaves or time the ripening of a grape, could I also stem a flow of blood?

I whispered to her ruined tongue as I shoved my weight against her to keep her still. "Heal. Stop bleeding."

She whipped her head from one side to the other and gagged on her own blood as Hesta forced a block of wood into her mouth to keep her from clenching it. I sensed the raw, angry edge of her wound and felt the blood flow begin to respond to my magic.

"Keep her head still." The man's voice wavered.

"Heal," I whispered again. "Stop bleeding."

But the force of the flow was too strong, the wound too profound.

I closed my eyes as the poker met its mark, the anguished cry of the girl matched only by the stench of burning flesh.

⌘

Hesta wiped the last of the blood from my hands. "There, now. Dress yourself and that's the end of it."

"Thank you." I reached for the simple, gray gown she'd brought to replace the ruined one.

She turned at the door. "This is best not spoken of."

I felt my jaw tighten. "I'm supposed to pretend this never happened?" My words were darts, sharp and unforgiving.

"That's not what I meant, my lady." She hesitated, then stepped forward and rested a hand on my arm. "I only meant that I shouldn't have let you help. You're Lord Nelgareth's guest—not one of the servants."

"I see." I tried to soften my words, but they still prickled. "I won't speak of it."

"We couldn't have done it without you, though. Truly."

I nodded, wishing I could erase the scene from my memory and the heaviness of failure from my heart. In the moment, I'd been certain the magic would do its work. But it hadn't.

"You're stronger than you look," Hesta said. "That'll serve you well."

She closed the door softly behind her. I stood, gown draped over one arm, knowing now that I couldn't leave. A man who had his servants' tongues cut out wouldn't hesitate to make good on his threats against Poppa.

Three hundred silvers began to sound like a fair price.

9

MARALYTH

Rain was pattering steadily against the windowpanes when a man dressed in azure-and-white livery and wearing an eye patch arrived to escort me to the room in which I'd met Nelgareth the night before. As soon as he saw me, he rose from his seat at the desk.

"Ah, thank you, Ed. Good evening, Lady Maralyth." His smile was warm, his eyes lighting as though he were glad to see me.

Ed bowed his way from the room as I dipped a stiff curtsy and headed toward the same upholstered seat I'd sat in before. He joined me, his hands wrapped around a steaming mug.

"The rain makes everything so damp," he said, raising the mug slightly as he sat across from me. "Otherwise I find I enjoy this much more at breakfast."

As if on cue, a servant arrived bearing a second steaming mug and placed it on the table beside me.

Nelgareth took a sip and made a satisfied sound in his throat. "Taste it. I insist."

Though I silently railed against Nelgareth's insistence, I sipped whatever was in the mug. To my delight it was sweet and spicy.

"It's *myar,*" Nelgareth said—my reaction to the drink must've shown on my face. "Made from warm milk and roasted tzala beans from the foothills of Northland. A drink your mother probably enjoyed in her youth." He waited for me to comment, but I remained silent. "So, which is it, my lady? Will we work together, or will I be forced to proceed without your cooperation?"

As if he were being *forced* to do anything. "I have one request."

He raised an eyebrow. "When you're queen, you'll be able to request anything."

I ignored his remark. "I want you to let my family know that I'm safe."

"I'm afraid it's too early for that."

"But—"

"I've spent years planning this," Nelgareth said. "I can't risk anyone finding out where—or who—you are. From today forward, you are no longer Maralyth Graylaern." He cocked his head. "Does this change your answer?"

My heart crumbled into pieces when I thought of Poppa and Nestar worrying about me. Grieving my loss. I hadn't expected Nelgareth to say yes—not really. But his refusal stung more than I'd expected it to. Nevertheless, I'd had all day to think about my answer.

I drew myself taller in my seat and met Nelgareth's gaze. "I'll accept my role. But I need to know how to justify the murder of a king."

Nelgareth smiled and handed me a leather, cylindrical case. "This may help."

Reluctantly, I took the case and removed the lid. A scroll was rolled inside; I tipped it out and, unrolling it on my lap, read.

ERRORS OF THE KING
Compiled by those who oppose his rule

My stomach tightened. Without question, the document in my hands was treasonous.

"Read it," Nelgareth said. "Take your time."

For a moment, I hesitated. But curiosity is a quickly ripened fruit, and I set aside my misgivings and continued to read. It was immediately clear that the author meant to portray King Selmar II in the worst possible light.

Arguments ending in the death of whoever had contradicted him.

Increased hostilities with Northland.

The suspicious death of his queen.

Other things were listed, too, that seemed they couldn't have much to do with the king himself: increased seasons of draught since the 799 Thungrave overthrow and decreased production from vineyard and field alike, for instance.

The magic sizzled inside me, whispering wordlessly of treachery. Was this truly my heritage and my birthright? And if I were queen, could I make a difference? I'd never known anything except the oppression of a king who squeezed his subjects dry and distributed wealth into a tight, small pool. What if, for instance, my plan to organize a vineyard cooperative could come to life on a grand scale? Might I change people's lives for the better?

Would accepting Nelgareth's three hundred silvers be only the beginning?

I began to carefully reroll the scroll. "I have questions."

"Ask."

"What if you're wrong? What if I'm *not* the Dallowyn heir?"

"I'm not wrong." Nelgareth's voice was soft as a caress. "Did you ever see your mother work her magic?"

Breath froze in my lungs. The question burned in his eyes and hung in the air between us.

"I did," he went on. "It was as . . . magnificent . . . as your own display last night."

He sipped his *myar* as though my world hadn't been tipped upside down. I wanted to slap him—to wipe that stupid, sentimental expression from his face.

"Swish has obviously been working for you for a while," I said. "Am I the only one he's ever brought to you?"

"No; there have been several." His shrug was almost disarming. "Only one was a true, full-blooded Dallowyn, like you."

I wrapped my hands around my mug, my heart racing. If there were someone else, why did he need me?

"His name is Shervan," Nelgareth continued, "a Brother of the Holy God in the Order of the Lily. I'm as convinced of his bloodline as I am yours, but I confess I'm relieved to have found a suitable replacement."

I narrowed my eyes. "Why?"

"For one thing, he's in his eighties. Still possible to sire a child, but not very likely."

Disgusting.

"Choosing a wife for him has proven to be a point of contention among the lords who are loyal to my cause as well," Nelgareth went on. "If I had a daughter of my own, the choice would have been easy."

I failed to see how it could be *easy* to marry your daughter to an old Brother who probably wanted nothing to do with her—but I couldn't let the revulsion worming its way through my stomach show on my face. "Did you have Brother Shervan kidnapped, too?"

Nelgareth's expression fell, and his words mellowed. "That's the second time you've used that word. Were you mistreated?"

"Yes," I said without hesitating. "They grabbed me from behind and put a sack over my head."

"I'm truly sorry."

I nodded. Maybe he *was* sorry, but I wouldn't absolve him that easily. Or maybe he was saying all the right things because, if I did end up on the throne, he'd want me to remember him favorably.

He let out a quiet sigh. "Our gentle Brother has long known his birthright, but has chosen a life of seclusion to hide it. He would have made a most reluctant king."

As if I were somehow less reluctant.

"How can Brother Shervan be sure of his birthright?"

He took a sheet of parchment from the table beside him and offered it to me. "I was fortunate enough to procure this from him; his family kept their heritage well-documented."

I took the sheet—it was old and stained, but the writing was clear. My pulse raced as I read a summary of the bestowing of magic to the first Dallowyn king, and how that gift would forever be in the blood of his descendants. *Only those springing forth from the direct Dallowyn line have the magic,* it said, *and no other.*

I read that sentence at least five times, my heart pounding.

If it were true, then I couldn't deny the heritage Nelgareth insisted was mine.

If it were true, then Mother had known—and hadn't told me.

I held out the document to Nelgareth. "I have no such written proof."

"You have your face," Nelgareth said, "which is so like your mother's. And you have your magic."

"But what of the Thungrave magic?" I asked. "The people may fear King Selmar, but they hold his power in awe."

"Their awe is based on lies," Nelgareth said. "The magic Tommas Dallowyn set free roamed the land and destroyed everything in its path. Once Selmar Thungrave acquired the magic, the land was safe. Selmar I was hailed as a sort of hero, despite the fact that he murdered Tommas to take the throne. It's a twisted story that the Thungrave kings have used to honor themselves over the past century."

"And you have enough support to attempt this?" It wasn't like I hadn't imagined the entire thing falling apart, with my ending up in a dungeon, accused of treason.

"I've been gathering support for some time," Nelgareth said. "Selmar has caused much unrest through his unpopular push to wage war on Northland, and it's worked to my benefit."

I thought of Nestar and the workers grumbling about this very thing. "A king can wage war where he wishes."

"But at great cost, if the war is unpopular. You will not wish to be at war with your neighbors, I think, when you are queen."

When. Not *if.* His confidence was astounding.

"So," Nelgareth said, placing his mug on the table and clasping his hands. "We'll begin your training immediately, and we'll present you to the loyal lords as soon as possible."

I'd noticed the signatures at the bottom of *Errors of the King,* but hadn't read them. "Who?"

"Tomlin Mallory of Keepings, Lorrin Trace of Tell Doral, Mat Evin of Laine. You will have the support of these men and their armies."

"Will there be a need for armies?"

Nelgareth offered the smile of a patient parent willing to overlook his offspring's ignorance. "A queen will always need the support of her lords' armies—especially during a takeover of power."

Dread spread through my stomach. "And how is that to be done?"

"We will take the lives of Selmar and his two sons. Then we'll establish your court quickly and, hopefully, without further bloodshed."

He spoke of killing as though it were nothing. But then, this was the man who had had his servant's tongue cut out.

"And . . . where will I be, when this takes place?"

"You'll be at the palace in Crownhold with everyone else," Nelgareth said. "The upcoming marriage of Cannon to Milchas's daughter is the perfect setting."

There had to be something in it for Nelgareth—some advantage I was overlooking. But for now, I let it go. If I won the throne, I would have more power than he did. Any decision to favor him would be mine alone.

"The wedding celebration is eight days long," he continued, "beginning with a welcome supper for early guests and culminating with the wedding ceremony at noon on the eighth day. We'll make our move before the wedding can take place."

I swallowed hard. "Who will you say that I am?"

"I'm going to present you as my ward, Maralyn Keele, the orphaned daughter of the late Lady Nelgareth's cousin once removed."

"Why would anyone believe that?"

Nelgareth's smile was nothing short of self-satisfied. "It's a fiction I created years ago, in the hope that one day I would need to use it. My wife's cousin and his wife have always lived a reclusive life in the north of Criminy. The wife died several years ago, and Keele himself died earlier this year. All I'll need to do is to apprise you of a few details, and it will be an easy enough role for you to assume."

Nothing about this would be remotely easy. Every word Nelgareth spoke pulled me in a dozen directions. To pretend to be someone else, to acquiesce to murder—it was beyond comprehension.

"The three hundred pieces of silver," I said, "for my father."

"I'll send it to him first thing in the morning, along with a pardon for the underpayment of his Firstfruits," Nelgareth said. "After you are queen, you'll be able to tell him the whole story."

"What if you fail?"

"I won't fail." Nelgareth leaned forward and raised his mug. "*We* won't fail."

I thought again of my plans for starting a vineyard cooperative in Windsbreath. How much more might I accomplish from the throne? Not alone, surely—I would have advisors and counselors and . . . Holy God. If everything fell into place, I would be queen of Perin Faye.

Queen!

I raised my mug, though my hand shook and my heart somersaulted.

"To Perin Faye," I said.

Nelgareth's smile was all teeth and triumph. "To Queen Maralyth."

10

ALAC

"Master Elred tells me his students have been asking to visit a vineyard." Zeth kept pace with me as I hurried to meet Cannon in the morning room.

"Is that so?" I'd hoped they'd be more subtle, but they were young boys, after all. I tried to hide my smile.

"Apparently your teaching skills stretch beyond history and geography."

"Apparently." But I saw the spark in Zeth's eye—he'd always encouraged my interest in wine, in his own, quiet way.

"Perhaps you should consider teaching as a vocation," he said as we approached the morning room.

I grunted. "No, thanks. If I hadn't come up with the vineyard idea, I might've thrown all three of them from the nearest parapet."

"Surely not, my prince."

I stopped by the thickly paneled archway to the morning room and faced him. "I don't know how you survive without a sense of humor."

"My suggestion that you teach was in earnest. The Academy in Tell Doral would be a perfect fit."

I couldn't help staring. "Can you honestly see my father agreeing to something like that?"

"Admittedly, no."

"If you can convince Father that I'd make a better vintner than second prince, though, let me know."

He raised an eyebrow and offered his usual bow before continuing on his way. I stretched a kink from my neck and entered the room. Cannon sat in one of two alcoves, his feet on the chair opposite his. He looked so much like Father with his pale hair and dark eyes that I almost recoiled. A steaming mug of *myar* sat on the round table beside him.

"Morning, brother," he said, his gaze intent on something outside the window. "I'd swear that was a peacock, but we haven't had any on the grounds for years."

"Maybe it's lost."

He absently lifted his feet from the other chair so I could sit. On cue, a servant brought me a tray of tea things, while Cannon continued to stare out the window. I thanked the servant, who withdrew quickly, eyes darting nervously to Cannon as she left.

Father had the same effect, tenfold. It was Cannon's birthright, and some days I felt sorry for him.

Cannon reached for his mug and made eye contact for the first time. Dark circles made his eyes look shadowed.

"Rough night?" I asked.

"Nothing I can't handle."

I wanted to ask him if it was harder to bear the weight of the magic in Father's absence—if he hungered for it even more. But magic was yet another topic we disagreed on, and I didn't want to go there.

"So." I poured the tea into my waiting mug—I preferred my *myar* in the evening. "Why did you want to meet with me?"

"Do I need a reason?"

My heart hitched. Sometimes he reminded me of the brother he used to be, before Grandfather died and Father became king. Before the magic had cast its shadow over our family.

"No," I said carefully.

He took a deep swallow. "Actually, I did want to talk with you about something."

Of course. I stirred cream into my tea and waited.

"Father's war effort continues to lose popularity," he said.

"It was never popular in the first place."

"True." He took another noisy slurp and set the mug down. "But it's one thing for commoners to grumble about it. It's another thing altogether when lords and underlords are digging their heels in."

I huffed. "No one digs their heels in with Father."

"Behind his back," Cannon said. "You know what I mean."

"I'm not sure what you're trying to say."

This was a perfect opportunity for Cannon to comment on my lack of intellect or inability to understand politics. Instead, he chewed his bottom lip and looked too serious.

"Let's say something happens to Father while he's away," he said.

I stopped my mug halfway to my mouth and put it down again, a vague chill running through me. "Why are you saying that?"

"Let's say it happened," he pressed. "Suddenly I'm on the throne, and then what? Everyone starts pressuring me to drop the campaign against Northland, and I don't have the experience to set them all straight."

"But you'll have the magic." I couldn't believe I'd said it. The magic I'd always hated—the magic I'd never wanted any part of—was suddenly the first thing on my mind.

"Yes." The strange glimmer that always lit his eyes when he thought about the dark magic made my stomach wither. "But I want to be more than just a sorcerer. I want to be a good ruler."

I stared, and probably my mouth was hanging open, because Cannon looked at me and frowned.

"You wouldn't understand."

"Why are you telling me this?" I asked.

"This place is going to be crawling with guests for over a week before the wedding," Cannon said, "and you're going to be involved with most of the planned events, in case you've forgotten."

I would very much have liked to forget. "So?"

"So, I need you to strike up conversations with the sons and daughters of the lords. Find out who's supportive of the war effort and who isn't. Fill them up with wine and beer and get them talking."

"To what end?"

"I need to know who my supporters are, before—" He raised his hand, palm up, and let it fall back to his lap. "I need to know."

"And then what?"

"Then you can help me sway people. Paint the war effort in a good light. Point out the reasons it will make us stronger. Richer."

This probably wasn't a good time to tell him I was against the war. "I still don't see why it matters."

"There's no glory in being king if your people don't stand with you," he said softly.

No one dared stand against Father—at least in his presence. He could call upon the magic in a breath, squeezing people's hearts with fear so that they nodded and bowed and gave him whatever he demanded. Fealty. An army. Executions. A rack of lamb after the cooks had already prepared a venison supper.

It's why people hated him.

It's why *I* hated him.

I looked at Cannon, whose gaze had wandered once more through the window. I'd never seen him look so . . . worried.

"I'll do my best," I said.

He nodded, his fingers absently tracing the edge of his mug.

"Is, uh, that all you needed?"

"I never said I *needed* you."

I set my teeth against the retort that almost flew from my mouth. This was the first half-decent conversation we'd had in weeks, and, for whatever reason, I wanted to savor it.

∝∾

Ellian's arrival day dawned sunny and dry, like any bride-to-be would want. I groaned as I rolled out of bed, knowing this was only the first wave of the horde of people that would soon show up at the castle.

The only thing more annoying than a wedding was the wedding guests.

I went outside to wait with Cannon for the arrival of his betrothed and the ridiculous entourage that would come with her. He stood at the base of the entry stairs, hands behind his back, silver circlet resting on his head like a too-tight ring. It caught the morning sun and flashed with the slightest movement. I was convinced he was aware of the effect and was doing it on purpose.

The first carriage could be heard clattering up the drive when I reached Cannon's side. Zeth stood opposite, and four men-at-arms were poised behind us. To the side, three Brothers of the Holy God stood in their midnight-blue cowls, a token spiritual presence in the castle of a king who bowed to no god. Father spent more time at his oversized desk than in the castle sanctuary.

"You don't need to be here," Cannon said.

I ground my teeth. "Father asked me to support you."

"Did he? I'll be sure to ask him to raise your allowance when he gets back."

"Try not to be an ass in front of your future mother-in-law."

The carriage was coming to a stop, effectively curtailing whatever Cannon might've said next. Behind it, a second carriage was well on its way. Cannon, all smiles, went to help Lady Milchas from the carriage, which was festooned in banners of green and orange—the Milchas colors. I couldn't help noticing that her dress was more appropriate for a formal ball than a journey in a carriage. But then, her daughter was going to marry the crown prince, so I guess that counted for something.

I bowed and greeted the lady and her husband, whose bald head shone almost as brightly as Cannon's crown. When I'd finished with the necessary small talk, I turned to see Cannon greeting Ellian, who had emerged from the second carriage. She was even slighter than I'd remembered—a pale, golden-redheaded thing who didn't even look to be the sixteen years she claimed. Cannon kissed her hand as if he might also eat it, and she laughed a little too loudly.

I had no right to feel sorry for her—she was destined to be queen, after all—but I did. I wouldn't wish the magic's dark legacy on anyone.

Cannon took her arm and drew her nearer to me. "You remember Lady Ellian, brother?"

I bowed. "How could I forget?"

"My prince," she said. "It's good of you to greet us."

"My pleasure, my lady." If I had to spit out one more formality, I might explode. But I had one more obligation before I could escape; I turned to Lady Milchas. "May I?"

She accepted my offered arm, and I escorted her up the steps, marveling at the way she started breathing hard when we were about halfway up. True, she was a bit on the plump side, but I guessed the real reason was that she sat and did nothing all day. When we reached the patio, she stopped and pressed her hand against her heart.

"Forgive me," she said. "Those stairs are formidable!"

I smiled until my teeth hurt. "Especially in a gown, I'm told."

One glance at Ellian proved otherwise; she'd reached the top and was smiling up at Cannon as they made their way through the door, apparently engrossed in whatever inane story he was telling her. I deposited the panting Lady Milchas inside the foyer, then bowed my way out the door.

I'd had enough formal nonsense for the morning; it was time for a ride.

⁂

The water was cool as it swirled past my feet. My horse grazed contentedly nearby as I sat on a flat rock with my feet dangling into the stream that lazed its way along the border of the meadow I'd chosen. In the distance, I could see the vineyard I'd taken Rupert and the others to not long ago, one of many small, local ones that grew just enough for their families.

"It is not for the mind of a prince to spend time learning a commoner's trade," Father had said when he discovered I'd been learning how to grow grapes.

I hadn't argued. But I hadn't stopped learning, either.

Glancing over my shoulder, I reached inside my collar and pulled out the blood locket, which hung from its chain around my neck. It was hard to remember the exact moment I'd decided to wear it; some time in the past few days, I'd stopped fighting it. It was hard to deny the vague sense of invincibility it gave me. As I sat with my feet in the water and my hand around the locket, I had to admit that my reason for coming to this secluded thicket had less to do with getting away from Cannon and his guests and more to do with the dark magic pulsing inside the locket.

I closed my eyes and wrapped my fingers around the locket, allowing its heat to slip beneath my skin. Father had set the spell to protect me, which was a good thing, I told myself. Preserving life wasn't evil.

If the magic inside were truly capable of keeping me from harm, what other good might it do?

I couldn't wipe the rotted grape from my memory, though. If the magic could do that to a grape, who was to say what—or who—else it could happen to?

I'd promised myself I wouldn't open the locket again, but I found my fingertips twitching to do just that. How could I understand something I couldn't observe? Ten seconds wasn't such a long time; maybe it was worth the risk.

My breaths coming hot and shallow, I slipped the chain over my head and opened the locket. The black mist was dense enough at first to obscure the blood beneath it.

One. Two.

It dissipated slowly, then more quickly, revealing the still-liquid, slightly pulsing blood beneath it.

Three. Four.

It swirled like a tiny cyclone above the locket, gathering speed and density.

Five.

I watched, spellbound, as the cyclone grew, until it was the size of a persimmon. Tentatively, I stuck the tip of my finger into its midst.

Six. Seven. Eight.

The mist spun tight around my finger, obscuring it to the first knuckle.

Nine.

I cried out as searing pain erupted in my hand.

11

MARALYTH

I'm Maralyn Keele," I said to no one, "a distant cousin of the late wife of Lord Nelgareth. He was kind enough to take me in after my father's death."

I stood in my favorite room—a sunlit parlor in the lower part of one of the turrets, its windows sweeping round a full half circle and welcoming in the morning sunlight. On the large table before me, an array of books and documents from Nelgareth's library lay in disarray. I'd spent the past week studying, familiarizing myself with maps, laws, politics, and the history of Perin Faye, though the latter I already knew quite a lot about. At home, we didn't have a library, but Poppa owned a few, precious books, one of which was a history of our kingdom. I'd spent many rainy days poring over its time-stained pages.

How many books might Poppa buy with three hundred silver coins?

Sticks and Pinion, Nelgareth's dogs, lounged on the floor nearby. I hadn't exactly befriended them—I wasn't quite ready for that—but they'd evidently decided that they liked me, which was a good thing. At least I no longer feared them.

In the evenings, Nelgareth quizzed me until my head ached. "Perin Faye hasn't seen a woman in power for over a century, thanks to the Thungraves," he said more than once. "After you've taken the throne, you mustn't give anyone the impression that you don't have the strength for it."

More than once, I was tempted to mention that I didn't plan on cutting anyone's tongue out. Apparently the now-tongueless girl had been sent back to her family, but I couldn't so easily forget what I'd seen—and what I'd failed to do.

It was difficult to reconcile the brutal, tongue-cutting Nelgareth with the man I spent hours with every day. He was ever gracious, ever patient with my studies. He spoke gently and respectably, and sometimes his gaze felt almost tender.

He's priming you to be queen, I'd remind myself. *Of course he's going to treat you well.*

I sighed and checked the list of conversational questions Nelgareth had given me to practice—next was "Is it true that your parents never left northern Criminy even to appear at court?"

The door swung open, and Ed entered with a bow. I never knew quite where to focus when I looked at him; my gaze always wandered to the eye patch.

"For you, my lady."

He gestured, and a manservant entered bearing a huge vase of flowers—brilliant blooms in oranges and burgundies unlike any I'd seen.

"Oh! But . . . why?"

"Compliments of Lord Nelgareth," Ed said. "To soften the burden of your studies."

I didn't like Nelgareth's presents—last night it had been a pair of silken gloves sitting by my supper plate. It felt too much like he was buying my favor. Or perhaps keeping me compliant.

"They're lovely," I said. "Will you place them on the table by the window?"

After Ed and the manservant had left, I turned so that my back was facing the flowers. I had a lot to review before my next meeting with Nelgareth. I knew better than to neglect to thank him, though. I'd become rather accomplished at expressing appreciation I didn't feel.

⚬≫⚬

I stood outside the closed door. It had been at least half an hour since Nelgareth left me there while he went in, and I was tired of waiting. Inside the room, voices rose and fell, but I couldn't make out a single word. Whether they were arguing or simply feeling the effects of too much wine, I couldn't tell.

For at least the fifth time, I smoothed the skirts of the teal-and-crimson damask dress Nelgareth had commissioned specifically for this meeting. The use of the Dallowyn colors felt forced, but it was hard to deny that the dress itself, with its embroidered bodice and slight train, was masterfully made.

Nina, my appointed maidservant, had done my hair in a magnificent swirl, gathering it into a coiled braid in the back with curled tendrils on either side of my face. Atop it she had placed, no doubt on Nelgareth's orders, the most delicate of tiaras. A hint of royalty, no more.

I sighed and wiped my sweaty palms on the dress, wishing the door would open so I could get this over with. On cue, the scrape of the latch on the interior was followed by Nelgareth's appearance in the hallway. He closed the door gently behind him before turning to me.

"Are you ready, Your Grace?"

I flinched at his use of the title. "I'm ready."

"And you'll remember everything I've coached you on."

"Why would I forget?" I snapped.

Nelgareth blinked. "Excuse me?"

I wanted to tell him to stop questioning my competency. Instead, I said, "Say little, be decisive but courteous, and defer to you."

"And thankful. You're ever so thankful for their support."

"If they give it," I said, taking his offered arm.

"Their support is already ours," Nelgareth said, "unless for some reason they are utterly unimpressed with you." He patted my arm with his other hand. "But I don't foresee that. I've prepared you well."

I didn't share Nelgareth's confidence, but I raised my chin as he opened the door and continued to hold my head high as we entered. Three nobles sat at a heavy, oval table, their fine clothing vying for attention in the dimly lit room. They rose as Nelgareth led me to one of two empty seats. I felt their stares as I stood in front of my designated chair, Nelgareth beside and slightly behind me.

"My lords," he said, "may I present to you Lady Maralyth Graylaern, rightful heir to the throne of Perin Faye."

I inclined my head, hoping I looked gracious instead of awkward.

The lords bowed—a bit stiffly, I thought, but then, I was an unknown, and couldn't expect much else.

"My lady, may I present Lord Mallory of Keepings, Lord Trace of Tell Doral, and Lord Evin of Laine." Then he gestured for me to take my seat.

Lord Mallory, on the far left, had the grandest air about him. His dark hair was pulled back into a low tail, the gray at his temples making him look regal instead of old. He wore a thin circlet of silver on his head—a lord's coronet, I guessed—and of the three, he was the only one who wore a cloak, folded just so over one shoulder. As I sat and the others followed suit, he remained standing.

"Nelgareth has just shown us the painting he's kept in hiding all these years," he said. "Your resemblance to Lady Nelgareth is astounding, my lady."

Say little, Nelgareth had said. I dipped my head once in acknowledgment and said nothing.

Mallory took his seat, and Nelgareth sat to my right. The other two seemed less impressed but equally interested as they settled into their chairs. Lord Trace was the oldest, easily sixty-five or seventy, with his gray, curly hair cut unusually short. On his left, Lord Evin was youngest and most striking—he couldn't have been more than thirty. His pale hair hung straight to his shoulders, and the corners of his mouth curved up as though he were perpetually smiling; it was disconcerting, so I looked away.

"She certainly favors her mother," Nelgareth said. "It's difficult to deny the relationship."

"As long as the painting is authentic, as you say." Evin's gaze rested somewhere behind Nelgareth; I turned my head and saw the painting of Connie Nelgareth—no, of *Mother*—hanging on the wall in full view.

The same chilled, sinking sensation I'd felt when I first saw the painting swept through me, crawling into the crevices of my heart and stomach and causing me to fist my hands tightly in my lap. The resemblance had shocked me then; this time, it made me want to rail against Mother and the truths she had never shared with me. It was as though I hadn't known her at all.

I looked at the auburn hair, so like mine. Had she truly used her magic to age her own hair so that it would turn silver-white? I turned away from the painting and fixed my eyes on Nelgareth.

"I would hardly have had time to commission this painting since Lady Maralyth's arrival," he said. "If I didn't believe she were the Dallowyn heir, we wouldn't be having this meeting."

"Ogden's been planning this well before you joined our ranks, Mat," Trace said in a voice both gruff and gentle. "There's no way he'd risk placing the wrong person on the throne. At any rate, Leon's widow told him herself about her true bloodline."

"We've had plenty of time to discuss the validity of Lady Maralyth's claim," Nelgareth said. "Her time is best served right now by answering any questions you may have."

The lords fidgeted while I bit back the indignation of Nelgareth's calling this *my* claim. I hazarded a guarded glance at each of them—none looked as though they particularly wanted to speak to me.

This was ridiculous. If Nelgareth wanted me to be silent, and nobody else was going to start a conversation, what was I even doing here?

Say little, indeed. I actually had quite a bit to say. "My lords, I'm sure you know that I was brought here against my will. I know firsthand the oppression of living under King Selmar's rule, especially because our vineyard is subsidized by the crown, allowing the king to control our business. Some days, all we have to feed our workers is bread and cheese. Sometimes not even the cheese."

I felt Nelgareth stir beside me, but I ignored him.

"We suffer far less than others," I continued, "and my father pays his workers as well as he can. But there are so many other vineyards—smaller ones—that don't have the ability to bring in any income. You can't feed your family on grapes." I paused to temper the passion that had begun to color my words. "I don't pretend to understand the workings of government or the intricacies of court life, but I'm learning."

If the lords were surprised at my sudden speech, they didn't show it. Evin, at least, had begun to sit forward in his seat.

"Life on a vineyard is very different from the life you will soon find yourself living," Mallory said. "How prepared are you for that change?"

A fair question. "Nothing in my life could have prepared me for this," I said, surprised at how steady my voice was.

"But now that you're here . . . ?" Mallory made a circular gesture with his hand.

"Lord Nelgareth is an excellent teacher," I said.

The lords nodded, Evin exchanging a glance with Nelgareth, but I couldn't see Nelgareth's expression.

"I have three daughters," Trace said, "and two granddaughters. I would not wish your fate on any of them."

His words weren't encouraging, but I understood his meaning. "Thank you. I'm quite anxious about my own father, who has no idea what's become of me."

"And in due time, he will know all." Nelgareth's tone told me I'd crossed an unspoken line. "At any rate, my lords, this is she on whom our hope rests. Have you any other questions?"

"It's hard to know what to ask," Evin said. "I suppose her health might be of interest? Her ability to bear children?"

Heat rose to my face and I fixed my gaze on the nearest wine goblet. Nelgareth cleared his throat.

"Of course I'll have the royal physician examine her," he said, "but she's young and healthy, as you can see. Were she sickly, I would have continued with our first plan."

Mallory harrumphed. "Which I for one was never excited about."

"My lady." Trace folded his hands on the table and leaned forward, his expression kindly. "In whatever way it might bring you comfort, I want you to know that I am willing and ready to pledge fealty to you. My men-at-arms will be ready at your command."

"I—" Did the king have any inkling that the loyalty of some of his lords was in serious doubt? "Thank you."

"I can't say I'm interested in offering comfort, my lady," Evin said. "But I appreciate your willingness to take the throne."

I inclined my head, not sure whether or not he was offering support. A furtive glance at Mallory told me that he was withholding comment, his forefingers pressed against his lips.

"What's next?" Trace asked.

"I will present her at the wedding festivities as my ward, and we will proceed with our plan."

"What about the others?" Mallory said. "I know Milchas is a lost cause, but what of Bentian and Malcom?"

"Bentian is firmly under the king's thumb," Nelgareth said. "As for Malcom . . . it's hard to say. He has expressed enough dissatisfaction over the past few years to make me think we could win him over, but I'm not sure I'd ultimately trust him."

"Our combined armies are more than a match for the others', if it comes to that," Evin said.

I placed my hands in my lap and tried to will away the unsettling truth that these men were talking about taking up arms against their own countrymen, all in the name of bringing me to the throne and protecting that throne once it was taken. It's what kept me up at night more than anything else. People would die—the king and his two sons, and anyone else who got in the way. I didn't know if I could wrestle this one to the floor. I told myself that *I* wasn't doing the killing, but in the end, what did it matter? There would be no coup without death.

"Let's spare Her Grace the sordid details," Trace said.

Hot panic suddenly shot through me, and I rose without thinking. Immediately, all four lords rose around me. I stood for several anxious heartbeats and attempted to compose myself.

"I'm not Her Grace yet," I finally said, my voice barely above a whisper. Then I remembered myself. "But thank you for your support."

Nelgareth placed his hand on my arm, a comforting gesture.

"Allow me to escort you out," he said.

I pulled myself together enough to offer a gracious little curtsy to the other lords. "It was a pleasure to meet you."

"The honor is ours, my lady," Trace said, his hand on his heart.

Nelgareth and I walked wordlessly out into the foyer. I was so relieved that the lords hadn't asked me any difficult questions. Only when he'd shut the door did he release my arm and turn to face me.

"You had rather a lot to say."

My cheeks burned hot, but I would not apologize for my words. Did he want to put a mute queen upon the throne? "Yes, I did."

"It was exactly what the lords needed to hear—strong words from the first female ruler in over a century."

His response surprised me. I nodded wordlessly.

"They say the best leaders are those who never sought leadership," he continued. "This bodes well for you."

"How does it bode for the lords?" I asked, finding my voice.

"They will expect to be rewarded for their loyalty, of course."

"And you will advise me on that?"

"As you wish."

I almost asked him how he stood to personally benefit. But he had sidestepped the question before, and I didn't want to risk angering him—especially since he hadn't mentioned the comment I'd made about Poppa.

"Will I . . ." It was hard to find words that didn't feel like I was choking on them. "Will I have to be there when the king and the princes are murdered?"

"Yes." He said the word gently. "It will happen at the wedding breakfast, the day of the wedding. You will be present along with all the lords and their families."

"What if I'm not convincing?" My fears bubbled to the surface. "What if they see through me?"

"They'll have no reason to suspect anything. You've done your work well." Nelgareth drew a folded sheet of paper from his breast pocket. "You may be interested in this."

Warily, I took the paper and unfolded it. *Receipt for the payment of three hundred silvers,* it read. Poppa's signature was scrawled across the bottom. I stared at it, my eyes burning with unshed tears.

"I'm a man of my word, my lady," Nelgareth said softly.

I closed my eyes briefly, then opened them. "Thank you."

He took my hand and kissed it. "I'll see you at supper, Your Grace."

The hollow touch of his kiss lingered long after we parted.

12

ALAC

I shook my finger; the mist wouldn't dissipate. Panic rose in my chest as the pain intensified. Instinctively, I closed the locket and held it against my breastbone. Warmth from the blood locket grew in my palm until it was almost too hot to hold. The pain decreased, then faded. I opened my eyes and sucked in a sharp breath when I looked at my finger. The nail had grown long and curved, as though I hadn't trimmed it in weeks. Possibly longer. Horrified, I bent my finger and examined the nail from all angles. It was at least three inches long. I stared at it until my vision darkened; then I pulled out my dagger and cut the nail off.

For a while, I sat and tried to make sense of what had happened. The grape, my finger—both times, the magic had worked in such a way that time had seemed to pass, leading to the rotting of the fruit and the growth of my nail. The blood locket had released the magic from my finger—but hadn't reversed the damage. And had the cloud of magic dissipated, or had the power of the locket destroyed it?

I knew the story of the free-roaming magic that had terrorized the land until my great-great-grandfather had performed the first ritual and taken the magic to himself—right before murdering Tommas Dallowyn and taking his newly won throne. The same magic was inside the locket, and I imagined it would behave the same way, though on a much smaller scale. Somewhere, that tiny spray of black mist was wending through tree and field, affecting anything that crossed its path.

Soberly, I hung the locket around my neck and tucked it inside my tunic. Regardless of the destructive powers of the magic once outside the confines of the locket, the power within it had done its job, protecting me by dispelling the magic attached to my finger. I didn't want to know what would have happened if the magic had run its course. Visions of a blackened finger falling off and rolling onto the ground made me more determined than ever to fight the temptation to open the locket again.

More than that, though, I wanted to understand the magic that, for over a week now, had kept me under its thrall. I'd always feared it— and because I feared it, I hated it. If I thought about it hard enough, it was probably the reason I'd always been content to be second born. If assuming the throne meant wearing the mantle of a dark power I didn't understand, I wanted no part of it.

Until now. I couldn't rest until I understood something of this stolen magic and its hold on my father—and his father, grandfather, and great-grandfather before him. I'd watched it consume Father; I'd learned to recognize the dark gleam in his eyes when the magic was moving within him. If I took the time to learn how it worked, perhaps I could wield the power in a less destructive way. Turn it from darkness to light.

Before it consumed me, too.

∾

It was another two days before I found a chance to approach Cannon alone. I'd watched him retire earlier than usual and figured I'd find him halfway through a bottle of wine in his apartments, which were just down the hallway from mine.

I stepped into leather slippers and told the guard at the door to stay where he was. If Tucker were on duty, he would've wanted to come along, which I wouldn't have minded.

I knocked twice and opened the door without waiting for Cannon to answer. In the dim candlelight, Cannon disentangled his face from Ellian's with a loud sucking sound, and I fought to restrain an eye-roll, for her sake. She leaped from his lap, smoothing her gown and turning her back to me in one, graceful motion.

"Your timing needs a little tweaking, brother," Cannon said, pulling a linen shirt over his bare torso.

"After the wedding, I promise not to make any surprise visits." I cleared my throat. "Apologies, my lady."

"None necessary," Ellian said, deftly fastening whatever Cannon had managed to open and turning to face me with a composed smile. "I hear little brothers are supposed to be a nuisance, at any rate."

It was hard not to smile back. "I'll try to work on that."

"Is there a reason for this interruption, or did you just want to make small talk with my betrothed?" Cannon asked.

"I need to talk with you about . . . certain things."

Cannon laughed. "It that code for something? Ellian and I aren't going to have any secrets, so say what you came to say."

"I can leave," Ellian said.

"You're not leaving." Cannon looked at her with an almost glazed expression and licked his lips. "Come."

He rose and extended one arm toward her. After a quick glance in my direction, she moved beneath his arm, which he wrapped around her shoulders. They both looked at me, waiting.

I lifted the blood locket from beneath my dressing gown and held it out. "Tell me what you know about this."

Cannon's expression changed immediately. He took his arm from around Ellian and stepped forward, reaching for the locket with one finger, which he touched briefly to its surface.

"It's about time you asked," he said.

"You knew about this?"

"Of course I knew about it. Do you think Father would leave you to your own devices with something like this?"

I dropped the locket back beneath the dressing gown. "You might've said something."

"He asked me not to," Cannon said. "Have you opened it?"

"Yes."

"Father said you would."

A slow shudder worked its way up my spine. "I think about it all the time."

"You won't be able to stop." Cannon's voice had gone hollow. "Not ever."

I stared at him in the silence; his eyes had shifted color, darkening slightly. I'd seen it in Father so many times that it didn't startle me.

Ellian moved forward. "I should go."

"No. This belongs to you now, too." Cannon's eyes were still on me. On the place where the locket rested beneath the fabric on my chest.

"Father goes on progresses every year," I said. "Why does he feel the need to protect me this time?"

Cannon looked, for a moment, reluctant. Then, hastily, he said, "Come with me."

∽∝∾

I'd hated my father's quarters ever since the night I'd first seen the ritual. Even now, when he wasn't there, anxiety crept through me and caught me in a stranglehold when I realized that was where we were going.

The double doors of his apartments were free from any guards—a sure sign that he wasn't in the castle. I hung back while Cannon turned the knob and pushed one of the doors open. He ushered Ellian in, and I forced myself to follow. The space smelled like Father—frankincense, pipeweed, red wine. And the strange, slightly burned scent that I had always attributed to the magic. Or perhaps it was my imagination.

A candelabra sat to the right of the doorway, and I took a minute to light three candles. I held one and gave the others to Cannon and Ellian, who looked ghostly against the dark backdrop of my father's chambers.

Cannon stopped near the table by my father's enormous bed. I knew he'd find a key in the drawer—it was where I'd found it years ago, when I sneaked into Father's chapel. But instead of opening the drawer, he reached into his pocket and pulled out his own key. He faced the paneled door to the right of the bed.

Ellian's eyes were large in the candlelight. "Is this his private chapel?"

"Yes." Cannon turned the key, and the door swung silently open.

I shuddered. It had been nearly a year since the last time Father had compelled me to join him here, to go over the ritual and make sure I understood what was required of me, should Cannon die without an heir. The long table to the left was the same one I'd hidden beneath as a boy, concealed behind the heavy, damask table covering. The single lamp, dangling above the altar, cast a red glow over everything.

"This," Cannon said, taking Ellian's arm, "is the secret of the power of the Thungraves."

Ellian stared, her mouth a small *O*. "Incredible."

"Our great-great grandfather saved the kingdom from a dark magic that destroyed everything in its path," Cannon went on. "With this."

"So the story goes," I said under my breath.

Cannon glared. "So the story *is*."

I let it go. I was here for information, after all.

Everything was in place, from the spotless altar cloth to Father's jeweled dagger resting on a crystal goblet, both of which I'd watched him use before. In the center of the altar sat a hammered gold dome— the "receptacle," Father called it. On the surface, it was a ludicrous display of wealth, encrusted with precious stones. But it held dark secrets that transcended its earthly value.

"What is it?" Ellian asked.

I stood an arm's length from the receptacle and stared at the small door on its front. "There's an hourglass inside." Father had never opened it in my presence, but I'd seen it on the night he'd performed the ritual.

"No one can touch it but the king." Cannon's voiced was hushed with what sounded like reverence. "When Father dies, it will be my turn."

Anxiety tightened my bones as Cannon reached for the small door on the receptacle. Ellian stepped back, probably so she could see better, short as she was. The door opened soundlessly.

Within the receptacle, an ornate hourglass sat, faintly glowing against the black velvet it rested upon. Instead of sand, the bulbs were filled with a luminous substance, most of which swirled in the lower bulb. It felt wrong, somehow.

"The breath, the blood, the words." Cannon stared at the hourglass as he spoke. "This is the breath."

Ellian swallowed, her expression rapt. "What is it?"

"The souls of the kings who have gone before and the raw magic of Tommas Dallowyn, who created this ritual to give his magic to the Thungraves."

"Why is most of the breath in the lower bulb?" I asked.

"A Thungrave king will always know when his time is growing short," Cannon said, "by the amount of breath left. Shortly before Father left for his progress, the breath sank alarmingly. He began to fear that he wouldn't make it home, so he wanted to be sure you'd be protected from the magic until I was able to perform the ritual."

"He's . . . dying?"

"Not this exact moment." Cannon's voice tightened with irritation. "It means he doesn't have much time left." He closed the receptacle and turned to me. "Our hold on this magic is the only thing that keeps it from destroying the entire kingdom. You know that."

It wasn't the right time to tell him I wasn't sure I believed that. "So, it'll just create mass destruction while I sit safely in the castle and watch?"

"Don't be stupid," Cannon said. "You'd be my heir—no one else would matter."

"Why does it call my name?"

"Not *it. They.* The spirits of the kings."

That definitely didn't make me feel better. "Why do *they* call me?"

"They know your blood." He walked to the right wall, where a squat, metal cabinet sat. He opened a squeaky door, rummaged for a moment or two, then shut the door and returned to the altar bearing a velvet scroll case. "This was supposed to wait until Father's death, but I think you should have it now."

"What is it?"

"The words. You can't complete the ritual without them." He handed me the scroll. "I've had these memorized since I was fourteen. Hide it somewhere safe."

I took the scroll, a chill creeping down the back of my neck. Here was the final piece of the ritual—the one secret entrusted only to the direct heir. "I'd rather not."

"Until Ellian gives me a son, you're my heir. You have to be ready."

I didn't want to think about the possibility of having to take

Cannon's place, but I'd rarely seen him so earnest. I nodded. "I'll be ready."

"And don't take this off." He pressed his hand against the blood locket beneath my dressing gown; it burned hot against my flesh. "Your duty lies with the throne, whether you like it or not, brother. If Father dies and you're not wearing this, you're as good as dead."

13

MARALYTH

A light breeze played with the wisps of hair around my face as I waited in the courtyard in front of the keep. The ride to the royal palace would be a short one—two hours, I'd been told—but the preparation for the journey had been nothing short of ridiculous.

By now, the story of Lord Nelgareth's ward—the unfortunate orphan of his late wife's cousin—had been widely circulated. That I would accompany him to the wedding festivities for Prince Cannon and his bride was unquestioned. In the past week and a half, I'd been fitted for enough dresses to cover every social engagement leading up to the wedding, as well as the wedding itself. I had a passing knowledge of the names of all the lords and their families and was hopefully ready to engage in conversation at court.

Now, in the late morning heat, I tried to prepare myself for what lay ahead. I was thankful the king wouldn't be there. Hanging over me hourly was the sickening reality that he would be murdered so that I could take his throne. And his sons with him. I constantly pushed it as far from my thoughts as I could, distancing myself from the dark work of others.

"My lady."

Hesta stood inches from my elbow; I hadn't heard her approach. "Take this." She pressed something into my hand.

"What—?"

"Hush." She lowered her voice. "If anything goes wrong—if you find yourself fleeing the castle for any reason—don't come here. It's the first place they'll look for you." She closed both hands around mine, which held whatever she'd given me. "This is a safe place," she whispered.

I felt too confused to know what to say. She gave my hands a final squeeze, then kissed me soundly on the cheek.

"You're brave and kind, which is more than I can say for most people," she said. "Whatever his plans for you may be, stay true to that bravery and kindness."

Then, as though we hadn't had any conversation at all, she gave a crisp nod and made her way back to the house. I peeked into the palm of my hand and saw a small, carefully folded sheet of paper. I tucked it deep inside the pocket of my gown and tried to calm myself.

When the footman finally offered me his hand, I grasped it firmly and stepped into the carriage, determined that I would prevail—and make a difference for my family and all of Perin Faye.

No matter how dreadful the path.

The inside of the carriage was almost as opulent as Nelgareth's home. My maidservant Nina and I sat across from each other on heavily tufted seats of fine damask, with velvet throw pillows tossed about. We rode in silence for some time. When I was sure Nina wasn't paying attention, I dug the paper out of my pocket and unfolded it. It was a simple map of a section of Silverton, with an X marked at the corner of two streets. Above the X was written, "Wennie's." Heart pounding, I refolded the paper and returned it to my pocket. How much did Hesta know, I wondered? And why did this "safe place" even exist?

I hoped I never needed to find out who Wennie was, but I breathed silent thanks to Hesta for her kindness.

Nina remained respectfully quiet until the gate of Crownhold could be seen in the distance. Then it seemed she could no longer contain herself.

"You must be excited to meet the young Prince Alac," Nina said.

I stared, particularly since he was on the "to be murdered" list. "Why?"

"I've heard he's quite charming, though apparently he keeps to himself a lot."

"If he keeps to himself, how does anyone know whether he's charming or not?"

"I . . . don't know, my lady." She gazed out the carriage window. "Perhaps he'll take his own wife, once Cannon is married."

"Perhaps." Or perhaps he wouldn't live to see his next birthday.

Anxiety fluttered its way up my skin and through my stomach as the city gate grew nearer. I'd said *yes* to the murder of three men so that I could take the throne; the weight of that truth was a burden I'd have to get used to.

By the time our carriage stopped at the palace gate, I was certain my heart would soon beat itself out of my chest. The terror of entering the castle we were attempting to take was almost too much to bear.

I peered out the window as our driver exchanged a few words with a guard. Ahead of us on the well-kept road, Nelgareth's gleaming carriage had already made its way to an expansive courtyard. Beyond that, I could just make out the turrets and battlements of the castle.

I can't do this.

But I took a great breath. *I will do this.*

We pulled into the courtyard, where Nelgareth's carriage had already stopped. I curled my hands around the sill of the carriage window and craned my neck to see beyond it. It was clear that several people were there, but the carriage hid them.

Nelgareth cut a fine figure in a richly embroidered tunic the color of a summer sky. I gathered my skirts and prepared to disembark, expecting the footman, but Nelgareth himself appeared at the carriage door.

I took his gloved hand and allowed him to guide me from the carriage, though I was capable of doing it myself.

"Remember not to speak until spoken to," Nelgareth said softly.

Did he think I was a child who couldn't remember simple rules of etiquette? But I nodded once and straightened my shoulders, trying my best to appear as though being presented at court weren't at all out of the ordinary.

We walked around the other carriage, which was parked near the base of a wide, stone stairway that led to a long patio. In front of the steps, flanked at a discreet distance by men-at-arms, stood the two princes—of similar height, though the one with a jeweled coronet on his white-blond head and a lady on his arm had to be Cannon. The other was Alac, then. His light hair hung in messy waves just past his shoulders, and he wore a circlet of gold upon his head, so thin it was barely discernible.

"Your Grace." Nelgareth bowed low. "It's a delight to be received by you."

"Lord Nelgareth." There was no emotion in Cannon's words, and his facial expression was practiced. "You may remember my brother Alac?"

"Of course." Nelgareth smiled and bowed again. "My prince."

A thin man to Alac's right cleared his throat. "It's good to see you again, Ogden."

"Ah, Zeth! Likewise."

My heart skittered at the name. This was the High Minister, who had the king's ear and his deepest trust. He was taller by half a head than anyone else and wore his hair in a thick, black-and-silver braid pulled forward over one shoulder.

"I can see you're keeping our princes in good form while their father's away," Nelgareth continued.

"They keep themselves in form, I assure you," Zeth said.

"Splendid."

With each word Nelgareth spoke, my stomach knotted more tightly. In a short while, the "splendid" princes might be dead, yet it was impossible to tell that Nelgareth felt anything but respect, and perhaps even affection, for them.

"This is my bride-to-be, Lady Ellian Milchas," Cannon said.

Ellian was all smiles. "My lord."

Now that I was closer, I could see that Ellian was no older than I. She was all grace and charm in her beautiful blue gown, her long, golden-red curls resting like sleeping kittens over the front of her bodice. I wondered if she loved Cannon, or if the match were purely one of state.

Will you grieve him when he is gone, Lady Ellian?

"And it gives me great pleasure to present my ward, Lady Maralyn Keele, daughter of my late wife's cousin once removed."

On cue, I dipped a small curtsy and forced myself to meet Cannon's, then Alac's gaze. "Your Grace. My prince."

"My lady." It was Alac who spoke; his brother merely nodded.

I wouldn't allow myself more than a cursory glance at Alac's face before averting my gaze. In the single heartbeat in which our eyes met, something nameless shifted inside me, as though it were making room for him.

I couldn't breathe. And then the moment passed.

"We're delighted to be here to celebrate your nuptials." Nelgareth was all grace and polish without a hint of the black deception beneath his smile. "Thank you for the honor."

Another carriage made its clattering way across the cobbled expanse, next in line for the princes' greeting.

Zeth stepped forward. "If you'll follow me, I'll see that you're brought to your rooms."

His gaze rested on me for a heartbeat too long, a silent assessment that made me feel every bit the false girl I was.

Nelgareth motioned with his head for me to go first. I glanced at the cowled Brothers of the Holy God who stood off to one side, perhaps to bless the arriving guests. They offered nothing, though; not even eye contact. I followed Zeth up the steps, the swish of my dress lost in the tumult of the arriving carriage. When I reached the patio, I turned briefly to take in the view and saw Alac looking at me.

He smiled.

The heat that flashed through me tightened into a cold knot in my stomach, and I turned away.

Zeth bowed us from his presence in the castle foyer, which opened to a height I'd never seen inside a building. At the top was a dome of colored glass, glowing with sunlight and reminding me of the sanctuary in Windsbreath. A matronly servant led us up a wide, stone staircase that curved its way up to a second story, where she then led us down a long hallway to a door on the right.

"For you, my lord," she said.

"Thank you, Berrie," Nelgareth said lightly, passing into the room as though he'd been there dozens of times. Probably he had.

I followed Berrie to the next door, which she opened.

"And for you, my lady," she said, stepping out of the way so I could enter.

The chamber was no finer than any of Nelgareth's. Even so, its beauty was breathtaking. Most of the back wall was taken up by a paned window that stretched nearly to the ceiling and into which a cozy window seat was built. To its right, a door led to what appeared to be a small balcony. The room itself contained a writing desk and two overstuffed chairs beside a hearth on the right wall. To the left, a doorless entryway led to a separate bedroom.

"Thank you," I said.

Nina entered quietly and made her way to the bedroom with one of my satchels. I found myself wondering where she would sleep.

"The Welcome Supper will be served at seven, my lady," Berrie said, offering a little curtsy before letting herself out.

I walked to the window seat, drawn to it in almost the way I'd always been drawn to vineyards and trees and all growing things. Kneeling on the deep cushion, I could see what had attracted me— the balcony opened to a lush garden below that included ornamental trees and arbors of table grapes ripening in the sun.

My chest tightened with longing for home, and I closed my eyes against the tears that wanted to spill forth. I could no longer allow myself such indulgences.

"They'll be bringing your things up directly," Nina said from the entryway of the bedroom.

"Have you been here before, Nina?"

"No, my lady."

I sank onto the window seat. "I'm not sure how to behave."

Nina chewed her lip. "I don't think there's any need to behave differently from how you normally would. The king isn't here, so that makes it much less frightful."

"Frightful?"

She nodded. "He's said to fly into a rage at the least provocation."

I knew that to be true from my near-memorization of *Errors of the King*. I offered what I hoped was a convincing smile. "We mustn't provoke him, then."

"Yes, my lady."

Staying away from his sons would be a good idea, too. The less I saw of them, the better.

A light rap sounded on the door, and Nina immediately went to answer it. My things, I supposed.

But she closed the door again after a brief exchange with someone and handed me a small square of creamy parchment—a handwritten note that made my heart drop to my toes:

> *Prince Alac requests the pleasure*
> *of your presence at his table this evening*
> *for the Welcome Supper.*

So much for avoiding him.

14

ALAC

I regretted sending the obligatory invitation the moment it left my hand. True, there was a certain sense of decorum I needed to stick with, now that the official wedding week was underway, but I wasn't sure what had induced me to invite a perfect stranger. Other than the way her hair had glowed in the sunlight. Or maybe it was her gaze, direct and matter-of-fact—like she was challenging me instead of flirting.

I couldn't even remember her name. Mara-something. Maralee? Probably I should find out before the Welcome Supper.

Cannon and Ellian were still making small talk with the self-important underlord and his wife from Draper's Down who had arrived minutes after Nelgareth, so I signaled to Tucker, who stood several paces from me, and took the palace steps two at a time.

"You could've acted a bit more princely just then," he said, catching up to me at the door.

"Next time you can strew flowers at my feet as I leave."

Tucker grinned. "Meet you at the stables, then?"

"Give me ten minutes to change."

It would be slightly easier to deal with playing host tonight if I could get away for a couple hours. Father would never have allowed it, and if I were perfectly honest, that was probably why I wanted to do it.

By the time I'd changed into my riding leathers and made my way to the stables, Tucker had our horses ready and waiting. I mounted, feeling the surge of freedom the saddle always gave me. This time, though, it was tempered by the subtle weight of the locket around my neck, which seemed daily to grow heavier.

"Did I actually see you hand off an invitation card?" Tucker asked, bringing his horse abreast of mine.

"I figured I'd get it over with."

"You could do a lot worse."

"I don't even remember her name." I urged my horse forward.

"Maralyn Keele," Tucker said, keeping pace. "And it's a good thing you keep me around."

"I'm not even sure why it's necessary to give out invitations in the first place. We're all going to be eating supper together, regardless."

"Not everyone gets to sit by a prince and bat her eyelashes, though."

I rolled my eyes. "She doesn't seem like the eyelash-batting type."

Which was definitely intriguing.

⌘

I'd never been this early for a supper party. Barely-on-time was more my style, though I tried never to be late for the sake of avoiding Father's wrath. Tonight, in his absence, there was no excuse for me to already be seated at the head table, fingering my goblet of wine like a nervous page.

Why should I be uptight about sitting beside some dead underlord's daughter? Mara-something Keele. Nine chances out of ten, Nelgareth was hoping to marry her off to me. Might as well get the initial meeting over with.

Guests filtered into the dining hall, which was our smaller, secondary hall—and the one I preferred. It seated no more than fifty, and tonight there would be fewer than thirty. Things would get more crowded tomorrow, and I'd have to find creative ways to excuse myself from the chaos.

"Wonders never cease." Cannon picked up the purple ribbon at the place to my left that signified a seat reserved for a lady. "Which is it? Lisbet or Nelgareth's whelp?"

"Lisbet's here?" I scanned the room but didn't see the dark-haired girl who'd been throwing herself at me since she was about five.

"Must be the whelp, then." He pulled out Ellian's seat and kissed her neck before she sat.

I greeted Ellian instead of favoring Cannon with a response. She was all smiles, as though life couldn't possibly have turned out better. She'd learn the hard way what life would be like once Cannon became king. Let her smile while she could.

Nelgareth lingered in the doorway as he usually did, quietly announcing his presence as though everyone in the room should stop and take notice. I didn't pay him any more mind than usual—my gaze was arrested by the girl on his arm. It was true I hadn't let myself pay too much attention earlier, but it was hard to ignore her now. It might've been her auburn hair, so striking against the ivory gown. Or maybe it was the way she stood there, assessing instead of fawning. As though she were taking silent measure of the room and everyone in it.

I leaned over Ellian's head and caught Cannon's eye. "She's no whelp."

15

MARALYTH

My dread of sitting at the princes' table wasn't lessened by the way Prince Alac rose when he saw us in the doorway. I half heard Nelgareth saying something to a servant about my having been invited to the head table; then we were making our way between the two long tables in the center of the dining room toward the small dais at the front.

I offered a deep curtsy. "Your Grace. My prince."

"I'll leave you in their good hands," Nelgareth said, bowing. All grace, all politeness.

Alac stood behind a chair, waiting for me. I walked to the side of the dais and stepped up, feeling ridiculously on display. I wondered how long it took to get used to things like this.

"My lady," Alac said, waiting for me to take the seat he offered.

His hair was pulled back into a tail, but it still looked slightly unruly. I offered the most gracious smile I could muster and took my seat beside Lady Ellian.

"Hello, again," she said. "It'll be nice to have you to chat with instead of being stuck alone between two bickering brothers."

"Surely they don't!"

"You'll see for yourself before the night is over. I'm sorry, what was your name?"

"Maralyn." It felt foreign on my lips.

"I'm Ellian." She laughed lightly. "Though I'm sure you knew that."

"I'm honored to sit by the bride," I said.

Cannon commanded her attention just then, and I settled back in my seat with a small smile at Alac, who reached for the flagon to his right.

"Wine?" He waited for my nod before beginning to pour.

"Bothshed Clarion," he said. "Not my favorite red, but it's nice and round. This is one of their best vintages."

My interest moved up a notch. "You know your wines?"

"It's a hobby of mine." He smiled. "But I won't bore you with it."

"Wine isn't a boring topic, my prince."

He looked at me as though he weren't sure if I was serious. "It's kind of you to say so."

You're brave and kind, Hesta had said. I felt nothing but false.

High Minister Zeth took the seat on Alac's other side, making my heart wilt a bit. He bowed his head as if I were a fine lady.

"This is Lady Maralee Keele," Alac said.

"Maralyn."

His brow wrinkled. "I knew I'd get it wrong."

He seemed genuinely embarrassed. Was this the dark, brooding, magic-laced prince I'd been reading about for the past week and a half? Perhaps he was an excellent actor.

For the rest of the meal, his conversation was divided between Zeth and me, which was a strange mixture of awkward and relieving. Ellian filled in the gaps by asking polite questions about my family and my interests, but Cannon was possessive of her attention, and she loved giving it to him.

This was a million times harder than I'd feared. Memorizing names and keeping my fictional story straight was the easy part. What really worried me was that I'd fail at presenting myself as a noble-bred girl, despite Nelgareth's assurances that I'd learned quickly and well.

I thought of our simple suppers at home—toasted bread and cheese, turnip soup, leftover scraps from lunch. Since arriving at Nelgareth's, I'd eaten the finest morsels imaginable, cooked and served by others; this meal was no exception. Who was feeding the workers at home? Would Poppa use some of his three hundred silvers to feast on meat every night, as I did?

By the time dessert arrived, I could no longer eat, the remains of my exquisite supper littering my plate like unwanted guests. I allowed my food to be taken and hoped I could fake eating the cream-drenched tart that had been placed before me.

"I don't care for apricots much, either," Alac said.

I was mortified that he'd caught me moving forkfuls of the tart around on my plate. A glance at his dessert, though, showed me he'd barely touched it.

"I like them," I said. "I'm just not very hungry."

He gave me a side-eyed glance. "I do believe you're telling the truth."

"Why wouldn't I tell the truth?"

"Most girls say 'I'm not hungry' or 'I'm tired' when they really mean 'This food is awful and I can't stand your company.'"

"You must know a lot of dishonest girls."

He smiled. "Yes. I suppose I must."

I was relieved a few minutes later when Nelgareth appeared. He bowed low.

"My prince," he said. "I must beg my ward's removal. It will be a long week at court, and she needs her rest."

"Of course." Alac rose as I did. "Thank you, Lady Maralyn, for supping with me."

I smiled and raised an eyebrow. "Thank you for getting my name right."

When I rose from my curtsy, Alac looked like he was holding back laughter. My stomach dropped, and I turned away quickly. I should never have allowed myself that moment of levity with the prince. It wouldn't happen again.

Once Nelgareth and I were free of the dining room, I felt I could breathe again, even though I hated feeling like he had me on a tether.

"How was your supper with the prince?" Nelgareth asked.

"Awkward."

"There will be many other ladies commanding his attention this week," Nelgareth said. "You won't have to worry about sitting with him again."

"Yes." I hoped he was right.

∞

I slept more deeply than I dreamed I would. In the morning, I was awakened by the arrival of a luxurious breakfast on a tray—soft-boiled eggs in a nest of sautéed mushrooms, several thin slices of ham, and two steaming buns dotted with sage—my favorite!—and served with butter and several jams in beautiful, cut-glass jars. And a mug of *myar,* of which I'd grown quite fond.

It felt decadent to sit in my nightgown and eat fine food in the privacy of a room in the castle. Perhaps it would eventually feel normal if I were queen, but I didn't share Nelgareth's confidence that that would happen. I'd saved Poppa's life and provided him with enough silver to keep him comfortable for years, but there was a good chance that the coup would end badly for me.

When I'd finished eating, I chose a simple, wine-colored day gown and sat at my dressing table while Nina did my hair. It still felt silly; I'd only ever worn braids or a low bun. I had to admit, though, that Nina had a gift for making even my untamable hair look beautiful.

"I'll prepare your gown for tonight before I go," Nina said when she'd finished.

I waited until she was occupied; then I made my way to the window seat, where I'd hidden Hesta's map in a crack behind the cushions. I pulled it out and studied it, my head swimming; I wasn't good at maps. Sighing, I refolded it and tucked it into my bodice. I'd find a better hiding place later, when I was alone. Once I had it memorized, I'd destroy it.

I left Nina to her business and made my way past the window seat to the balcony door. Sweet scents of fruit and flower met me the moment I stepped outside. Feeling freer than I had for the past two weeks, I curled my hands around the railing and breathed deeply of the summer air. Beneath me, rows and circles and undulating lines of flowers created a dazzling picture, with carefully placed trees creating depth. In the center of the garden, a fountain, its four spouting fish sitting at the quarters of its circular edge, sent its tinkling music over the soft breeze. Even the vineyards, in all their wild beauty, couldn't rival the artistry of this garden.

I sat upon a small bench and noticed a miniature fig tree in the corner of the balcony. It was planted in a large, brass pot, and stood perhaps four feet tall. I moved closer, feeling somewhat sorry for a tree consigned to such an existence. Several fruits, smaller than regular figs, were nearly ripe, while others sat hard and green among the dwarfed branches. I stroked the leaves, magic humming in my fingertips. A fierce longing, like the need to draw breath when underwater too long, rose up within me.

Tentatively, I brushed my fingers over the nearest almost-ripe fig; it seemed to dance beneath my touch, begging for the quickening I could give it. The nudge within me grew to an uncontainable ache.

Would it be so bad to use such a small amount of magic? I glanced over my shoulder at the door I'd left ajar, then leaned forward and peered at the garden beneath me. Except for Nina in the bedroom, I was completely alone.

"Ripen," I whispered. "Be sweet."

In the space of two breaths, the fig beneath my fingers deepened to a purple-brown, its added weight bending the branch from which it hung. Deftly, I twisted it and allowed it to fall, warm and plump, into my hand.

"Excuse me, my lady. I hope I'm not intruding."

I stifled a gasp and held the fig to my breast as I turned to face the doorway. Prince Alac stood there, his mouth quirked into a decidedly mischievous grin.

16

ALAC

Lady Maralyn looked as though I'd caught her stealing a piece of fine silver. She rose, the fig still clasped to her chest.

"My prince."

"You can call me Alac," I said. "And you can eat the fig, too." I nodded toward the fruit hidden in her hand.

Her cheeks reddened. "That doesn't seem appropriate."

"Eating a fig?"

"No, calling you Alac."

"Well, I insist. On both counts." All during supper, she'd never given me the impression that she was in the market for a proposal. I couldn't stop marveling at her matter-of-fact honesty and the way she spoke to me as if I were a human being instead of royal second prize. "So, uh, did you sleep well last night?"

"I did."

"I'm glad to hear it," I said. "I'd hate for you to feel exhausted after your first night here."

"That's very kind, my prince."

"Alac."

She curtsied and said nothing, and I felt more like an unbroken colt than a prince. Perhaps my spontaneous desire to break with protocol was another reason no one took me seriously.

"Forgive my intrusion." I placed my hand on my heart, hoping it would help her know I was being sincere. "Greeting guests gets awfully boring, and mostly they talk to Cannon, anyway."

"Do they?"

I suddenly felt stupid and wished I'd come to her quarters with a better plan. "Um, would you like a tour of the garden?"

The strangest expression crossed her face, nothing like the polite-if-obligatory gratefulness I'd expected. "Yes. Thank you."

I stepped back so she could go through the doorway before me, and her shoulder barely brushed my chest. The blood locket beneath my tunic grew warmer—or perhaps it was heat of a different kind.

She waited for me by the door, her maidservant standing expectantly by her side; clearly she'd asked her to accompany us. Which, of course, was the right thing to do. I tried to hide my disappointment.

"After you," I said, allowing them both to pass through before me.

We made our way to the Queen's Garden, which Maralyn's quarters overlooked. Now that I had her (almost) to myself, I couldn't think of anything remotely intelligent to say. This girl was so *different*. She didn't have the courtly beauty that so many noble girls liked to show off, but I'd never seen eyes like hers, set in an oval face framed by that *hair*. Her father had been some minor underlord, nobody I'd have been able to name, certainly. That might account for the way she carried herself—unaffected, natural.

Sending her that invitation had been the smartest thing I'd done in weeks.

We entered the garden from the west side, and I guided us to the wide path that led directly to the fountain.

"This is generally a favorite of our guests," I said, finally finding my voice again. "There's a story about the fish and how they were once alive—but I can never tell it right."

She glanced at the fountain ahead, but then her gaze drifted to the grape arbors. "Your vines are healthy. You must have excellent gardeners."

"Yes." I'd helped tend them sometimes, but I didn't feel like telling her that. "They're good grapes, too."

"Grape harvest is my favorite time of year," she said, her words soft, almost wistful.

"Why?"

The question seemed to fluster her. "I . . . my father grew some grapes of his own."

"Oh. I'm sorry." This was Nelgareth's ward, who'd recently lost her father. I needed to stop being stupid. "Winemaking fascinates me. I always wished we had vineyards here."

"So you're interested in the growing as well as in the drinking?"

"Yes," I said. "Almost more so."

"It's more work than you may think." Maralyn brushed a strand of hair from her face and tucked it behind her ear. "From a distance, things often seem more romantic than they really are."

"That's probably true," I said.

By now we'd reached the fountain. A Brother passed silently, pruning shears in hand, offering me a slight nod as he went about his business.

"Are there many Brothers of the Holy God at the palace?" Maralyn asked.

"Not since my mother died." She had found solace in her faith and supported the Brothers' charitable efforts. "Father keeps a small number on hand to keep the sanctuary running."

Because faith and sorcery are generally at odds.

"Tell me about the garden," she said, not looking at me. "There are flowers here I've never seen before."

"Happy to." Except, I didn't know much about the flowers, other than that my mother had valued them so much that, when once a late frost destroyed a section of the garden, she'd wept. "This has been known as the Queen's Garden since the castle was built, but my mother was especially devoted to enhancing it."

Maralyn trailed her fingers along the edge of the fountain as she made her way toward a raised bed of deep purple flowers to the side of the left-hand path. I hoped she wouldn't ask me any specific questions.

"These," she said, squatting. "They're shaped like roses, but they're smaller. And I don't see any thorns."

"No thorns," I said.

She looked up, making direct eye contact for the first time. "You don't know what they are, do you?"

"If you please, my lady," her maidservant said softly. "They're a variety of lisianthus. They bloom in late spring, but a skilled gardener can coax a second blooming in late summer to early fall."

"They're lovely," Maralyn said, rising. Her gaze was still on me. "You don't have to pretend to know about the flowers, my prince."

I thought I caught the hint of a smile before she turned and continued along the path. "What about these?" She stopped again, this time beside a row of flowering bushes where butterflies danced. "Nina?"

"We've always called them glory bushes," Nina said, "because of how the butterflies glory over them. I honestly don't know the horticultural name for them."

"Cannon and I used to catch butterflies this time of year," I said. "We used the finest nets so their wings wouldn't be damaged."

"No creature wants to be caught, no matter how fine the net," Maralyn said softly. She bent to pick a flower.

"Careful," I said, reaching. "This one *does* have thorns."

I touched her hand just as her fingers brushed the nearest blossom. A strange vibration swept down my arm and into my hand, so startling that I sucked in a quick breath. The blood locket around my neck flared hot.

Maralyn pulled her hand away as though I had slapped her. "What are you doing?"

"I . . . I only meant to protect you from the thorns, my lady."

She looked at me with an expression that wasn't so much fearful as it was stunned. My heart slammed against my chest as I thought of some way to smooth this moment over. I had no explanation for what had to have been some sort of magical response—the locket still felt uncomfortably warm against my skin.

"Forgive me," Maralyn said. "I have a headache."

"Shall we return to your rooms so you can rest?" Nina asked.

"Yes."

But she stood for what felt like an entire minute, alternately staring at me and making what looked like an effort to compose herself. I began to flatter myself that she was waiting for me to offer to escort her back. Finally she curtsied, a stiff gesture that told me she wanted nothing more to do with me.

"I look forward to seeing you tonight," I offered.

But she walked away without a backward glance. Which was fine. Whatever had just happened between us didn't need to happen again. At least, that's what I told myself as I walked in the opposite direction.

The magic around my neck told a different story. Dark, desperate, hungry.

For the first time, I began to be frightened of myself.

17

MARALYTH

I adjusted a shoulder of the aqua gown that had been made especially for the Wedding Mingle—a traditional supper for wedding guests at the palace. The feigned headache had excused me from further contact with Alac for the rest of the day. I couldn't explain what happened in the garden, but it had deeply unsettled me. In all the years I'd been ripening grapes and removing blight, I'd never felt anything like it.

A sharp knock at my door made me jump. Nina hurried to answer while I took one final look at my reflection and wondered what I could do about the worry crease that seemed always visible between my eyebrows. I tried to smooth it as Nelgareth entered and bowed.

"I've come to escort you to the Mingle." He was dressed in yet another tunic I'd never seen, this one a deep crimson with silver embroidery threaded throughout.

"Thank you," I said, taking his proffered arm.

"You look lovely," he said as we started down the hallway—soft and low, as though he wished no one but me to hear the compliment.

Uncomfortable warmth crept up my neck. "Thank you."

We walked in silence down the corridor and the stone staircase. When we reached the bottom, Nelgareth turned left, taking us down another hallway through which others were also walking toward the wide-open double doors at the end. Every ten paces or so, a guard stood against the wall to the left and the right. Each time I passed a pair, guilt stabbed my heart.

Betrayer.

Usurper.

Murderer.

Whether the coup succeeded or failed, any blood that was spilled would be on my hands as well as Nelgareth's. My greatest consolation was that Poppa was safe.

When we finally reached the doorway to the king's hall, the opulence took my breath away. The walls were solid gilt, with huge paintings in carved wooden frames hung at even intervals—royal portraits with oil-paint eyes that stared at the living around them. Large, round tables dotted the hall, draped in fine linens and set with dishes that gleamed in the candlelight. A bowl of fresh flowers sat at the center of each table, and the chairs were festooned with covers of deep purple velvet, twelve per table.

Most of the lords and underlords and their families had arrived; a few would come tomorrow. Already there were so many strange faces, so much sound of talking and laughter. I was drowning in people.

"This way," Nelgareth said softly.

He led me toward a table near the dais, on which there were two ornate thrones. Cannon and Ellian sat there, greeting those who approached them and looking very much like they were playing king and queen. Wishing we could have taken a table closer to the back, I sat in the chair Nelgareth pulled out for me.

"Lady Maralyn."

I looked up to see Alac standing behind the chair next to me. He gave me a formal head bow, which made him look particularly awkward.

"My prince." The words tasted of dust.

"Is someone sitting here?" He gestured to the empty seat on my right.

"Apparently not. But—"

"We're supposed to mingle, so, if you don't mind . . . ?"

Nelgareth bowed, meeting my eye with a distinct "I'll be watching" expression before he withdrew. I tensed.

Stop waiting for me to make a mistake.

Alac sat beside me as two other boys appeared at the table, hanging like flies to picnic food.

"Mind if we sit here?" the tall, thin one said.

A flutter of annoyance crossed Alac's face. "Traman Connoly and

Bertram Maynard, my lady. Their fathers are underlords from Sailings Port."

"Bertram's the fat one, my lady, in case you mean to tell us apart."
Traman was lanky and long-limbed and looked as though he were
growing out of his tunic where he stood.

Bertram punched him, and I found myself wondering if every
noble-bred boy in Perin Faye was an idiot. They jostled each other for
a few seconds before Bertram won, taking the seat next to mine.

Alac seemed as unimpressed as I. He leaned closer and said in un-
dertones, "Is your head feeling better?"

"Yes. Thank you." I folded my hands in my lap and looked across
the room, hoping to dissuade further conversation. Lord Mallory,
in his silver coronet and a midnight-black tunic, took a seat beside
Nelgareth at a table near ours, offering me the briefest nod as our
eyes met.

"That's Mallory, Lord of Keepings," Alac said. "Thinks quite a lot
of himself."

Of course he wouldn't expect me to know Mallory—or any of the
lords I'd already met in secret. "Does he?"

"He and his wife both." He gestured with his chin to the short,
round man taking a seat at the table to our right. "That's Bentian,
Lord of Draper's Down and incredibly boring. He's also my uncle."

"Your uncle?" Was he going to point out every lord and underlord
present?

"My mother's brother," Alac said. "That's my Aunt Jenina beside
him."

Discomfort crept along the surface of my skin as I forced myself to
look at the lord and lady of Draper's Down, one of the three lordlands
that did not support Nelgareth or know of his plans. "Firmly under
the king's thumb," Nelgareth had said of him. That made sense now.

His wife caught my gaze and offered a polite smile. I smiled back.

A servant arrived bearing a large flagon, from which he poured
red wine into our waiting goblets. Fionna red—I knew that bouquet
like I knew the feel of my own teeth in my mouth. I curled my hand
tightly around the goblet's stem and forced back the swell of home-
sickness that threatened to overwhelm me.

An exquisite girl with raven hair and dimples like craters in her cheeks glided into the seat on the other side of Alac and commanded his attention. Relieved, I angled myself slightly away from him, which, unfortunately, opened me more directly to Bertram, who was laughing raucously at some joke I'd missed. He took his goblet and drank as though it were water, making embarrassing guzzling noises. Then he slapped the table several times, nearly knocking my goblet over.

Ugh. If I had to eat my meal beside this toad, I wouldn't be able to stomach it. I glanced at Alac; he was listening to the chatter of the dark-haired girl. He laughed at something she said, and my stomach squeezed unexpectedly.

It was warm laughter, the kind that made you want to laugh along. *This would be easier if you were cold and horrid.*

"There you are!" A tall girl and someone who looked like she could be her sister stood behind Bertram and Traman. "We'd hoped you'd sit with us tonight. We're over. . . . *there.*" She pointed with a long, delicate finger.

Bertram and Traman were on their feet in seconds. They followed the girls without so much as an "excuse me."

I breathed a sigh of relief and took a swallow of my wine.

"I don't suppose you'd mind some more refined company?" Ellian stood where, a moment ago, the other girls had stood, her eyes bright.

I smiled. "I'd love some."

She sat, tucking her skirts neatly around her and folding her hands on the table, behaviors that seemed, to me, to be very practiced.

"Where's your bridegroom?" I asked.

Ellian shrugged. "This is the part where we're supposed to . . . mingle. I didn't get to speak with you much last night, so I thought I'd give it another try."

I smiled. "Cannon seems quite fond of you."

"He is! But sometimes he forgets to share me with others."

"That must be nice."

"Not always!" She laughed. "I mean, it's wonderful. Of course it is. But—well, I need to meet people I don't know. I don't want to be the kind of queen who doesn't remember anyone's name at her own court, despite how my husband may dote on me."

Her answer surprised me. At least she was being honest, though, which was more than I could say about myself.

The meal arrived at the same time a broad, middle-aged woman in a bright blue gown sat on Ellian's other side and bombarded her with questions. Trapped between two people engaged with others, I made myself small and focused on eating. The food was sumptuous, despite my meager appetite—delicate whitefish in a citrusy sauce, roasted turnips, and tiny pastries filled with spicy, minced meat.

I'd almost finished eating when Alac turned to me once more. "Forgive me, my lady. I meant to start a conversation, but . . ." He tilted his head toward the beauty, who was in the midst of what seemed to be a joyful reunion with another finely dressed girl. "Are you enjoying your meal?"

"Yes," I said. "And the wine."

"The wine, yes." He lifted his own goblet. "Graylaern Fionna is my father's favorite."

His expression was earnest—kind, even. I found myself drawn toward conversation even as my heart railed against it.

"Do you have a favorite, my prince?"

"Alac. Please."

"Prince Alac, then." I wouldn't allow myself the intimacy of his first name alone. Couldn't.

"That's a slight improvement." He smiled. "I think it might be my favorite, too. Though, on a summer's evening, I prefer the Fionna white."

I nodded, pushing my heartache deep inside where it wouldn't show. "That's my favorite, too."

He raised an eyebrow. "You know it? I was certain we commanded the entire Fionna white inventory each season. Or at least most of it."

I swallowed a mouthful of turnip with difficulty, realizing my blunder. "I'm not sure how my father came to have some, but I've never enjoyed a wine more."

"I'll see that you have more while you're here."

"Thank you," I said, considering my next words carefully. "You know about the Great Blight, of course."

"That's when Graylaern Vineyards was subsidized by the crown," Alac said.

"Other vineyards were decimated, too, and they never recovered." I met his gaze. "There are so many small, family vineyards across Delthe that don't have the means to produce enough wine for profit."

"We have all the wine we need—not just from Delthe, but from Fanley and Tell Doral, too."

"For *nobility,* yes. But wouldn't it be nice if these vintners could make a living selling wine to the local market?"

"I . . . guess I've never thought about it."

Of course he hadn't. "I didn't mean to go on." I really needed to keep my mouth shut about wine.

"Actually, I'd love to talk about this more," Alac said. "Perhaps sometime soon?"

I needed to end this dangerous trajectory. "Perhaps," I said as blandly as I could, and then pointedly turned my attention to the woman on Ellian's left, who had embarked upon a story of a particularly early frost that had spoiled her gardens and heralded the longest, coldest winter she could remember.

I remembered it, too, barely. I was three, and I woke up to the sound of shouts and calls in the middle of the night. I had padded to the kitchen and looked out the window to see row after row of glowing fire pots in the aisles of grape vines, and among them, large winged creatures creating crazy shadows as they beat their wings up and down, up and down.

Fairies, I'd thought. Or perhaps winged horses had come to earth from their kingdom in the sky. But then Mother had come from the other room, a pair of the long, white wings cradled in her arms.

"Stay inside, little Mara," she'd said, kissing the top of my head. "I'm going to go help warm the grapes."

It must have been terrifying, I now realized, to live every day in fear that someone would recognize her, despite her silver hair. No wonder I couldn't remember the sound of her laughter. I hadn't heard it often enough.

As dessert was served—a steamed pudding swimming in cream— there was a lull in conversation, and Alac returned his attention to me.

"I think I've had enough of the crowds," he said.

I traced lines in my pudding with my spoon. "You're not used to this?"

"Not really. There's not much need for me to be present at any official functions, and, except for the Council of Lords every spring, we don't usually have this many people at court."

He was infuriatingly normal. Incomprehensibly relatable. "Royal weddings are exciting for most people."

"People with very dull lives."

I smiled—without effort, without meaning to. Horrified, I hid it by stuffing my mouth with pudding.

"Were you planning on attending the javelin throw tomorrow?"

I swallowed the pudding. "I . . . hadn't really . . ."

"I'm not participating, but some of the fellows are impressive."

"I'll ask Lord Nelgareth what his plans are for me."

"Fair enough."

I returned my attention to my dessert, spooning more into my mouth to give my trembling hand something to do. I could barely taste it.

∝∾

I spent the last, dizzying hour of the Mingle being introduced to more underlords and their wives than I could ever remember. Nelgareth's demeanor was gentle when speaking of the recent loss of my father, Underlord Keele, whom almost nobody knew because he had apparently always sent a representative for the yearly Council of Lords.

Nelgareth had chosen my fictional family well.

I hung on Nelgareth's arm, the dutiful ward, grateful to be presented at court and excited for the upcoming royal wedding. Every smile, every nod, every word of thanks for offered condolences stripped away another layer of my humanity.

Nelgareth was quiet as he escorted me to my quarters. When we reached my door, he released my arm and turned to face me.

"Prince Alac seems to have taken quite an interest in you," he said.

I bristled. "Why do you say that?"

"It wasn't an accusation," Nelgareth said mildly. "Only an observation."

"I haven't encouraged him," I went on, words squeezing between my teeth. "I never asked for his attention."

Nelgareth considered me for a moment. "It might serve you well, my lady, to stop assuming that people are finding fault with you."

I opened my mouth and closed it again. Was that what I was doing? Had always done?

I sighed. "This isn't easy."

"There was nothing wanting in your performance tonight. People will remember . . . and come to love you."

I smiled automatically, but a chill ran through me. Would people love me after such a grand deception? Did falseness beget affection?

He kissed my hand, holding it a second too long before releasing it.

"Good night, my lord." I hastily entered my quarters and closed the door behind me, grateful for the darkness pressing against me, blocking everything out.

Except Alac's smile. And that was the one thing I wanted to erase most of all.

18

ALAC

Once Maralyn left the Mingle, my desire to stay dwindled. I remembered my promise to Cannon, though, and reluctantly engaged in some half-hearted conversations about Father's war effort. It was soon apparent that there wasn't much substance behind anyone's aversion to it; most sons and daughters of nobles didn't concern themselves with issues outside their daily lives.

"It'll throw the economy into ruin," one underlord's son spouted. "Do you have any idea how much wine is currently exported to Northland?"

I knew how tightly Father controlled all exports and how he funneled profits into the royal treasury. "It would definitely affect trade" was all I could come up with in reply.

"War is so terrible," one particularly vacuous girl named Dhalia said. "Your father should know better than to bring something so terrible upon us."

I rolled my eyes and she didn't even notice.

Truth was, I agreed with them all, though I couldn't say so. If Cannon expected me to miraculously turn the tide in favor of Father's war plans, he was delusional.

Half an hour of mindless chatter, and I was spent. Tucker wasn't on duty, so I didn't have him to talk to, and the swarm of girls who seemed always ready to demand my attention was more than I felt like dealing with. I downed a final goblet of wine—more than I needed, really—and left.

I'd be glad when this damned wedding was over and everyone would go back where they came from.

"Leaving so early?" Nella's arms were filled with endless folds of a shimmering green fabric.

"It's brain-numbing in there." I gestured to the bundle in her arms. "What's that?"

"Lady Donita's gown. She spilled wine all down the front of it, so I'm taking it to the laundress for her."

"She's wearing her undergarments in there?"

Nella clucked. "Go on, then. Sometimes I despair of you."

But I heard the affection in her words, as always. "At least I didn't spill any wine."

It was too early for sleeping, and once I'd stripped down and thrown on a nightshirt, I pulled out a thin, leather book with a gold-stamped title that I'd kept hidden for years. Then I reached beneath my bed and dislodged the loose stone that had concealed my boyhood's illicit treasures for as long as I could remember. I pulled out the velvet scroll box that Cannon had given me before we'd parted the night before, then laid it and the book on my desk and lit some extra candles before sitting down.

I spread the book open; the binding was broken enough that the pages lay flat. The words were old and familiar and had terrified me when I'd first read them. I was ten, and I'd discovered the book, dusty and forgotten, in a locked cabinet in the library. The words inside had unraveled the secrets I'd pondered and feared since watching Father slice his hand with that glowing dagger. And it had settled in my heart, once and for all, that I never wanted anything to do with the Thungrave magic.

I allowed myself one self-conscious glance at the door before lifting the blood locket from beneath my tunic and curling it into my hand. Without thinking, I began to stroke it with my thumb. A warm hum rose up from it, and I caught myself and moved my hand away.

I turned to the first page, where the title was echoed in a bold hand in thick ink: "The Gift of the Holy God," and beneath it "The Dallowyn Magic and Its Counterpart." No author's name was included; I'd often wondered who might have penned it.

A strange thrill went through me, and my hand trembled as I

turned the page. Before, I'd read the words of this volume with loathing, because it confirmed without a doubt that Father's magic wasn't truly his.

The same bold handwriting marched in meticulous lines on the next page. This was a tale I'd known all my life, but had been taught to relegate to the sphere of myth. It spoke of the early days of Perin Faye, when Daxion, the first Dallowyn king, received his crown from the First Brother of the Holy God, and with it the magic that ran through all living things—beast and fowl, tree and vine. It was the magic of time itself, and was given into the hands of the king to wield as its chosen master, keeping it from those who would use it without the Holy God's blessing.

I turned to a page that was marked with a bit of ribbon and fell open easily. My own notes in the margin highlighted this passage:

Time is neutral. Therefore, the Magic, which is wrought of time, is neither good nor evil on its own. When freely given, it provides life and light. When stolen, it turns on itself, bringing power at great cost. And if this stolen Magic is set free, it will consume everything in its path in the same way time itself eventually does—by bringing it to death and rot.

When I'd first read the words as a boy, all I could think of was Father with that dagger, spilling his blood into a crystal goblet. Later, when I learned I, too, might have to offer my own blood someday, I became more convinced than ever that it was wrong. The rightful magic of the old Dallowyn line required no blood sacrifice—it was freely given.

The words "bringing power at great cost" especially frightened me. When my mother died, I was convinced that she had been part of the "great cost" of Father's ill-gotten magic.

Like all the Thungrave queens before her.

There was no redeeming the fact that the magic was stolen. But what struck me now was that magic set *free* was destructive. Both times I'd opened the blood locket, it had dispersed something that had worked the way the book seemed to say. The first time, a single grape rotted; the second time, my fingernail grew several weeks' length in a few seconds.

And if this stolen Magic is set free, it will consume everything in its path . . . by bringing it to death and rot.

The magic itself was supposed to be neutral. What if I learned to use the magic in the locket for *good*?

I pulled the scroll from its case and unrolled it—it was smooth and supple, as though time hadn't touched it. I read the words—silently, as Cannon had urged me. Giving utterance to them outside of the ritual was frowned on for reasons even Father didn't seem to understand.

> *Spiritis eque sanc deu*
> *Coram regibi spiriti alme*
> *Habitisi medum moriari*
> *Me sume te prestiqui sinte*
> *Tempori aterni.*

My lips buzzed with the desire to speak the text out loud. The words were meaningless, the language ancient and arcane.

I flipped the scroll facedown onto the desk with my palm.

I couldn't deny the struggle—the more I fought the magic, the more I craved it.

And then I had a new idea that swelled inside me like sudden hope. What if, instead of trying to bend the magic's will toward good, I found a way to return it—contained in the receptacle, maybe—to the Holy God? Maybe it was too late for Father, but what if I could give Cannon the chance to be king without being enslaved by this dark power?

I turned back to the beginning of the book. It was going to be a long night.

19

MARALYTH

Truly there could be nothing so boring as watching men and boys throw javelins.

I sat beside Nelgareth, sipping chilled peach cider and applauding when I was supposed to—for four interminable hours. Fortunately, I only saw Alac from a distance, since Nelgareth had insisted I sit with him.

The ladies-only supper that night was worse. I was lucky enough to secure a seat at the end of one of the long tables, which made me feel less hemmed in, but the conversation was exhausting. The girl beside me, who looked barely old enough to be presented at court, did nothing but gush about her favorite lordling's javelin performance. Across the table and down a little way, the beautiful, raven-haired girl kept throwing me glances that were decidedly unfriendly. Odd, since I hadn't spoken so much as three words to her.

By the time dessert arrived, I'd reached my limit. I excused myself after only a spoonful or two of the warm berry pie, which was too sweet, and hastened from the dining hall. The men-only supper had been set up outside beneath a sprawling pavilion, which sounded much nicer. I imagined both meals would continue for some time; musicians were tuning their instruments as I left, and I passed servants pushing carts of sweet liqueurs in the hallway.

Perhaps I could beg Nina for a foot rub.

"Lady Maralyn."

I spun, unable to hide my surprise at hearing Alac's voice.

He tried, unsuccessfully, to hide his laughter. "I didn't mean to scare you."

"You didn't scare me, my prince." He couldn't see the way my heart was trying to scramble out of my chest.

"I was actually coming to find you in the dining hall; looks like I almost missed you."

"Yes. I couldn't think of a single, other thing to say about javelin throwing."

It was hard to read the expression on his face—amusement? Admiration? I felt my cheeks grow warm and I wasn't sure why.

"I wanted to ask if you were planning to come on our picnic excursion to Crossford Falls tomorrow."

"I haven't decided."

"Not that it'll be much more exciting than this evening, but there's an exceptional waterfall. It far surpasses the fountain in the Queen's Garden."

I shrank inside myself, remembering the unfortunate and inexplicable surge of magic that had happened near the fountain. "Does it?"

"Marginally." His grin disarmed me. "Will you come?"

"I'll have to ask Lord Nelgareth if—"

"I've already asked him. So . . . will you come?"

I stifled a sigh. "Yes. Thank you."

"Excellent! We're meeting in the courtyard at half past eight. My carriage will be at the front."

His carriage? This was such a bad idea. "I'm sure that's not necessary, Prince Alac."

He opened his mouth—probably to remind me to call him "Alac"—but then seemed to think better of it. He smiled instead. "It's my pleasure."

I scrubbed his smile from my memory as I hastened to my rooms, weary to the bone from playing this game of deception and knowing I had to keep it up.

Six more days. I could do this.

⁓

I stood by Alac's carriage feeling frightfully conspicuous. A man-at-arms who didn't seem any older than Alac approached and offered a slight bow. His hair was a mess of unruly curls that seemed intent on escaping from his loose military bun.

"Lady Maralyn?" he said, and waited for my nod. "Prince Alac is running a bit late, and he asked me to keep you company."

There was a growing crowd gathered around the other carriages; I was hardly alone. Still, I had to admit it felt better to have someone to talk to while I waited for Alac. Except, I wasn't quite sure how to conduct myself. Did ladies generally engage in conversation with guards who had been sent to keep them company? Nelgareth's training hadn't covered this.

Apparently, silence was correct; the guard didn't address me further, so I didn't offer anything. Slowly, the others began to file into carriages. I couldn't help noticing the questioning glances some were casting my way.

I wished Alac hadn't singled me out so publicly.

Finally, he appeared, walking lightly down the steps and speaking words at the windows of the other carriages until he made his way to me and the silent guard.

The guard turned to me, his expression playful. "Should I announce him? He hates that."

"I . . ."

"Lady Maralyn!" Alac had obviously heard him. "Don't let Tucker get under your skin; he only *thinks* he's clever."

"I was simply trying to soften your intimidating presence." Tucker's words were warm and easy; clearly these two were good friends.

I offered Tucker what was likely a stiff smile. Even their playful banter was painful and surreal. Would Tucker also lose his life when the attack came?

"Joining us?" Alac asked his friend.

"No, thanks, Your Greatness," Tucker said. "I should really act like I'm on duty."

"You *are* on duty."

Tucker grinned before taking several steps away from us and striking an on-duty pose. I made a grand effort to split my outer self from the turmoil in my heart. "You seem to know each other well."

"He's my best friend," Alac said. "He's also a member of my personal guard."

Definitely someone who would fight to the death to protect his friend. "Are you always under personal guard?"

"Technically, yes," Alac said. "But Tucker and I have an understanding, so sometimes I get a break. He'll give me a wider berth at the picnic."

"Not that I don't have anything better to do," Tucker called.

"Are you finished?"

"I'll just maintain my discreet distance, shall I?" Tucker laughed as he turned to face the other way.

"Ready to go?" Alac offered his hand.

I hesitated—the last time our hands touched, the magic had done something I didn't understand. But a noble girl would never refuse the hand of the prince, so I took it. Nothing happened. I sighed with relief and stepped nimbly into the carriage.

It was far less opulent inside than I'd expected. Soft leather seats faced each other with a few neatly embroidered pillows scattered on each. Alac sat across from me, and within moments we began to move.

"I hope you don't mind my asking you to ride with me," Alac said. "I just wanted a few minutes alone, so we could talk."

Why, why, why did he insist on pursuing me? "I'm happy to talk, my prince, if that's what you'd like," I said brightly.

"I wish you'd call me Alac. I get tired of always being attached to a title."

I smiled. "It's not every day one meets a prince who doesn't want to be called a prince."

He shrugged. "It's different for Cannon. I'm just the backup plan."

"Surely you're more than that."

"I've made my own plans," Alac said, "and they have nothing to do with palaces or politics."

"What do they have to do with?"

"Wine." A flicker of insecurity crossed his face, like he wasn't sure he should go on.

"Ah, yes. You mentioned your interest in wine." It was the last subject I wanted to discuss.

"I've been funneling money into a manor on fifty acres in Tell Doral since I was sixteen. After Cannon and Ellian are settled, I'm going to start a vineyard."

"Can you do that?" The question sounded foolish as soon as I'd uttered it.

"Why would anyone want to stop me? I'm the invisible one around here."

I felt sorry for him for half a moment, but quickly recovered. "A lot of families with less than an acre would love the opportunity to do something like that."

"Actually, my plan is to create jobs," Alac said. "I know there are a lot of wine growers out there, like you said before. I'd learn from them, and they'd be able to support their families and contribute to a not-royally-controlled winery."

"But you *are* royal."

"Yes. But I'm not the king."

"You couldn't provide a job for every vintner in the kingdom," I went on, careful not to let my passion show. "If the others could band together somehow—create cooperatives—things might be different."

Alac nodded slowly. "That's not a bad idea."

Not a bad idea? It was brilliant, and I wished he'd say so.

He cleared his throat. "There's a small vineyard just outside the palace gate. I spent a lot of time there when I was young."

"Learning to grow grapes?"

"Yes," Alac said. "But I want to experience the whole process, from vine to goblet." He made a face. "I hope I don't sound stupid."

"Not at all! It's just not very . . . princely."

"Unprincely is what I do best."

I laughed—and immediately wished I hadn't. His expression softened in such a way that I knew he was pleased he'd made me laugh. It was getting easier and easier to talk with him, and I didn't like it. I tried to imagine him dead.

Dead, dead, dead.

"I don't think we're going to see any sun today," I said, feigning deep interest in the clouds outside the carriage window.

"I choose to remain optimistic," Alac said. "Though, honestly, I think the picnic might be boring."

"Why?"

He shrugged. "Did you notice we left three empty carriages behind? A lot of the men opted for archery instead of a picnic, and the rest of the ladies were put off by the weather."

"Is the picnic going to be that dreadful?"

"Absolutely. But the waterfall is . . . well, breathtaking."

"I love waterfalls." Not that I'd ever seen one.

"I'll be happy to show it to you."

I offered the smile that was expected and tried in vain to stop enjoying his company.

We soon arrived at a lovely expanse of grass bordered by tall, thin trees. Alac hopped out of the carriage and offered me his hand as I disembarked. Through the trees, I could hear the crashing song of the waterfall.

"What do you think?" he asked.

"I think it's going to rain."

"The clouds will clear." But he darted a less than hopeful glance at the sky.

"It's lovely here. Truly."

Around us, everyone was disembarking, and I could see that Alac was right—it was mostly ladies, standing in clusters while the tents and food tables were being set up. Tucker appeared from somewhere and offered me a slight bow of his head and a smile.

"I hope you realize you stole my seat of honor in the prince's carriage."

"Shut up, Tucker," Alac said before turning to me. "They should have everything set up soon."

"My prince!" The dark-haired, dimpled girl was making her way toward us, her yellow gown an explosion of color in the gray morning.

Alac groaned under his breath, but bowed politely. "I see you've decided to brave the weather after all!"

Dimple-girl's smile seemed fashioned specifically to deepen the crevices in her cheeks. "Of course I have!" Her eyes fell on me and her smile faltered a hair.

Suddenly I understood her cold glances from the night before.

"Lady Lisbet, this is Lady Maralyn," Alac offered. "We were just discussing how tiresome it is when someone interrupts a conversation."

I swallowed a snort as Lisbet's lips parted, her dimples melting to mere hints. She offered a perfunctory curtsy. "A pleasure."

I inclined my head. "The pleasure is mine."

Her eyes were on Alac, though. To an awkward degree.

"I was hoping you'd take Carolee and Nan and me to the falls," she said.

Alac looked like he'd rather eat a snake. "In a little while, perhaps?"

Lisbet positively bounced her away across the grass to her friends.

"Well, I suppose I should start making my rounds." He flashed me a lopsided smile. "See you in a bit? If I may, that is."

I returned his smile and offered a slight nod, not trusting myself with further words.

I wandered over to the crowd, feeling terribly alone. Lisbet caught my eye and whispered something to the girl beside her, making me wish I'd stayed at the castle.

By the time the tarps were stretched over food tables and piles of blankets and pillows for guests to lounge upon, the first spray of rain had begun. Those who had wandered through the trees to peek at the waterfall found their way back, filling their plates and goblets and making themselves as comfortable as possible out of the drizzle. I caught myself searching for Alac and wondering when he'd take me to see the falls. Horrified, I lowered my gaze, cheeks burning.

This would have been easier if he were arrogant or hateful. But he was neither.

I chatted idly with a few people sharing my corner of a blanket, and warded off a flirtatious comment or two from an overly hopeful boy who didn't even look old enough to shave. The drizzle continued, persistent and depressive, and the grumbling beneath the tarps became as oppressive as the weather. I finished my tiny finger sandwiches and rose to brush the crumbs from my dress.

"Lady Maralyn."

Alac stood in the drizzle. "I believe I promised to show you the waterfall?"

"That's what she needs—more water," Flirting Boy muttered behind me. He was rewarded with silly giggles.

I straightened my shoulders and smiled. "I'd love to see it," I said.

"As long as you don't mind the rain . . ."

"It's barely a sprinkle," I said.

Alac looked . . . relieved? Delighted? And why did I care? He offered his arm and I accepted, though I immediately regretted it.

It was impossible to hate him when he was treating me so well. Which, if I admitted it, was all he'd done since we met.

Tucker joined us, keeping a respectful distance as we made our way through the trees toward the falls.

"Does he always trail you?" I asked.

Alac laughed and turned around. "Hear that, Tucker? She wants to know if you always trail me."

"Of course I didn't hear it. I'm too busy trailing you."

Confusion washed through me as I tried to emotionally distance myself from their teasing. This wasn't at all what I had expected. Alac was too real—too *human*. Nelgareth may have spent years formulating his plan and hoping to find a missing heir, but for me, this was fresh. Uncomfortable.

"We grew up together," Alac said. "As soon as Tucker joined the military, I requested him for my personal guard. He doesn't seem to mind. Especially since I pay him well."

"I heard that."

"You were meant to."

I found myself smiling before I realized the futility of enjoying this moment.

He's a Thungrave. Don't forget it.

I had never expected him to be kind. Or funny. Or actually concerned about whether or not I were interested in something.

My sigh was long and deep, a shuddering breath that ran the length of my spine. I was grateful for the growing sound of the waterfall, which obscured it.

Tucker waited in the trees while Alac and I continued to the banks of the river, which churned and hissed with the power of the waterfall.

"Don't get too close," Alac said over the noise of the water. "The spray makes everything slippery."

"It's beautiful."

And it was. The water streamed down in four distinct channels, dancing around rocks and outcrops and creating never-ending patterns. I could've stared at it forever.

"I can see why you chose this spot," I said.

"Not that anyone else is particularly happy about it."

"Then they needn't have come."

Alac looked at me with eyes I couldn't read. Suddenly flustered, I returned my gaze to the falls.

"I couldn't agree more, Lady Maralyn."

"Mara." As soon as I said it, I wasn't sure why I had.

"Mara?"

"It's what my family called me." Finally, I spoke something true. And it would certainly be easier to answer to a name I was used to.

I could hear the smile in his words, though I still wasn't looking at him. "Mara, then."

Desperate to dispel the awkward moment, I picked up a stick and tossed it into the frothing water. That's when I heard the growl.

Fear pricked my skin like a thousand pins. I turned my head toward the sound to see a wild dog not fifteen paces away, teeth bared, wolverine eyes fixed on me. White froth dripped from its maw.

"Don't move," Alac said.

I couldn't have moved if the earth had shifted; this was the terror of my childhood, facing me. The sound of cries from across the vineyard. Blood on the table where Mother stitched the mauled worker. Sleepless nights brought on by the single bark of a lone dog somewhere in the distance.

The dog lowered its head and growled again, the tumult of the water nearly swallowing the sound. Slowly, Alac withdrew a dagger from his boot, and even more slowly aimed it at the dog in a defensive posture. He whistled, setting the dog barking.

I thought of Tucker, waiting in the trees. Probably he couldn't hear anything because of the falls. The dog's barks turned back into growls, the hair on its neck standing straight. Alac took another cautious step forward.

Above me and to the right, a tree branch hung just out of reach. If I could jump to grab ahold and swing my legs up . . .

The magic awoke beneath my skin, amid the trees and the falls and the frothing dog. What could I do with it, though? I hadn't been able to staunch the bleeding of the girl's cut tongue. How would I stop the attack of an animal gone mad?

Then, suddenly, the dog lunged toward me, and Alac leaped between us, dagger out. I screamed and jumped for the branch—and missed. I landed hard as Alac lost his footing and the dog knocked him onto his back, teeth bared. Without hesitating, I extended both hands, palms forward.

"Be still. Sleep."

The magic leaped forth in a surge of heat and ecstasy. As I watched, the dog wobbled a bit, its ears drooping. Moments later, it lay still at Alac's side.

He scrambled to his feet and took several steps backward. Then he looked at me.

"What did you do?" His words were almost a hiss.

"I . . ." Dear Holy God, what *had* I done? I let my arms drop to my sides.

"Turn away," he said.

I knew what he was going to do, but I didn't need to hide from it. The dog wouldn't sleep forever, and when it awakened, it would attack again. Poppa had taught me long ago that any creature that foamed at the mouth was dangerous.

Alac slit its throat, then wiped his dagger clean in a patch of thick undergrowth. After he'd replaced the blade, he looked at me again. The drizzle chose this moment to thicken into the rain everyone except Alac had been certain would fall; he stood blinking through the downpour, waiting, perhaps, for me to explain myself.

I had no words.

"Was it magic?" he finally said. His voice sounded hollow.

I lowered my gaze and said nothing.

"For the sake of the Holy God, tell me what just happened."

His words didn't hold the anger I expected them to. I took one, tremulous breath and looked into his eyes. "I saved you."

He stared at me for what felt like a full minute, rain streaming from his hair and face, mouth open as though unspoken words had frozen it.

Then he turned and left me standing with the dead dog. I watched him disappear through the trees and felt my false world close in around me.

20

ALAC

I stood naked while a manservant Nella had insisted upon gave me a vigorous towel-dry, as though the rain needed to be purged from my skin. Tucker entered, closing the door softly behind him.

"Always nice to see more of you."

"Shut up." I stepped away from the servant. "That'll be all, thanks."

He bowed and gathered up the towel and my wet clothing and left, while I slipped into my undergarment. I grabbed the dry linen shirt the servant had left draped over a chair and pulled it over my head while Tucker straddled my desk chair and sat on it backward.

"You couldn't be that upset about a little rain," Tucker said.

"This has nothing to do with rain." I began to pace aimlessly, but Tucker knew better than to try to stop me. "See that book on the desk behind you? That's supposed to have the answers I need. And then . . ." I threw my hands up and kept walking.

"You want to explain that a little better?"

"It's Lady Maralyn."

"So you *did* fight and storm off."

"No." I raked my fingers through my still-wet hair. "Something happened while we were by the falls."

Tucker whistled low. "Talk about moving fast."

"That's not what I mean!" I blew out a stream of air. "There was a wild dog. It jumped at her, and when I went to stab it, I stumbled. It would've ripped into me if she hadn't stopped it."

Probably he was staring at me, but I was too busy pacing to take notice. "She stopped it . . . how? And for the love of the Sacred Church, will you stand still?"

I forced myself to sit in one of the tufted chairs I never used. "Magic. I swear it."

"Did she say so?"

"She didn't have to. One minute the dog was coming at me with its teeth bared, and the next it was . . . asleep. When I questioned her, all she said was, 'I saved you.'"

"Cruce."

"I should have suspected something when I first met her," I went on. "Our hands touched in the garden, and there was this . . . surge. I assumed it was the blood locket, even though I couldn't figure out why it would do that."

Tucker shifted on the chair. "Maybe you should take the necklace off."

"It's not a necklace."

"Pendant of doom, then."

"This doesn't have anything to do with that." I clawed at my hair again. "There's no way she'd have magic like that unless she had Dallowyn blood. And if she does, it's likely she doesn't even know it."

"How could she have magic and not know where it came from?"

"Most people don't know the truth anymore," I said. "Common knowledge says all magic is stolen—except for my father's. Which makes it sound like it's legitimately his."

"And it's not."

"No, it's not."

Tucker eyed the flagon of wine on the table next to me and crossed the room. "You shouldn't even be spending time with her." He poured it into two goblets and took one for himself. "You know that."

I took the other goblet and swirled the wine, considering my words. "I've only just met her," I said as evenly as I could. "It's just . . ." I took a deep swallow of wine. "She's . . . intriguing. You have to admit it."

"Fair enough. But even if you had serious intentions, it's not likely your father would agree to the daughter of some obscure underlord."

"She's Nelgareth's ward now," I couldn't help saying. "That might count for something."

"*Do* you have a serious interest in her?"

"I've only known her for a few days. That's not even possible." I drank another mouthful of wine. "I like talking with her."

"You know what I think?" Tucker gestured with his goblet. "I think you should've spent more time with Loralie this summer. Or that other one—the one with curly hair?"

I rolled my eyes. "Brinda. Not my type."

"So what are you going to do about Maralyn?"

I grimaced. "I'm going to have to question her."

"Sounds terrifying."

"For her or for me?" I emptied my goblet in a series of gulps. "Will you bring her here? Tell her I need to talk with her."

"That'll melt her heart, for sure."

"I'm not trying to melt her heart," I said. "I need to ask her about putting wild dogs to sleep."

Tucker set his goblet on the table with a thunk. "I'll go get her."

"Thanks."

At the door, he turned to face me. "You might want to put some breeches on before I get back."

I reached for the rest of my clothing as soon as the door had closed behind him, my innards in a thousand knots. I had about ten minutes to think of a way to ask questions that wouldn't put her on the defensive or shut her down or scare her.

All this, without letting on that she'd scared *me*.

21

MARALYTH

I stood by the window that looked out to my balcony, ignoring my wet clothes. Nina had met me outside the solarium upon my return, but I'd assured her I could take care of myself. Now, alone, I was wracked with the fear I'd held at bay all the way back to the palace—in a different carriage.

I'd used magic to save Alac's life. And no story I could come up with would hide the truth.

That he'd left me standing in the rain was enough to make me realize the danger I was in. I'd jeopardized Nelgareth's entire plan. I knew I should tell him, to give him a chance to make a contingency plan.

Like sneaking out of the castle at night. Or something.

I was terrified to tell him. And terrified not to.

I'd come to the castle ready to hate both princes, but there was nothing about Alac that inspired loathing. And now I'd revealed my deepest secret to him when I should have let him die.

Hastily, still trembling, I unknotted my wet hair and peeled my sodden dress and undergarments off, draping them over a bench in the bedroom before struggling into what seemed like the simplest and most comfortable gown in the wardrobe, a cream-colored linen with a softly scooped neckline of tiny jewels.

I'd barely finished when someone knocked at the door.

I pressed my hand over my mouth, heart hammering in my chest. Perhaps, if I were quiet, whoever it was would leave.

More knocking. Then I heard a male voice, faint on the other side of the heavy wooden door.

"Lady Maralyn?"

Tucker.

Hiding was inexcusable. I smoothed my hair self-consciously and answered the door.

Tucker inclined his head and raised an eyebrow. "You look rather . . . rained upon, my lady."

I tucked hair behind my ear as heat rose to my cheeks. "I've barely had a chance to change."

"Forgive me." He seemed amused. "I've been asked to escort you to Alac's quarters."

The weight of the castle itself pressed against me, so that I could barely speak. "Why?"

"To talk, apparently. May I?" He offered his arm.

I nodded and accepted, though I would rather have jumped from my balcony into the gardens below. Had Alac told him about the dog? The magic?

He waited while I pulled my door softly closed. "Too bad about the rain today."

"Yes." I had no capacity to make light conversation.

"I hear the sky seers are declaring a sunny day for the wedding, though."

I knew he was making a joke, but it wasn't even mildly funny. When the wind whispered to me that it brought a storm on its tail or clear skies in the morning, it never lied. Perhaps sky seers had drops of Dallowyn blood they weren't aware of.

My unresponsiveness was obvious enough that Tucker didn't try to force further conversation. When we arrived at the door of Alac's apartments, he knocked, then opened the door and gestured for me to enter first.

"My lady," he said.

Alac's expression was softer than it had been when we parted, but it was also guarded.

I curtsied. "My prince."

"Lady Maralyn."

"Well, now that we've established who you both are . . ." Tucker raised an eyebrow, but Alac didn't respond. "I'll, uh, be outside the door."

My heart fluttered like a trapped moth as Alac waited for Tucker to leave. At the sound of the door closing, he gestured to a small table, where two goblets and a large flagon sat among a cluster of fat candles.

"Wine?"

"Please." Though I didn't want any.

"Fionna white, as promised."

He poured, then handed me a goblet. I sat at one of the two heavily upholstered chairs on either side of the table and waited while he took the seat across from me.

"Do you fear my father?" he asked.

It wasn't the question I'd expected. "I've never met him."

"You know what I mean." The palest hint of irritation had crept into his voice. "People say he's evil. A sorcerer. You must admit you've heard rumors like that."

"Yes, I have."

"I've grown up fearing him," Alac said, "and it was the same when my grandfather was on the throne. I was afraid of him, too."

"Why are you telling me this?"

He took a long swallow of wine, then rested the goblet on his knee and met my gaze with startling directness. "I've grown up in the shadow of my father's stolen power. I know magic when I see it."

Words froze behind my teeth. I sipped some wine to calm my nerves, but the cool Fionna white flooded my mouth with memories of home. With great effort, I willed away my anxiety, forcing myself to be an ice-carved representation of myself.

"I saved your life," I said.

"*How?*" He leaned forward. "*How* did you save it?"

Had I a heart of granite, I would've let the wild dog kill him. But now, as he waited for my answer, I realized how ill-prepared I was to play this double role. In a million lifetimes, I would not have stood by to watch him die.

I took a wavering breath. "I told it to go to sleep."

"And it . . . listened."

"Yes."

"You've done this sort of thing before?"

"I've never seen a rabid dog before."

"Damn it, you know what I mean."

Discomfort gave way to a sense of danger. If he knew his father's magic was stolen, then he also knew where it rightfully belonged.

I knit my words into a lie before I set them free. "I don't know why I can do it. I always could, but I've never told anyone." That part, at least, was true.

Alac rolled his goblet between his hands slowly, as though he were rolling out his thoughts before giving them voice. "So, you've always had this . . . ability."

"Yes."

"Only you? Or your family, too?"

My heart knocked like a relentless woodpecker against my breastbone. "Only me."

His hand drifted toward a barely visible chain around his neck. "The Holy God gave his magic to the Dallowyns. It was never meant for the Thungraves—or anyone else."

"I didn't steal it."

Breathe, Mara. Don't get defensive.

It was like telling my heart to stop beating.

"How can it be that you're not a Dallowyn, then?" Alac said, more to himself than to me.

I watched him wrestle with his own question, my grip terror-tight on my goblet. The candlelight played on his face, softening him. Making him feel approachable.

Too human.

I am stone. I am ice. I am not here to humanize you.

Alac reached inside his neckline and pulled out the chain. On it hung a strange-looking locket, which he held between thumb and finger.

"My father gave this to me the day before he left," Alac said. "His blood and mine are inside it." Something strange passed over his face, a brief struggle of unnamed emotion. "It's supposed to protect me while he's away. Insurance, in case anything happens to him."

It felt as though my voice were drying up inside me; when I spoke, it was in half whispers. "Protect you from what?"

"From his magic." His gaze was so intense I could almost feel it. "I've never wanted this. I've never seen anything of magic that wasn't destructive or terrifying. So what kind of power can put a wild dog to sleep and save a prince's life?"

My tongue, my teeth, my lips wouldn't move. I stared, making a valiant effort to keep any trace of emotion from my face.

I am stone. I am ice.

"Magic is from the Holy God," I said slowly.

"My father says the same thing," Alac said. "But why are you able to do *good* things?"

"I don't know." I couldn't look at him. I didn't know where to look.

"I've never seen my father save someone's life or restore someone to health or . . . anything like that. It was dark magic, and that was the end of it. But you've shown me that it *can* be used for good."

"But—" My throat caught and I swallowed hard. "I'm not supposed to have magic. If anyone found out—"

"*I* found out. Did you expect me to escort you to the nearest dungeon?"

My words were air. "I don't know what I expected."

"I swear I won't tell anyone. Well, Tucker knows. But he's safe." His expression became earnest. "Will you help me learn to find the good in the Thungrave magic?"

This was impossible. I hardly understood my own magic; it simply happened and always had. No one taught me what to do or to say. It was like breathing.

"If it's true that magic like mine comes from Dallowyn blood, doesn't that make me your enemy?"

It was a small smile, but it warmed his face. "*Are* you my enemy?"

"No, my prince." *Liar.* "I wouldn't have stopped the dog if I were." *Liar, liar, liar.*

"Well, then," Alac said. "Perhaps I can consider you a friend."

"Perhaps."

I smiled because it seemed the right thing to do. But the smile came easily, and I realized with heartsick certainty that, in a different situation, I would have been delighted to call him my friend.

To feel the warmth of his smile.

"You don't seem to fear your magic," Alac said.

"And you fear yours."

"It's not mine," Alac said. "It's meant to be passed to the firstborn son."

"If it's not yours, why do you want help with it?"

"It *could* be mine, if Cannon becomes king and dies without an heir. I don't want it, though."

"Why not?"

"I saw my father complete the ritual that gave him the magic," Alac said. "I watched him open his mouth so wide you'd think his jaw would snap. And then the magic rushed in, like air and darkness mixed together. Through his mouth and inside him." He drained his goblet and placed it on the table. "He was never the same afterward."

In the wake of Alac's words, mine felt small. "And that's what you'd have to do . . . if you were king?"

"Yes," he said. "But I've never wanted to be king."

I hadn't expected a royal son to be opposed to the throne. "Not ever?"

"No. Mostly because of the magic." He reached behind his neck and unclasped the chain on which the locket hung; then he held it in his palm for me to see. "That time in the garden, when I felt something—when we both felt something—I thought it came from the blood locket." He paused, his gaze fixing mine so firmly it was almost palpable. "Now I'm not sure it did."

I swallowed. "I don't know anything about your father's magic."

"I'm talking about *your* magic, Mara." He took my hand, enfolding it in a grasp so warm and gentle that confusion welled up in me like a fountain. "I thought maybe I could find a way to return the magic to the Holy God and be done with it. But I'd rather be able to use the Thungrave magic the way you use yours."

His gaze was too intense, and I could hear him breathing—too shallowly. He was as nervous as I was.

But my own nervousness was compounded by the proximity of his face. The faintest hint of stubble shadowed his jaw, and his mouth turned up just so at the corners. His nose was sprinkled with pale freckles that danced onto his cheeks, barely visible. In the few days

I'd spent at the palace, I'd never allowed myself to look this closely at him.

I took my goblet and drank deeply, if only to hide my face for a few seconds. When I set it down, Alac released my hand and held the locket before me once again. A strange thrill crept through me.

"I resented my father when he gave this to me a few weeks ago," he said, gazing at the strange amulet. "I've always hated the magic. Feared it." His eyes met mine, and an odd light was in them. "Knowing what you can do, I fear it less."

The ghost of his touch still warmed my hand; I fisted it tightly in my lap. "So, there's blood inside the locket?"

"Yes," he said. "I keep telling myself I won't open it again."

Curiosity burned in me more deeply than fear. "What happens when you open it?"

With one deft motion, he flicked the locket open. At first, nothing happened. Then a fine, black mist rose from it and swirled in the air, a tiny, silent storm. It gathered itself into a cohesive mass and flew directly toward my face—and into my eyes.

I screamed as blindness overcame me.

22

ALAC

I watched in horror as the black mist seeped into Mara's eyes. She teetered where she sat, dropping her goblet, and I lunged forward and caught her by the shoulders, terrified that she'd been blinded, or that she would begin to age where she stood, her beautiful face creasing and wrinkling beyond recognition.

Tucker blew in as I eased Mara farther back on her chair. She looked at me, then, her expression dazed but her eyes clear and focused.

"What happened?" Tucker asked.

I ignored him, kneeling by Mara's side and keeping my hands on her shoulders, still fearful that some dreadful change would come over her.

"Can you see me?" I asked softly.

She nodded. "Yes. I'm fine."

"Will someone please tell me what happened?" Tucker asked.

"I opened the locket," I said, "and the black mist came out and went into her eyes."

Tucker gave me a look that would've made me wither if I weren't so concerned about Mara. "I told you to get rid of that thing."

I released Mara's shoulders and reached for the locket, which had slid to the floor. I slapped it shut.

"I'm not sure what happened." It sounded lame, but I found I had no words to describe what had come over me. Moments before I'd opened the locket, I'd heard my name again—clear, cold, disembodied. In the moment, I had an overwhelming urge to become one with the magic. In the aftermath, I felt nothing but revulsion.

Tucker knelt on Mara's other side. "With your permission, my lady?" At her nod, he took her wrist—so delicate—and pressed his fingers to her pulse.

I should have thought of that.

"I'm well enough," Mara said. "Truly."

"Pulse is a bit rapid, but steady," Tucker said.

Desperate to feel useful, I picked up Mara's goblet from the floor and poured more wine into it. "Drink," I said.

Wordlessly, she took the goblet and drank a little; her swallow was loud in the silence. I sat, the blood locket still clasped in my left hand. Disgusted, I placed it on the table.

Mara looked at me, her eyes clear and unaccusatory. "You're looking at me as though you expect me to drop dead."

"I—" There was no way to hold anything back. I glanced at Tucker, who was still kneeling by Mara's side, and then I returned my gaze to her. "The first time I opened the locket, that black . . . whatever it is . . . landed on a grape. Tucker and I watched it rot before our eyes." Mara nodded, waiting for me to continue. "The next time I opened it"—I threw a sheepish expression at Tucker; he didn't know about this next one—"it surrounded my fingertip, just here." I pointed. "My nail started to grow really fast—the growth of several weeks, at least. It was painful."

Tucker and Mara were both staring at me, but Mara's expression was more thoughtful than horrified. "How did you stop it?" she asked.

"It was the locket," I said. "That's the only way I can explain it."

"And what happened to your finger?" Tucker asked.

I held it up for them both to see. "It's fine. I trimmed the nail and that was that."

Tucker made a sound in the back of his throat and said nothing.

I leaned closer to Mara, so I could see her eyes. I half expected her to draw back, but she sat still and met my gaze evenly. "How are you feeling?"

"Silly for having screamed."

"But your eyes . . . ?"

"They feel fine. *I* feel fine." There was, perhaps, the slightest tremble in her voice, but mostly she was surprisingly calm. "It's hard to explain. One moment the magic was there, and then it was . . . gone."

I had felt it, too—the sudden disappearance of the magic's tingle, the way it made my skin thrum with energy, like the air before a thunderstorm.

"Maybe the locket protected you," I offered.

"Give it to me," Tucker said. "I'll give it back when the king returns."

"No," I said, a gnawing hunger tearing at my insides even though a minute ago I'd placed the locket on the table with revulsion. "You'll have to trust me."

"It's not you I don't trust," Tucker said. "It's whatever *thing* is inside that amulet."

I was eager to say something—anything—to Mara to redeem what had just happened. I'd seen the fear in her eyes when I questioned her about her magic. I hadn't meant to scare her; I'd meant to learn from her.

And I had to admit it—despite everything, I'd just wanted to see her again.

But who was I kidding? A few conversations and a walk by a waterfall weren't going to make her suddenly consider me in a favorable light. Even if she *had* given me permission to use her pet name.

A "passing fancy," Tucker would call it. I'd had enough of those in the past couple of years—I knew what that felt like.

This felt different.

"I'm sorry, my lady," I said, inwardly cringing at how formal I sounded. "I shouldn't have opened it."

"You meant no harm," she said.

"All the same. I feel stupid."

Tucker snorted. "I'm glad you said it first."

"You're not stupid, Alac." Mara's voice was soothing, like a balm upon a fresh wound. "You've been handed something you don't understand."

"Thank you." I wanted to say more, but words felt suddenly mixed up inside my mouth, and my heart was pounding. Something about those amber eyes and the long lashes that moved languidly when she blinked.

She meandered across the room, her gaze sweeping the surroundings as though she were looking for something—anything—else to look at. "If there's nothing else you need me for . . ."

"Oh. Of course not. I mean, you should go." I was a stuttering fool.

"I don't suppose you have any more of that Fionna white? An extra flagon?"

"You can have the rest of this." The flagon was half filled; I retrieved it from the table. "Tucker can carry it back for you."

Already she was at the door. "I don't need an escort, thank you." She stepped back and allowed Tucker to open it.

"Mara." I handed her the flagon, which she accepted. "Will you help me?"

"No, my prince," she said to the open doorway. Then she faced me. "I'm sorry."

Tucker withdrew quietly as I sat for several long minutes after Mara left, trying to decipher her parting expression. Regret? Pity? Disdain? I couldn't place it, and I didn't like it.

Damn, that girl. Blood locket and strange black mists aside, I'd never felt so discombobulated in my life.

23

MARALYTH

I leaned against the door to my quarters, breathing hard and glad that Nina hadn't returned yet. The flagon of wine had been nothing more than a decoy—an attempt to divert Alac's attention long enough for me to take what I had really wanted—the thin volume I'd glimpsed on his desk, its title pressed in letters of gold on its cover:

THE GIFT OF THE HOLY GOD
The Dallowyn Magic and Its Counterpart

I didn't know how soon he'd miss it or if he'd suspect that I'd taken it. But the opportunity had presented itself too completely for me to ignore. This was exactly the sort of thing I needed.

I'd worry later about how to return it.

I stroked the page, my fingertips itching with the lifeblood of the flax plant from which the linen paper had come. This was a book I would have loved to read when I was a girl, hiding in my room and healing the bruised plums I wanted to snack on.

For the rest of the evening and well into the night, I immersed myself in the book. First I read things I already knew—how all magic came from the Holy God, how King Daxion Dallowyn had received the magic from the First Brother of the Holy God, how Selmar Thungrave I had murdered Tommas Dallowyn for the throne after performing the ritual that allowed him to claim the magic for his own bloodline. This much Nelgareth had instructed me in himself.

The first half of the book ended with a simple list of the Thungrave kings and the dates on which their reigns began:

799—Selmar I
823—Gregar I
862—Donal I
892—Selmar II

The second half of the book spoke of the properties of the stolen magic, which were so different from the magic I was born with. It was spelled out in such detail that I felt overwhelmed. And more than a little frightened.

One passage that was marked in the margin, like several others, by notes in what I assumed was Alac's handwriting, drew my attention so that I read it more than once:

> Time is neutral. Therefore, the Magic, which is wrought of time, is neither good nor evil on its own. When freely given, it provides life and light. When stolen, it turns on itself, bringing power at great cost. And if this stolen Magic is set free, it will consume everything in its path in the same way time itself eventually does—by bringing it to death and rot.

I thought of the black mist creeping into my eyes. For a moment, I'd been blinded—but then everything felt normal. My eyes weren't "consumed"—unless there was some slow magic at work in them. A terrifying thought.

Alac had mentioned a rotted grape and a fast-growing fingernail. These both spoke of the death and rot brought by the passage of time. If the mist hadn't disengaged from Alac's finger, would the finger have died and rotted, like the grape? And what would happen if there were enough mist to enshroud a whole person? I shuddered at the implication.

The magic in Alac's locket was a small piece, though—contained. What about the magic in the king himself? What would happen if this magic were set free instead of passed to his heir?

What would happen if all three were killed at once? Where would the magic go?

The supper Nina had procured for me grew cold as I continued to read, the truth of the situation growing clearer with each passing breath. Especially when I read this:

> The very body and soul of each Thungrave king become the dwelling place for the stolen magic, which is held at bay by bone and sinew, mind and spirit. The magical protection of the firstborn reduces the likelihood that he will die before his father, but what if both perish? Without the ritual passage of magic from father to son, the magic will be free to reap its destruction at will. The ritual, therefore, is of utmost importance, and should be carried out without delay following the death of the king.

King Selmar wasn't the true enemy—the stolen magic was. By murdering the king and his sons, Nelgareth would unleash the power that had been behind the Thungrave takeover a century ago. What danger might that pose? If it could rot a single grape, could it destroy a vineyard? Steal the life from anything it encountered? Demolish an entire kingdom?

It was nearing midnight when I finished the book. Murdering the king and his sons had always felt wrong—now it felt doubly so. Without any notion of what might happen if the magic had nowhere to go, it was too big a risk to take.

And I needed to let Nelgareth know.

❧

I was properly attired for the Presentation of Wedding Gifts—a pale pink dress in keeping with the tradition of wearing pastels as a soft background to whatever bold color the bride-to-be might wear as she and her groom received their presents. A silly tradition, but the dress was light and cool.

Nelgareth arrived promptly at nine to escort me. For once, I was relieved to see him.

"Can we talk privately after the Presentation?" I asked.

"Is something wrong?"

"Possibly."

Nelgareth nodded. "We'll meet in the Queen's Garden afterward."

We said nothing more, and I arranged my face into what I hoped was pleasant and anticipatory. Though, to be honest, I couldn't fathom watching Ellian and Cannon opening gifts all morning.

It was as bad as I'd expected. The same, round tables used during the Mingle were dressed in linens of palest pink and yellow and set up on the palace's main lawn. Yesterday's rain had vanished, leaving a sky scoured clear of clouds and air that felt end-of-summer cool. Servants wove among the tables with trays of bacon-stuffed muffins, cheeses, and cold strips of beef. In the center, a large, round platform had been erected, where Ellian and Cannon sat on throne-like chairs, surrounded by a pile of packages and chests. Ellian's vibrant purple dress stood out like an ink blot.

As firm as my resolve had been to not look for Alac, I found myself scanning the tables. He sat with the bride's parents and his aunt and uncle at a table closest to the front and draped in deep-red table dressings instead of pink—and he was already looking at me when I found him. Unwanted heat coursed through me, and I lowered my gaze.

Nelgareth led us to a table not far from theirs, and I busied myself with placing a napkin on my lap, as though giving my hands something to do would take away the guilt of having stolen Alac's book.

Maybe I should have simply asked him for it. In the moment, it hadn't crossed my mind.

The opening of the gifts commenced, and Cannon looked as bored as I felt. Ellian, however, was a glowing vision of excitement, and I gave Cannon credit for giving her this moment.

Just when I thought I wouldn't be able to make myself watch Ellian gasp over yet another set of fine linens or an oversized necklace, she opened her final gift. As soon as the applause died down and the musicians began tuning their instruments, I turned to Nelgareth.

"I'm leaving now."

It was hard not to see the trace of disapproval in his expression; the Presentation wasn't officially over yet. But he leaned close and whispered his answer.

"I'll follow you shortly." I didn't like the feeling of his breath against my ear.

I made my way to the Queen's Garden and sat by the fountain for what felt like far too long. When finally I saw Nelgareth approaching between rows of flowers, my stomach knotted. I slid to the end of the bench to give him room to join me.

He swept his gaze across the garden, determining that we were alone. "What do you wish to speak about?"

I gathered my courage. "King Selmar's magic."

Nelgareth frowned. "What of it?"

"I've been studying it," I said. "There's an elaborate ritual that takes place to pass the magic from father to son. But if there's no one to pass it to, it has nowhere to go."

"Tommas Dallowyn is long dead. Once the Thungrave bloodline has been extinguished, this will be over."

"I think you're wrong." I squeezed my hands together. "You already know it's stolen magic. The only thing that can contain it is the body of the king it inhabits. I don't know what will happen if the king and both his sons die."

"You will take the throne, which is the reason you're here. I have not made these plans lightly, or without much study. The death of the Thungraves will mean an end to their tyranny."

"Their tyranny, yes," I said, "but not the magic."

"Where did you learn this?"

"From a book."

"And where did you find this book?"

"I . . ." I wanted to lie, but if I lied to everyone, where would I find my truth? "I took it from Alac's quarters."

"Alac's . . . quarters?" Nelgareth raised an eyebrow, waiting for me to confirm.

"Yes," I said, ignoring his implied question. "He hates the magic, my lord."

"The magic doesn't even concern him." His voice had grown an edge. "Cannon is the heir."

"Until Ellian has a son, Alac is next in line."

"You're talking about them as though they have a future." Nelgareth glanced furtively around the garden again before lowering his voice. "I've been watching Alac, and it's clear his interest in you has grown. You've been doing an excellent job of receiving his charms without seeming too . . . taken."

I sucked the insides of my cheeks. "But?"

"But I'm not sure it's wise to visit the prince in his own chambers."

Stay calm, Mara. Show him that you can respond without being defensive.

"He asked me there himself, and his personal guard was present."

"Why did he ask you there?"

"To talk with me." Now was not the time to mention the wild dog.

Nelgareth looked at me, assessing. "It's not wise to give your feelings free reign, my lady."

I felt a flush rising to my cheeks. "I've known him for a few days. I don't have *feelings*."

"Capturing the attention of a prince is a bit intoxicating. I'd like you to remain sober until we've completed our mission. Three more days—it's that close to our grasp."

I took a deep breath and centered myself. "You're right, my lord. We're so close."

Nelgareth rose. "I look forward to escorting you to the ball tonight."

Something in me snapped to attention—an awareness of the way he looked at me that I hadn't noticed before. "Yes. Thank you."

"I would like to claim the first dance, as well."

"Oh." Surely this wasn't what it sounded like. "As you wish."

"Until tonight, then." He offered his hand, and I took it, allowing him to raise me from my seat. "I'm convinced that Selmar's magic will die with him, and that will be the end of it. Don't worry yourself over this anymore."

"Yes. I'll try."

Lies. How many more would I tell in the next three days?

I watched him leave. Then I turned to the fountain, soaking in its soft music.

Nelgareth was wrong—I knew it deep in my bones. I had to stop this coup before it happened. Before Nelgareth, in his arrogance, unleashed a dark, untamed magic that could prove more dangerous to our kingdom than any Thungrave king.

I'd said yes to the throne. But it was time for me to say yes to Perin Faye instead.

24

MARALYTH

Nelgareth arrived at my door earlier than I'd expected. Nina finished the final touches on my hair while Nelgareth poured two goblets of wine from a flagon he'd arrived with.

"A drink before we dance," he said.

Something inside me clenched tightly.

With a single look from Nelgareth, Nina curtsied her way from the room, closing the door softly behind her. Nelgareth handed me a goblet, then sat in one of the overstuffed chairs by the darkened hearth.

He raised his goblet. "To you," he said.

I drank without having first raised my own goblet. Already, I felt the hanging weight of yet-unspoken motives for this early arrival.

"Come. Sit."

I sat primly in the chair across from him, mindful not to crease the voluminous skirts of my ball gown—a gold damask that, to me, looked too queenly.

"You're aware that I have no children."

"Yes." Discomfort curled through me.

"A cousin stands to inherit my lordland, though I can't say I'm too happy about that. He's not the brightest star in the sky."

"I know nothing of these matters." I sipped my wine and looked anywhere but at his face.

Nelgareth went on as though I hadn't spoken. "Before I found you, I was ready to place our reluctant Brother Shervan on the throne. My hardest decision, then, would have been which lord's daughter would make the best queen. Now, I'm faced with a similar decision for you."

My insides crawled. "I have no intention of marrying some lord's son simply to satisfy someone's ambition."

"That's not my intention."

There was no doubting what he would say next, but I didn't want to hear it. I rose, but he leaned forward and took hold of my wrist.

"Once you're on the throne, you'll have me to thank for putting you there," Nelgareth said, eyes dangerous. "You'll also have me to thank for *keeping* you there."

I tried to pull my wrist free, but he tightened his grip, his nails digging into my flesh. Fear clawed at me, but I pushed it aside. "You're hurting me."

A muscle in his face twitched, and he drew even closer, his words soft and menacing. "This conversation is *not over.*"

He released my wrist. Heart thudding against my chest, I rose and crossed the room, waiting by the door with my back to him until he joined me. We walked through the corridors without speaking, though a thousand angry words pressed against my teeth, struggling for freedom.

I held them back.

༄

The hall was magnificent, more dimly lit than usual and draped with garlands of flowers. Musicians were setting up to the left of the dais, and round tables were pushed to either side in rows, leaving a wide, open space in the middle for dancing.

So many winter evenings, Mother had danced with me near the hearth, teaching me the steps and praising me every time I mastered something. I'd never dreamed she'd once danced at court—or that I would one day be doing the same.

"Apologize to Lady Ellian for leaving early today," Nelgareth said. "I'll meet you for the first dance."

I withdrew my arm from Nelgareth's without looking at him. All his praise, his professed confidence in me—it wasn't because I was the Dallowyn he'd dreamed of, but because I was the means of placing *him* on a throne by my side.

Forcing myself to appear calm—and compliant—I made my way over to where Ellian stood chatting with a group of fawning girls. Lisbet was among them, her gorgeous hair swept back so perfectly that she looked like a painting. She averted her gaze as I approached.

"Maralyn!" Ellian seemed genuinely glad to see me. "I was just telling the others how the tapestry Lord and Lady Ollem gave us smelled strongly of cedar and cellar. I think it must've been in storage for *years*!"

I smiled, wondering why she would publicly ridicule a wedding gift and reminding myself that she was sixteen and as spoiled as every other noble girl here. "I'd like to apologize for leaving the Presentation of Wedding Gifts a bit early."

"Did you? I hadn't noticed." She took my hand. "You look exquisite this evening. Doesn't she look exquisite?"

The others muttered their agreement, and I felt myself growing warm. "Thank you, Lady Ellian."

"Just Ellian, please. It'll be tiresome having to be 'Your Grace'; I'd rather enjoy my name for as long as I can."

"You're not queen yet, my love." Cannon wrapped his arm around her and kissed the side of her head, while all the girls, including me, curtsied. "Are you ready to dance? They won't start without us."

Ellian giggled, and they walked away without taking anyone's leave. I turned awkwardly to the other girls—I'd spent little time with them and didn't feel like I belonged.

"If you'll excuse me," Lisbet said, "I've promised Prince Alac the first dance."

I watched her go, marveling at her obviousness. Then I excused myself from the others and reluctantly searched for Nelgareth. He smiled when he saw me, as though nothing ugly had passed between us. It made my skin crawl.

The music began. Nelgareth was an excellent dancer, but his hands felt sweaty whenever I touched them, and his gaze made me so uncomfortable that I finished the dance without making further eye contact. When it was over, I offered a deep curtsy, as though I'd had the most enjoyable time ever. Then I hurried to a table near the wall and sat, accepting a goblet of wine from a passing servant and breathing out my growing revulsion.

In a thousand summers, I would not marry that man.

I searched the crowd for Alac, telling myself it was because I needed to speak with him and not because I was eager to be with him again.

It's not wise to give your feelings free reign.

I swallowed the memory of Nelgareth's words with some wine and slammed my goblet onto the table. What did it matter what I felt about anyone? In three days, either I would be queen—or I would be dead.

"You look utterly bored." Tucker was dressed in a fawn-colored tunic, his curls slightly less messy than usual.

I smiled, thankful for his gift of putting me at ease. "I believe I'm the only girl who isn't trying to find a husband."

"You're sure about that?"

"Quite sure."

"Well, then, I suppose it's safe for you to dance with this oaf."

He stepped aside, and Alac was there, the jewels in his tunic winking in the candlelight.

"Lady Maralyn." His bow was formal. Almost self-conscious.

"My prince."

"Really, you two," Tucker said. "Have you forgotten you're on a first-name basis?"

I felt my face flush. "Alac, then."

"Will you dance with me?" Alac asked. "The music's starting again."

"Yes." And suddenly I was smiling. "I need to talk with you, anyway."

He grinned. "Works for me."

We took our place—second in line—for a stately pavane. It was a regal dance, slow and pompous, and one that I could manage without missing a beat.

We danced without speaking at first, my hand resting on his, our steps light and perfectly synchronized, as though we'd danced together dozens of times. Cannon and Ellian were in front of us, leading the long procession through the courtly dance.

King and queen, everyone was surely thinking. And what of me, dancing with Alac behind them? Did they think he'd chosen me purposefully for this dance?

Had he?

I swallowed the dark dread that tried to crawl up my throat and choke me.

Ellian will never be queen.

"I thought you said you wanted to talk," Alac said.

"I do," I said. "I was concentrating on the dance."

And trying to ignore the warmth of his hand against mine every time we touched. It felt like truth instead of deception, life instead of death.

"We've got half a dance left."

I turned to look at him, though I was supposed to face forward. "I have a request."

His smile radiated heat that warmed a place in me I didn't think I'd allowed him access to. "Anything."

"I want to see your father's private chapel."

"Why?" I heard hope in the single word.

I turned to face forward again, careful to keep in step with the music. "I . . . may have borrowed a book from you."

"*You* took it?" He waited for my single nod. "I've been looking everywhere!"

"I'm sorry," I said. "I read it last night. I have no idea if I can help or not, but I want to try."

"You could've asked me for it."

"I was afraid you'd say no. Will you show me the chapel?"

He nodded once. "Meet me at the base of the stairway to the guest wing at midnight?"

It was my turn to smile. "I'll be there."

Nelgareth be damned.

25

MARALYTH

It was almost half past twelve before Alac arrived at the stairway.

"Sorry I'm late," Alac said.

I gave a little shrug and took his arm when he offered. It felt strong and sure beneath the shirt's fabric, and my stomach did a strange, twisty thing that left me feeling mildly flustered.

We walked through a hallway I'd never seen and up a curved stairway that led to a broad foyer lined with long, rectangular windows one against the other, affording a view broken only by the strips of lead between the panes. I imagined that, if it hadn't been dark, the view would be glorious. I remembered seeing these windows on my first approach to the palace, down the pristine cobblestone lane and through the lush trees. From up here, one could probably see past the lane to the colorful roofs of the town, and beyond.

A view that could be mine, if I were queen.

"My father's apartments," Alac said, gesturing to a grand double door set in the center of the wall facing the windows. "Normally it would be guarded, but as it stands . . ."

He opened the door a crack and peeked in, as though he feared the king might be hiding in there. Then he pushed it open and stepped aside.

"After you."

Knowing I was stepping into the chambers of a king was inebriating. The front room was enormous, stretching the entire length of the hallway outside, with a large stone hearth at each end. A yawning archway draped with sheer curtains opened to a second chamber beyond, with wide windows reflecting light from the open doorway onto a canopied bed. The walls of the main room were hung floor to ceiling with ivory velvet, upon which was mounted all sorts of framed artwork and small tapestries, and the furniture was gilded—every single piece.

"This way," Alac said, heading toward the bedroom.

A door stood to the right of the grandiose bed. Alac opened a narrow drawer in the bedside table and withdrew a key. I waited while he unlocked the door. It swung open on well-oiled hinges, and a dusty, faintly metallic odor wafted out. We stepped inside.

Alac let out a low sigh as he closed the door behind us. "I hate it in here."

I followed him into the dark room, lit only by a single lamp in a red sconce that dangled above the altar. To the left sat a long table draped with a cloth and littered with candles and candlesticks. Alac lit a few while I walked toward the altar, my skin buzzing. It wasn't the same sensation as when I ripened grapes beneath my fingers or whispered away a touch of frost. It was an intense feeling that set me on edge.

A hammered-gold container, like a miniature, domed building, sat in the center of the altar. It was overlaid with an intricate, swirling pattern of silver vines and inlaid with precious jewels—ruby, emerald, sapphire. On the front was a little door, not much bigger than my two hands together. Its knob looked like it was made from a large, uncut diamond.

Alac came up silently to my left. The air felt heavy and expectant, and the stillness was so profound that I felt I shouldn't breathe.

"This is it." Alac's words were hushed.

"What's in it?" I asked.

"The source of the stolen magic."

Exactly what I'd wanted to know.

I glanced at Alac; his gaze was fixed pointedly on the dome, his hands grasping the altar cloth so that I thought he might accidentally pull it down, bringing the dome with it. So slowly that, at first, I didn't realize he was moving, Alac reached toward the dome. He paused when his hand was directly in front of the door, then curled his fingers around the knob and pulled the door open. His body shuddered so violently that I thought he might fall over.

"Alac?" The word trembled inside my mouth.

"The breath," he whispered.

In the shadowed light, it was hard to see what was inside the dome. It looked like it might be an hourglass, or some other item fashioned from metal and glass.

Alac's arms fell to his sides. "See the top bulb? It's almost empty."

I looked and saw that it was, indeed, an hourglass. Swirling inside was a gently glowing *something* that moved like a living thing. Alac was right—most of the swirling substance was in the bottom bulb.

He turned to me. "Once my father is dead, Cannon will be the only one who can receive the magic. When he does, the top bulb will be full again—and my father's spirit will join the others inside here."

My own magic burned within me, responding to its stolen counterpart in waves. "Tommas Dallowyn's magic."

"Yes," Alac said. "He basically tore it from his own blood."

"That must've taken a powerful blood magic." The undulating mass made me uneasy.

"The sorcerers who trained him were hunted down by Wexen's supporters after Tommas murdered him," Alac said. "Their secrets died with them."

"If there's a way to transfer the magic to a person, there must also be a way to transfer it back to where it was taken from," I said slowly.

"To the Holy God?" Alac's words were colored with hope.

"Yes." But it seemed unfathomable.

"I'd like that to be true. But I'd also like a chance to use this magic for good, the way you use yours."

"I was born with mine," I said. "This is blood magic."

"So how can we undo blood magic?"

I didn't know.

His voice dropped lower. "The spirits of the Thungrave kings are here. My father will be next to join them. And then . . . I'll be one step closer to the throne."

The tone in his voice had coaxed gooseflesh on my neck and arms. "How do you know the spirits are here?"

"They call my name."

I swallowed. "You can hear them?"

"Sometimes."

He didn't elaborate. I shivered; magic was something I understood, but voices of dead kings wasn't.

"We should go," Alac said.

We walked silently from the chapel; I waited while he locked the door and replaced the key in the drawer. With every step through the king's darkened chambers, the conviction in my heart grew.

"I want to help you," I said, heart pounding. "I'm just not sure how."

Alac's expression was so grateful I almost cried. He looked at me for several heartbeats, as though he didn't know what to say. Then he smiled.

"Maybe we could—"

The door opened; I stifled a gasp as Alac and I froze.

High Minister Zeth stood in the doorway with a stunned expression on his face.

26

ALAC

"Z eth." I didn't know what else to say. I couldn't imagine what he was thinking.

"My prince. My lady." Formal as ever. "Word has just come that your father will arrive within the hour. I came to see that his private chapel was in order."

My stomach tightened. "He's more than a day early."

"So it would seem." But his gaze was on Mara.

"I should go," Mara said.

Zeth moved to one side so she could slip past him. She'd almost gone when I called out, "Can we talk over breakfast?"

She threw me a quick glance I couldn't quite read. "Yes."

After she'd gone, Zeth turned to me. "I wouldn't presume to pry, my prince, but—"

"It's not what it looks like. She . . . wanted a tour." It wasn't completely false. "Will he want to see me?"

"He may."

He wouldn't, and we both knew it. "You won't tell him about this, will you?"

"It wouldn't be wise to upset the king upon his return, my prince." He stepped closer. "You're wearing it, I presume? In case he asks me."

Every muscle in my body tensed. "He can ask me himself."

I spent the next hour pacing in my room, telling myself I was stupid for waiting for a summons while questioning why it would bother me not to have one. I'd finally given up and changed into my nightshirt when the knock came at my door. Of course. I answered, barely giving the servant enough time to finish telling me that my father had requested my presence in his study before closing the door in his face.

Hastily, I redressed. Then, leaving the blood locket visible at my neck, I walked the dark corridors to Father's study.

Guards stood at either side of the door, a sure sign that he was inside. I knocked the required three times.

"Come."

As always, his voice, even through the thickness of the door, brought a chill with it. I opened the door, bowed, and closed the door behind me.

"Your Grace."

Father sat at his desk, the candelabras fully lit, the magic hanging in the air around him, a presence far more tangible than I'd felt before. Cannon stood behind him to the right, arms folded, hair looking as though he'd rolled out of bed in the middle of a tempestuous dream. Or perhaps from Ellian's embrace.

"Did you wear the locket as I instructed?" No greeting, no apology for the late hour.

"Yes."

"Give it to me."

I held his gaze, the icy oppression of the magic that always kept him at a distance seeming thinner, more easily breached. Slowly—reluctantly—I slipped the chain over my head.

I dropped the locket onto his desk. "How was your journey?"

He ignored me, reaching for the locket and weighing it in his palm. "Something has shifted." He looked up. "Did you open this?"

"You told me not to."

His gaze was slow and penetrating. "I'll ask one more time. *Did you open this?*"

"No." It wasn't the first time I'd lied to him.

He handed the locket back. "Your lack of curiosity disappoints me."

"Just like everything else about me."

He stared at me, those magic-dark eyes penetrating my bones. Then he picked up a quill and started writing, not giving me another glance. "Music on the Green is tomorrow at one o'clock," he said. "Don't be late."

I glanced at Cannon, whose expression was darkened by the same oppressive presence that always hung around Father. Normally, I would back out of the room, never daring to turn my back on the king. But he wasn't even looking at me.

I turned and left, pulling the door sharply closed behind me.

It wasn't until I'd crawled into bed that I allowed myself to think of Mara. Her willingness to help was more than I'd hoped. I'd send someone to escort her to breakfast in the morning room, and I'd make sure we weren't disturbed. For the first time, I felt hopeful.

A creeping worry swelled in my chest, though. *Would Father know she had magic?* Despite the terrifying strength of his power, he wasn't omnipotent. But what if his magic recognized the Dallowyn blood in her veins? The blood locket had tried to protect me the first time my hand brushed against hers, and it held a small fraction of Father's full power.

Cruce. It would have been better for her if she'd never come to the palace at all.

27

MARALYTH

I awoke early, my heart racing with anticipation and dread. I feared Alac expected me to have an answer for him, and I didn't. But breakfasting alone with him was more appealing than I dared admit.

Somehow, I had to save him.

I'd barely finished dressing when Nina answered a knock on the door, which I expected might be Tucker or someone else from Alac's personal household. Instead, servants arrived with an elaborate breakfast cart—and Nelgareth.

The dread in my heart doubled.

"Good morning," he said. "I've taken the liberty of bringing you breakfast, and I hope you won't mind if I join you."

Unease tapped at my heart as I offered a curtsy. "Thank you, but I have other plans."

"Do you? Well, you'll have to change them."

"Shall I finish your hair, my lady?" Nina asked.

"No, thank you," I said, twisting it into a low knot as I spoke. "Go have breakfast."

"You'll wait outside the door first," Nelgareth said, "to turn away anyone who might come calling."

Nina curtsied, threw me a nervous glance, and went out the door.

Anger and fear warred within me. I balled my hands into fists while the servants laid everything out—poached eggs drizzled with creamy sauce, shaved lamb, jelly-filled pastries, steaming *myar*. I wanted to beg the servants not to leave, but the door closed soundly behind them.

"I confess I don't like the way they brew their *myar* here," Nelgareth said. "We'll have to see about that." He gestured for me to sit across from him.

I sat. "Why are you here?"

"I told you our conversation last night wasn't over," he said. "I'm here to finish it."

I set my jaw. "You're going to propose marriage."

"Not propose. Plan." He sipped his *myar,* eyeing me over the rim of his mug and waiting for me to react.

I sat taller and schooled my voice to be as firm and even as his. "Your rank is lower than mine, my lord. When the time is right, I will be the one doing the proposing."

Nelgareth set his mug down very deliberately. "How do you think your father is spending his three hundred silvers, Maralyth Graylaern? Do you think he's happy? Safe?"

My chest tightened. "Are you going to threaten his safety every time you want something from me?"

"I'll threaten you whenever necessary, my lady." He sliced into an egg with the side of his fork; the yolk pooled onto the plate, like golden blood.

I pushed my own plate away.

"It's settled," Nelgareth said, chewing. "I'll draw up the papers this afternoon."

"I'd rather die," I said.

"I'll make sure that doesn't happen."

Damn him. If I wasn't killed during the coup, I'd find a way out of this.

Nelgareth wiped his mouth. "The wedding breakfast is two days from now. Everything's in place."

Two days. That's all the time I had to save Alac.

I nodded as though this were nothing to me . . . as though chatting about murdering kings and princes were a normal part of conversation at meals.

"Only the lords and their families are invited to the traditional breakfast," he continued, "along with family members of the bride and groom. It will be a small, manageable crowd."

"I hate violence," I said.

"It will be less violent than you may suspect," he said. "I'm not a violent man."

I'd completely lost my ability to hold back. "You don't consider *cutting out a servant's tongue* violent?"

He placed his fork down, clearly caught off guard. "A man who doesn't protect the integrity of his household is an open target. That doesn't make me violent."

"I'm sure your servant would disagree."

"You're young. You'll understand this sort of thing once you've been on the throne for a few years."

"I hope to *never* understand that sort of thing."

He finished his meal in silence; I left mine untouched. As soon as he left, I'd send a message to Alac. Perhaps it wouldn't be too late to meet him for breakfast.

"At any rate," Nelgareth said, as though we'd been talking all along, "I feel it's best for you to stay in your quarters until the morning of the wedding."

I stared, disbelieving. "Why?"

"Because I wish it," Nelgareth said. "You've had enough freedom the past few days. You don't need the young prince distracting you any further."

"He's not a distraction!"

Heart in a furious panic, I rose and made a run for the door, but he was fast and caught me before I got there. He took me roughly by the shoulders and turned me to face him.

"It will do you well to remember that I won't forget anything you've said or done, once I'm queen!" I spat.

His eyes grew cold. "And it will do *you* well to remember to whom you are most indebted." He pulled me so close that our noses touched. "Until later, my betrothed."

He left, and moments later I heard the scrape of a key in the keyhole. I ran to the door and tried it—it was locked. How he had even procured a key, I didn't know.

I slammed the door with my fist, then turned and leaned my back against it, eyes closed.

"Alac." I felt utterly responsible for his fate.

And utterly despicable.

And now I was a caged bird, expected to sing upon her release as she alighted on the throne and married the man who had placed her there.

But it wasn't the throne that needed taking—I knew that now. It was the magic, stolen a century ago and ruining the lives of four kings—and an entire kingdom.

I wouldn't waste time lamenting. Abandoning the breakfast, I fetched Alac's book from the dressing-table drawer and took it out to the balcony. If I couldn't meet with Alac, then I would study the book myself. There had to be something in there that I'd missed. Something that would free Alac and the others from the curse.

If I failed, at least I'd be able to say that I'd done what I could to save the kingdom a different way.

∞

No day had ever seemed longer.

By the time the light was fading, I'd come to no clear conclusion on how to free Alac from the magic he so despised, but I did begin to formulate a plan that might—hopefully—save his life.

Supper had long since passed, and Nina, who had been given the key and permission to sit with me until bedtime, sat quietly embroidering while I went through my plan for the tenth time in my head, knowing that I was either desperate or mad, or possibly both. Nina attempted for the second time to conceal a yawn, and I realized I'd waited long enough.

I rose from the window seat. "I'm sorry you've been kept here so long."

"It's no bother, my lady," she said, gathering her embroidery. "You would have been lonely this evening without someone to sit with you."

Her tenderness pricked my conscience and heightened my nerves. Aside from gentle nudges to birds and insects, the wild dog had been the first living creature I'd worked my magic on. I wasn't confident it would be the same with a person. I had, after all, failed to staunch the bleeding tongue.

"I appreciate your kindness," I said, placing my hands on her shoulders. Then, to the magic gathering beneath my palms, I said, "Rest. Go to sleep."

Nina's eyelids fluttered as she looked at me with a question forming on her lips. Then her eyes closed and she began to crumple to the floor. I caught her, a deadweight in my arms, and eased her the rest of the way down.

"Sleep deeply," I crooned, my hand upon her brow. "Let not the slightest sound awaken you."

I watched her for a full minute, her breathing even and soft, her mouth slightly parted. Then I dug into the pocket of her dress to retrieve the key nestled within. Taking a single candle in a holder and Alac's book, I unlocked the door, then locked it again behind me. The hallway was dark and quiet; it was past eleven, and most people were in bed by now. Hopefully that included Nelgareth.

I crept quickly by his door, pulse racing. As soon as I'd made it past, a sense of exhilarated freedom coursed through me. I hurried through the darkened hallway and prayed to the Holy God that I wouldn't be seen.

28

ALAC

It was hard to believe how dull a day could be without Mara in it.

Hearing that she had taken to her room with a headache only made me feel slightly better. It hadn't assuaged my fear that I'd frightened her off.

Music on the Green had lasted until well after sunset, though no one really seemed to be enjoying themselves. The festive tone of the past few days had left since Father's arrival; it now seemed all the guests had rehearsed their lines prior to speaking, so careful was the conversation. I'd finally excused myself before the final set of songs, ignoring Father's disapproving look and making my way to the stables. A night ride was just what I needed to clear my head and prepare myself for tomorrow, which would consist of a long and boring wedding rehearsal.

It was later than I'd meant to return, so at least I wouldn't accidentally run into any giggling girls hoping for a moment alone with me. The only girl I was interested in didn't giggle, and it was unlikely I'd see her any time soon. Marvan, who'd been pulled from a card game to take his station at my door for the night, hung several steps behind me.

Light from a single candle illuminated a figure skulking just outside my door. I slowed, wondering if any of the lords' daughters would be brazen enough to come looking for me.

"Let me go first." Marvan pressed ahead, but I kept up and arrived at my door at the same time. Someone stood several paces away, her face a play of light and shadow from the candle she'd placed on the floor.

My heart somersaulted. "Mara?"

"I need to speak with you."

I glanced at Marvan, who seemed to be stifling a smile. "Come in."

We left Marvan at his post, and I found myself grateful it wasn't Tucker tonight. Mara's arrival was so unexpected—and had my head spinning so fast—that I didn't think I could handle his teasing right now.

Several lamps were already lit; I took Mara's candle and lit several more with it while she took the same seat she'd sat in the day before, when the black mist had gone into her eyes. *The Gift of the Holy God* sat on her lap.

"Is your headache better?"

She frowned. "Headache?"

I shifted, wondering what mistake I'd made. "Um, I was told you had one."

"I didn't. Lord Nelgareth insisted I stay in my chambers today."

Odd. "And now you've sneaked out."

"Yes." She handed me my book. "I shouldn't have taken this without asking."

"I would've given—"

"I know." Her eyes blazed with an intensity I hadn't seen before. "I've done much studying and have come up with something a bit worrying." She opened the book to a page she'd marked and turned it around to face me. "Read this passage."

I took the book and read aloud. "'The journey toward transferal is wrought with—'"

"Not there," she said, pointing to the next paragraph. "Here."

I allowed myself to enjoy the moment that her hand brushed mine as she moved it out of the way. Then I read once more.

"'As the time of transferal draws near, it's natural for others in the near bloodline to find themselves drawn to the magic, of which they will have little understanding. As such, there is conceivable danger to remaining offspring, as the magic seeks to make its way fully and completely to the legitimate heir, and to destroy all else. A royal mother carrying an unborn child—a younger sibling to the heir—will be at particular risk during this time, though a mother carrying the heir can be a conduit for the transfer of power, should the need arise.

In general, though, any offspring, born or unborn, will be in as much peril as everyone else.'"

I looked up. "I already know about the danger."

"Are you still wearing the locket?"

"Yes." I couldn't tell her that I no longer wanted to part with it.

"Alac—" An odd, desperate expression broke out on her face, and she rose. "Will you be greatly missed if you don't attend the wedding breakfast?"

"I wouldn't say I'm ever *greatly* missed."

"But could you?"

"I could. Why?"

"Can you meet me at the falls that morning instead? I . . . think I may be able to help you. But I'd like to return to the place where I put the dog to sleep. I have a theory."

"How will you get there, though?"

"Saddle a horse for me, and tell one of the stable hands to expect me."

The entire thing was madness. Yet something about the way she looked at me made me want to say yes over and over.

"I could do that."

Now that I'd said yes, I couldn't tell whether she was relieved—or anxious. She offered the smallest smile, but it wasn't convincing.

"Mara? What is it you're not telling me?"

She looked stricken for a moment, but recovered quickly. "I'm sorry. It's just that . . . you've asked for my help, and I'm afraid I'll fail."

I smiled. "But you're willing to try."

"Yes." She folded her arms around herself. "I should go."

Her face was soft in the candlelight. Like a painting. Like something I wanted to touch. "Shall I walk you back?"

"No." For a moment she stood staring at me, and I imagined what it would be like to kiss her. But then she abruptly said, "Good night."

I watched her leave, then stood in the silence of my quarters for a long time afterward, staring at the door.

I wanted to believe there was more to this than the magic. Could it be that at least part of her wanted to be with me? Alone?

It was too much to hope for. I threw my clothing on a heap and climbed into bed with the book, wondering what else its pages had revealed to her.

And wondering if, when she crawled into her own bed, she thought even a little bit of me.

29

MARALYTH

My heart thudded against my chest as I made my way back to my apartments. As I turned a corner, a dark, hunched figure emerged from a recessed stairwell just ahead. I pressed myself against the wall and held my breath. Who would be creeping about this late? Besides me, anyway.

The figure paused, and in the dim light I could see it was one of the Brothers of the Holy God, cowl draped over his head. I waited, and soon the Brother made his way down the hall, slippered feet silent against the stone. When the hallway was quiet, I continued on, hurrying past the stairwell that I was now convinced led to the castle sanctuary. I had no idea what hours the Brothers kept, but it seemed likely there would always have been a certain number of them awake.

Had I left Alac's a moment sooner, the Brother might've emerged at the moment I crossed his path. For as careful as I thought I'd been, I'd been at great risk for being caught.

It sobered me, but it also confirmed how determined I was to save Alac from the fate he didn't deserve. I'd deal with my own fate afterward.

Nina still slept soundly where I had left her. I slipped the key back into her pocket.

"Be refreshed," I said. "Rise."

She opened her eyes and gave a small sound of surprise—and perhaps dismay. "My lady?"

"I hated to wake you."

"I'm sorry, I . . . did I fall asleep? I can't remember."

"It's no matter. You've spent a long day in here with me."

"Thank you. I'm quite embarrassed."

I smiled. "There's no need. I'll see you in the morning."

After she'd gone, I undressed quickly and crawled into bed, thinking of nothing but Alac. If he'd been present during the attack, my hope was that the locket would protect him. Asking him to meet me at the falls was a last-minute idea, and he'd said yes so easily that I felt guiltier than ever.

He thought I wanted to be with him—I could tell by the way he looked at me. Yes, I was trying to protect him. Save his life. But he didn't know that. Couldn't know that. And once he realized I wasn't going to show up, the danger would hopefully have passed.

It was an imperfect plan, but it was all I could think to do. If Alac were missing from the wedding breakfast, I was certain Nelgareth's intentions would be carried out, anyway. There would be an immediate hunt, surely. But he would at least have time to get away.

After that, I didn't know. If I were declared queen, that would make me Alac's immediate enemy. And he'd figure out pretty quickly that I'd sent him away because I knew about the coup.

No matter. There was no time for anything else. I could spend the next day in my rooms without feeling like I was doing nothing. I'd be Nelgareth's well-behaved ward, waiting for her chance to attend the royal wedding.

But oh, Holy God. Tomorrow would surely be the longest day of my life.

30

ALAC

The mind-numbing boredom of the following day, which was filled with wedding rehearsal, final wardrobe fittings, and playing host, was offset by thoughts of meeting Mara in the morning. I lay awake for hours that night, thinking about her and trying to imagine what she'd come up with. I'd long given up trying to find hidden answers in the book, and the irrefutable ache that kept growing within me for continued communion with the stolen magic made me fear for my sanity.

I hated the way I craved it, the way it gnawed at my gut like an insatiable hunger. Mara was my only hope—and I sort of hated that, too.

Cannon's wedding day dawned gray and bright, as though the clouds couldn't make up their mind. I dressed in the tunic I'd already planned to wear to the wedding breakfast, but with riding leathers and boots beneath. By now, guests would already be filtering in to the king's dining chamber for what was to be the most intimate gathering, meant only for the families of the bride and groom, plus the seven lords and their families. Even still, it was a ridiculous amount of people, most of whom I either didn't like or didn't care to know. Mara couldn't have chosen a better time to ask me to meet her somewhere else.

I waited another five minutes; then I opened my door. Tucker stood at his post, arms folded.

"You've been taking your time in there," he said.

"I wanted to wait until most of the guests had arrived before leaving."

"Are you sure this is wise?"

I shot him an incredulous look. "Did you actually just say that?"

He shrugged. "I'm coming with you either way. It's just . . . I think you'll be missed."

"For three minutes, maybe." I started walking down the hallway toward a back stairwell, and Tucker matched my pace. "She put a wild dog to sleep, Tuck. And the black mist in her eyes didn't faze her. Whatever she's got, I want it."

"That's not all you want."

"You have to admit she's incredible."

"Not my type, but I've seen worse."

I gave him a side-eye. "You've seen worse?"

"Remember that cross-eyed girl with boils all over her face?"

"Very funny."

By now we'd reached the bottom of the steps, the doorway of which opened into a narrow corridor leading to the kitchens and other work areas, with a door at the end opening to the grounds not far from the stables. I took a quick glance in the opposite direction, where the hallway opened into the grand foyer. The king's dining chamber was behind the other staircase and not visible from our perspective. No one would see me leaving.

I was about to turn when a flash of crimson silk caught my eye. There, her arm threaded through Lord Nelgareth's, walked Maralyn, her face all smiles, on her way to the wedding breakfast.

I stared, disbelieving. My heart felt hollowed out, like a dead tree, as I watched them disappear into the hallway leading to the dining chamber. Tucker's firm grasp on my shoulder jarred me.

"Looks like she had a change of plans," he said.

"Or maybe this was her plan all along."

"What, to get rid of you? What does it matter whether you're at breakfast or not?"

My pulse pounded inside my ears. "I don't know. But I'm going to find out."

I squared my shoulders and walked in the direction of the dining chamber.

31

MARALYTH

My heart was a hundred-pound weight as I entered the dining chamber on Nelgareth's arm. Already, the room was filled with guests, many in their seats. A long table was set against the middle of the rectangular head table to make the shape of a *T*. Cannon and Ellian sat in their seats of honor at the center of the head table on either side of the king's chair; Ellian's golden-red hair was twisted back from her face and dotted with tiny, fresh flowers the color of buttercream. Her smile never faltered and her cheeks were in a permanent state of blush—the perfect bride.

"My lady." Lord Mallory, silver circlet on his head as always, took my hand and kissed it, his gaze holding unspoken meaning. "What a wonderful day today will be. All the kingdom will celebrate."

"Yes, my lord," I said. "Everyone loves a wedding."

Duplicity. Doublespeak. I'd become far too good at it.

Nelgareth pulled out a seat for me near the head table, indicative of his influence in King Selmar's court. He then sat to my left.

I thanked the servant who filled my goblet with sparkling wine. The king had not yet arrived, and Alac's seat at the head table was, of course, empty as well. My stomach twisted into yet another knot as I thought of Alac riding to Crossford Falls, expecting to meet me there. I reached for the goblet and scanned the table—and my very breath froze.

Alac was crossing the room, his expression dark, his gaze fixed on his place at the head table. I watched him, sick dread spreading through me.

Why hadn't he gone to the falls?

He kissed Ellian's hand, his face momentarily softening into a smile. Ellian's parents, Lord and Lady Milchas, sat to Ellian's right; he greeted them as well, and then took his seat on Cannon's right.

Our eyes met, and in that single heartbeat I saw anger and disappointment so profound that it was almost palpable. Then he looked away, and I wanted to jump to my feet and scream for him to leave, to run, to get as far away from the castle as he possibly could.

Dear Holy God, how can I sit here and watch his murder?

Regardless of my attempts at guarding my heart, he'd wormed his way in. If I landed on the throne, I would spend the rest of my life regretting the loss of this funny, kindhearted, thoughtful prince who defied everything I'd come to believe about him and his family.

It was a fathomless loss. Unavoidable and shattering.

I felt the darkness before I saw that King Selmar had entered—a heaviness that seemed to squeeze the breath from my lungs. At once, everyone rose, and I scrambled to my feet as well. The king waved us all casually back to our seats as he made his way to the head table. Greetings of "Your Grace!" and "King Selmar!" rang out as our monarch took his seat and reached for the goblet beside his plate. He raised it, and his gaze swept the dining chamber.

"To the wedding day," he said.

His words were friendly enough, but his voice sent a chill through me and made my hands buzz. Despite my aversion to swallowing anything, I drank sparkling wine when everyone else did, and a strange tingle went down my throat, as though the wine were crying out on its way down. I coughed and put my goblet on the table with a too-loud clunk.

King Selmar's gaze rested on me; his eyes were dark, like his irises had been swallowed by too-large pupils. My magic thrummed beneath my skin.

"I'm honored to present my ward to you, Your Grace." Nelgareth was fawning. Cooing, even. "This is Lady Maralyn, recently entrusted to my care."

King Selmar inclined his head; it felt like a strange benediction. Then, when our eyes met a second time, something shifted. His already dark eyes seemed to grow darker still, and he leaned slightly forward in his seat.

The magic raged within me; I tried to tamp it down, to tame it into submission. It burned in my fingertips and on my tongue.

"Lady Maralyn." He spoke my name as though it were a question.

I bowed my head and counted to five, trying desperately to look subservient and nonthreatening. When I looked up, his full attention was still on me. Around us, the room grew strangely hushed.

"It's her first time at court, Your Grace." Even Nelgareth's confident voice sounded thin in the presence of what seemed like immeasurable power. Every breath I took felt charged with it. Choked by it.

I was certain the king had sensed my magic; I felt turned inside out and wrung. But he sat back, his scrutiny suddenly ended.

I averted my eyes, breathing through a tiny "oo" to still my pattering heart. Conversation swelled once more, though it remained subdued. Strained.

I'd sworn to myself that I wouldn't, but I looked at Alac again. He was conversing with Lord Bentian, who sat beside him. Lady Bentian and a young married couple completed the seating on that end of the head table. A cousin and his wife, if I were correct.

Would they *all* die because they shared the king's blood? My pulse rushed in my ears and my throat felt like it was closing.

Soft music began to play from a band of musicians in a far corner, and the food was served with relish. Everything on my plate was more beautiful than any morsels I'd seen—strips of spiced meat curled into the shapes of flowers and garnished with a snowfall of goat cheese and delicate herbs, including sage; large, golden mushrooms stuffed with minced shellfish and cheeses; beetroots cut to resemble blossoms the color of blood.

Blood.

I forced tiny nibbles into my mouth, chewing until I had no choice but to swallow. Despite Ellian's smiles and the pleasant music, the atmosphere was quiet, pressed into submission by the presence of the king and his magic.

Did no one else notice? I was sure that Alac must.

King Selmar seemed disengaged—there but not there. "Bored," some might label him—but it was more than that. He was dark and brooding, and his beringed fingers often drummed on the table as though he were merely biding his time. I finally stopped looking at him altogether.

"You're not eating," Nelgareth said softly.

I swallowed the bile that tried to come up my throat and took another small taste of the stuffed mushrooms. Everything was dust in my mouth. I rinsed it down with another swallow of the wine and almost choked, coughing violently into my fisted hand and trying not to be conspicuous.

Nelgareth handed me a napkin. I tried to thank him, but another fit of coughing stole my words.

Dessert was served, and though I'd barely eaten a quarter of what was on my breakfast plate, I couldn't bear the thought of a single spoonful of the rich, vanilla custard that sat like a cloud in front of me. For the dozenth time, I stole a glance at Alac, who was attacking his own custard with gusto.

Holy God, what was Nelgareth waiting for? The slightest sign that something was about to happen might give me a chance—the wildest, most unbelievable chance—of saving Alac. It flew in the face of all the reasons I'd accepted the role of usurper. It would complicate everything that had been planned for so long.

But I couldn't sit here and do nothing. Alac Thungrave didn't deserve to die.

Finally, Nelgareth rose, and the room quieted. My heart stuttered. I tried to smile the way so many others were smiling, but my face was baked clay that might crack. I hazarded a glance at Alac; heat flashed through me as I realized he was staring at me, and probably had been for some time.

"Why?" he mouthed silently.

I swallowed a silent sob. "I'm sorry," I mouthed back.

Nelgareth cleared his throat. "I'm pleased to present the traditional flagon of wine to the wedding couple and their families—the finest from my own cellars."

"That's because you steal all the best wine," someone called out, followed by much laughter.

Nelgareth's face crinkled with mirth. *Liar. Murderer.* He gestured toward a servant who was making his way to the head table, pushing a small cart that held a quarter cask and a jewel-studded flagon, along with several brilliant crystal goblets. My already knotted stomach squeezed tighter as I recognized him.

It was Ed from Nelgareth's keep. What was he doing here at the castle, serving wine?

It struck me like a thousand cyclones. *Poison.*

"This is one of the best vintages of Graylaern's Fionna red—889," Nelgareth said. "If you'll do the honors."

Ed bowed and filled the flagon from the cask. He placed the flagon on the table between the king and Cannon, then took a small goblet from the cart and poured it half-full of wine. With much grace, he swirled it, smelled it, and sipped. Then, nodding, he offered the small goblet to the king, who waved it away.

"Very good, Your Grace," Ed said, bowing his head.

One by one, he filled the rest of the goblets and handed them out to everyone at the head table.

Holy God. The poison's in the goblets.

I flinched as Alac curled his fingers around the stem of his goblet. My heart beat so fast I felt lightheaded. King Selmar raised his goblet.

"To Prince Cannon and his bride—long may they live, long may they reign."

He drank.

The others at the table raised their goblets.

I flew to my feet as though my chair were burning. "Alac, don't drink it!"

He froze, the goblet partway to his mouth. For one iced moment, the room was utterly silent.

In the next instant, Ed pulled a thin stiletto from his sleeve and deftly slit Cannon's throat.

Cannon sat for several seconds, a look of surprise on his face, blood exploding down his chest, before falling forward onto the table. Ellian screamed, and Alac dropped his goblet onto the table. The room erupted into a frenzy of pushed-back chairs and the drawn swords of men-at-arms at the entryway.

Nelgareth rose triumphantly. "Long live the house of Dallowyn!" he cried as the king slumped forward.

32

ALAC

Cannon's blood flooded the table as Father crumpled from his chair to the floor. In the confusion, it took me too long to comprehend what was happening.

This was an attempted takeover. And I would be next to die.

Someone was screaming nonstop over the clash of iron as weapons were drawn and engaged. I pulled the dagger from my riding boot, then fell to my knees at Father's side. He lay on his back, his face twisted and blue. He gasped for breath as though there were a fist around his throat.

"Father." I was sure he didn't want to see me. I was less than nothing to him.

He turned his gaze to me; a trickle of blood oozed from one nostril as he tried to speak. "You are king." He grabbed my hand and pressed it to his chest.

"Father . . ."

"The breath. The blood. The words." He made a strangled noise as he tried to breathe. "Before it's too late."

Something in his face changed . . . softened. The darkness in his eyes faded, and for the first time since I was nine, blue irises looked at me with such emotion that a sob caught in my throat.

"Alac. I'm sorry."

I cupped my other hand around his face; he pressed his cheek to my palm and closed his eyes, his body shuddering before going still.

The clash of swords rang above us; I looked up to see an unknown guard fall to Tucker's sword.

"What in damnation is going on?" Tucker shouted.

My answer died in my mouth as a sharp cold brushed the hand that still held my father's face. When I returned my gaze to him, a trail of mist began to rise from his mouth, dark and undulating and growing in size and density as it continued to issue forth. The cold wind it created chilled me to my core, and I released my father's face and moved back.

I knew that wind. I knew that black mist.

Sounds of melee gave way to sharp cries and renewed screams. I rose and backed away as the mist took a greater, denser form than anything I'd seen. It filled the air above my father's body, vaguely human-shaped but more formless monster than anything else. I could almost hear it breathing.

"To the queen!" Nelgareth shouted. "To the queen!"

The queen?

As I stumbled backward, away from the black mist, I scanned the frenzied room for Mara. I found her quickly, backed up against a wall, her face a mask of horror as she beheld the magic that was ever expanding, ever encroaching upon the limited space in the room.

She'd called out to stop me from drinking the poisoned wine. She'd known what Nelgareth had planned.

Long live the house of Dallowyn, Nelgareth had cried.

Holy God. Mara *did* have Dallowyn blood.

And had known it all along.

"Alac!" Tucker's voice seemed miles away. "Get behind me!"

Nelgareth jumped onto the table, his eyes wild. He looked down at Father's body, a look of triumph on his face. "Your sorcery is useless now. Long live the queen!"

The black mist moved forward, almost as though it were responding to Nelgareth's words. He stood in defiance of it, while others in the room either cowered against a wall or fled in terror.

Then, suddenly, the mist was upon him, closing in on him the way it had closed in on the grape and on my fingertip. He yelled and tried to break free, but his struggles seemed to thicken the magic, tighten its hold on him. His yell turned to a long cry of pain. I watched in horror as, through the dark mist, he aged before my eyes. His body writhed, jerking at strange angles as his hair lengthened and whitened, his skin wrinkled, his backbone twisted and hunched.

I knew he was dead when the yelling stopped. But the magic didn't release him. His corpse grew rigid, then limp, and then it began to darken and rot.

Tucker pulled on my arm. He might've been pulling all along. *"Cruce,* Alac. Come away!"

I stumbled backward a step or two. Others were running from the room in all-out panic. The mass of magic, having finished with Nelgareth, gathered itself up and rose higher, higher, until it had seeped through the ceiling, leaving behind a blackened mess of flesh over dried-out bones.

"Your Grace."

I looked up to see Zeth, face white, standing before me. "We must secure the castle."

Holy God. I couldn't even comprehend what had just happened.

And what an absolute idiot I'd been.

"Your Grace." He rested his hand on my arm.

I closed my eyes. Opened them again. Looked at my brother, face-down in a still-widening pool of his own blood.

"Yes," I said, and my voice did not sound like a king's. "We must secure the castle."

∞

The wedding decorations in the king's hall whispered of celebrations silenced. I sat at the head seat of a hastily-brought-together table of state, an untouched goblet of mulled wine at my elbow. Tucker and my entire personal guard had been called to duty, in addition to Father's normal complement. Zeth sat to my right, looking tired and stricken.

Men I barely knew—Father's military, spiritual, and accounts ministers and a man named Brigg whose role I couldn't remember—sat at scattered seats around the rest of the table, their expressions ranging from anger to disbelief. Suddenly I wasn't only visible, I was king. And I needed to take counsel from virtual strangers.

Except for Zeth, whom I at least knew. I decided I'd trust what he said over anyone else.

"Nelgareth must've been planning this for a long time," Allan Enroth, the military minister, said. "Our next step is to uncover which of the lords were conspiring with him. That'll give us an idea of the size of their army."

I frowned. "But . . . they failed. I'm alive."

"Yes, Your Grace," Zeth said, "but so is the usurper."

The weight in my stomach grew heavier. I kept seeing her face, hearing her voice calling to me. *Alac, don't drink it!*

She'd been part of Nelgareth's plan, but at the last minute she'd tried to save me. Why? It haunted me as much as her duplicity goaded me.

"It will be easy enough to determine which are the traitorous lords," Brigg said. "They won't dare remain in the palace after this failed attempt to take the throne."

I remembered now—Brigg was the lordland minister. If anyone should have been aware of possible treason, it was him. That explained why he looked so remorseful.

Zeth rested his hand on my arm. "Would you like Brigg to take charge of rooting out the false lords?"

I didn't care about false lords—I only cared about finding the girl who'd lied to me from the moment I'd met her. Who'd conspired all along to take my father's throne.

The false lords would die—and so would she.

"Yes," I said. "Every lord in the castle is under house arrest. See that no one leaves."

Brigg bowed his head. "Yes, Your Grace."

The title settled into my bones as though it had always belonged there. I'd been king for an hour, and without the magic weighing me down, I felt I could actually do this.

Be king.

Except.

The locket was hot against my breast, and every breath I took reminded me it was there, protecting me. Calling to me.

When I paid attention, I heard the cold, thready voices of the dead kings, calling my name and begging me to listen. I was sure I heard the timbre of Father's voice among the others, beckoning me to the magic he'd never shared with me in life.

Not this Thungrave king. The magic will not master me.

"Minister Frederin, I leave it to you to begin preparations for a double funeral," Zeth said.

Frederin seemed too overwrought to think about much beyond the mug of mulled wine he held squeezed between his pudgy hands. "Yes, of course." His gaze drifted to the ceiling. "Will it dissipate, do you think?"

Of course—it wasn't the death of the king that had him upset; it was the magic that had been set free and now hung, a dark funnel, over the castle directly above Father's private chapel. Or so Zeth had told me.

"It won't." This was something I could talk intelligently about. "It's waiting for me to perform a ritual that will allow it to inhabit me, the way it inhabited my father. But I have no intention of doing that."

Frederin looked as though he wasn't sure he was relieved or frightened by my answer. The others shifted in their seats and said nothing.

"The magic was stolen a century ago," I continued, "and stolen magic turns on itself and becomes destructive. My father became a different man the day my grandfather died. I don't want the same thing to happen to me."

Frederin's eyes were large as moons. "Not *stolen,* surely, Your Grace. A Dallowyn bastard gave the Thungraves their magic of his own volition."

"And he was murdered so the magic would stay in their bloodline—and Selmar Thungrave took his throne!" The more words I spoke, the more fiercely my heart burned within me. "The Thungraves were never meant to have the magic."

"Is that why you don't intend to complete the ritual?" Zeth's voice was quiet.

I looked at him and for a moment saw what looked like hope in his eyes. "Yes."

"But what of the loosed magic?" Brigg asked. "If it won't dissipate, what will happen?"

"I don't know," I said. "But I'll figure it out."

"And meanwhile there's at least one person at large who needs to be found," Enroth said. "The young woman whom Nelgareth apparently planned to put on the throne."

"Maralyn Keele." Her name was bitter in my mouth. "Nelgareth's ward."

Or was she?

"I've already sent men to Nelgareth's keep, since it's likely she would have been instructed to retreat there," he continued. "The castle and grounds are also being searched."

"I'll find her myself." I spoke the words almost without thinking first, but as soon as I said them, I knew I had to be the one—to find her, to face her, to ask her why.

To condemn her.

"That's out of the question," Enroth said. "You're king now—the last surviving Thungrave. Your place is here, under guard."

"My place is out there, finding the girl who wants to be queen."

"Commander Enroth is right," Bart Lellen, the accounts minister, said. "The people have lost their king and his heir; they will want to know that their new king is safe in his castle."

"They won't want any such thing." My words had a sharp edge, and I didn't care. "People hated my father. Feared him. And as long as they think I'll turn out the same, no one's going to care whether I live or die."

Brigg cleared his throat. "With due respect—"

"Today has nothing to do with respect," I said. "I'm going to find her, and that's the end of it."

Silence fell like night. Brigg took a noisy swallow of his wine and Zeth folded his hands meticulously upon the table.

"We should send men directly to the Keele estate in Criminy," Enroth said.

My throat tightened. "I suspect you'll discover there was never a daughter named Maralyn." There was no denying her Dallowyn blood now.

"Perhaps," Enroth said. "But we need to explore every option."

"Yes," I said. "But ultimately, she's mine to find."

"There's a chance my men will find her first," Enroth said.

I met his gaze, the coil of hot determination growing tighter in my gut. "If they do, I want her alive. And brought directly to me."

33

MARALYTH

The stitch in my side was so great that I stopped, doubled over, behind the stables. My entire body trembled, from my teeth to the soles of my feet, and I feared I'd be found at any moment.

When the guests had scattered, I'd lost sight of everyone. The coup had failed—because of me—and I knew that my capture would be the king's priority. *Alac's* priority. Others may not have known who Nelgareth was referring to when he declared the throne for the Dallowyns, but Alac did.

It would have been all too obvious.

Chaos was spreading rapidly across the castle grounds as guests continued to stream out, voices raised in terror, and guards sounded the alarm.

I had to get out. But how?

I ran away from the castle, toward the narrow swath of trees that grew just inside the castle wall, rimming the sprawling lawn. I reached an ancient corn oak that was wide enough for me to hide behind.

I looked up. The castle wall loomed just beyond the reach of the tree, solid and impossible to climb. I compressed my lips, thinking. Climbing trees was one thing—climbing stone walls without any purchase was another. I scanned the other trees in this small stand, but none were close enough for me to make use of their branches to gain height and leap onto the wall.

Sounds of chaos and fear echoed across the grounds, and my heart beat faster. Magic tingled in my palms and fingertips, calling to the leaves, the stems, the branches.

The magic belongs to me. It saved Alac from the wild dog; it can save me from capture.

I knelt beside the oak tree and plucked an acorn from its nesting place among the roots. It grew warm in my hand as I walked to the wall and dug a small hole in the ground with my finger, then placed the acorn inside it.

"Grow," I said. "Become a tree."

I'd never produced this level of life before; a ripened bunch of grapes was a far cry from creating an entire tree from a seed. But the magic flowed from me in a joyful rush, and the acorn cracked and sprouted beneath my palm before I'd drawn more than three breaths. As I continued to pour out the magic that sprang hot and ecstatic from my hands, a sapling unfurled, growing in girth and height faster than my sight could keep up with.

I scooted back as the tree continued to grow, branches spiraling outward, leaves unfurling. The ground cracked and swelled above the invisible roots as they reached deep into the earth; the trunk fattened and darkened with bark that was marked by the passage of time. I was swept up in a power so immense that I felt one with it. No hiding, no fearing what I was. Utter freedom—and the joy of pouring forth life, as the Holy God had intended.

In watching the tree grow before me, I lost sense of the passage of time. It might've been five minutes or more, but it felt like seconds. Or days. When the tree had grown to a size capable of bearing weight, I withdrew my magic, and the growing ceased. A beautiful corn oak stood before me, its lower branches extending above and beyond the wall. I laid my hand on the tree, which was warm and tingly.

"Thank you," I whispered.

Then I climbed, as I had done since I was a child, sliding my way along the length of the lowest branch that stretched inches from the top of the wall. When I reached it, I dropped, landing on my feet and taking only a moment to steady myself. I craned my neck as far as I dared, but the castle entrance wasn't visible from here. The wall stood at least twelve feet high, so jumping wasn't an option. I sat, then hoisted myself onto my stomach so that I dangled feetfirst off the edge. Then, carefully, I lowered myself as far as I could without letting go.

About a seven-foot drop. I could do this.

I closed my eyes and let go.

34

ALAC

I stood in Father's chambers. His death felt less close here. Less real. Or maybe that was my heart, pushing away anything that might feel like grief. The father I loved had disappeared a long time ago.

I closed my fist around the blood locket. Did it know the king was dead? That I was supposed to be its new master?

The stolen magic, with nowhere to go until I claimed it, seemed to have fastened itself to the castle. Before I left to search for Mara, I had to see for myself.

I unlocked the chapel door and opened it slowly. At first, nothing seemed out of place—it was quiet and dark, and the single, red lamp hung above the altar, lit. But the blood locket grew hot beneath my tunic as I took my first step into the room, and the whispers immediately assaulted me.

Alac. Alac. Alac.

My gaze was drawn upward, and I could see the thick, black mass of magic pressing against the ceiling, undulating in waves. Above the receptacle, a tendril reached down, spreading thicker as it rose, like a funnel. Over and over, it touched the top of the receptacle and bounced back, as though repelled.

"Cruce."

How easy it would be to simply perform the ritual and take the magic as my own. Any threat this loose magic might pose would be immediately taken care of, and I could claim my rightful throne without any further trouble.

But allowing the magic to consume me would mean the end of who I was. And I wasn't ready to do that—not when there was a chance of getting rid of this curse forever.

Mara—whoever she was—had lied and committed treason. But she was a Dallowyn with magic far different from what I'd grown up knowing and fearing. If she truly had a way to contain or destroy the magic that had ruled my family for generations, I would force her to do it.

And then she would pay for her crimes, even if it ripped my heart clean through. She was the poison I'd drunk, instead of the cup Nelgareth had intended for me. Even now, I could hear her voice, see the soft curve of her lips when she smiled.

Damn her.

I closed and locked the door, but instead of placing the key back in the drawer where Father kept it, I stuck it into my pocket. My chapel, my key. Ears still ringing from the haunted whispers, I made my way out of Father's apartments and into the window-lined king's hallway.

"Your Grace."

Ellian stood there, dressed in black, her eyes red. Her hair, which earlier had been a masterpiece of flowers and braids, hung in waves down her back.

"My lady." I looked, but saw no escort. "Should you really be alone right now?"

She twisted a handkerchief between her hands. "I wanted . . ." She stifled a sob. "I wanted to see if I could hear him."

"Hear . . . who?"

"Cannon." Her voice was a hoarse whisper. "He said the souls of the dead kings become part of the magic. He wasn't yet king, but I thought . . . I wondered . . ." Her lower lip quivered and she looked at me imploringly.

Tears weren't one of my specialties. I tried to make my voice gentle. "Come away from here, Ellian. It's a dark place, filled with dark magic."

I offered my arm, and after hesitating, she took it. As I walked her past the rows of windows, the clouds finally broke, and sunshine bathed the hallway in glorious gold.

It would have been a perfect wedding day.

"I'm sorry," I said.

"He was your brother," she said. "It's your loss, too."

A wave of nausea roared through me as I pictured Cannon splayed across the table in his own blood.

My brother.

My onetime childhood friend, first lost to the magic and now lost forever.

I wouldn't allow myself to think about whether my last words to him had been kind.

"Yes," I said softly.

We walked in silence until I'd taken her all the way to her quarters. From behind the closed door, I could hear violent weeping.

"My mother," Ellian said.

"If there's anything I can do . . ."

She squeezed my arm and clung for several seconds before releasing me. "You can't bring him back."

"No. I can't."

She looked at me; tears were streaming down her face. "So much blood . . ."

If I closed my eyes, it's all I could see. The blood.

"I'm sorry," I said again.

I stood outside the door after she'd closed it, listening to the renewed wailing from within and wondering if Ellian might come to understand that she'd been freed from a life that would have brought her little joy.

"You didn't deserve this, Cannon," I whispered. Then I walked away, anger coiled like a serpent in my gut.

⚬⚭⚬

Tucker stood with his hand cupped over his eyes, looking up. "Seems like it's just . . . waiting for you."

The same heaviness that struck me every time I thought of the magic weighed me down further. "It is."

"Look at that, there." He pointed.

I looked, and a new level of dread threaded its way through my stomach. A long tendril of the black cloud was peeling off from the main bulk, like yarn from a skein. It wove through the air like a snake, stretching thin and finally breaking free.

"*Cruce,*" I whispered.

A second tendril broke free from another point as a third began to take shape. I scanned the sky and saw several more dark tendrils of magic undulating through the air in the same general direction.

"Maybe they'll dissipate," Tucker said.

But I knew they wouldn't.

"Let's go," I said.

We mounted our horses and rode to the gate, where the guard had been tripled. The uneasiness among the men was obvious; several of them continued to throw glances at the dark cloud hovering over the castle.

"Who opened the gate when guests wanted to leave this morning?" I asked the nearest guard.

"We did, Your Grace."

"Did you take any notice at all of who was leaving?"

"Not much. We tend to pay more attention to who wants to come *in*." He glanced nervously at the magic cloud.

"And you've been ordered to allow no one to exit without my permission?"

"Yes, Your Grace."

I looked at Tucker. "I'm assuming she got out. She'd be foolish to do anything else."

"If she's hiding anywhere on the grounds, they'll find her," Tucker said.

Part of me wanted to stay within the confines of the palace wall and join the search. But it seemed so much more likely that she would have made her way outside.

I motioned for the guard to open the gate. "That would make things easier."

Not that anything felt easy right now. As the gate opened, I urged my horse forward, determined to find Mara and stop the magic before it spread any farther.

Though I was certain she would've been smart enough to stay off the main roads, we took a well-worn path that bordered the edge of the nearby vineyard. It had occurred to me that the familiarity of the vineyard might have lured Mara here to find safety. Anyway, it was worth a try.

"We can't just barge onto this person's property," Tucker said.

"I'm the king," I said bitterly. "That should count for something."

We were approaching the small gate at the entrance when I reigned in my horse, stunned by what I saw. About half of the vines on the first two rows were completely dead, withered and brown as though they'd died a long time ago. Beside and behind them, the vines were flourishing, their leaves green and healthy and looking the way they should just past harvest.

I glanced at the sky, but there was no sign of magic.

But I knew its handiwork. I'd seen it before.

I'd watched Nelgareth writhe and age and die while encased in it. The single grape it had rotted was nothing in comparison.

There was no sign of Mara in the vineyard. And no one had seen her.

"Is it true?" one long-whiskered worker asked. "Is the king . . . dead?"

"I am your king," I said.

I left as he was still bowing, Tucker behind me.

⚬≫⚬

For the rest of the afternoon, Tucker and I made a methodical search in all directions from the palace, asking passersby once or twice if they'd seen a girl in a crimson gown who looked like she was lost. As the sun was setting, we turned toward the palace to make a final sweep on our way back, concentrating on wooded areas that afforded better hiding.

"She can't have gone far," Tucker said. "She left without any money or food or even proper shoes for traveling."

"She's got magic," I said. "There's no telling what she could do."

The sky was still light as we made our way back through the palace gate, where I gathered immediate information that Mara hadn't been found on the castle grounds. I hated to lose search time, but with night falling, Mara would have to sleep, too.

At the stables, I dismounted and gave my horse to a stable hand. "I'm going to walk the grounds a bit," I said.

Not that I expected to find anything. I just couldn't get it out of my head that Mara wouldn't simply disappear—that somewhere, somehow, she would have left her mark. The way she'd left it on my heart.

Damnable girl. I'd dig every trace of her from my mind like flesh from a rotting corpse.

I walked beyond the stables and across the hawking grounds to the trees that skirted their southernmost edge. Beyond them, the palace wall stood, tall and imposing. Much of my boyhood had been spent there, climbing the trees and generally staying as far away from court as possible. Once, I'd fallen asleep in a makeshift tree house in one of the oak trees—it was a miracle I didn't fall to my death.

I approached the trees now, my heart struggling to reconcile old memories of the Cannon who had been a big brother I wanted to look up to with the brother he'd become. Despite the violence and unfairness of his death, I found myself struggling to feel anything more than the injustice of it.

Or perhaps the horror was too fresh. I could give myself that grace, at least.

I stopped by the oldest of the corn oaks, on the outer edge. The light was fast fading, but I could see that something was different about this stand of trees I'd spent so much of my childhood in. There, to the left of the ancient oak and so close to the wall that it seemed they'd grown up together, stood a young corn oak, tall and lithe and definitely not belonging there. I walked over to it and laid my hand on its trunk, which stood mere inches from the wall.

It buzzed beneath my hand, and the blood locket warmed against my chest. As though it knew Mara's magic.

Looking up, I saw that its branches reached up and over the wall—a perfect escape for someone who wasn't afraid to climb.

For someone who had the ability to grow a tree where none had been before.

Heart hammering, I removed my weapon and laid it on the ground. Then I wrapped my hands around the lowest branch and swung myself up, my limbs tingling with magic. I climbed, easily matching the height of the wall and shimmying across a branch until I reached the flat, stone top. I lowered myself onto it and stood in the failing light, scanning as far as I could see.

It was a good drop to the earth below, but not impossible. From here, where might she have gone?

"Mara?"

The word ushered from my mouth without permission, as though it had come of its own accord. If she had fallen and were hurt, she might well be lying in the shadows against the wall, unable to move and knowing it wasn't safe to call for help.

"Mara?"

But silence met me.

As I made my way back to the castle, a sharp cry rang out. I was trying to determine where the sound had come from when a second, longer cry, like someone in pain, erupted from the direction of the stables. I ran, hand on the hilt of my sword, until I came upon a guard I didn't recognize, kneeling in the grass halfway between the stables and the Queen's Garden. He was middle aged, his hair a mixture of dark and gray, his sinewy hands pressed to the sides of his head.

"Are you hurt?" I asked.

The guard lowered his hands and looked up, and my heart nearly stopped.

It was Tucker, looking nearly sixty years old.

35

MARALYTH

I found my way through the streets of Crownhold by sheer luck. Every tavern and public meeting place was clogged with merrymakers intent upon celebrating the royal wedding, despite the fact that nothing had been provided for them to do so. I made my way through knots of people, hurrying but not running, trying desperately to blend in while moving as quickly as I could.

Getting through the city gate would be hardest—unless I could make it look like I was traveling with others. Not many people were leaving, though; it seemed much of the city had decided to declare a holiday. I wondered in a panic how quickly the horrible news would spread once it made its way out of the castle. And how quickly soldiers would arrive, combing the streets to find me.

Then I saw my chance—at least a dozen colorfully dressed merchants were leaving in a group, along with several donkeys and a small cart. I slipped into the midst of them, toward the back, hoping my expensive gown would blend in with the brightness of their clothing. I was almost through the gate when a commotion of shouting and hoofbeats sounded behind us.

"In the name of the king, close the gate!" someone yelled.

I hastened through, forcing myself to keep pace with the group for ten paces, twenty. The gate, which had swung closed behind us, suddenly began creaking open again. A quick glance over my shoulder revealed a cluster of soldiers on horseback who clearly meant to search outside the city wall. I veered to the right, toward a stand of trees, trying to stay inconspicuous. I was out of time, though, so after a few steps, I ran.

The trees weren't far, but it felt like I'd never reach them. Voices rang out, men shouting words I couldn't discern. Gathering the skirts of my unfortunate dress into a wad in one hand, I climbed the first tree with branches low enough to access, cursing my lack of a good pair of Nestar's breeches. I'd always climbed as fast as he could—even faster, once he grew lanky and leggy and unable to swing up with the agility of his smaller, lighter sister.

Our childhood days of tree-climbing served me well as I pulled myself into a crook high enough to make it virtually impossible to see me from the ground.

And I waited.

The bark gouged my back through the delicate fabric of my dress as I leaned back, sounds of pursuit far below shoving spikes of fear through my stomach with every call, every snapped branch. I held my breath as an insect made its way across my face, leaving a tickling trail that I didn't dare slap at.

When finally it was quiet, I stayed where I was, making sure the search party had moved on. Even then, I climbed down slowly, ears pricked for the slightest sound. I stopped at every branch and waited until I was sure it was safe to continue. By the time I landed, I was convinced that the men were gone.

It took me a minute or two to get my bearings. Even then, I couldn't be completely sure I was right. Until I made it to the clearing, I wouldn't be able to map my way to the main road.

Which was probably swarming with soldiers by now.

I had no food, no water—not even shoes that were appropriate for outdoors. To survive, I'd have to do my best to find my way to Wennie's, though I had no idea what I'd be looking for. A house? An inn? At least I'd been smart enough to memorize Hesta's map, which I'd never truly believed I'd need.

After knotting my gown on one side to make walking easier, I scooted through the remaining trees until they thinned, then ended near a fenced paddock. Several horses were at the far end, but I didn't have time to add horse thievery to the already-heavy charge of usurper.

In the sky above the horses, a single, black strand snaked through the air, stretching and thinning in turns. The magic within me pressed against my skin, and my heart caught.

This was Thungrave magic. Had the entire mass broken into pieces? Panicked, I cupped a hand over my eyes and scanned the rest of the sky. There was another—and another. The strands snaked lazily through the air like faceless creatures. Fear burrowed, hard and true, into my heart.

If magic were on the loose, then Alac hadn't performed the ritual yet. But what horrible things would it accomplish as it spread? I had to find a way to stop it—as soon as I found my way to safety.

When I was sure my path was clear, I followed the fence to its corner, which lay at a dirt road. A house sat to my right, so I turned left, following the path until I was close enough to another line of trees to dart into its shadowed depths. My hunch that the path led to the main road was correct, but my relief was instantly clouded by the presence of riders from the palace who seemed in the process of setting a guard along the road.

I would have to cross their line of watch in order to continue to Silverton. And I'd have to stay off the road to do it.

In the end, I crawled just beneath a ridge that ran along the outer edge of the trees, low enough to be obscured from immediate view and high enough that I was able to see the road if I lifted my head. When the ridge flattened out, I stopped, heart hammering, and lay flat. In the distance, a horse whinnied, and the breeze carried a single shout.

I had no choice but to go deeper into the woodlands that lay sprawled to the south, sometimes hugging the road and other times opening into fields or thickets. Possibly nobody expected me to try to travel alone—on foot—all the way to Silverton. If anything, they might suspect I'd retreat to Nelgareth's keep, where I'd be easy to find. Hadn't Hesta told me not to return there if I had to leave the castle?

I'd have to stay hidden, like a rabbit in the wild, and hope I didn't get lost. Two hours by carriage, more than twice that on foot . . . and I had no idea how long through the trees and wild lands. Hopefully I'd find my way before darkness fell.

With no other choice before me, I set off, not allowing myself to think what would happen to me if I were caught.

⁘

The sun was low in the sky by the time I admitted I was lost. Faint with thirst, I knew I needed to worry more about finding water than I did finding the road. Sounds of pursuit had long since disappeared, but I'd kept moving, desperate to see the outermost buildings of Silverton before night closed in. Now, I veered from the direction I was almost certain would lead back to the road, and instead looked for signs that a spring or stream might be nearby. At first, I searched frantically, scanning the scrub and tree roots ahead of and around me, looking for water.

A wave of dizziness forced me to slow down, then stop. I closed my eyes, licking my dry lips and trying to think logically. It was nearing sunset; birds would be flying toward water sources. Swarming insects, like gnats, would also be prone to hover where water lay.

I changed my focus, paying attention to the birds and looking for clouds of insects that I'd normally avoid. When dusk had thickened almost to the point at which I couldn't see, I found it—a shallow, burbling stream that cut through the trees like an exuberant song. Half stumbling, I made for its bank, falling to my knees and scooping up mouthful after mouthful of the cool, delicious water.

When I'd drunk my fill, I used the remaining light to find somewhere to sleep. By the time I'd curled into the hollow of a tree with roots like arms reaching for a hug, exhaustion had taken the edge from my fear. I'd avoided capture for an entire day, and the morning light would bring with it hope of finding Silverton and the help I needed.

I closed my eyes against the darkness and thought of Poppa, safe in his bed with no knowledge that I was alive, or of anything that had happened. And I thought of Alac, whose life I'd saved and who had probably put a price on mine.

I didn't blame him. But I longed to tell him my side of the story—all of it. For reasons I couldn't understand, I dreaded his loathing of me more than I dreaded the possibility that he wanted me dead.

"I'm sorry, Alac," I whispered to the night.

36

ALAC

"What just happened?" Tucker's voice sounded like gravel; as soon as he'd spoken, he brought his hand to his throat and tried to stand.

"Tucker." I knelt, steadying him and then easing him onto the ground. "Are you in pain?"

"It's fading." Then he caught sight of his hand, and horror bloomed across his face. He held both hands in front of him, staring. "*Cruce.*"

I looked up. From here, I had only a partial view of the funnel of magic above the castle. But in the failing light, I could see the strands as they twisted themselves free and took off through the air.

"How did it catch you?" I asked.

Tucker was still staring at his hands. "I . . . I'm old." He touched his face, stroking downward with his fingers and tracing his jaw down to his neck. "How can this even be real?"

I took him by the shoulders. "How did it catch you, Tucker?"

He looked at me with haunted eyes. "I don't know. None of the strands seemed low enough to pose a threat. Then suddenly I turned around and one of them was upon me. It was like . . . being smothered by nothing."

"But you got free."

"I don't know how," Tucker said. "It just . . . left. Kept moving." His eyes darted around, searching. "Nowhere is safe."

His words pierced me. The strands had seemed inconsequential, threading themselves free from the mass of magic hugging the castle. Perhaps I'd deceived myself into believing they would go away on their own. I looked up again in time to see another strand wending its way through the dusky sky, like a fledgling creature searching for its mother.

"Let's get you inside." As if I could guarantee safety anywhere.

And yet, the magic hovering over Father's chapel seemed intent upon staying there; it wanted—if magic could want—to claim the next heir. The strands that broke free weren't heading into the castle or even attempting to reconnect themselves to the main mass. They simply . . . dispersed.

And they were deadly.

Tucker rose—a bit stiffly, but otherwise he didn't seem to be too encumbered by his sudden aging. "How am I supposed to protect you like this? *Cruce,* how am I supposed to do anything?"

"We'll figure it out."

But the cold truth inside my heart whispered that Tucker had just lost at least forty years of his life, and there was nothing I could do to get them back.

❧

"Holy God," Nella said for at least the third time, as Tucker settled onto the cot I'd had brought into my own rooms. He'd refused the bed, saying he wasn't *really* an old man, and Nella had helped create comfort by bringing fine linens and pillows.

"Maybe it'll fade by morning," he said as he rolled over.

"Would that it were true." Nella tucked him in the way she'd tucked me in so often after Mother's death. "I don't think I'm going to be able to sleep tonight, myself."

I squeezed her shoulder. "The magic seems to be moving out and away from the castle. You're probably safer in here than anywhere else."

She raised an eyebrow. "Has anything ever been safe here?" When I didn't answer, she kissed my cheek. "I'll stay a while, if you'd like."

"I would, actually," I said. "I have some things to attend to."

"Go on, then. I'll make sure he's sleeping soundly before I leave."

I smiled my thanks and left, grateful for the bit of elixir Nella had given me to add to Tucker's wine. Fast and deep sleep would be far better for him than lying there worrying. It would be bad enough in the morning when others saw what had happened to him. At least we hadn't had to deal with that yet.

It was only a matter of time until fear turned to panic. Already several members of the castle staff had fled their posts, wanting to get as far away from the "terrible, dark cloud" as possible.

I stood in the hallway outside Father's chambers for an hour or more, alternately pacing and staring out the expansive windows at the night sky. I couldn't see any magic strands, but I knew they were out there, slowly peeling themselves free from the knot of magic hovering over Father's chapel.

I had the power to stop this. If I completed the ritual and took the magic into my body where it wanted to go, the black cloud and the terror it was producing would stop. Were I braver or more selfless—or if I lusted after the magic the way Cannon had seemed to—the choice would have been easy. But receiving the stolen magic and allowing it to possess me for the rest of my life was something I'd never wanted.

I didn't want to lose myself to the darkness. But even more, I didn't want to perpetuate the same heartless rule of my Father and all the Thungrave kings before him. I'd watched his compassionate eyes cloud into darkness; I'd felt the withdrawal of his warmth and his ever-increasing need to be in control. To exert his will. To create a kingdom that met his every need and fed his hunger for power.

If I performed the ritual, that was who I'd become. Mara was the only person who might be able to do something about the renegade magic that continued to issue forth, but it could take days—weeks—to find her. I could stop it right now, instead of risking my subjects' safety—their lives—so I could avoid transforming myself into a monster.

Yet here I stood, hesitating, wrangling with the horror of giving myself over to the very thing I'd always railed against. Always hated.

With a sigh, I faced the door to Father's chambers. Despite all the reasons I wanted nothing to do with this legacy of magic, I couldn't deny that the current need was greater.

I was king, after all. And despite a lifetime of never desiring the throne, I found myself wanting to rule. Wanting to save my people from the magic more than I wanted to save myself from it.

I pushed the door open and made my way to the chapel within.

The presence of the black cloud felt even more oppressive as I stepped inside the room—or perhaps it was my heightened awareness that my own body would soon house it. In the silence, it seemed I could hear a slight, continual hissing, and when I looked up, I could tell, even in the dimness of the chapel, that a thick layer of the cloud hung ominously from the ceiling, funneling down to a point above the receptacle, as before.

I walked toward the altar, feeling wooden. Everything I needed to perform the ritual—the dagger, the crystal goblet, the receptacle— were in place on the altar. Except the scroll from Cannon, which I now pulled from inside my pocket and laid carefully beside the other items.

The breath. The blood. The words. This wouldn't take long.

I wiped the sweat from my palms and took a long, slow breath. Then I unrolled the scroll and read the words silently, forming the syllables on my lips to practice speaking them.

> *Spiritis eque sanc deu*
> *Coram regibi spiriti alme*
> *Habitisi medum moriari*
> *Me sume te prestiqui sinte*
> *Tempori aterni.*

The words were as meaningless as before—foreign. But as I mouthed them, a distinct whisper echoed in my ears:

> Breath of the Holy God
> And spirits of the kings before me
> Dwell within me until I die
> And then let me join you
> For time eternal.

For time eternal. Dread took root in my stomach as I remembered that, once I assumed the magic, I'd belong to it forever. My spirit would join the other dead kings in the receptacle—and I'd never be free.

But it didn't matter. I had to do this.

I placed the scroll beside the dagger, then stood directly in front of the receptacle. I reached for the diamond knob, but I stopped and fisted my hand in the air before touching it. Great God, this was hard. It would have been easier to go to my death than this.

Determined to see it through, I opened the receptacle door in one swift motion. The hourglass sat as before, except that the top bulb was now completely empty. The breath swirled restlessly, violently, in the bottom bulb, glowing with unearthly light.

Alac.

Was that Father's voice? Shaking myself free from the terror that tried to steal my ability to move, I reached for the hourglass, sure that, once I touched it, the magic would draw me to itself. There would be no changing my mind.

I curled my hands around the posts on either side of the hourglass; they were so cold they burned. My breaths were loud in my ears as I waited for the top bulb to fill.

The swirling intensified, and the cold posts warmed. My heart slammed against my chest as I felt a surge of power welling up from within the hourglass. The blood locket burned hot.

Alac. Alac.

The voices were mournful, pleading. Imbued with sorrow so deep I felt I'd drown in it.

Searing pain tore into me, and I yelled and tried to let go of the hourglass—but it seemed my hands were fastened to its posts and I couldn't pull them free. Blinding light forced me to close my eyes as the pain intensified, ripping through me like a thousand knives, a thousand swords, a thousand flaming arrows.

I was going to die.

Soft, warm hands closed over the top of mine, though my pain was so great that the touch didn't seem quite real. Somehow, they pulled me away from the hourglass, and within seconds, the bright light and searing pain faded to nothing.

I opened my eyes. Ellian stood there, her face alight in the glow of the hourglass.

"You can't take the magic," she said, her words tremulous.

"I have to take it," I said, "or it will destroy everything."

"It no longer sees you as king." She took a sobbing breath. "I'm carrying Cannon's child."

37

ALAC

I wasn't quite sure where to look. Ellian's words hung in the air between us, a revelation I hadn't considered a possibility.

"Are you sure?" The question sounded stupid after I'd voiced it, but I didn't know what else to say.

"Yes," Ellian said. "It happened when Cannon visited me a couple months ago."

I closed the receptacle door and found that I was shaking deep in my frame, deep in my belly. I'd been prepared to accept the magic I'd always hated; I thought I'd save the kingdom with a few short syllables and some drops of my own blood. But the cloud of magic raged above me, unmovable and untouchable.

"How do you know it's a son?"

Ellian's hands went to her abdomen, perhaps unconsciously. "Cannon told me I'd be drawn to the magic—that I'd feel stirrings I wouldn't understand—once I was carrying the heir. Since Cannon's death, it's been unbearable."

"But until this child is born, I'm still king."

"The breath, the blood, the words." Ellian's voice was hollow. "Cannon's blood is in this child."

It was all about the blood. I knew that.

"Is this why you came here last night?"

She hesitated. "Yes. I thought if I could hear Cannon's voice, he could instruct me somehow." She gazed at the receptacle. "I don't know what to do."

"There's nothing you *can* do."

Tommas Dallowyn had overlooked a serious flaw in his ritual. The magic could not discern the difference between a grown man and an unborn child.

I looked up at the swirling blackness and felt its palpable presence, its inherent need to destroy. "How long until . . . ?"

"Seven months," she whispered.

Cruce. "As long as this magic is uncontained, it's going to create a wake of destruction. Seven months from now, there may not be a kingdom left for your son to rule."

"If there were some way for me to take it for him . . ."

"It would kill you as soon as you touched the hourglass." Like it had tried to kill me.

"But it didn't hurt me when I pulled you away just now," Ellian said softly. "It knows there's a tiny king inside me."

How stupid of me. If the magic was already drawn to Ellian's unborn child, of course it wouldn't kill her.

"You're right. You'll be safe until the baby's born," I said. "But no one else will."

"What's to be done?" Ellian asked.

"We need to find Maralyn Keele."

Ellian's expression darkened. "The usurper."

"Yes. She's the only one who might be able to stop the spread of this magic."

"She had your father and Cannon killed so she could take the throne! Why would you trust her to do anything?"

"I'm not going to *trust* her to do it," I said. "I'm going to *command.*"

"She deserves to die."

I took the scroll from the altar and curled it into my hand. "Yes. But Perin Faye deserves a chance to be free of this damned magic first."

Ellian grabbed my sleeve, her expression pained. "My son—"

"Deserves to be free of it, too."

She released her grip. I left her in the shadow of the magic, her anguished wail echoing behind me.

❧

I wasn't used to wearing the breastplate outside training rounds. It seemed prudent, considering I had no idea who might be out there on Mara's side, happy for an opportunity to slay the remaining royal who was irritating enough to have avoided being murdered.

Thanks to Mara. But I couldn't go there.

Tucker's expression was grim as he mounted his horse, his now-old face lined and craggy in the dim morning light.

"You feeling up to this?" I asked.

He glared at me. "I'm not *that* old."

"But you've aged," I said gently. "It happened in a matter of seconds, but it's real. You may not think you're sixty, but your body does."

"Cruce."

"We'll figure it out."

"You keep saying that." He sighed, which was something he didn't often do. "Is this it, then? I've lost most of my life, and I'll just . . . die?"

"I don't know, Tuck."

"You say you think Mara can take care of this crazy magic."

"I hope she can," I said. "I don't know for sure."

"What if she can't?"

"One thing at a time," I said. "We have to find her first."

He clucked softly and urged his horse to walk. "Anyway, it gives me the advantage of anonymity, in case we need it."

"Now you're sounding more like yourself." I brought my own horse alongside his and we made our way to the gate.

By now, the castle grounds and the immediate area had been thoroughly searched. Mara might have decided to hide in town, but I strongly suspected she had at least attempted to make it to Silverton. Nelgareth had to have had some sort of plan in place in case the assassination attempt failed, to keep his chosen queen safe. If she was already at Nelgareth's keep, things would be admittedly trickier.

Nelgareth was dead, though. And I had no idea who would inherit his lordland—he had no sons. Best-case scenario? Utter chaos and the scattering of those who had supported the cause.

Twelve hand-picked men waited at the gate—the rest of my personal guard plus seven more that I trusted to do what I asked them to, which was mainly to make sure Mara wasn't harmed.

Regardless of what happened later, I needed her alive.

Deven, who'd been a member of Cannon's guard for at least a

decade, brought his horse next to mine. "I know everyone's been over this, Your Grace, but I'd feel better if you stayed here. We can do this without you."

"I know you can," I said. "But I need to be there when we find her."

He frowned but offered a short nod. "Yes, Your Grace."

"Four couriers have been sent ahead to Silverton with the same flyers that are plastered across Crownhold," Marvan said. "They were hastily printed, but the likeness is good."

The memory of Mara's face was bitter. "And it says wanted alive?"

"Yes, Your Grace."

Several of the men were staring at Tucker. I raised an eyebrow in his direction, and he cleared his throat.

"I had a little mishap with a magic strand," he said. "We'd best keep an eye on those things."

"Tucker Dane?" one of the guards said, his eyes round. "Is that you?"

"More or less." Tucker was trying too hard to sound cheerful. "I still have my wits about me, so don't worry."

The unease was palpable as we turned our mounts and headed through the open gate. I glanced over my shoulder and looked at the dark funnel that hung like a storm over the castle, its tendrils slowly but perceptibly stretching forth like snake tongues.

Tucker came up beside me, our knees almost touching. "I swear we could outrun one of those strands . . . they're so slow," he said. "I can't believe I was stupid enough to get caught in one."

"Nothing stupid about it," I said.

"Are they sentient, do you think?"

I frowned. "No, I don't. Magic doesn't . . . *think*."

"It's just that . . ." He lowered his voice. "A minute before it happened, I was looking up at the magic cloud. The strands were all stretching straight out—not down. Why would it suddenly dive for me?"

"I'm sure it didn't dive for you." I shuddered, wondering what might make the magic change direction like that. Then I remembered the buzz of magic beneath my hand when I'd touched the oak tree, and the way the blood locket had warmed against my skin.

Had the strand of magic somehow responded to that? Been drawn to it?

I kept the thought to myself. If it were true, I'd have to add guilt to the list of emotions I should've been feeling—but wouldn't allow myself to feel.

It was an easy ride to Silverton, less than two hours. We'd be fanning out, though, combing the woods and countryside in a thorough sweep that could take several days. If Mara had traveled this way, she would likely have stayed off the road, and might possibly have gotten lost.

Though, this was the girl who'd put a wild dog to sleep. I imagined she could probably tell the trees to point her in the right direction if she wanted.

We divided ourselves into pairs; I stayed with Tucker, of course. All eyes were on me, waiting for my command. I reminded myself for the tenth time that morning that I was king. Everyone would look to me first.

Until Ellian's son was born.

"Maralyn is small," I said, "and smart enough to stay hidden if she sees us. Just remember that I want her alive and unharmed."

A soft chorus of "Yes, Your Grace" rippled through the group before we spread out to begin our search. I knew it didn't matter who found her—only that she was found.

But in the seething depths of my heart, I wanted it to be me.

38

MARALYTH

I was lost.

It hadn't been easy to admit it. It seemed, at first, that I was on the right track; the sun rose before me, so whenever the trees momentarily thinned, I had to shield my eyes. But after a while, the forest became denser, and it was more difficult to tell if I was walking east.

When finally I came to a small clearing, startling several does and a fawn, the sun was far to my left. Somehow, I'd turned south. Breathing away the panic that tried to strangle me, I focused on making a logical decision. If I turned east at this point, I'd likely end up to the south of Silverton, and could miss it entirely. It seemed like a better idea to turn around and head north for a while, and then turn east. I'd have to be careful not to go too far north, though, and risk hitting the main road.

Having thus decided, I turned around, making my way uncertainly through trees that should have been familiar, but weren't. By the time I'd reached a small stream, I had to admit I had no idea where to go from there. I followed it for a while, more worried about dying of thirst than of being captured by Alac's men.

The stream had just widened a bit when I stopped, my gaze riveted by a swath of trees on the opposite bank that were simply . . . dead. Compared to the thriving, green trees around them, this cluster of eight or ten looked as though they'd been dead for decades, their branches bare, their boughs twisted and brittle. One of them had fallen into the midst of the others.

With a sinking heart, I waded across the stream. Even before I reached the dead trees, I knew. My magic spun in my fingertips and swelled in my chest as I approached the nearest tree and put my hand on its dry bark.

The dark magic had left its signature like mold on a rotten vegetable. I shaded my eyes with my hand and searched the bits of sky unobscured by the leaves. Several long, dark strands were just visible.

Clearly, the magic was still dispersing from the castle. Probably growing. Which meant that Alac hadn't performed the ritual.

When I reached a rolling meadow near sunset, I knew I could go no farther. My shoes were shredded and my feet ached. I'd drunk my fill before leaving the comfort of the stream, but my stomach ached with emptiness. I found a small mulberry bush and ripened the berries beneath my fingers for a meager supper. Then I crawled into a hollow behind an ash tree and prayed no one would find me.

The throbbing in my feet was more of a deterrent to sleep than the hunger; I woke often during the night, worrying about the stolen magic and what it was capable of. When I could finally sleep no more, I stood and studied the lay of the land. The sky was pale in the east, and I tried to map in my mind whether I'd gone far enough north to head toward the sun—or if I'd become absolutely turned around. I feared the latter was true.

Heading east seemed smartest. The trees seemed thinner in that direction, which might mean the end of the forest. The pain in my feet was bearable as I set off, and I wished more than anything for a decent pair of shoes. By the time the sun had fully risen, I was limping.

I heard the horses before I saw them—a soft nicker and the stamping of an impatient hoof. Drawing back so quickly my head swam, I pressed myself against a thin tree and assessed. The horses were tethered, but there were no signs of a camp. It was as though the riders had left them there and gone off on foot.

My heart hammered against my ribs. Even if these weren't Alac's men, it wasn't in my favor to be found alone by strangers. With my feet in this sorry condition, I wouldn't even be able to run.

I'd just decided it would be safer to hide when someone grabbed my arm. I yelped, immediately trying to twist myself from his grasp.

"Is it her?" The second man—one of Alac's personal guards—stepped forward as I continued to struggle.

"Who else would it be?" My captor shifted around so that he was facing me. "Lady Maralyn Keele, isn't it?"

I set my teeth. "No." Which wasn't a lie.

"I'm sure it's her," Alac's guard said. "Let's take her to the king."

Dread like the weight of a thousand boulders sank into me. *The king.* Alac.

I stopped struggling, and the soldier holding me loosened his grip slightly. His expression was almost pitying, as though he didn't relish having to take me forcibly before the boy who had every right to demand my death.

"I have a daughter almost your age," he said. "For her sake, I'll handle you gently."

I didn't want him to handle me at all. My gaze darted from him to the other one and back again as panic crept up my throat and squeezed. I couldn't let them take me to Alac.

"He and Tucker can't have gone far," Alac's guard said. "It's been no more than a quarter of an hour since they set off."

Alac is with them?

The guard nudged me to walk with him toward the horses, while the other one drew his sword, as though I were in any position to put up a fight. The trees and ground and sky thrummed with the magic of growing things, calling to me as I struggled to concentrate on what I needed to do. For five or six steps, I allowed myself to be led like the prisoner I seemed to be. Then, with voiceless breath, I spoke to the vines growing up the trunks of the two nearest trees.

"Grow. Save me."

The vines burst into motion, twisting and churning and growing thick and long. At first, the men didn't notice them. But as the vines made their way from the trees and slithered along the ground toward us, my captors stopped short.

"*Cruce,*" one of them breathed.

In the next moment, the vines wrapped themselves around their ankles, pulling them to the ground, where they landed awkwardly, the sword tumbling from the hand of Alac's guard. I jumped out of their way as the vines continued to twist around their legs and arms and torsos, holding them captive as I hurried away as fast as my wounded feet would allow.

"What sorcery is this?" one of them yelled as I spoke to the tether of the nearer horse—a silvery-gray mare that was much too big for me.

"Rot," I whispered. "Dissolve to nothing."

The leather crumpled to dust, falling away as the horse tossed its head in apparent surprise. Bracing myself against the pain, I stepped up into the stirrup, grunting as my foot took the full force of my weight. A quick glance at the men showed me that they were completely incapacitated, bound by the vines so that they could barely move.

With great effort, I swung myself onto the saddle and took the reins. "Be still," I sang to the vines. "Hold them."

Then, amid calls for help from the vine-enrobed soldiers, I urged the horse toward the east and took off, my aching feet dangling well above the stirrups.

I didn't dare to look back.

39

ALAC

I stared at Deven and Marvan as they pulled the remaining bits of vine from their arms and hair. "You're sure it was her?"

It was an inane question; of course it was her. Who else would speak to the plants and call them to her bidding? I didn't want to admit that someone had found her before I did. Or that she'd escaped.

"You might've warned us that she's a sorceress, Your Grace," Deven said.

I pressed my lips together and didn't allow myself to contradict him. In their eyes, Mara was no different from my father.

"Which way did she go?"

"East," Marvan said. "Toward Silverton."

"We're up against more than we realized," Deven said. "This is no mere girl caught between Nelgareth and the throne. The horse's tether was just . . . gone."

"Let's ride together," Tucker said. "If we don't overtake her, we'll be able to find her once we get there."

"No." I said the word more loudly than I'd intended. "I need to do this alone."

Deven looked incredulous. "Forgive me, Your Grace, but that's a terrible idea. This girl uses *magic*! Look how easily she got away from the two of us."

"I have to agree," one of the others said, and several grunted assent.

"What's going to stop her from doing something similar if she feels cornered by over a dozen armed men?" Might as well play on their fears to assert my will. "This is my battle. Mine's the throne she almost took. I'll find her and deal with her myself."

"I'm coming with you," Tucker said.

I opened my mouth to protest, but I realized it would be good to have him along. He was the only other person who knew Mara. And there was also the burning hope in my chest that she might be able to help him. If we terrorized her into submission and took her by force, she wouldn't be willing to help anyone.

That's the story I told myself, at any rate. Mostly I wanted to find her because she was my own, personal failure. I hadn't been able to see past my feelings to the truth of who she was—an imposter. A traitor. I'd feasted on every lie that dripped from her mouth and grown fat on the sweetness of her company.

"Ride back to the castle," I said. "Tell them I commanded your return."

To a man, they shifted uneasily. It was ingrained in them to protect their prince. Their king.

"As you wish, Your Grace," Deven finally said.

I turned to him. "And say nothing of what happened here." I didn't need stories of her sorcery to reach the castle before I brought her there myself.

After they'd ridden away, Marvan awkwardly sharing Deven's saddle, Tucker clapped me on the shoulder. "Good to know I can tell my king how things are and get away with it."

"Keep it up and I'll make you call me 'Your Grace' when no one else is around."

"Seriously, though," he said. "Be careful."

"I don't think she's going to attack me with vines."

"That's not what I mean." He raised an eyebrow. "Your heart's more ensnared than Deven and Marvan were."

"My heart has nothing to do with this," I said darkly. "She's a traitor, and she's going to die."

Tucker looked like he was going to say something else but thought better of it. He clucked to his horse and headed east.

~∞~

It was less than an hour's ride to Silverton. We stayed off the main road, wary of any of Nelgareth's men that might be at large, searching for their missing queen. Or for me. By the time the town was visible on the horizon, my jaw ached from clenching my teeth. Tucker was mostly silent, leaving me alone with my thoughts. A thousand iterations of the first words I'd say when I found Mara marched through my brain, none of them feeling right.

We reached the postern gate and were admitted without consequence. I sighed with relief to think that Nelgareth had at least not had the forethought to post his own men there. Or perhaps his arrogance had been too great. His keep was directly off the main road, so Tucker and I cut across a field and approached the heart of the city from another direction, picking our way along a stream and pushing through a copse of spindly trees until we reached an accessible side street.

"Remarkably smelly back here," Tucker said.

"Spoken like a spoiled castle dweller."

He shrugged. "Maybe it's my old nose."

I was more thankful for his sense of humor than I could express. "Riding through the streets calling her name probably isn't the best approach. Should we stable the horses?"

"Might as well," Tucker said. "Let's find a decent inn and take it from there."

I hadn't been to Silverton since I was seven or eight—before Mother died, before Father had taken the magic and transformed into someone I didn't know. Nelgareth and his wife had hosted a magnificent party, and all the lords and their families were present. I hadn't been as excited about that as I was about the promise of an old-fashioned jousting match. Right before the match started, Cannon had shoved me so that I fell into a pile of horse dung. Mother was distraught and sent me inside to be bathed and my clothing laundered.

I missed the joust. And Cannon never owned up to pushing me.

We secured lodgings for the horses at one of the larger inns to the south of midtown, as well as taking a room.

"I've been thinking," I said as we dumped our saddlebags into a corner. "Now that we're here, we should try to blend in. She already knows that men on horseback were sent out to find her; I'd rather not alert her to our presence before we find out where she's hiding."

"If she's even here." Tucker laid his sword on the bed—it was less conspicuous to carry only daggers.

"You heard Marvan—she rode east. Someone in town will probably take her in, and once they learn they're harboring a fugitive, they'll hand her over."

Tucker frowned. "Except for the fact that anyone who might be hiding her will be loyal to her cause."

I couldn't let myself believe that.

Tucker didn't say anything else; he simply unbuckled his breastplate. I did the same before pulling my unruly hair back into as tight a tail as I could fashion.

"That just might be your new look," Tucker said.

"It rivals yours, for sure."

He threw a nearby candlestick at me. "Let's go."

I laid my sword beside Tucker's and followed him out the door, my heart in a strange tangle, telling myself it wouldn't faze me when I finally saw her.

I was lying.

40

MARALYTH

The first thing I did when I reached the postern gate was to set the horse free. It took more effort than I'd expected, but finally the beast responded to my shouts and firm slaps on her hindquarters and took off in the direction we'd come. My feet ached with every step, which made me even more thankful I'd had the horse. Noblewomen had a lot to learn about what real shoes looked like.

My progress through the city was slow. I had to rest every ten minutes or so, not only for the pain in my feet but also for the hunger in my belly. Twice I took handfuls of water from rain barrels at the backs of buildings, but other than that, I had nothing to sustain me. Over and over in my head, I reviewed the map that I'd committed to memory.

At first, I didn't pay attention to the fluttering signs posted here and there. When I finally stopped to read one, my legs almost gave out beneath me.

WANTED ALIVE AND UNHARMED:
MARALYN KEELE, TRAITOR
REWARD: 1200 SILVERS

That was four times the amount Nelgareth had sent Poppa after I'd agreed to the coup.

The drawing of my face was accurate enough to make me uneasy. I ducked behind a nearby butcher's shop and tore a thick swath from the hem of my dress. I draped it over my head and tied it beneath my chin; it made a raggedy scarf, but at least it helped obscure my face.

After that, I stuck to the shadows. There were so many signs that I lost count; I began to wonder if even Wennie's would be safe.

It took me at least two hours to find Silverton's sanctuary, the one landmark Hesta had drawn on her map. Its pale gray stones and windows of deep-blue glass set it apart from the more modest buildings around it. From there, it was easy to find the streets Hesta had labeled.

The building that Hesta had marked "Wennie's" on the map was an inn, its door weather-beaten, its large, square window thick with grime. Now that I'd found it, anxiety crept through me, and I hesitated in the street to the point of feeling ridiculous. Then, if only because I was tired of standing on my sore feet, I crossed the street and entered the inn.

My first glance of the inside told me that it wasn't open for business, though the scent of something savory cooking made my stomach roil with hunger. The front room, where tables and chairs should've been, was a hodgepodge of furniture to one side and a huge, age-worn table to the other. The bar was piled with books, lanterns, boxes, and various other things. One end of it was cleared off as a sort of working area. A shockingly blond-haired woman looked up and put down her pen when she saw me.

"Can I help you?"

"I . . . Hesta sent me."

"Hesta." She breathed the word instead of speaking it. "Sit down. You look exhausted."

I stumbled to the nearest couch and sank onto it. The woman hurried from behind the bar and knelt beside me.

"Let me see those feet."

No questions—not even my name. I winced as she took one of my feet in her hand, examined it, and then pulled off the ruined shoe.

"Nasty blisters, but we'll clean and bind them," she said. "And then I'm sure you'd like something to eat."

She left, and I peeled my other shoe off, marveling that I'd made it this far once I saw the state of it. I looked around; there was something comforting about the inn's casual disarray. Probably because I'd just spent two nights in the woods.

She returned with a bucket of water, some cloths, and a small, black jar. I sat with my legs extended across the sofa, and she got to work gently bathing the first foot, cleaning the blisters and patting my foot with a cloth to dry it.

"Are you the Graylaern girl?" Her words were soft, and she continued to focus on my foot.

My true name! She knew more than I'd dreamed anyone would. "Yes."

"Is it true about the king and Prince Cannon?"

The horror of that morning flooded back—the blade slicing across Cannon's neck, the blood, the expression on the king's face as he slumped in his chair. I shuddered.

"It's true."

She worked silently for a while, dabbing ointment from the black jar onto my foot and binding it with strips of soft fabric. Then she began bathing my other foot.

"You must be Wennie," I finally said.

She looked up. "Yes. And you're safe here. At least for now." She continued her ministrations to my foot.

"I have no money."

"You don't have to pay me." She curled her hands around my freshly bound foot and lowered her voice, though no one else was in the room. "It's an honor to offer you a room, Your Grace."

My bones went soft at the use of the title. How much had Hesta known? Who else might know?

Wennie must've read my thoughts. "There are more Dallowyn supporters than you know. A lot of us live right here."

An entire inn full of supporters?

"You don't need to call me 'Your Grace.'" The title didn't feel wrong—it felt world-heavy, like something I couldn't carry.

"As you wish," Wennie said. "But I'm sure you'll get used to it after a while."

I nodded and said nothing.

"There are rumors," she then said, "about strands of dark magic tearing free from the castle and traveling east. Is it true?"

"Yes." I couldn't bring myself to tell her about the dead trees.

"Well. We'll all do what we can to protect you."

There's no way you can protect anyone from this.

She rose. "Stay there and rest your feet. I'll bring you some supper."

I smiled my thanks, grateful for her kindness. In a short while she brought me a bowl of steaming tomato soup, thickly seeded bread with butter, and a tankard of water. It was like something Mother might've served, and my heart clutched as tightly as my stomach.

After I'd finished my second bowl, Wennie came to the table and held out a key.

"Here you go, love. It's the door across the hall from the washroom." She pointed to a dark hallway to the right of the bar. "Small room, but you don't need more than that right now, do you?" She smiled.

I took the key, grateful for any room at all. "Thank you, Wennie."

"After supper, I'll see about some shoes and fresh clothes. For now, you might want to rest a bit. The supper horde can get noisy."

I rose, wincing as I put weight on my tender feet, and walked gingerly to the dark hallway. The door across from the washroom was slightly narrower than a normal door, as if the room had been squashed into the back corner of the building as an afterthought. The key turned easily in the lock, and I slipped into the room and locked the door behind me.

Wennie hadn't been kidding when she'd called the room small. There was barely enough space for the bed, which was pushed up against the far wall. A narrow window sat in the wall to the left, up too high for anyone outside to see much—a comforting thought, considering this was the ground floor.

I sat on the bed, which groaned beneath my weight as though it would rather I didn't use it. The room was dim, the window shuttered and too small to leave in much light. I sighed, the last few days crashing around me like waves in a tempest.

I had absolutely no idea what to do next.

It would have been easy to run home to Poppa and Nestar, where no one at court would know to look for me. But I couldn't ignore the steady tide that seemed to be sweeping me toward a throne I'd agreed to accept—and had then sabotaged. I feared Alac would perform the ritual and take the magic as his own. Yes, that would contain it, but it would also destroy him.

I didn't want him to be destroyed.

His taking the magic wouldn't ultimately do anything for our kingdom, at any rate. It would be more of the same oppression we had lived under for a hundred years, this time at the hands of someone who'd never wanted it in the first place.

Someone kind and funny who cared about people instead of power.

Despair welled up inside me. I'd saved Alac's life, but what had he received as a result? The aftermath of the murder of his family and the loosing of stolen magic that had the power to age anything with which it came into contact.

I hugged myself hard, remembering Nelgareth's cries as the magic aged him, and how those cries had gone suddenly silent. He'd been destroyed by the magic he'd thought he could overcome by killing the king. I couldn't pretend I was sorry, but the horror of his death hung over me like heavy fog.

I wasn't aware of falling asleep. A knock on the door woke me, but it was so soft I wasn't sure at first that it was a knock at all. When the knock came a second time, I hurried to unlock the door.

It swung open with a groan, and I cried out in joy.

"Nestar!"

41

MARALYTH

In one, giant leap, I was in his arms. He crushed me to his chest so that I could barely breathe, while tears warmed my cheeks and washed away some of the horror of the past few weeks.

He drew back, holding me by the shoulders. "Are you well?"

"I am." I frowned at the purplish smudge beneath his eye. "What happened to your eye?"

"Bit of a fight."

"What are you doing here?" It almost didn't seem real. "How did you find me?"

"I always find you," Nestar said.

A loud cry came from the front room. I frowned and slipped past Nestar into the hallway; he followed me. Some sort of commotion was happening near the door, but a knot of people made it impossible to see.

"You stay there," Nestar said, already moving up the hallway.

I followed him.

I could just make out the top of Wennie's head as Nestar and I pushed our way through the gaping crowd. When we got as close as we could, I saw that Wennie was sitting on the same couch I'd sat on earlier, when she was tending to my feet. She had her arm around a very old woman, whose long, wavy hair was pure white. The woman's gnarled fingers were folded tightly in her lap, like she was holding herself together with them.

Wennie stroked her hair, and the woman cried out again, as though she were in terrible pain. Someone pushed past me, brusque and insistent.

Swish.

Disgust rose like bile in my throat. What was he doing here? Suddenly, Wennie's inn felt far less safe.

"Who is this?" Swish squatted in front of Wennie and the old woman.

Wennie looked up, her expression colored with fear. "It's Vita."

Several people gasped or murmured, and a deep sense of dread punctured my heart.

"*Our* Vita?"

Wennie nodded, and Swish pressed a fisted hand against his mouth. Nestar draped his arm around me and dipped his head toward my ear. When he spoke, his words trembled.

"She's not much older than me."

My heart plummeted to my ruined feet.

"What happened, Vita?" Swish's voice was gentle in a way I didn't think him capable of.

"I was napping." Vita's voice sounded spent, as though a lifetime of using it had worn it thin. "I woke up in a black cloud. I could hardly breathe. And then . . . the pain . . ." She pressed her hand to her chest and began to rock.

Nelgareth's writhing, aging body pierced my memory. There was no doubt that Vita had been caught in a magic strand. It was amazing that she'd survived at all—somehow, she must've gotten free.

My hands thrummed and tingled, the magic restless and insistent. If could I ripen grapes or restore a vine to health after it was blighted, I could reverse Vita's aging.

Couldn't I?

I hesitated. What if I tried—and failed, in front of all these people?

Without warning, Vita fell forward, landing on the floor in utter stillness. I watched, horrified, as Wennie knelt by her side, pressing her fingers to the side of Vita's neck.

"She's dead," she said softly.

Someone cried out, and a distressed murmur filtered through the crowd. I stood, numb, disbelieving. If I had acted faster, maybe I could have helped.

Swish stood and faced the crowd. "I need someone to tend the body," he called out. "The rest of you—go about your business."

Then his gaze fell on me, and my insides turned to ice.

The crowd unknotted, sluggishly at first, and a girl and a middle-aged man stepped forward to collect Vita. Swish moved close to me, his gaze darting momentarily to Nestar.

"Wennie said you were here." Swish's bottom lip was scabbed and his hair was as messy as ever.

"I have nothing to say to you." I looked again at Vita, translucent and withered and utterly still.

"Probably you have a lot to say," Swish persisted, "and I want to hear it."

"I'll come, too." Nestar's words had an edge.

"Fine. We'll go to my room." I shouldered past them both and pushed through the slowly dispersing crowd.

When we reached my room, I sat on the bed and motioned for Nestar to sit by me. Swish could sit on the floor—or stand the whole time, for all I cared. I turned to Nestar, noticing his unshaven face and longer-than-usual hair in addition to the bruise beneath his eye.

I reached over and squeezed Nestar's hand. "Tell me how you found me."

"Can't that wait?" Swish asked, leaning against the door and crossing his arms.

"No, it can't." If anyone were going to be bossy, it would be me.

"When you disappeared that morning, we couldn't make sense of it," Nestar said. "Father was almost physically ill with worry."

Oh, Poppa. "What did you do?"

"We started searching in shifts—we couldn't leave the fields unattended. When we realized Swish was gone, too, it seemed obvious he had something to do with it, but we couldn't put the pieces together."

"Sharp as ever," Swish said.

Nestar leaned forward, jaw tense, eyes boring into Swish. "You can shut that dung-filled mouth of yours, or I'll shut it for you."

"You've tried that once already."

Nestar's bruise and Swish's scabbed lip suddenly made sense. "Stop it, both of you. Nestar, go on."

"We all knew Swish was a Dallowyn supporter," Nestar said. "I had no idea how that might be connected to you, but I left home and started searching for people who knew him. It took me a couple weeks, but their trail led me here."

"Does Poppa know?"

Nestar glanced at Swish again. "No, he doesn't."

"Once he stopped hitting me, I explained to him why it was important to keep your location a secret," Swish said.

"Wennie's actually the one who sat me down and explained things," Nestar said. "I was too angry to listen much, but at least she kept me from beating this bastard to a pulp."

"Look," Swish said. "I get it. I took her, and everyone was worried. I've already explained why I did it, and I'm pretty sure you don't have a problem with the fact that your sister is the rightful heir to the throne."

My heart twisted a little. I'd been sure Nestar would want to bring me home. "Is that true?"

"Only if it's what you want, Mara."

I took a long breath. "It is. But it's complicated."

"Tell us what happened," Nestar said.

I glanced at Swish; he was looking at me.

"I know it's hard to believe," he said, "but I'm on your side here."

"Is this the part where I make friends with the person who kidnapped me?"

"I'm not your friend," Swish said. "I'm your supporter. Your subject. The whole reason I brought you to Nelgareth is because I've wanted to see a Dallowyn on the throne for most of my life. You have the right to hate me, but I hope you'll never have cause to question my loyalty."

"An apology wouldn't be such a bad idea," Nestar said.

Swish cast him a dark look before returning his attention to me. "I'm sorry. I wish there could've been another way."

I didn't feel like discussing it, so I nodded curtly and let the subject drop. Then I told them everything—from my first day in the palace until I ran from the dining hall as the dark magic engulfed Nelgareth. I didn't mention how I'd used magic to escape from Alac's men; only that I'd stolen one of their horses and made my way to Silverton. Nestar and Swish listened without interrupting, their gazes intent.

Nestar, especially, seemed to breathe in every word I spoke. When I finished, he let out a low whistle.

"It sounds like someone else's story," he said. "Not yours."

"I know."

Swish was frowning. "Why didn't you let Alac drink the poison?"

I met his gaze without flinching. "Because he didn't deserve to die."

"And the others did?"

"No one deserves that sort of death," I said. "But Nelgareth's plan was already in motion. Alac never wanted the throne or his father's legacy, and I wanted to come up with a different way to free Perin Faye from the oppression of the magic."

"What different way did you have in mind?" Nestar asked.

"I haven't figured that out yet."

Swish huffed. "Maybe our would-be king should perform his damned ritual instead of letting strands of stolen magic wander around the kingdom killing things."

"That's easy for you to say," I said crisply. "You have no idea what it means to be possessed by dark magic."

For once, Swish didn't have an answer.

"Wennie said that a lot of Dallowyn supporters live here," I said.

"Everyone here is a Dallowyn supporter," Swish said. "A band of rebels, right under the king's nose."

"How did you find all these . . . rebels?"

"When Nelgareth hired me to find him magical folks, I was already connected with a lot of people—many of them right here at Wennie's. But there are others, too, all over Delthe and in other lord-lands, too. Folks who have little bits of magic they're afraid to do anything with, plus the people who support them."

"You have *magic*?"

Swish looked at me for a moment, then stepped forward and pressed his hand onto my knee. Within a few seconds, heat radiated from his hand as though it had been warmed over a fire. I gasped, and he removed his hand and returned to his place by the door.

"It's not much," he said. "It helps if your tea's grown cold, or if you're having trouble lighting a fire in your hearth."

I couldn't help staring. "Are you a Dallowyn?"

"Yes," he said, "but not in the direct line, like you."

"How do you even know that?"

"Just because your mother chose to keep you from knowing doesn't mean that the rest of us have forgotten."

It was still hard to grasp that there were people out there proud of their Dallowyn heritage instead of terrified by it—or ignorant of it.

"My mother said nothing. Ever."

"She had more reason to be cautious," Swish said. "You're obviously in the direct line. And Nelgareth's brother attempted a coup—and failed. It's no wonder your mother ran."

Indignation beat at my breast. "How do you know all that?"

"Do you think I was out there blindly looking for magical people? Nelgareth told me enough to help me know what to look for."

"You didn't work alone, though." I remembered the others who had been with him.

"We've had a network in place for almost four years," Swish said. "Folks outside the castle—and inside."

"How does everyone communicate without getting caught?" I was admittedly impressed.

"One of the Brothers of the Holy God from the castle sanctuary is on our side. He receives messages from inside the castle and sends them outside through children."

"Children?"

Swish shrugged. "Feed a hungry child, and you've got a loyal messenger," Swish said.

"I suppose a Brother would arouse the least suspicion."

And then I remembered the night I'd encountered the shadowy Brother skulking down the hallway. Might that have been our informant?

It was hard, in the dark, to tell friend from enemy.

I turned to Nestar. "Did Swish tell you all this?"

"Yes. Once I finally agreed to listen."

For a moment, my voice faltered. "Was it hard to hear?"

Nestar shook his head slowly. "Not as hard as you might think."

I returned my attention to Swish. "What about the other people you brought to Nelgareth? What happened to them?"

"Never saw them again."

Horror wove through me. I absolutely believed Nelgareth capable of putting them to death.

"I need to find a way to return the stolen magic and stop the devastation."

"Agreed." Swish looked pointedly at me. "But first, Alac Thungrave needs to die."

I let Swish's words sink into the air around me, where they settled hard and heavy. He was ready to remove the main obstacle to my throne, and now wasn't the time to argue Alac's right to live. Or to let Swish know that Alac was out searching with the men he'd sent to find me.

"We'll talk in the morning," I said, making my tone as dismissive as I could.

After he left, Nestar and I sat on my bed talking until I could barely keep my eyes open. The timbre of his voice spoke of home, and his eyes reminded me so much of Poppa's that twice I had to brush tears away.

I spoke in greater depth about everything that had happened since the day I'd been kidnapped. He asked questions—some that were easy to answer, like what the inside of Nelgareth's keep looked like or how well guarded the castle was, and some that weren't easy at all.

"So, what are your feelings for this prince?" he asked after I finished telling him about my walk in the garden with Alac when my magic first responded to his.

"I've told you—he's a decent person. Kind and funny and not what I expected at all."

"You know what I mean."

I did know. But it wasn't something I'd allowed myself to think about, let alone give voice to. "I like him."

"Like . . . ?"

"Nestar, I spent a week with him. That's hardly enough to time to get to know him, let alone . . . *feel* things."

"And yet you saved his life. Twice."

I closed my eyes. "I was supposed to let everything unfold. In the end, I couldn't do it."

"And sabotaged everything Nelgareth put into motion."

My chest tightened with anger. "Nelgareth also wanted to *marry* me! Should I have gone along with that, too?"

"I'm only saying . . . you've said you're willing to take the throne, and you have a lot of people supporting you—probably more than we could know, once word gets out that a Dallowyn queen is at large. So if you're going to do this thing, then you have to accept everything that comes with it. No matter how hard."

"Like having Alac put to death."

"Yes."

I knew he was right. It was easier to think about this when Alac wasn't here; when his eyes weren't crinkling in thought, or the light wasn't hitting his face just so. But that didn't mean I wanted to.

"It feels wrong." My words felt flimsy, like moth wings.

"He's your enemy, Mara. If you think for a minute he won't have you tried and executed for treason, you're dreaming."

I saw the concern in Nestar's eyes. And I saw truth.

"I know," I whispered.

"You can do this, Mara."

I wasn't sure I could.

"Thank you for coming for me," I said.

"I couldn't not come." He ran his fingers through his hair. "Poppa wanted to come, too, but I convinced him to stay. It would be too much for Kenton to handle with both of us gone."

"It didn't bother you not to be there for harvest, did it?" I asked.

"No." His answer had come quickly, as though he didn't have to think about it. "I was too busy worrying about you—and planning all the ways I'd make Swish bleed."

"Does Poppa know?"

"Know what?"

"That your heart isn't in the wine, like his."

"I—how do you know that?"

I smiled. "Haven't I always told you I know the grapes better than you do?"

"Yes, but I figured you were just trying to irritate me."

"I was telling the truth," I said.

Nestar sighed. "No, I don't think he knows. And I could never tell him."

"What *do* you want, if not the vineyards?"

"I want to make a difference somewhere other than in the wine cellars of nobility," Nestar said. "I don't know what that looks like. But fighting for what you believe is right? Standing up to tyranny? Setting the right person on the throne? Sometimes I feel . . . I don't know. Like I was born for this."

"Then maybe you were."

He tousled my hair. "I couldn't let Poppa down like that, Mara."

"It would let him down more to know you were doing something that made you unhappy."

"Do you always know the right thing to say?"

"Usually."

He kissed my forehead. "Right now, I just want to protect you."

I leaned my head on his shoulder, allowing myself one last moment to be his little sister.

Instead of his queen.

42

ALAC

For the rest of the day, well into the evening, we searched the streets and stables and inns of lower Silverton. As the day progressed, a sense of panic continued to rise among the people. Everywhere, there were whispers of dark magic and devastation, and some people were leaving town. Twice, I got a glimpse of a magic strand, floating ominously above the rooftops and disappearing. It was hard to ignore Tucker's trepidation, though he did a good job of trying to hide it.

The public room of the inn we were staying at was strangely empty that night. There weren't even any servers, and the owner himself brought us our plates of goat shank gravy over boiled potatoes and tankards of beer.

"You're traveling, are you?" he said, his eyes darting nervously to the darkened windows.

"Yes," I said, trusting my several days' growth of beard and uncharacteristically tied-back hair to assuage any notion that I might resemble the "unremarkable younger prince." "My, uh, father and I are just passing through."

"You've heard about the king, then? And the cursed magic running rampant?"

"Some, yes." I drank my beer and tried not to act overly interested.

"There's no rhyme or reason to it," he said. "Like a sickness you're afraid to catch."

"You've lost a lot of customers, I see."

"Two thirds, at least! As if running to the countryside is going keep them safe."

I glanced at Tucker; he was stabbing at his potatoes, obviously not enjoying the conversation.

"What about you?" I said to the owner. "Are you going to stay?"

"I've got nowhere else to go," he said. "I guess I'll take my chances with that blasted magic getting at me while I'm abed."

He went off to deal with the only other table that had someone sitting at it. I waited until he'd engaged them in conversation before leaning closer to Tucker.

"So tell me. If you'd seen the magic strand before you got caught in it, would you have been able to get away?"

"Probably," Tucker said. "Whenever I see one, it doesn't seem to be moving particularly fast."

"So, if we take turns keeping watch tonight, we'd have time to react if one of them turns up in our room?"

Tucker drank long and deep from his tankard. "We can do that. But this is starting to feel like a losing battle."

"We have to find her, Tuck," I said.

"We'll find her," Tucker said. "It just would've been easier if there were more than two of us."

I jammed a forkful of food into my mouth, choosing that over answering him. It had been hard to see past my burning need to be the one to find Mara first—to make her face me and admit her deception. I wondered now how my rash decision had affected our chances of success.

"I think we should focus on the inns and hostelries," I said. "If she does have supporters here, they're going to be holed up somewhere secure."

Tucker nodded. "With room for a crowd."

"You think she's got that many people on her side?"

"Who's to say? We should be ready for anything."

"The wanted posters are on every street corner," I said. "There has to be at least one person in this town loyal to the crown and willing to turn her in."

"We can stop at the constables' first thing to check," Tucker said. "If she's there, we can save them the trouble of transporting her to Crownhold."

I sighed. "In the meantime, let's ask our friendly host for a list of inns. We can map our route before bed."

"There's one other possibility," Tucker said softly. "She might be dead."

I ignored the ice that coated my veins. "Until that's a known fact, I won't believe it."

For the small amount of hope I held that Mara could help me do something about the magic, her death would be the end of any hope at all.

43

MARALYTH

When I entered the main room the next morning, dressed in a pair of breeches and a floral tunic that looked like it belonged on a curtain rod, a crowd of residents had already gathered at the large table, their conversation low and intense. Several heads turned as I approached, and Swish caught my eye and gestured to the seat beside him.

"Morning, Your Grace," he said. There was no note of irony in his voice. "Feet feeling any better?"

"Yes, thank you." Wennie's salve had worked wonders.

I sat down and gazed at the sea of faces, some bleary-eyed, others alert and responsive. My insides convulsed when I recognized the horse-toothed boy and the beefy girl sitting halfway down the table. The other kidnappers.

Swish didn't miss the moment. "Burt and Telda," he said. "Yes, I paid them, and yes, they're loyal, or they wouldn't be here."

Telda offered me a somewhat sheepish nod. I nodded back, then looked away.

I was glad to see Nestar take an empty seat at the other end of the table. I couldn't help noticing how well he blended with this collection of people—as though he belonged here.

Wennie set a tray of steaming mugs on the table, offering me a little smile as she wiped her hands on her apron.

I took a deep breath. "Wennie, is the door barred?"

"I'll do it now," she said, crossing to the door.

I folded my hands on the table and tried to look . . . queenly. If these were my people, then I needed to let them know that I was willing to take charge.

To hold court.

"Ladies and gentlemen," Swish said, "I give you the rightful queen of Perin Faye."

The "hear, hears" and "my queens" caught me off guard. I sat a little taller, pulse racing.

"King Selmar and the crown prince are dead, and"—I swallowed the dryness in my throat—"I'm here to claim the throne from Alac Thungrave."

People cheered. Several sets of hands passed down a steaming mug of tea for Swish and one for me as well. I curled my hands around it, grateful for the soothing aroma.

"There's a price on my head," I continued, "so my first concern is— can you keep me safely hidden?"

"We'll hide you here until we can find a more secure location," Swish said. "Nelgareth's keep would be ideal, but it's too risky to move you there right now."

There were mumbled sounds of assent, and I found myself surprised to find this level of commitment. If this group of outcasts felt so strongly about the throne, what was it like around other tables in other inns and public houses?

"The coup failed," Telda said. "How will you take the throne?"

"Nelgareth's army was prepared to come defend the new queen," Swish said. "They still are."

"I appreciate your support," I said. "You have my word that, if the path is cleared, I will accept the throne of Perin Faye. But right now the strands of magic are a much more urgent problem."

"Can you stop them?" someone asked.

"I don't know," I said. "But I need to try. If I don't find a way to stop this magic from destroying everything in its path, there won't be a kingdom left to rule."

More nods of assent. I looked around the table and saw that everyone's attention hung on me like spiders on a web. "As long as Alac doesn't perform the blood ritual needed for him to receive the magic, I have a chance to find a way to stop it."

This was when I needed to tell them to find Alac and bring him to me, dead or alive. It's probably what they wanted to hear. Nestar's words from last night rang in my ears.

He's your enemy, Mara. If you think for a minute he won't have you tried and executed for treason, you're dreaming.

But what if I needed him? What if this was something we had to do together?

Or what if I was telling myself that because I couldn't bear to sentence him to death?

This wasn't about my feelings, though. The people around this table wanted me for their queen, and I owed them as much truth as I could offer.

"Alac was part of the group he sent out to search for me," I said. "He could be in Silverton even now."

Swish stared. "How do you know this?" He probably meant, "Why didn't you tell me this yesterday?"

"I escaped from two of them, and they mentioned that he was nearby."

"*Escaped* from?" Nestar's brow was furrowed. "You said you stole a horse."

"It was a bit more complicated," I said.

Sudden, repeated pounding on the door made most of us jump. Wennie had just set a bowl of porridge on the table; she turned and walked to the door.

"Who's there?" she called.

"Let me in, Wennie!" The voice was female—and frantic. "It's Julan!"

Wennie unbarred the door and stepped back, allowing Julan to burst into the room, almost losing her balance as she stumbled forward.

"It's not safe here," she said, gasping for air. "It's not safe anywhere."

"What are you talking about?" Swish's voice was calm and even.

"Magic strands," Julan said. "They're dipping low and catching people unaware. I've heard tales of entire herds of sheep lying dead in the fields. And the trees. Have you seen them dying? Here and there, trees have fallen over, their branches and trunks half-rotted as though they've sat there for decades."

I rose, dread weighing my heart so that each breath I took felt labored. Vaguely aware of others also rising, I walked around the table and stood in the doorway. I looked at the street, which at first appeared full of normal activity. But then I noticed the difference—a shopkeeper hastily piling things into a cart; a cluster of men charging down the street, sacks on their shoulders; a woman running, calling to someone I couldn't see.

I tasted their panic. I intimately knew its source.

"I have to go," I said to no one specific.

Then I stepped outside.

At first, I saw no sign of the magic strands. Even as I craned my neck and searched the morning sky, everything seemed clear. There was no hint of the devastating wisps of magic that seemed to travel of their own accord.

"Come inside," Swish said near my ear.

I ignored him, stepping into the street and continuing to search for any sign of the magic. I could feel the panic around me, palpable and insistent; surely these people weren't packing up and leaving for no reason.

And where did they expect to go? I hadn't observed enough strands to determine if there was a pattern to where they traveled. If this continued, then, truly, nowhere was safe.

A high-pitched scream came from the cross street to my left. I ran around the corner of Wennie's inn and stopped short—a wisp of magic, the length of two horses and no wider than my own shoulders—wended down the street. A woman with a child in her arms cowered against a wagon, her face contorted by terror.

Swish's hand curled around my shoulder. "*Cruce.*"

The magic within me surged and roared beneath my skin with a jubilance I couldn't account for. At the same time, I was inexplicably drawn to the dark magic strand. Shrugging out of Swish's grasp, I ran toward the woman.

"Maralyth, what are you doing?" Nestar's voice.

The strand continued to stretch toward the woman, who in her terror couldn't see that it wasn't moving quickly; she might've easily gotten clear of it.

And then, suddenly, I knew what I had to do.

"Move away!" I called.

Her eyes darted to me and she tightened her grip on the child. I ran until I was between the strand and the woman; then I took her by the shoulders and gave her a shove.

"Go! You're safe!"

Someone screamed, someone else yelled, and I faced the magic strand with my arms outspread. The cold of a hundred winters sliced through my skin and bones and heart, and my vision went black.

Then Nestar's hands were on my shoulders, and I opened my eyes, the sensation gone.

"Is she safe?" I asked.

"What just happened?" Nestar's words were tinged with fear.

Swish and several others, including the woman with the baby, stood several paces away, staring. Nobody else spoke.

A wild and reckless joy filled my breast, because finally *I understood*. I looked at Nestar through unbidden tears. "The magic belongs to me. It always has." Then I turned to face the others.

"Find Alac Thungrave and bring him to me alive."

I did need him, after all.

44

ALAC

Tucker and I slept in shifts, with several lamps burning so we could see the slightest bit of magic. The blood locket continued to lie warm against my flesh; during my watch, I often caught myself curling it into my palm and allowing the soft thrum of the magic to sing its wordless song to me.

The fact that it was no longer an option for me to complete the ritual didn't make things any easier. Without any way to control the magic, it would continue to kill and destroy anything in its path. I knew this—and yet a part of me rejoiced.

I could become king without becoming my father.

By the time the first hint of light squeezed through the shutters into our cramped room, I was more determined than ever to find Mara. I rose, rubbing my eyes with my knuckles, and called to Tucker, who lay dozing on the solitary bed.

Cruce, he looked so old.

"It's barely light," he said groggily.

"Light enough," I said. "We have a lot of inns to visit."

"Fine." He sat up and stretched, grimacing as though it pained him. "They'd better serve good beer."

"It's too early for beer." I threw his tunic at him. "Let's go."

⁂

Despite my carefully planned list, we had to backtrack several times to hit inns and hostelries we'd missed, which wasted a lot of time. Most of the establishments, like the one we were staying at, were oddly empty, as people continued to head for the countryside or wherever it was they were running to feel safe.

Nobody had seen Mara—or even seemed like they were trying to hide something.

We searched until the light had faded and our stomachs were growling. Tucker had slowed down as the day progressed, to the point where I started to worry. He seemed a bit better over a supper of a thin soup with questionable strands of meat in it; I mostly ate hunks of bread soaked in the salty broth.

"You up to taking first watch, old man?" I asked later as we walked up the stairs to our room.

"I only *look* old, remember?"

I wasn't so sure.

When Tucker woke me a couple hours later, he looked like he could barely keep his eyes open. I knew I couldn't let him take another shift. I settled onto a chair to spend the rest of the night looking out for rogue magic strands and worrying about Tucker. What if I was wrong, and Mara wouldn't be able to help him? What if we never found her?

At first light, I woke Tucker with new determination.

"We're going to find her today," I said.

But he looked at me with half-closed eyes and a sorry attempt at a smile. "I hate to say it, but I'm feeling my age—again." He stretched his arms and repositioned himself, looking more like a grandfather than my best friend. I hoped I wasn't imagining it, but he seemed older.

Worry pinched my gut, but I tried not to let it show. "You're just a little gray for nineteen, is all."

"I feel like an old man. I *am* an old man." He closed his eyes. "I keep thinking it's a bad dream."

I looked at the creases on his face and the way his mouth was drawn in at the corners. We had no way to know what effect this sort of sudden aging would have on him. A man who had actually aged forty years might easily have twenty left. But I feared more and more that Tucker might only have days.

"Take your forty winks, old man. I'll be back in a few hours. Sound good?"

No response.

"Tuck?"

Concern turned to fear as I pressed my hand against his chest and shook him gently.

This time I shouted. "Tucker!"

But he remained utterly, terrifyingly still.

45

MARALYTH

I rose before dawn and dressed quickly, not even bothering to put my hair up. Nestar and Swish and at least a dozen others were leaving at sunup to comb Silverton for Alac, and I needed to brief them before they left.

Nestar was already sitting at the table when I entered the front room, his hands around a mug of tea.

"You're not looking very queenly this morning," he said.

I rolled my eyes. "I'll be sure to hire half a dozen ladies-in-waiting later today."

When it seemed everyone was there, I stood at the head of the table, where everyone sat eating bowls of cold, leftover cabbage soup. Wennie placed a steaming mug of tea in front of me, and Nestar offered me a nod of encouragement before I began.

"First of all, thank you," I said. "My priority is to stop the magic from devastating our kingdom. The source of the magic is in the castle, and that's where it needs to be stopped. I need Alac Thungrave to get me safely inside."

"That's a huge gamble, Your Grace," Swish said.

"Yes, it is." I avoided Nestar's gaze as I continued. "And if we can't find him quickly, I'll have to go without him."

"Mara, you can't just walk up to the castle gate," Nestar said. "They'll arrest you."

I turned to Swish. "What have you learned about the state of things at Nelgareth's keep?"

"He kept a skeleton army there, and the rest of his forces were apparently camped in some secret location, in case they were needed to establish your throne after the coup. I don't know what's become of them."

"Can you find out?"

"I'll send a message to Hesta."

"Good. If it takes an army to get inside the castle, that's what we'll do. But I'd rather find Alac." I faced the group around the table. "It's going to be hard searching for someone you've never seen, so I'll try to describe him as best as I can."

I closed my eyes briefly, and the memory of Alac's face smiled at me. For a moment, I swam in emotions too deep to navigate. Then I emerged, and, standing tall, I described Alac to my supporters. My subjects.

I told of his light, wavy hair that he usually wore loose. I described his height, his build, the way he walked. Eyes and jaw and the curve of his mouth—I created a painting of Alac with my words.

"And if you look closely"—I felt my cheeks burning—"he's got pale freckles on his nose and cheeks."

"Remember, we're not looking for someone who looks like a prince," Swish said. "He might look like any other person on the street."

"And also remember that I want him alive and unhurt."

Several thuds sounded from the door, as though someone were kicking it. Wennie hurried to the door while I stood with my heart pounding.

Wennie unbarred the door and Burt burst through, holding his hands out as though he were carrying something. His face was etched with pain.

"I went to take a piss behind the barn," Burt said, "and somehow got my hands caught in one of those blasted strands."

I was across the room before Burt had sat on the nearest tuffet. "Let me see," I said, kneeling beside him.

"Don't touch them!" he said.

I didn't touch them—it wasn't necessary. I could see they'd been aged beyond what seemed possible. The skin was wrinkled and hung loose between gnarled, deformed knuckles. Both hands were covered in spots, and the long nails were yellowed and cracked.

"Do something." Burt's words were more of a moan. "You've got to help me."

This, from one of my kidnappers. The magic within me cried out, begged me for release. "I don't know . . ."

Nestar came up behind me. "Try, Mara."

I heard the others gathering around and noticed several curious onlookers hovering just outside the door. Then I looked again at Burt's ruined hands. I couldn't do nothing—they looked like they belonged on a dead man. This was no time to fear failure.

Despite his plea not to touch him, I rested my fingertips on his wrists and closed my eyes. "Reverse. Be young."

The magic leaped forth in a glorious tumult, more eager and vibrant than ever.

Then, suddenly, Burt was on his feet, whooping like a crazed little boy. "She did it! She healed them!"

He was moving so much that I couldn't even see the hands. I rose, feeling the sense of awe that pervaded the room. Most eyes weren't on Burt—they were on me.

"Stop jumping around and let me see," Swish finally said.

Burt held out his hands. "Look at this! Thought I was going to lose them."

The anxiety in my heart settled; Burt's hands were whole and smooth again. There didn't seem to be anything wrong with them.

Nestar squeezed my shoulder. People started cheering. And then Burt knelt before me, one fresh hand on his heart.

"My queen," he said. "I'm yours to the death."

One by one, the entire group knelt. Nestar. Swish. The strangers near the door.

Everyone.

Kneeling before *me*.

"Long live Queen Maralyth!" Swish called.

Everyone echoed him, voices raised. I felt breathless, but I held my head high and smiled with gratitude.

Nestar and the others swallowed down the rest of their breakfast and headed out to search for the boy whose life I'd saved twice—but probably wouldn't save a third time. I stood in the doorway, watching them fan out in the street, and then I turned to go inside.

"Your Grace." A slender, brown-haired girl about my age placed her hand on my arm. "My sister was caught by the magic yesterday and won't come out of the house now. She looks older than our mother. Could I . . . could I bring her to you?"

How could I say no? "Of course," I said. "But please don't speak of it to anyone."

She nodded solemnly. "Yes, Your Grace."

She returned an hour later with her sister—and five other people, one with an ornery goat in his arms.

By the time I'd undone the ill effects of the dark magic on each of them—including the goat, whose back legs had gone lame—seven more people had arrived.

"We can't keep the door open all day," Wennie said.

But I knew I couldn't turn these people away. "Set guards. Two by the door, two across the street, two farther off. They can make sure everyone who comes has a need and alert us if there's trouble."

Wennie looked doubtful for a moment, but then she shrugged. "Let's do it."

It was late when Nestar, Swish, and the others returned by twos and threes, none of them having had any luck finding Alac. It was later still by the time I'd healed the last person in what had turned out to be a long line.

"How many cows and horses did you turn away?" I asked Wennie wearily.

"Eight," Wennie said.

"And that doesn't include the folks who waited in line to ask me if I could come to their homes."

"You'll be glad to hear my news of Nelgareth's keep," Swish said. "There's a complement of twenty-two men ready to escort you to the castle at your command. And they've sent a runner to your army in the field, to let them know you're alive and well and ready to take your throne."

My army. "How can so many men stay hidden?"

"It's what armies do," Swish said.

Holy God, I didn't want to start a war. "One more day. If we don't find Alac tomorrow, we'll attempt to take the castle by force."

"Which means getting you to the keep tomorrow night," Wennie said.

"Yes. But I'll spend the day healing as many people as I can. We just need to find a different place. Somewhere outside of town."

"If you're going to be outside all day, I'm coming, too," Swish said.

"So am I," Nestar said.

I smiled—mostly at Nestar. "Fine. But we'll need people to replace you in the search for Alac."

"We're going to send out everyone we can," Swish said. "We'll find the bastard, I swear it."

46

ALAC

ruce. Not now. Not like this.

"Tucker, it's not over. Damn you, it's not over."

I took his shoulders in my hands and shook him, his head lolling like a cloth doll.

His eyes opened. "What are you doing?"

"Holy God, Tucker!" I jumped back, my heart in my teeth. "I thought you were dead."

"You were pretty close to snapping my neck, so you might've been right." He sat up—slowly, like it took great effort.

"You weren't responding."

"I was *sleeping.*"

"No one sleeps that deeply. Seriously no one."

He rubbed his eyes with his thumb and finger. "I've never been this exhausted."

"Maybe I should stay with you?"

"It'll be a little hard to find Mara that way."

I rubbed my hand against the beard that had thickened daily. "Will you at least drink a little wine before you go back to sleep? Get something in your stomach?"

"If it'll make you feel better."

"It will." I reached for his half-full goblet from the night before and placed it on the table by his bed.

"Guess I'd better get used to needing a lot more sleep," Tucker said, taking the goblet.

I heard the sorrow in his voice. And the fear. He hadn't needed extra sleep when the magic had first aged him.

"I'll be back in a few hours," I said. "You can come with me then."

He drank some wine and grimaced. "Only if you bring me something better to drink."

"Beer," I said. "Definitely."

I closed the door softly behind me, more determined than ever to find the girl who had turned the universe upside down.

∞

When I returned at lunchtime, luckless and discouraged, Tucker was sitting downstairs eating fried potatoes and bacon. My heart lightened when I saw him.

"You're looking better," I said, sitting across from him.

"Younger, I hope you mean."

I didn't answer; he looked older every time I saw him.

"No luck?" he asked.

"None. But I'm sure that'll change when you're with me."

I inhaled my own plate of potatoes and bacon and downed a tankard of beer, and then we set out again. Our pace was slower, thanks to Tucker's age, but I tried not to let my frustration show.

Near suppertime, we walked through the door of an inn that looked as though it might have been converted into some sort of dwelling; instead of pub tables and rows of stools at the bar, there were couches and tuffets and one huge table to the right, where two young men sat playing cards. The bar was cluttered with supplies and had no seats, and a blond-haired woman stood behind it filling a basket with what looked like parcels of food. A man with haphazard hair leaned against the front of the bar. They both looked at me.

"Do I know you?" the woman asked.

It was a strange greeting. "No. I'm looking f—"

"This isn't an inn." Her voice was smooth and unruffled. "It's a private residence."

"I'm sorry," I said. "I didn't mean to intrude."

The men at the table had gone silent—watching. The man by the bar turned around slowly. Tucker shifted beside me; I sensed his unease.

The woman came out from behind the bar, repinning her lopsided bun as she walked. "You're not intruding." Her tone had softened, but her expression was guarded. "The magic strands have us all on edge. Maybe I can direct you to a decent inn or hostelry?"

"Thank you," I said, "but we're actually looking for someone. A girl with dark red hair who was lost in the woods somewhere between here and Crownhold."

A chair scraped softly as one of the men at the table rose. The man with the wild hair strode forward.

Tucker grasped my shoulder. "She's not here."

I knew he was warning me, but I wasn't going to walk out that easily. These people knew something. "Her name is Maralyn. Lady Maralyn Keele."

"And what might your name be?" the wild-haired man said. "Alac Thungrave, perhaps?"

Cruce.

The woman rushed to close the door behind us while the other two men pressed in. All three men wore daggers.

"She's wanted by the crown," I said. "Anyone harboring her will be considered complicit in her crimes."

"She *is* the crown," Wild Hair said, "and she's commanded us to bring you to her."

My chest tightened. Tucker and I were both armed, but we were outnumbered—and Tucker was in no shape to fight.

"This old man doesn't know me," I said. "I paid him to help me search. Let him go."

Wild Hair pursed his lips and looked Tucker up and down. "That so?"

"Let him go, Swish," the woman said. "He has nothing to do with this."

Swish shook his head. "We're not taking any chances." He unsheathed his dagger and turned to one of the other men. "Lock him in Mara's room."

They took Tucker's dagger—and mine, too. I felt the steel of a blade at my back as I watched Tucker being led down a narrow hallway. The woman fetched a ring of keys from behind the bar and followed them.

Damn them all. I should never have sent the rest of my men home.

I looked at Swish, whose smug expression made me want to throttle him. "I'm not the one committing treason here."

He smiled. "But you're the one who's outnumbered."

The others returned from wherever they'd locked Tucker, and the woman grabbed the basket from the bar.

"I'll carry her supper," she said. "I should've thought to send it along with you when you left this morning."

"It's a good thing I was here just now." Swish gestured with his dagger to the other men, who each took me by an arm. "I'm right behind you, Thungrave. Don't try anything."

If only he knew how desperately I wanted to see Mara. But I threw him a sullen look before the other men pulled me toward the door.

∞

Less than half a mile from the city gate, a steady trail of people was making its way toward a stand of ash trees off the main road. Some were limping, some were carrying small animals—a goat, a suckling pig—and one or two were being borne in wagons. We made our way through the trees, my captors tightening their grip on my arms as we drew nearer to the crowd. Swish was so close to my back that I could hear him breathing.

The trees ended at a broad, grassy depression that was easily missed from the road. A thick cluster of people cluttered the area, and a single, mournful cow on a lead mooed as though she'd lost everything dear to her. In front of the crowd stood some sort of hastily rigged tent.

The afternoon sun was warm, but the sweat on my brow was more from apprehension than heat. At least thirty or forty people stood in a tight semicircle near the front; we arced around them to the left, and finally I could see.

There she sat, beneath the tent, her hair pulled loosely back from her face, her lips parted. My heart hitched for a single moment before thick rage nearly blinded me; I curled my fists against it and willed myself to stay calm.

Mara held the hands of a woman sitting in front of her, who cried out suddenly as Mara released her hands.

"They're normal! They're normal again!"

As the woman rose, thanking her profusely, one of the others beneath the tent stepped forward and took the woman's arm, leading her away while a young girl pushed her way through the knot of people, a wiry, old man on her arm.

"No need to push," the man leading the woman away said. "Maralyth will be here until sunset."

Maralyth?

Perhaps I'd heard him wrong.

As if under a spell, I watched as the man knelt before her, so unsteady that the young girl kept a grip on his arm. Mara placed her hands on his shoulders and spoke quiet words. I held my breath as the transformation took place—white hair turning brown, bent spine straightening. The locket burned beneath my shirt, and I closed my hand around it.

When Mara lowered her hands, the man was young again, and it was clear the girl was his daughter. She threw her arms around his waist and squeezed him while he expressed his thanks. He rose without effort and turned to the crowd, his face bright with the miracle he'd just received. Everyone cheered, and the man made his way through them.

We stopped just near the front, and Swish stepped forward.

"Your Grace," he said.

Mara looked up, and her face froze when she saw me. It seemed a universe of time that we regarded each other, the rawness of her betrayal warring with something far less ugly within my breast.

She rose slowly, gathering herself up like a flower springing from the earth. The man beside her moved almost imperceptibly forward; from the corner of my eye, I thought I saw him reach for a weapon at his waist.

"My lady." The words felt tight coming out of my mouth.

She curtsied. "My prince."

Any warmth that might've crept into my heart at the sound of her voice froze into midwinter. Even now, she was playing a game. Pretending.

I hazarded a glance at the man behind her; he seemed my age, and his face was shaped like hers. A brother, maybe? He stepped back, but his hand was on his weapon. Mara stepped forward. She wore breeches and a tunic that was too big for her—and she was as beautiful as ever.

And as treacherous.

"Damn you," I whispered.

Instead of answering, she addressed the crowd.

"A moment, please," she said.

Mara's probably-brother moved to gently urge the crowd back; the woman from the inn placed the basket on the blanket and helped him, hushing those in the crowd who were begging for a turn. The men grasping my arms let go and joined the others. Together they made a subtle arc around Mara, their expressions wary. Mara was a stone, an unmoving tree. If she was afraid of me, she didn't show it.

"Who are your friends?" I felt my voice would break from the strain of keeping it low.

"Friends."

My jaw tightened, and I forced the anger deep into my bones where it wouldn't show. "I've been looking for you."

"And we've been looking for you."

Cannon's blood. Father's choked-out last words. Ellian's screams. It all came rushing back with such force that I sucked in air through my teeth.

"Do they know you're a traitor? That you stood by while my father and brother were murdered in your name?"

Swish grabbed me by the neck. "Speak with respect or not at all, Thungrave."

"Swish, stop! Let him go." It wasn't a plea—it was a command.

He gave me a single shake before releasing me; I coughed once and tried to look at least a little dignified.

"I know how to stop the magic," Mara said evenly, "and I need your help."

So this was why her motley gang hadn't killed me on sight. She needed me.

But could I even believe her?

She turned to Swish. "Keep him at Wennie's until I'm finished here."

"Yes, Your Grace," Swish said. I wanted to take her by the hair and slam her into the ground. Yell at her face until she shrank away, small and defeated. Throw her from a high wall and watch her fall.

But that wouldn't solve the problem of the magic.

"Let's go, Thungrave."

He grabbed my arm and led me away.

47

MARALYTH

I watched Swish and the others lead Alac away. Nestar put his hand on my shoulder.

"Be careful, Mara," he said. "He may not see your heart, but I do."

I whirled to face him. "This has nothing to do with my heart."

The effort to heal the people and animals now seemed twice as great, though my magic flowed as smoothly as ever. Each time another strand would appear in the sky, someone would cry out, and I would stand and beckon to it—and it would come.

And each time my body drank in another strand, the crowd would cheer and hail their queen.

When the light had nearly faded, we sent the crowd home, which wasn't an easy task. Nestar and I walked back to Wennie's in mostly silence. With every step, my heart beat more wildly, knowing that Alac was waiting.

Knowing he hated me and probably wished me dead.

The front room was crowded and chaotic. Everyone looked at me as I walked in; it was clear they were eager to see this play out.

I found Swish. "Where is he?"

"Locked in your room." Swish handed me a key. "Are you ready to see him?"

"Yes. Alone."

"Not a good idea," Nestar said. "At least one of us should come with you."

"No," I said. "This is between Alac and me."

"There's an old man in there with him," Swish said.

I frowned. "What old man?"

"Thungrave claimed he was helping him search for you."

I thought for a moment. "If I want you to remove the old man, I'll call for you."

I headed toward my room, trusting Nestar to stop Swish from trying to interfere. When I reached the door, I forced myself not to hesitate. I turned the key in the lock and pushed the door open.

Alac stood there, his expression aloof—except for his eyes, which burned into me with a fire I couldn't name. Was afraid to name. His hands were tied. Wordlessly, he turned and sat on my bed. Then I noticed the old man sitting to his left, his head against the wall. He looked vaguely familiar, and when he sat up and looked at me, he seemed to know me, too.

Horror rose inside me as I recognized his eyes and the slope of his nose. "Tucker?"

"Believe it or not," he said.

Holy God, he looked ravaged—as though his lifeblood were fast fading. I'd seen so much of this over the past two days, though, that my reaction was short-lived. I knelt on the floor in front of him and laid my hand on his arm.

"Renew. Be young."

The wrinkled skin and white hair faded, and in the space of a minute or two, he looked like himself again.

I waited through several moments of breathless silence as he stared at his hands.

"*Cruce,*" he said before looking at me. "I . . . really don't know how to thank you."

"How do you feel?" The concern in Alac's voice made my heart ache.

Tucker slapped his hands against his chest. "Like myself. Like . . . I'm alive." He looked at me. "Thank you, Lady Maralyn."

"Or is it *Maralyth?*" The warmth in Alac's voice was gone. "The names are awfully similar; I wouldn't want to make a mistake."

"It's Mara. You needn't call me lady."

"No, I needn't." His expression crumbled momentarily, like he'd lost his resolve to be angry. But then his jaw hardened again. "Let me be clear. You're complicit in the deaths of my father and brother, and you conspired to take the throne. In that light, I owe you nothing—except maybe a death sentence."

My insides felt like dust. I pressed my mouth into a tight line and waited for him to continue.

"You said you need my help to stop the magic," he said. "How?"

"In the morning, I need you to take me to the castle and guarantee my safe passage," I said. "I need access to your father's chapel so I can claim the magic."

"*Claim* it?"

"Remember when magic sank into my eyes and seemed to disappear?" I waited for his nod. "The other day, the same thing happened with a larger strand of magic. And since then, I've absorbed many of the strands into my body. The magic came from the Dallowyns—and that's where it belongs. With the Dallowyns." I dared to meet his gaze. "With me."

Alac thought for a moment. "You're talking about wisps and strands. How do you know you could bear the entire amount?"

It wasn't as though I'd never thought about that. "I don't know. But I have to try."

He pressed his fist against his mouth, thinking. I waited, not wanting to upset what felt like a delicate balance.

"Two things," he finally said. "First of all, Tucker goes free."

An incredulous sound leaped from my throat. "So he can fetch an entire army to rescue you? I don't think so."

"Really, Alac, I'd rather not be a game piece," Tucker said.

"We're all game pieces here." Alac's eyes bored into mine. "You're asking for safe passage into a palace where everyone sees you as a murderer and usurper. I won't give it to you unless you release him."

Had I honestly thought he'd give me what I wanted without a price? "What's the second thing?"

"When I take you there, it will be as my prisoner."

My heart shuddered. If I'd had any small hope that Alac would soften when we met, that hope was now snuffed.

"You're hardly in a position to call *me* a prisoner," I said.

"This is *your* castle," Alac said. "When we're in *my* castle, it'll be a different story."

Yes. Quite different.

"I'll stand trial?" I hated the way my voice quavered.

"Yes."

"I see."

"You'd do the same thing if you were in my position," Alac said.

"If I were in your position, I would hope I'd listen to the whole story before passing judgment."

"My father and brother were *murdered*."

"And you weren't." I said it quietly, making myself keep eye contact.

"She has a point," Tucker said.

"You say you know how to stop the magic," Alac said. "You've lied at every turn, yet here I am, having to trust you, anyway. You know you deserve to stand trial for what you've done."

His words dug deep. "Will it be a fair trial?" My voice felt suddenly small.

"On my honor, yes," Alac said.

I hesitated; then I looked at Tucker. "Come with me, before I change my mind."

"You up for it, old man?" Alac asked.

"You can stop calling me that now," Tucker said. "And yes, I'm fine."

Alac let out a long stream of air. "Let the rest of my guard and the others who came on the search know that I'll be bringing Mara to the castle in the morning. Have them wait for us at the city gate."

Tucker nodded, then rose and followed me through the door, which I locked behind us. Swish and Nestar stood at the end of the hallway; their hands went to their daggers when they saw Tucker.

"Release this one," I said.

"Not an old man, after all," Swish said.

"No," I said. "And as part of my negotiations with Alac Thungrave, he goes free."

Swish narrowed his eyes. "Negotiations? He's our *prisoner*."

"And he has the power to either agree or disagree to get me safely inside that castle." I gestured toward Tucker with my chin. "Let him go."

Nestar and Swish exchanged glances. Then they lowered their weapons and stepped aside.

"As you wish, Your Grace," Nestar said, his words deliberate.

Tucker walked between them, then stopped and looked over his shoulder. "Thank you for . . . well, forty years, at least."

I nodded once and watched him go. Then, without looking at either Swish or Nestar, I returned to my room and unlocked the door. Alac looked up as I entered, but said nothing. I locked the door and sat on the other end of the bed.

"They let him go," I said.

Alac offered no words of thanks. He only looked at me with eyes that burned with accusation and unasked questions.

"Why haven't you performed the ritual?" I asked.

"I tried. I couldn't do it, because Ellian is pregnant with Cannon's son."

My breath caught. "But how could she know it's a boy?"

"Apparently the magic knows." He looked at me blandly. "Why are you doing this?"

"I care about the people of this kingdom." I said. "About everyone whose lives have been affected, one way or another, by stolen magic."

"My father's life was affected, and so was my brother's." Alac's words were edged in ice. "Did you care about them?"

A whisper was all I could muster. "I'm sorry."

"You're *sorry*?"

"I didn't want you to die." I hated the way my voice trembled.

"Am I supposed to thank you for that?"

I ground my teeth together until my jaw ached. When I'd subdued the angry words that wanted to come out, I trusted myself to speak.

"I don't need your thanks. I only need you to get me inside the chapel."

He was silent for several heartbeats, and he wouldn't look at me.

"Who are you?" he finally said, so softly I almost missed it. "How did you become Nelgareth's pawn?"

I weighed how much to tell him. The hard glint in his eyes reminded me to be careful.

"I was kidnapped," I said. "Nelgareth was paying people to find . . . magic users."

"And how did that turn into agreeing to murder my family?"

Self-control dissolved, and the words that came out were lined with a hard edge. "Your *family* was part of the long-standing scourge on our kingdom—a line of despotic kings that used their power to intimidate and manipulate, instead of ruling justly. Who brought prosperity to themselves instead of to their kingdom. You said yourself that you feared your father from the day you saw him perform the ritual. Why is it hard to understand that I might've believed that Perin Faye would be better off without him?"

"And better with you."

"It isn't about better—it's about birthright."

Alac's expression darkened. "The throne of Perin Faye is *my* birthright. Not yours."

"Then you have nothing to worry about." I was sure my words sounded as bitter as they tasted. "I'll stop the magic, and then you can have me tried and condemned—and the throne is yours."

A pained expression crossed his face, but he hid it quickly. "I suppose I'll be staying here for the night?"

"Not *here,*" I said. "I'm sure they'll put you somewhere."

"Would you at least do me the dignity of cutting this cord?" He lifted his hands. "It's not like I'm going anywhere."

I hesitated. Between the two of us, I was the one who had told all the lies. I knew I could trust him. "I'll have them cut it."

"I'd appreciate that."

I rose, my heart flooded with the realization that I had missed him. That my greatest personal loss had been his friendship—and the way he looked at me that made my stomach feel weightless. I'd secretly hoped our conversation would've gone better.

"I want to leave at first light," I said.

"My horse is stabled at The Bent Fork."

I nodded and opened the door, and he followed me to the front room. The buzz of conversation stopped as we entered, and Swish and Nestar approached us.

"Alac is going to take me to the castle in the morning," I said, loud enough so everyone could hear. "His horse is stabled at The Bent Fork, so someone will have to bring it here tonight."

Swish's words were taut. "Is there anything else, Your Grace?"

"Yes. Please cut the cords on his hands. He's given me his word that he won't try to leave."

❦

Nestar knocked on my door right as I was ready to blow out my candle for the night. I sat up in bed.

"What's wrong?"

"Nothing," he said. "Only that we've decided to follow you at a distance."

"Who's 'we'?"

"Swish and me and several others. You may trust Alac Thungrave, but we don't."

"Nestar, I—"

"The others don't know you well enough, Mara, but I can tell there's a piece missing in your story."

I sighed. "It doesn't matter. I have to do what's best for Perin Faye."

Concern spread across Nestar's face. "Tell me what you haven't told the others."

"After I take care of the magic, I'm going to be his prisoner."

"What!"

"Nestar, I have to do whatever it takes to contain this magic."

"But you'll be condemned to death!"

"The entire kingdom will be condemned to death if I don't do this."

"You've got an army, Mara. Let them fight for you."

"What army will fight for an imprisoned queen accused of treason?"

He sat heavily on the bed beside me and wrapped me in a hug. We stayed that way for a while, and it felt like all the nights he'd held me during thunderstorms, when I was little and silly and afraid of loud noises. Then he let me go.

"If the worst happens," I said, "tell Poppa how much I love him."

"He knows how much you love him." He rose to leave. "I'd rather tell him that you're queen."

48

ALAC

I slept on a lumpy sofa with someone different guarding me every couple of hours. Each time I woke throughout the night, I thought of Mara, just down the hall, so close. The room I was in felt empty, like there was nothing to breathe when she wasn't there.

Probably I should never have tried to find her on my own. This entire mess was my fault, as Tucker had been quick to point out.

Mara seemed confident that she could take care of the magic, but that wasn't what I was worried about. It was far easier to condemn her to death when she wasn't sitting across from me, wisps of hair framing her face and brushing her cheeks as she spoke.

Damn her! I couldn't forget what she'd done—how she'd deceived me. But what if she successfully reclaimed the magic? How would I look if I handed the girl who'd just saved the kingdom over to be tried and sentenced for treason?

I'd be the monster then, instead of her.

Did that even matter, though? She deserved to die.

Even though she'd saved my life. Twice.

My heart and head were tangled in an endless knot. And I'd be damned if I let my heart win.

✺

Maralyth's brother stood with my horse outside the inn. He looked at me with daggers in his eyes.

"See that nothing happens to her," he said.

"I've already given her my word," I said. "I don't need to answer to you."

The door opened and Maralyth stepped out—dressed not in breeches this time, but in a light-colored gown that hugged her waist and made me forget why I would ever want to be angry with her.

"Good morning," she said.

I couldn't answer. When I saw her face, listened to the distinct lilt of her voice, all my convictions wavered. I'd fallen for her from the moment she'd first stepped out of a carriage in the courtyard, and I didn't feel capable of unfalling. Every word poised on my tongue felt like it would lumber forth with a clumsiness that would let the world know that this girl unraveled me.

I couldn't let her know that. Couldn't let it show for a minute.

She's a traitor and a liar. Stop thinking of her in any other way.

She turned to her brother and the others who had come outside. "When the magic threads disappear, you'll know I was successful."

"Be careful, Maralyth," Wennie said softly.

My horse was eager to be on his way. Mara mounted with more grace than I'd expected, and I swung up behind her, excruciatingly aware of how close we were sitting. The thought of spending two hours smashed against that dress was nearly unbearable.

The trip wasn't a long one, but I feared it would seem interminable. I could smell her hair, feel her breathing. I was aware every moment of how my thighs were pressed against her, the heat of her igniting me no matter how I tried to fight it.

This was absolute madness. The girl had conspired with traitors to take the throne, and had almost succeeded. And here I was, burning for her like a lovesick donkey.

I grew steadily angrier until I noticed, to the left and right of the road, great swaths of dead trees. It was arbitrary; everything would look green and normal, and then we'd come upon three or four or fifteen trees that were twisted and barren.

"Is that—?" I said.

"Yes." I felt her sigh. "It's so widespread."

I looked up warily. A twisted strand of magic, almost creature-like, hovered for a moment over the treetops before fanning out and heading east.

"*Cruce,*" I said.

"Your locket will protect you," she said, "and I can take care of myself."

I half expected her to begin healing the trees, but she sat, silent and still, in the saddle and did nothing. The devastation seemed to get worse as we neared Crownhold. Then I saw the first bodies lying in the road—a horse and its rider, both looking as though they'd been dead for weeks.

Mara turned her face away. I couldn't help staring.

Half a mile later, we came upon another dead body, not quite as decomposed as the others, amid another cluster of dead trees and foliage. I steered the horse around it, only to encounter another one not a hundred paces away.

"Stop," Mara said. "He's not dead."

I reigned in the horse and she dismounted so quickly I almost didn't realize what she was doing. Without hesitating, she ran to the person's side. He was old and frail, barely able to sit up with her help. I watched, mesmerized, as she laid her hands on his shoulders. Beneath her touch, he grew young and strong, the way Tucker had—a boy who looked barely fifteen. Within moments, he was standing and embracing her, whole and well. They spoke quietly for a minute, and then he made his way toward Silverton.

I helped Mara back into the saddle. "What did you say to him?"

"I told him to go home to his family and tell them to remain hopeful."

She'd acted like a queen. Spoken like a queen. The knot in my stomach tightened.

We continued through the devastation—another dead horse, a wild dog that looked as though it were ready to drop of old age, and a carriage that had run into a tree, its driver slumped and rotten.

As we neared the city gate, the magic's effects became less evident, until soon there was mostly green. Perhaps Crownhold itself had been less touched because of the magic's propensity to travel. I was about to ask Mara what she thought about it when the sound of hoofbeats arrested me.

"That'll be the men I sent Tucker to gather."

I reined in and slowed to a walk. Moments later, at least sixteen riders rounded the bend, wearing the green and orange colors of Milchas, Lord of Fanley. In the midst of them, on a speckled-gray palfrey, sat Ellian, her hair in a dramatic twist on the top of her head. She looked very much the queen she didn't quite get to be.

"Lady Ellian," I called. "You're looking well this morning."

Milchas, her father, rode up beside her. When I saw that his hand was on the hilt of his sword, a dull warning rang in the back of my head.

"My prince," he said. "Your absence at the palace has been sorely felt."

"It was my intention to find Lady Maralyn," I said, "and I've done so." I waited for his response, but he gave none. "I was expecting some of my own men, but I'm glad to have your assistance in their absence."

Milchas turned to Ellian and looked as though he were waiting for her to speak. She met his gaze briefly, and then she looked directly at me, her chin raised.

"How is it that you came to find her?"

"It wasn't easy, I assure you."

Her expression hardened. "It seems obvious to us that you've been conspiring all along."

"Who is conspiring?" I kept my words light, though my pulse had begun to race.

"You and that *usurper,*" she practically spat. "The wine may have been in your cup, but you never intended to drink it."

"That's ridiculous."

"You are both equally responsible for the deaths of the king and Prince Cannon." She turned to her father. "Take them."

49

MARALYTH

Milchas's men closed in around us, a tight circle of horses that allowed no escape. I felt Alac tense behind me.

"This is a mistake," I said, wishing I could hide the tremble in my voice. "Prince Alac had no foreknowledge of the attack."

Ellian looked at me with eyes that held a sea of emotion. "I'm not listening to your lies. Bind them both."

Panic rose thick in my throat as I was forced to dismount and stand while my hands were bound behind me. It was like being kidnapped all over again, except this time I knew exactly where we were going—and why.

We were each tethered to a horse, then herded like cattle through Crownhold to the castle gate. Once inside, several men dismounted and, after removing us from the tethers, led us through the back entrance of the palace.

"This is ridiculous," Alac said. "I didn't conspire to kill my own father."

Silence.

"I'm sorry, Your Grace," one of the men finally said. "Lady Ellian has invoked the right of royal widow, and in your absence, her plea was upheld."

"The right of—but they were never married!"

"They would have been, had the crown prince not been murdered. Minister Frederin concurs."

Alac held his tongue for the rest of the forced walk. My thoughts were with Nestar and the others. They'd done a good job of staying well enough behind us that Alac never knew they were following.

Had they been close enough to see what happened? Would it even have made sense? And if it had, what could they possibly do?

When we reached the entrance to the dungeon, which was flanked by two guards, my heart quailed. Why would some of the crown's strongest supporters be so quick to wrongfully accuse the heir to the throne?

The stone staircase leading underground was lit at intervals by flickering torches set in iron holders. How many people were down here? Enough so that the stairwell was kept lit for the guards? During my stay in the palace, I'd never had a hint of what was going on in its bowels.

The steps were treacherous, especially with my hands tied behind my back. I faltered, so that the man behind me grabbed my arm and urged me downward; I almost lost my balance. By the time we reached the bottom, fear had encapsulated my heart, cold and immoveable. One of the men unlocked a thick, wooden door, then stepped aside.

The cell smelled of rot. It held nothing but a wooden bench and a chamber pot, and the earth floor was scattered with old, dirty straw. High on the left wall, a small, narrow window, lined with iron bars, mocked me with a promise of fresh air.

They cut our bindings and shut the door behind us with a resounding thud. The scraping and jolt of the bar on the other side offered a sense of finality that made my lungs feel too heavy to draw air.

Alac walked over to the wall and leaned both hands against it, head bowed. Not daring to encroach upon his personal torment, I sat on the bench, which was narrow and rough but better than the floor.

When Alac's silence became uncomfortable, I decided to break it.

"Did you think she was capable of this?"

"No." Alac spoke to the wall. "I knew she was eager to be queen, but . . . not this."

"Perhaps it's the magic," I said. "She's carrying the Thungrave heir, after all."

Alac turned to face me. "The night I tried to perform the ritual, she appeared just as I was failing. She told me she was hoping Cannon would somehow instruct her from the grave concerning the transferal of the magic to their child. Nothing she said made me suspect she'd try to take the throne herself."

"Her father might've influenced her—or even commanded her."

"I can't imagine Milchas coming up with something like this."

I had no answer. Figuring out the reason behind Ellian's behavior wasn't going to help us break free from this cell.

Something scuttled through the straw. I drew my feet up onto the bench and wrapped my arms around my legs, not wishing to be surprised by rat feet across my shoes. A sinking sense of dread enveloped me as I realized we had no answers—no way out.

Unless.

I rose and shuffled through the straw to the door. Placing my palm against it, I could feel the ancient, dull throb of life still whispering inside the long-dead wood. Magic almost spilled forth unbidden; I withdrew my hand.

"I can get us out," I said.

"How?"

"The door is mostly wooden. I can make it rot away."

Alac sank heavily to the floor and crossed his legs. "There will be guards."

Of course there would. I returned to the bench and drew my legs up again, away from the rats.

We sank into silence.

Holy God, how he must hate me. I wanted to think of something—anything—to say to fill in the empty minutes. To somehow lessen my growing fear. But words eluded me.

"Didn't it bother you that my family had to be murdered so you could have the throne?"

His question came out of nowhere, an arrow in the dark landing in the center of my conscience.

I sighed; nothing I said was going to sound right. "I tried to explain to Nelgareth about how killing your father would release the magic with nowhere to go. He chose to keep me in my room until the wedding breakfast instead of listening to me."

"You knew there was poison in those goblets."

"I didn't figure that out until moments before the wine was poured."

"And you said nothing—until my father had already drunk."

Words grew hot on my tongue. "Are you accusing me of wanting the throne, Alac Thungrave? Because I did. I do. Perin Faye was a prosperous kingdom with little poverty when the Dallowyns ruled. I grew up as the daughter of a vintner famous across all seven lord-lands, and yet there were nights when we barely had enough food to fill our bellies. You've never known hunger, or the fear that the crown would take even more of your father's earnings than it had the year before."

"I've known more fear than you can imagine."

"You know *nothing*." I didn't care how angry I sounded. "You've spent your life in luxury behind palace walls and never showed the least interest in a throne that might very well have been yours."

"I've changed my mind." Alac's words were tight. "I care about the people of Perin Faye, and I'm ready to be the king my father never was."

My heart thrummed relentlessly in my throat and my ears, Alac's revelation about his desire to be king so unexpected and raw. "So, here we are, then."

"Yes. Here we are."

A gloom settled over us, darker than the corners of our cell. I leaned my head against the cold, stone wall and closed my eyes. I thought of the magic strands, continuing to age and destroy everything and everyone in their path; I thought of the dark knot of magic in the chapel somewhere above my head, waiting to claim an innocent child as its next victim. I'd made it this far, only to be thwarted by the mother of the next Thungrave king.

It had all been for nothing.

A scraping at the lock jarred me from my stupor, and I sat up, my back railing against the sudden movement. Someone opened the door and placed a metal platter on the floor.

"Alac."

I looked up at the familiar voice; it was Tucker.

Alac rose. "What happened?"

"Lower your voice." I'd never seen Tucker so serious. "When I arrived last night, I could tell something was wrong. So I didn't say anything about you or Mara—I just returned to duty and tried to figure out what was going on."

"Didn't anyone question you?" Alac asked.

"Yes, but—look, I don't have much time."

"Can you get us out?" I couldn't help asking.

"I intend to," Tucker said. "But I can't just leave the door unlocked; it would arouse suspicion. And the dungeon master takes the key ring to his quarters every night."

"We don't need a key." Hope flared in my chest. "I can get rid of the door."

Tucker raised his eyebrows. "Well, then. Let me see what I can do about swapping our men for some of the guards posted along the way. Just, uh, don't do anything strange to the door until I can take care of the rest."

"Thank you, Tucker," I said.

He locked the door behind him, but this time I didn't feel quite as trapped. After a cursory check for rats, I crossed the cell to the platter, which contained two mugs of water and two hunks of dark, brown bread. Alac handed me one of the pieces of bread, and I grabbed a mug and returned to the bench, where I ate and drank woodenly, my eyes on the too-small window.

"They must have a special store of dry bread," Alac said through a mouthful.

I cupped my own bread, which was dry and difficult to chew, between my hands, instinctively reaching out with my magic to the heart of the grain from which the flour came. "Be fresh," I whispered, and the bread softened beneath my touch.

I crossed the cell and rested my hand on Alac's bread to freshen it. My fingers brushed his as I worked my magic, and an unbidden thrill traveled up my arm and into some hidden place inside me.

"Thanks," he said gruffly.

I returned to the bench, my heart beating too quickly.

After a while, we spoke of what it would mean for the king of Perin Faye to stand trial. We didn't mention the obvious fact that my own trial would be swift and sure—I'd allowed myself to be declared queen, which was treason, clear and simple.

Our words eventually faded along with the afternoon sun through its small portal. When it had grown almost completely dark, sounds from outside the door rattled me into attentiveness. I rose from the uncomfortable bench and squinted as torchlight stabbed my dark-deadened eyes. Alac rose as well, and we stood there, momentarily blinded. My stomach roiled with hunger and I dearly hoped it was a tray of supper.

Ellian, dressed in an evening gown of white damask that almost glowed against the darkness of the cell, stepped in. In one hand, she held a torch aloft, and in the other she held Alac's book, *The Gift of the Holy God*. Behind her stood two guards, also bearing torches. And behind them stood High Minister Zeth.

His face was unreadable in the torchlight. Had he so quickly shifted his loyalty to Cannon's widow?

"Where is it?" Ellian snapped.

"Where is what?" Alac's tone was flat with understated defiance.

"The scroll with the words. The one Cannon gave you."

"And what would you do with that?" Alac asked. "You can't take the magic."

"Not for myself, no. But for my son."

"If you try, the magic will kill you," Alac said softly. "You saw what happened to me."

"That happened because I carry Cannon's son, the true heir! As his mother, I can receive the magic on his behalf. Do you think me incapable of studying the Thungrave magic? I was destined to be queen!"

"That doesn't mean—"

"*A mother carrying the heir can be a conduit for the transfer of power, should the need arise,*" Ellian said, shaking the book as she spoke. "That's what it says, right here!"

I almost pitied her for the way she hungered for magic that wasn't hers.

"Let me end this," I said. "Your son doesn't need to be a slave to this magic."

She turned on me like a striking snake. "You are a *traitor* and deserve to die. I have nothing to say to you."

"The magic will kill you," I said.

Ellian stood taller. "You're *wrong*. I've already opened the receptacle—without being harmed. The magic recognizes the true heir." She turned again to Alac. "All I need is the scroll."

"You can't have it," Alac said.

Barely contained anger twisted Ellian's face; in the play of light and shadow, she didn't even look like herself. "I'm going to ask you once more."

"And I'm going to say no once more."

"You'll rot in here, do you know that?" But her voice trembled in a way that didn't match the force of her words.

"And meanwhile, the strands of magic will increase and spread over the land, aging and killing everything in their path."

"*Your* fault! Give me the scroll and I will take the magic and end the destruction."

Alac hesitated, and for a moment I thought he would give in.

"I'm not giving you the scroll," he said.

"Fine." She stepped aside and motioned to the guards, who moved forward. "Perhaps you'll change your mind in the morning, when your lady friend is taken for questioning. They have ways to make her talk that will send her screams all the way to your ears."

Alac swallowed audibly. "Ellian, stop this."

She narrowed her eyes—to me, she looked like a child playing at being queen. "You conspired to have your brother killed. But his son is going to be the king you could never be, if it means flaying every inch of skin from her bones."

"Your Grace, let me stay and talk sense into the boy," Zeth said.

Ellian crossed her arms and looked petulant. "You're welcome to try, High Minister. The guards will stay with you."

"Let them wait at the entrance," Zeth said gently. "I'm in no danger here."

I expected Ellian to protest, but she handed him the torch and swept from the cell.

Zeth affixed the torch into a holder on the wall, and, surprisingly, sat cross-legged in the filthy hay. Alac and I sat on the bench.

Alac's words had an edge. "What are you playing at, Zeth?"

"I've always been fond of you, and I truly wish you no harm." Zeth's words were quiet, unadorned. "But my one, great secret is that I'm a Dallowyn."

It was the last thing I'd expected him to say. I glanced at Alac—he looked stunned.

"In fact," Zeth went on, "I've supported the Dallowyn cause for many years." He looked at me. "It's because of me that your supporters have been able to receive messages from inside the castle."

Alac found his voice. "How? What messages?"

"I donned a cowl and assumed the role of a Brother of the Holy God, sneaking out at night. Hungry children make good messengers."

Just as Swish had told me! I remembered the Brother I'd seen skulking through a dark hallway in the palace. Had that been Zeth, sneaking out to send his messages?

"If you're a Dallowyn," I asked, "why not claim the throne for yourself?"

"I'm a descendant of Tommas, Wexen's bastard son," Zeth said. "I have no magic and no claim to the throne."

I stared at him—we both did—silence curling around us like winter bedding. He touched his long braid, which hung, as usual, over the front of one shoulder.

"All the men in my family have plaited their hair in the front, just so—our secret symbol of loyalty to our name and our heritage." He crossed his hands over his heart. "I'm afraid you now know everything about me."

Realization dawned. "Did you write *The Gift of the Holy God*?"

"Yes, with help from the extensive notes of Tommas Dallowyn himself. But the part I left out—for obvious reasons—was that Tommas sired a son before Selmar I murdered him. The son, of course, had no magic, since Tommas had removed it from his own bloodline. He was raised in hiding and given his true identity when he was old enough to appreciate it. Once he was grown, he hoped he could somehow right the wrongs of his father and restore Perin Faye to Dallowyn rule."

"But he didn't," I said.

"No, he didn't." Zeth sighed, as though his words were weighty. "My father was zealous about the Dallowyn cause, but he died young.

I continued his search for Dallowyn descendants shortly after his death. My sleuthing led me to a remote monastery of Brothers—the Order of the Lily, where I found a full-blooded Dallowyn wearing cowls and spending his days in prayer."

"Brother Shervan," I whispered.

"Yes," Zeth said. "He wasn't young—past forty, certainly—but still able to sire children. I convinced him to agree to a secret marriage with the youngest daughter of the Lord of Draper's Down, who'd opted for a religious life over an unsavory marriage chosen by her father. It took less convincing for her than it had for Brother Shervan."

"Nelgareth mentioned him," I said. "He meant to place him on the throne if he didn't find someone . . . younger."

Zeth nodded, not looking at all surprised. "Shervan's young wife miscarried their first child several months into the pregnancy. She was forced out of the convent, which turned out to be a good thing. I provided her with a small cottage where she could enjoy conjugal visits with her husband, and sometimes I also sneaked her into the monastery." He allowed himself a small smile before continuing. "It took almost a year," Zeth said, "but she conceived again. And this time, she bore a healthy daughter, whom they named Fawn. Shervan was so thrilled to be a father that he wanted to abandon his life at the monastery, but I counseled him not to do it. Stealth was so important for our plan to succeed.

"When Fawn was four, her mother died giving birth to a stillborn child. Under my influence, Fawn was brought to the convent, as was the practice for orphans. She was placed under the care of the very Sisters who had cast her mother out. And Shervan was able to spend time with his daughter."

"Did she know he was her father?" I asked.

"No," Zeth said. "But she did know that she was a Dallowyn—and that she would have to keep that—and her magic—a secret. I was busy gathering information, finding out who would support a Dallowyn claim to the throne, when Fawn was suddenly adopted by a noble family. It was all done secretly, and we had no idea where she had gone. My well-laid plans lay in tatters—and Shervan was unwilling to begin again with a new wife. He mourned the loss of his little girl."

He fell silent, and when he turned his gaze toward me, it was almost fatherly. "You can guess, can't you, who that little girl was?"

"My mother."

"*Cruce.*" It was the first sound Alac had uttered since Zeth began his tale.

"I eventually learned that she'd been adopted by a family in Northland whose own daughter had succumbed to an illness," Zeth continued. "It's a great scandal in Northland to be childless, so they adopted a girl the same age—and she took the other one's place."

"And she grew up to marry Nelgareth's older brother," I said, "and made the mistake of telling him her true bloodline."

"Yes." Zeth looked thoughtful. "The only puzzle piece I couldn't find—and apparently Nelgareth did—is what actually became of her. What's your real name?"

"Maralyth Graylaern, of Graylaern Vineyards. My father married my mother after his first wife died."

"Maralyth Graylaern." Alac spoke my name as though he were testing it, to see if it was really mine.

"When I first saw you and noticed how much you looked like your mother," Zeth said, "I was convinced our Dallowyn queen had made her way to the castle that was rightfully hers."

That explained why his gaze had lingered uncomfortably long when we first met. "Did you know about the coup?"

"I suspected," Zeth said. "Nelgareth would never have been careless enough to let his plans reach the ear of the king's High Minister."

"If they had, would you have tried to stop it?" Alac's jaw was so tight I almost saw it trembling.

"Nelgareth was a powerful man," Zeth said.

"Coward," Alac said. "That's no answer at all."

"I'm sorry to disappoint you, my prince." He rose with some effort and brushed the straw from his robe. "Don't give Ellian the scroll. I will do whatever it takes to dissuade her from carrying out her threats."

"You'll do *nothing*." Alac rose and stepped forward. "Your words mean *nothing*."

"I know you feel—"

Alac shoved him. "Get out of here. Spin your webs with someone else."

I rose quickly, ready to stop Alac from doing anything more. Zeth gave me a sidelong glance. Then he bowed and retrieved the torch from the wall.

At the door, he turned and looked directly at me. "If there's any way I can help, I will."

"Get. Out." Alac's words were pressed through clenched teeth.

Zeth pulled the heavy door open, then pulled it shut behind him, leaving us in utter darkness.

50

ALAC

In the black silence, my breaths sounded disproportionately loud. I heard the creak of the bench as Mara sat on it. Shuffling across the dirt floor with one arm out, I found my way to her, hitting my boot against the side of the bench before acclimating and sitting beside her. She shifted away from me.

"All these years." My voice trembled with anger. "He's been High Minister *all these years,* and it was a lie."

"But if he can convince Ellian to—"

"I don't want him to do *anything.*"

She sighed—a tremulous sound that made me want to touch her. "I'm sorry. For everything."

"But you still want the throne."

"I just apologized to you!"

It was my turn to sigh. "There isn't any way around this."

"Right now, we're on the same side," she said, "whether we want to be or not."

Was being locked in the same cell the same as being on the same side? I wasn't sure.

"Unless Tucker finds a way to clear a path for us, they'll take you for questioning in the morning. She wasn't kidding when she talked of flaying you." I realized in a maddening moment of clarity that I didn't want anyone to hurt her. "If Tucker doesn't come through, I'll have to tell her where the scroll is."

She was silent for a moment. "If you give her the scroll and she's successful, you will at least have saved the kingdom from the strands of magic."

"And handed them a power-hungry, sixteen-year-old sorceress."

"Yes. And nothing will have changed."

From the darkness of this dungeon, I had the power to save Perin Faye from an onslaught of magic run amok by handing it to Ellian. She'd still see to it that Mara and I were both put to death, but at least the stolen magic would once again be contained.

"You should have let me die," I said. "It would've been less complicated."

"Yes," she said, "but I wouldn't have been able to live with myself."

Did I mean something to her? And if I did, why should I care? I leaned my head against the wall and lapsed into silence. The heat of her body, inches from mine, made me aware of every movement, every breath I took.

"I can't believe you're Doreck Graylaern's daughter."

"Yes." Her voice sounded misty. "I miss him every day."

There was an openness in her words that I'd never felt. Or perhaps that was because, in the complete darkness of our cell, we were both stripped of anything else that might come between us. A portion of my well-tended anger softened to pity.

"You said you were kidnapped."

"I was."

"Who kidnapped you?"

"Secret Dallowyn supporters that Nelgareth paid to find someone in the direct Dallowyn line," she said. "One of them worked for my father."

"But how did the daughter of Doreck Graylaern end up with Dallowyn blood?"

I didn't think she'd answer; already it felt as though I'd pushed my questions to the limit. But to my surprise, she launched into a tale that kept me utterly captivated—a bride given to Nelgareth's older brother when Nelgareth himself had wanted her; a failed coup and a runaway wife who ended up marrying Doreck Graylaern.

"What made you say yes to Nelgareth?"

"He offered to forgive a Firstfruits discrepancy in my father's records, and to pay him three hundred pieces of silver. He also threatened my father's life."

Something deep inside me shifted. "You said yes under duress?"

"I did," she said. "But your father's errors were well documented, and his reign of terror well known. I began to think I might be able to make a difference."

"As queen."

She hesitated for only a moment. "Yes."

A storm of emotion battered me from the inside; I felt almost as though I were a ten-year-old boy, wanting to ask questions with answers that might scare me.

"Why did you save me?" The question stumbled out, awkward, cracked.

"Because . . ." I could feel her unspoken words pressing against the air between us. "You're kind. And you care about people. And you didn't deserve to die."

I tried to swallow the dryness in my mouth. "And my father and brother did?"

"No one deserves to die." Her words fluttered like bits of paper. "But the plan was in motion and I'd committed to my part. Up to the very day of the attempted coup, I believed I could make things better for the people of our kingdom. But I'd gotten to know you, and . . ." Her voice trailed off.

"Didn't you stop to think that, by saving me, you'd sabotage Nelgareth's entire plan, anyway?"

"Yes," she whispered. "But I wouldn't let myself think about that. I only wanted to save you."

My heart beat relentlessly against my skull, my neck, my chest. I knew in the depth of my soul that I'd never meet anyone like her again; not that I'd have the chance. The same mess she'd created in my heart before the coup—before life exploded—was there, twisting me into knots with every word she spoke. This damnable, conspiring girl had lied every day I'd known her—until now. And through everything she'd shared in this black cell, I began to see that what I'd known of her was very much the same as what she was showing me right now.

She was quiet for a little bit. Then she said, "Please forgive me, Alac."

The way she said my name drained anger from my heart like water. But could I forgive her?

"If Nelgareth hadn't had you to use for his plan, he would've used someone else," I said.

"But I said yes," she said.

"Which made it easier for him."

"Alac, I—" She hesitated, drawing words from some unknown depth. "I can't pretend you and I aren't at serious odds. Nelgareth's army—*my* army—is ready to fight for my right to the throne."

"No army can help you do what you really need to do to save this kingdom," I said.

"Yes," she said softly. "That's true."

In a moment of either boldness or sheer stupidity, I reached blindly for her face. When my fingertips found her cheek, she inhaled sharply, as though I'd startled her. The softness of her cheek as I cupped my hand around it shot fire into my loins with such force that I almost forgot how to breathe. I lost my fingers in her hair as I stroked her cheek with my thumb, brushing the edge of her lips just enough to feel her breath on my palm.

"I wish things could've been different for us," I said.

"Me, too." Barely audible, but echoing in my heart like an entire chorus.

I drew her to me until our noses bumped. The heat of a thousand flames threatened to consume me, but I guided her mouth to mine and brushed it with a single kiss. Soft. Sweet as wine. And not nearly enough. Then I wrapped my arm around her, and she rested her head on my shoulder—so naturally that it was like she'd been doing it her whole life.

I offered a silent prayer that Tucker would come through. If he didn't, I'd give the scroll to Ellian in the morning. Because there was no way in damnation I'd let them lay a hand on Mara.

Even if it was the last kind thing I'd ever do for her.

51

MARALYTH

I had no idea how long I'd been sleeping. Alac's arm was still around me, strong and warm. His very presence made the darkness less smothering. I shifted, trying to alleviate the stiffness in my legs, and his other arm came up around me, though he slept.

The memory of his kiss danced before me, my lips tingling as though it had happened moments ago. Everything I'd fought had come boiling to the surface, a tempest in my heart that could no longer be contained. He'd asked me why I'd saved him, and my answer hadn't begun to express what my heart didn't have words for.

There was no sign that morning was anywhere close; it was likely I'd only slept for an hour or two. A rapid rustling through the straw set my nerves on edge; mice in the pantry were one thing, but rats in a dark dungeon made my skin curl.

It seemed the world was ending. Every sound, however faint, made me jump through my skin, hoping against hope that Tucker had returned. There was no scrape of a lock, though. No whispers at the door.

We'd sit here until morning, Alac and I, and when the men came to drag me away, Alac would give up the scroll's location to Ellian, and what then? My opportunity to claim the magic would be forever gone—and so would Perin Faye's one chance to be free from the Thungrave curse.

The longer I sat in the smothering darkness, the more restless I became. What if Tucker never showed up? We'd have given up hope of escape without even trying.

I couldn't sit here and wait for fate to spell out its hand like that.

Alac stirred, and I gently extricated myself from his arms, not

wanting to wake him yet, in case he tried to talk me out of this. My
eyes pressed against the dark in a futile attempt to make out the di-
mensions of the cell. Another smattering of animal footsteps almost
made me change my mind—but I gritted my teeth and sank to my
hands and knees on the floor. I cringed as I crawled, the filthy hay
giving way to the dirt beneath it with a limp crunch. I felt my way to
the wall, which grazed my head sooner than I'd expected to reach it.
I rose, hands splayed across the stone, feeling. Sensing.

I moved to the right, groping for the door, heart pounding, eyes
blind. The magic burned and hummed beneath my skin, reaching out
to the life that was once in the wooden planks of the dungeon door.

"Mara?" Alac's voice sounded groggy.

"I'm by the door," I said.

"What are you doing?"

"Freeing us."

The bench creaked as he rose. "Is Tucker here?"

"No," I said. "I'm tired of waiting."

He said nothing more, merely waited in the dark to see what I
would do. My hands found the door, and I pressed them against it,
power roaring in my palms.

"Rot," I said. "Become dust."

The wood shifted beneath my hands, cracking and buckling and
softening, as though seasons passed with every heartbeat. I heard
movement from the other side of the door, the creaking of armor. The
door became dust, its handle falling to the floor, its iron bar crashing
onto the threshold. The startled guard reached for his weapon, but I
stepped forward and extended my hand toward his chest.

"Be drowsy," I said. "Sleep."

He staggered once, then fell heavily to the floor. Alac was by my
side in a heartbeat, blinking in the flickering torchlight, which felt
brighter than a million stars to my light-deprived eyes.

"*Cruce,* Mara."

"There were two guards at the entrance to the dungeon when they
brought us," I said. "I don't think I can put them both to sleep at once."

Alac thought for a moment. Then he took the sword from the
sleeping guard.

"You go through first and take the one on the right," he said.

I nodded, not wanting to give voice to my fear that one or both of us might not be fast enough. We made our way up the treacherous stairs, our footsteps light and careful. By the time we reached the door at the top, my heart had nearly beat its way out of my chest. The door's handle was on the left; I curled my hand around it and counted to three.

I pulled it open and leaped through to the right. The surprised guard reached for his sword as I pressed my hand against his arm and willed him to sleep. He dropped like a stone as a loud cry issued from the other guard.

I turned in time to see him draw his sword as Alac attacked. Their weapons clashed, and the guard called again for help.

Soon the whole castle would be awake.

I ran in a short arc around them, trying to get a clear view of the guard as the two fought. The last thing I needed was to accidentally put them both to sleep.

The moment appeared suddenly, and I extended my hand toward the guard. "Sleep."

He staggered, then fell to his knees, his sword clattering to the flagstone. He crumpled the rest of the way as Alac leaped around him and gestured.

"This way."

Footsteps were fast approaching—the guard's yell had done its damage. Alac and I ran down the dimly lit hallway and around the first corner, where we pressed our backs against the wall and listened.

"Damn," Alac whispered as the footsteps continued to draw nearer.

We were in a minor corridor leading to meeting chambers and rooms for less important guests—running this way would only take us farther from the king's chapel. But Alac gestured to the first door on the right, which stood ajar. Could we make it?

"Split up," came a command as our pursuers approached the intersection.

Too late.

The first guard turned the corner and saw me, his shouts echoing to the others that we'd been found. His grip was steel as he pulled me by the arm into the main corridor. I extended my free hand toward him, but he reacted before I was able to speak the words, taking my wrist and twisting my arm behind my back. I yelped in pain, the magic burning within me as it stuttered to a halt.

Alac stepped forward. "Let her go, Ulmer, you oaf."

"I serve Queen Ellian—not you."

We were quickly surrounded by five or six other guards, and the fight went out of me.

"Drop your sword," Ulmer said.

Alac's gaze darted from one end of the line of soldiers to the other, as though weighing his chances. Then, slowly, he lowered his arm. The sword clattered angrily onto the stone floor.

Ulmer's grasp on my arms tightened. "I'm not sure how they escaped."

"We'll figure it out once we've taken them back," another guard said. "Someone's going to take the blame."

Two of the others moved in and took Alac by each arm. He struggled once, then seemed to think better of it.

"Let's go," one of them said.

Then, suddenly, the guard directly in front of me fell forward in a spray of blood, a blade protruding from the front of his neck. Cries rang out and the soldiers turned to fight their unseen assailants. Ulmer drew his sword as he pulled me back away from the fighting. As soon as he let go, I raised my palm toward him.

"Sleep," I whispered, then leaped out of his way as he folded himself like a parchment at my feet, his sword clanging to the floor. I grabbed it, though it was too heavy for me, and ran away from the chaos, pressing my back against the wall and trying to make out what was happening. The soldiers who had been holding Alac had joined the fight, and Alac retrieved his own sword and entered the fray.

It was over quickly, and five guards lay dead. Averting my gaze, I walked toward the group of soldiers that had launched the deadly attack. One of them stepped forward.

"Is there a reason you didn't wait for me?"

Tucker! And I now recognized the others with him as members of Alac's guard.

"Mara decided you were taking too long," Alac said.

"It took a bit of subtlety," Tucker said. "The timing had to be right."

"I couldn't risk losing the opportunity," I said, placing Ulmer's sword carefully onto the floor.

Tucker raised an eyebrow. "Good to know who's boss."

I turned to Alac. "We need to get to your father's chapel."

"Ellian might've posted a guard, but we should outnumber them," Tucker said.

Alac looked at me. "Mara can take care of them."

We moved catlike through the corridors, Tucker leading and the rest of Alac's guard flanking and following. By the time we'd climbed the stairway and reached the window-lined corridor outside the king's chambers, I was trembling inside my skin, fearful with every step that someone would hear, someone would see. I hoped Tucker was wrong about the additional guards.

But two figures stood in half-shadow on either side of the chamber door. Instinctively, I hung back, allowing the guards to approach.

"Do I know you?" Tucker said to the nearer guard.

"I serve her royal highness, Queen Ellian."

"Is that so?" Alac's voice.

"Is there a problem?" Clearly he was someone from Ellian's household; he didn't seem to recognize Alac.

I stepped forward, both hands raised toward the guard. "Sleep."

His knees buckled, and he fell to the floor, silent. The other guard's eyes went wide, and he dropped his sword with a clatter. We left both guards to two of Alac's men, who set to binding and gagging them. The rest of the guards took posts on either side of the door, alternately staring at me and exchanging glances with each other. Tucker stood with Alac.

I placed my hand on Alac's as he reached for the knob. "What if she's asleep in there?" I whispered.

"Then I guess we'll be waking her."

We slipped through the door, and I closed it gently behind us while Alac fumbled in the dark with a flint to light some candles. Moments later, soft candlelight danced across the magnificent room, so fit for a king. Or a queen.

My breath caught as we entered the sleeping chamber, the mounds of pillows on the bed fooling me into thinking someone was in it. The bed was empty, though, its covers unrumpled.

Instead of opening the drawer of the bedside table, Alac reached inside his tunic for the chain on which the blood locket still hung. The key hung beside the locket; Alac set down his candle so he could unlock the chapel door.

But it stood slightly ajar.

For a moment, nobody moved. Then Tucker stepped forward, sword ready. He pushed the door open; it swung soundlessly on well-oiled hinges. The only light inside the chapel came from the red lamp hanging above the altar and a much paler glow from the receptacle beneath it.

I stepped closer, just behind Alac. My skin buzzed, and the enormity of the magic within the chapel caused the magic within me to sing with fierce longing. And then my blood froze in my veins.

Ellian stood before the receptacle, her hands on the hourglass, her arms wet with blood.

52

ALAC

It was as though Ellian hadn't heard us. She stood, statue-like, dressed in nothing but a white shift stained red by the blood that poured down her arms. In one hand, she held the jeweled dagger; the other hand held tightly to the door of the receptacle. The blood locket burned against my chest.

I gentled my voice. "Ellian."

Slowly, she turned her head. Her eyes were dark, haunted. Like Father's. Her face twisted into a sneer of rage so ugly that she seemed more monster than girl.

"Who let you out?"

"No one," I said. "We left."

"I've searched everywhere," she said. "Give them to me."

"I have nothing to give you."

"Give me the words! They're mine. They're *mine.*"

"She's gone mad," Tucker said under his breath.

"Step away," I said. "There are no words."

"Sleep," Mara breathed, hand extended.

Nothing happened.

Ellian turned back to the receptacle, magic funneling up from it like a possessed storm, reaching to the mass on the ceiling that seemed twice as dense as the last time I'd been here. "The breath. The blood. The words."

"Ellian, step away."

"Keep her talking," Mara whispered. "I need to get between her and the receptacle."

She didn't wait for my response; she simply moved forward, light from her candle dancing before her. Tucker circled around to the right, sword poised.

Ellian took the dagger and made a long slice on the back of the already-cut hand that held the receptacle door. If it caused any pain, she didn't show it. She continued to stare at the hourglass, its pale luminescence creating a strange, bluish aura around her.

"This isn't safe," I said, realizing how stupid that sounded. "Step away."

"The magic doesn't want you." Ellian's voice was wooden. "It wants me. My son."

"The words are gone," I said. "It's over."

"It's *not* over."

Mara was less than an arm span away from her. I saw her make the slightest signal to Tucker, who stood ready to disarm Ellian and pull her away from the receptacle.

In a hot second, Ellian grabbed Maralyth around the neck and pointed a dagger at her throat. "Give me the words or I'll kill her."

Mara caught my gaze, offering the tiniest shake of her head.

"Ellian, put down the knife."

"Give me the words!"

Tucker made the slightest movement in Ellian's direction. The mantle of magic that surrounded her swelled like a sudden storm, shoving Tucker back with such force that he hit the wall and lay utterly still on the stone floor. Mara cried out, and Ellian tightened her grip on Mara's neck.

Ellian's words were cold and hollow. "Give me the words, and she lives."

I didn't believe her. But I had to do something—anything—to stay her hand and find a way to thwart her so that Mara could take the magic.

"Fine. I'll get the scroll. But if you touch her while I'm gone, I'll burn it where I stand, so help me Holy God."

"You have fifteen minutes."

"Alac—" But Ellian jerked her forearm against Mara's neck, causing her to cough.

I met her gaze, trying to reassure her with the subtlest expression that I'd figure things out. Even though I had no idea what I was going to do.

"Fifteen minutes, Alac Thungrave," Ellian said.

Cruce. That wasn't enough time to think of anything.

∾

I ran through corridors and up and down stairs like a madman, trying to come up with a plan. When I reached my quarters, I threw myself through the doorway and lit the first lamp I could find.

The chambers had been ransacked. Desk drawers were open, papers and books and bottles of inks scattered everywhere. My bed had been torn apart, the covers and pillows thrown all about. There wasn't a single trunk or shelf or drawer that hadn't been torn into or cleared off.

At least I'd hidden the scroll well.

I fell to my knees and removed the loose stone beneath my bed. The scroll case was tucked inside the empty space, where I'd left it.

Ellian would recognize the case—she'd seen it before. But, as far as I knew, she'd never seen the actual scroll. At least, I hoped that was true.

I rummaged through the mess and found a fresh scroll and writing materials. Was there time for ink to dry? I didn't know. I was out of options.

I unrolled the real scroll and weighted it down with whatever I could grab—a book, a letter opener. Then I copied it, changing a word or a letter here and there, rendering it useless.

Holy God, please let this ink dry.

It had to have already been at least ten minutes. When I felt like I could wait no longer, I rolled the false scroll into the case and held the real one to the lantern flame—it went up in smoke with an unnatural hiss.

Scroll case in hand, I ran back to my father's quarters, knowing I'd have to act fast once Ellian realized the words weren't real. Or even faster, if she decided to slit Mara's throat regardless of my handing over the scroll.

They stood where I'd left them, the dagger still pressed to Mara's throat. Ellian's bright eyes rested on me the moment I walked through the chapel door. Then her gaze fell to the scroll case in my hand.

"That's it." Her eyes glowed with magic lust. "Bring it to me."

"Release her," I said, "and I'll give it to you."

"No." She dragged Mara backward, so that they were pressed against the altar. "Lay it by the receptacle, and I'll release her."

I fought the panic that rose in my chest, wondering if I could be quick enough to outsmart Ellian and the magic. Slowly and deliberately, I walked to the table on the left—the one I'd hidden beneath all those years ago. I opened the scroll case and withdrew the fresh scroll. Then I took a lit candle from the table and held it aloft, the scroll in my other hand.

"Put the dagger down," I said, "or I'm burning the scroll."

Ellian's eyes went wild, like the rabid dog that attacked me by the falls. "You're as stupid and willful as Cannon always said!" She released Mara, but continued to press the dagger into her neck. I could see a thin trail of blood where the blade had cut her, running between her collar bones and inside her clothing.

Tucker stirred. I forced myself not to look at him as I slowly closed the distance between us, scroll held before me, eyes on Mara. As soon as I was close enough, Ellian snatched the scroll and made a triumphant sound in her throat.

"The breath, the blood, the words," she whispered.

She unrolled the scroll—awkwardly, because one hand still held the dagger to Mara's throat. I held my breath while she read, waiting for her to notice that something was wrong.

But she didn't.

She faced the altar and dropped the dagger next to the receptacle, Mara forgotten. And she began to recite the words I'd written.

Mara threw me a look of horror, but I shook my head and motioned for her to move away from the altar. Before she had a chance to, though, Ellian stopped reading and turned to face me. Her expression was horror-filled, and her mouth worked silently for a few seconds.

"What have you done?" she croaked.

"Saved Perin Faye from another monster," I said.

Her face went blank. Then livid. Just as Mara reached for the dagger, Ellian yelled with rage unlike anything I'd heard, thrusting Mara away from her with strength that belied her size. Mara fell against the altar as Ellian came at me, dagger poised to kill.

The blood locket was still in my hand. Instinctively, I fisted it and held it out, arm extended. It burned hot—so hot I wanted to drop it. But I yelled through the pain as a white-hot stream of light burst from between my fingers and hit Ellian in the face.

She yelled and dropped the dagger, then pressed her hands against her cheeks, face contorted with pain.

"Stop! It's mine!" She staggered toward me. "It's mine!"

She threw her head back and let out a long, high-pitched scream. The light enveloped her, so blinding I closed my eyes.

Then it was over. Ellian lay in a heap, eyes staring, a single stream of blood running from the corner of her mouth.

I dropped the locket; it clattered to the stone floor as my palm throbbed in the cool air. By now, Mara was on her feet again. Above her, the dark cloud raged and swirled, a tornado of power that made my skin itch and my heart yearn, even now.

Tucker rose to his feet and said something I couldn't hear. I shook my head, unable to tear my gaze from what was happening. Maralyth reached for the receptacle and I almost cried out, making her stop. I'd touched the hourglass, and it had tried to kill me. But she took it in her hands and removed it from the receptacle effortlessly. Then she turned around and held it above her head, arms straight.

I stood, drinking in her wild beauty even as my heart writhed with terror that I was losing her. That the magic was too great. Even now, I knew I'd give up everything if only I could have her. She closed her eyes and threw her head back as the dark pillar moved from the receptacle to the hourglass, pulling the rest of the magic like a tether. The cloud descended toward her, thick tendrils reaching and spiraling around her, encasing her, squeezing into her like fingers of death.

And she began to age.

Her hair lengthened, whitened. Her skin wrinkled like crumpled paper and her body twisted. Still the magic came, faster and more furiously.

I lunged forward and a scream tore through my throat as Tucker pulled me back, away from her destruction.

Away from her death.

53

MARALYTH

I was fire.

Wind.

A universe of exploding stars.

The magic came to me like a wayward sheep, like a retreating army, like a swarm of bees. I opened myself to it, a yawning portcullis to my soul, and it rushed through, all ice and motion and the complexities of time. I drank of it like a parched traveler, swallowed it in great, heaving gulps. It rushed in through my hands, my mouth, my heart.

I felt it claim me. Time rushed through me like wind, stripping my youth and twisting my bones like old tree branches.

Then the aging stopped—and reversed. I felt myself strengthen, straighten. My tired frame grew strong and I wanted to laugh. To sing. To dance to the edges of eternity.

Every breath I took was pure magic. Every beat of my heart was bathed in the dark mist that filled me fuller than I'd ever felt. The weight of it pushed me to my knees, and still it came, barreling into me without hesitation, without mercy. The magic already inside me welcomed it, made room for it, melded with it.

I was blinded by the thickness of the mist. Deafened by the roaring of the magic.

I was too small. Every inch of me had been filled, yet the magic continued to pour in, and I had nothing left. I fell to my side and curled into the hourglass, too exhausted to do anything more while the magic had its way with me. I tried desperately to stretch myself beyond capacity, to make space where I knew there was no more.

And still the magic came, relentless and determined.

Then it was over. The hourglass in my hands grew dark. In the silence that followed, I lay still, afraid at first to even attempt to move. The last whispers of the dead kings, free at least, echoed in my head until they faded to nothing.

When my breathing felt normal, I rose slowly to my feet. The silence around me was profound. I looked up to see Alac standing there, Tucker's arm braced around his chest.

My heart beat furiously against my breastbone as I stepped forward. Alac's expression was unreadable, with so many emotions vying for attention that I couldn't separate one from the other.

"Mara."

I walked forward, holding his gaze like my life depended on it. He straightened, and Tucker removed his arm from Alac's chest. I stopped several paces away, drinking in the curve of his mouth and the shape of his face as he regarded me wordlessly. His face was wet with tears.

"I thought I'd lost you," he said.

A kingdom had been saved, a curse broken—and his first words were for me. I wanted to say all that and more. I wanted to tell him that the victory would have been empty without him. That all along, my heart had known, in its own way, that it would never be able to let him go. Crown or no crown. Kingdom or no kingdom. Magic or no magic.

But no words came. I stood mute, the magic settling into my bones and veins and head as though it had always been there.

He picked up the locket and held it out. "This is yours."

I took it from him, and our fingertips brushed, sending heat beyond the magic's capacities into my deepest insides. The magic in the locket pulsed into my palm and shot effortlessly up my arm, disappearing inside me. Alac sucked in a sharp breath as though hit with sudden pain.

I dropped the locket, which was now cold and impotent, its magic gone. Alac looked at me, his eyes hollow. Looked at me, as though I had cut off his arms.

But then something in his face changed.

"It's gone. The heaviness."

"You were never meant to carry it," I said.

I forced myself, then, to look at Ellian's broken body. She looked so small and empty. And young.

I knelt beside her, wishing I'd been moments quicker before she'd turned on me. "It wasn't her fault."

"Yes, it was." Alac's words sounded bitter. "The magic is strong, but there's still a choice involved. Ellian made hers."

The magic inside me was a silent, swollen tumult. I felt, for the first time, whole.

54

ALAC

I felt as though I'd bathed in the waterfall at Crossford, clean and re-freshed and able to breathe deeply. I'd grown so accustomed to the weight of the magic that I'd forgotten what it felt like to be without it.

To be free.

And there stood Mara, face bright, eyes alight with what could only have been joy. For a hundred years, the magic had been illegitimately claimed and forced into destructiveness. Now she basked in it—wore it the way the night sky displayed its stars.

She was stunning. And oh, she was alive.

I stared for long seconds at Ellian's body, horrified that it had come to this. What chance had she had, really, against the magic? Mara was right—ultimately, it wasn't Ellian's fault.

I knelt, ready to take the body, but Tucker placed his hand on my shoulder.

"I'll take her," he said.

"You hit that wall hard," I said. "Probably you shouldn't carry any-thing right now."

"I'm not an old man anymore."

"I'll do it." I hadn't meant to kill her. The magic had done that on its own.

Yet I had wielded it. I wondered darkly if that's how my father had justified the deaths of those who had fallen lifeless at his feet over the years—it was the magic, not him.

I lifted Ellian's body and cradled it in my arms, her head and one bloodied arm hanging limp. I turned and walked from the chapel, Mara and Tucker close behind. I laid the body on one of the ornate sofas in the sitting room, arranging the arms and hands just so before straightening to face the others.

To face Mara.

"'Thank you' doesn't seem like the right thing to say."

"You don't need to say anything," she said quietly.

"How did you know what to do?"

"I didn't," she said. "I opened myself to the magic, and it came to me. It was a matter of trusting it. Knowing that it was mine."

Hers.

The queen's.

"I heard the voices of the kings," Mara continued, "the ones you said kept calling you."

I shuddered, remembering.

"They weren't calling your name because they wanted you to join them. They were trying to warn you."

I clenched my hands into fists and thought of how the darkness had lifted from Father's eyes moments before he died. *I'm sorry,* he'd said.

"Trapped in death—just as they were trapped in life."

"They're free now," Mara said softly. "I felt them leave."

I wanted to feel sorrow for this final loss of my father, but all I felt was unspeakable relief. The magic was where it belonged now, the curse broken. Perhaps sorrow would come another day.

"I'll see that the body is taken care of," Tucker said.

"Wake Zeth and let him know what's happened," I said. "He can let her parents know." The matter of Milchas's complicity could wait.

"On my way."

"Thanks." I turned to Mara, feeling awkward. "I'll walk you to your quarters."

"That's not necessary." Mara wouldn't look at me.

"Yes, it is." I'd just lost my place in the world. I wasn't going to lose one last opportunity to be with her.

I offered my arm and, after hesitating, she took it. We left the room without a backward glance.

55

MARALYTH

Every inch of me was alive with magic. My skin tingled so that I was sure Alac must be able to feel it through the fabric of his sleeve. We walked in silence, though, and with each step the gulf between us seemed to grow. At the base of the stairway leading to my quarters, he stopped and turned to me.

"What comes next, Mara? Do you intend to take my throne?"

I regarded him in the dim light, trying to read in his eyes the emotion I couldn't discern in his words. "You never wanted the throne. What changed?"

"*I* changed," he said. "And now the curse is gone, and you've taken the magic that's rightfully yours. As king, I can rule without it."

"Do you *want* to?"

"Do *you*?"

The magic sang within me, calling to the wooden trestles in the ceiling, the flowers in the garden. Its reach was beyond anything I'd known, and I felt as though all of Perin Faye dwelled within me. But I couldn't say that to him—not now, while he stood there questioning his future.

"I want what's best for our kingdom," I said. "And I think you do, too."

He nodded. "I do. I'm just not sure what that is."

I reached for his face, but he caught my wrist, gently, and moved it away. "It's late. We should sleep."

My heart suddenly weighed twice as much. "Yes."

The depth of his gaze was greater than I could measure. He looked as though he might say something more, but he remained silent until it became clear that there wasn't anything else to say.

I offered a polite smile. "I can find my way from here."

I turned and walked up the staircase and didn't allow myself to look back at the boy who was not born to be king.

⁓⁓⁓

I stood on my balcony, its undersized fig tree now heavy with several ripened fruits, reminding me of all that had transpired since the day I'd first seen it. The air was cool and fresh, hinting of autumn, and a precise half-moon, nearly set, lent a silvery light to everything below.

Magic swam along the surface of my skin, danced among my bones, flowed in and out of my lungs with every breath. It was always awake now, always ready to do my bidding. I stood at the rail and gazed over the gardens to the vista beyond, my spirit weeping for all the devastation and loss. Yet there was much I could do to restore what had been destroyed. I lifted my hands, palms out, over all that I could and could not see.

"Reverse," I said. "Be restored."

As the magic leaped forth, I became one with every tree, every vine, every blade of grass in the magic's all-encompassing path. It rushed forth like a charging beast, like a storm, restoring the lost years to everything and everyone who still had life. I couldn't bring back the dead; I didn't want to. My heart broke even as the healing flowed, knowing that, for some, the loss had been irreversible.

When I sensed the magic had finished its work, I lowered my palms, which tingled joyously, and went back inside.

I sank into sleep that came quickly, born of the relief of a measureless weight lifted.

⁓⁓⁓

Pale light streamed through my window—bright enough to let me know that the sun had risen hours ago. I rolled onto my back and stretched, luxuriating in the memory of last night's victory, though so much was left unresolved. Moments later, there was a gentle knocking on my door. I slid into my dressing gown and answered.

Zeth stood with two maidservants.

"Good morning, Your Grace," he said.

"Zeth . . ."

The maidservants bobbed curtsies and entered, neither making eye contact with me. They went about their business—whatever that might've been—while I stood staring at Zeth.

"I've taken the liberty of securing guards at your door," he continued. "And I'll have breakfast sent directly."

"Zeth." I wasn't even sure what to say next. "I'm . . . not queen. Not unless—"

"Your army is afield, Your Grace—they arrived at dawn. But I'm sure this can be a peaceful transferal of power. It's my greatest wish that it will be."

"Where's Alac?"

"In his chambers, I'm sure."

"Ask him to meet me in the king's hall in an hour."

Zeth bowed. "Yes, Your Grace."

He left, and I turned to the maidservants, who stood quietly, their hands folded before them. "Is there any way I could get a bath?"

"Yes, Your Grace." Had Zeth instructed them?

This was wrong. I didn't want Alac to simply roll over and allow Zeth to usher me onto the throne that Nelgareth had cleared for me. Almost cleared.

I was bathed and dressed by the time my breakfast arrived. Hungry as I was, I gave myself only enough time to eat a few bites of egg-and-cheese tart. I wrapped a steaming cinnamon biscuit in a napkin and brought it with me as I exited, addressing the guards as I walked away.

"Please attend me to the king's hall," I said.

I'd taken so much from Alac. I would not accept the throne unless he gave it to me.

56

ALAC

I'd been awake since before dawn, my brain sorting through everything that had happened—and what this morning would bring. Now that the sun was at least high enough to cast light into my apartments, I splashed water on my face and lathered it well so I could shave the beard I'd grown in Silverton. I heard the knock through the thickness of the towel as I dried my face.

"Come in."

Enroth entered, dressed in full military uniform and looking as though he'd been up for hours. "Your Grace," he said haltingly. "A great army has arrived, bearing the standards of four lordlands."

"Which?" Aside from Nelgareth, I'd never learned how deep the treachery had reached across the seven lordlands.

"Delthe, Keepings, Tell Doral, and Laine."

My smile was bitter. "With that sort of opposition, Milchas never stood a chance. Make sure he's taken into custody immediately."

"Yes, Your Grace," Enroth said. "Your own troops await my orders."

I grabbed my dressing gown. "Show me."

We walked in silence down shadowed hallways and up the winding stairs of the northern turret. From the battlements, I could just see the army, to the north and west of the vineyard, their colors bright in the morning sun.

"How do they even know she's here?" I asked, mostly to myself.

"Apparently your enemies have been gathering support for a long time." He hesitated. "Considering the rumors, I find I'm questioning the prudence High Minister Zeth's presence at court."

"I'm fully aware that he supports the Dallowyn queen, Enroth."

"I see." It was clear that he didn't see.

I let out a long stream of air. "I need to get dressed. Keep me apprised."

He nodded as I turned and left. Not that I had any idea what to do next; getting dressed simply seemed reasonable. And gave me time to figure out what to do.

Zeth was waiting outside my chambers. He bowed, and I froze.

"Good morning," he said.

No title. Not even "my prince." But why would I expect one?

Words tightened my throat until I had to let them out. "Have you come to move me out of my royal apartments?"

"Of course not. There hasn't been a transfer of power."

Yet, he meant. "Did you even know whether or not Mara would be able to claim the magic?"

"I didn't," Zeth said. "I trusted the magic to instruct whoever finally came to the throne."

"That was a huge risk."

"I've learned to live with taking risks. It was my own ancestor who bribed Wexen for the magic and killed him to take the throne. Restitution was mine to make, more than anyone's."

"Even if it included murder."

"I'm sorry about your family, Alac. Please know that."

"You had no love for them."

"No, I didn't. But—" He looked, for a moment, unsure of how to continue. "It's safe to say that, had I known of Maralyth's plan to save your life, I would have supported her."

I wasn't ready to believe that—not yet. "Did you need something?"

"Only to deliver a message from Lady Maralyth," Zeth said.

At least he hadn't called her queen. "What message?"

"She would like you to meet her in one hour in the king's hall."

"I'll be there." There really wasn't anything else to say.

I had one hour to decide what was right.

❦

I stood outside the doors to the king's hall, familiar angst rushing through me as though I'd been summoned by Father. Strange, how my brain would go there, though everything was different now. I straightened my tunic—chosen with more care than I'd admitted to myself—and entered the hall.

Father and Cannon lay in state on the dais, carefully preserved so that their bodies might last for weeks before showing signs of decay. To allow people from all reaches of the kingdom to file by and pay their respects, if they so desired.

Not many would do so. I was momentarily engulfed by sadness—not for my loss, but for theirs. For Cannon's, for never knowing life outside the shadow of the stolen magic, and for Father, for losing himself so completely and never finding his way back.

A movement caught my eye. Mara stood several feet from Father's body, dressed in a deep blue gown with sleeves so full they hung almost to the floor and gold stitching that caught the light.

All that was missing was a crown.

As I watched, she placed her hand on Father's head. I walked toward her, my boots sounding obnoxiously loud in the cavernous space, but she didn't stir. I kept walking until I stood across from her, Father's body between us.

"You're not bringing him to life, are you?"

She opened her eyes languidly, as though my question hadn't startled her. "No. I can't do that."

"Would you, if you could?"

"I don't think so." She removed her hand from Father's head. "I was only asking his forgiveness."

I nodded, wishing I hadn't walked in during such a private moment.

I cleared my throat. "You wanted to see me?"

"Yes." She walked to the table of state that was still set up where we'd left it. Probably unconsciously, she sat in the king's seat. Queen's.

Perhaps it hadn't been unconscious, after all.

I sat beside her, drinking in her beauty like it was the last time I'd see it. I already knew what I wanted to say to her, but I thought I'd let her speak first.

"My army is on the field," she said, "ready to use force to ensure I take the throne."

"I know."

"And what about your army?"

"Waiting for orders from my military minister," I said.

Mara gazed across the hall as if her thoughts were strolling about, revealing themselves to her in whispered fragments. "This doesn't have anything to do with them. It's between you and me."

"I agree."

"We could let them fight," she went on, "and agree to abide by whichever side won. But I suspect it would be my army's victory; Nelgareth and his allies are a force to be reckoned with."

"I'm sure they are." I wasn't sure where she was going with this.

"But I want to know what *you* want, Alac Thungrave."

Her expression was so earnest that, for a moment, I couldn't find words. When I did, they felt inadequate.

"I'd like to be a good king," I said softly.

"I see."

"There's more." I swallowed the sense of inadequacy that rose inside me like a waking beast. "I've been thinking over my actions since the attempted coup. About how I became so focused on finding you and making you pay for your crimes that I was ineffective. I sent twelve men back home because I wanted to find you myself. And then I sent Tucker back to the castle to summon a guard, all the while assuming nothing could possibly be going wrong here."

"Making mistakes doesn't mean you aren't going to be good at something."

"No, it's doesn't," I said. "But then I thought about you. How you made yourself available to your people, to help them and keep them from being afraid. How you willingly came with me, knowing you'd be imprisoned, because you were willing to sacrifice yourself for a chance to stop the magic. I made most of my choices out of anger; you made choices because you knew they were right."

"I wasn't always sure what was right," Mara said.

"Even so."

She rolled her lips between her teeth and was silent for several moments. Then she folded her hands on the table. "So you do want to be king, and you don't. What is it you want?"

I couldn't tell her I wanted to spend as many waking minutes as possible with her, peering into the depths of her heart and feeling the warmth of her body pressed against mine. Or that the best thing that had come out of this whole, horrible affair was that I'd met her, even though she had come to sanction murder and steal the throne. Or even that I felt, for the first time, like I had the chance for a real life. Not an invisible life as the disposable second-born to a king, or even the life of a ruler on a throne I'd never been prepared for.

"I want you to be queen," I said. "You freed Perin Faye from a century-old curse. You freed *me.* You deserve the rule that's rightfully yours."

She seemed . . . relieved? "And you deserve the freedom to choose the life you want."

"You saved my life," I said. "And since I never got the chance to save yours in return, I guess I can give you a throne instead."

She smiled. "A fair exchange."

"See how easy this was?" Except for the way my heart was pounding.

"If you must know, I'm terrified. I feel . . . unprepared. And alone."

"You won't be alone," I said. "I'll serve you any way I can."

"Thank you, Alac."

She reached for my hand, and I took hers in mine and brought it to my lips, kissing it again and again, tasting the sweetness of her skin and swearing I could feel her trembling.

"Perhaps it's time to talk to the leaders of our armies," she said.

Reluctantly, I released her hand. "You're right."

✑

The meeting of Enroth and the captain of Mara's army was brief. After it was settled that I was voluntarily handing over the throne, word was brought to Nelgareth's—Maralyth's—men that the kingdom was now in the hands of their chosen queen.

Later that afternoon, the king's hall was filled with all the noble families who had been sequestered in the castle after the events of the fateful wedding breakfast. Many soldiers and officers were also in attendance, as well as scores of commoners that Mara had insisted upon allowing in. I caught a glimpse of Nella standing near the servants' entry to my left; she gave me a little nod of encouragement.

"I've always hated public speaking," I said, which made her laugh. Then I faced the crowd.

"After an entire century, the curse of the Thungraves is no longer upon us, thanks to this woman, a true Dallowyn and rightful heir to the throne of Perin Faye. With full heart, I pledge my fealty to Queen Maralyth."

I knelt at her feet, feeling as though I had just bestowed a gift on the entire kingdom. Cheering erupted across the hall. As I rose and swept my gaze across the mass of people, I noticed that some were standing stupidly, staring instead of cheering. But Maralyth didn't seem to notice. She stood, head high, expression serene, facing her people.

I stepped off the dais, thus leaving my royal life forever behind me. No regrets. No sudden realization I'd made a mistake.

And as Maralyth addressed her people for the first time, I had a glimpse of what was to come—a new era for Perin Faye and a chance for me to find my true place in this world.

For the first time in my life, I felt completely free.

57

MARALYTH

The crowd was unbearably large. Zeth and Alac flanked me as guards led us up the aisle of the overflowing hall. I scanned the pressing faces, desperate to find Nestar among them. It was futile, though; there must've been a thousand people in there.

Once we made it into the main foyer, where the crowds were being held back with rope barriers, I touched Alac's arm. "Can you find Nestar for me?"

He nodded, then signaled to Tucker, and the two of them turned toward the crowd. Zeth continued to walk with me to the morning room, a cozy retreat I was glad he'd chosen for me, despite the fact that it wasn't morning.

"That was a beautiful speech, Your Grace," Zeth said.

"Thank you." It had been surprisingly easy to address the horde of people—I just pretended I was talking to Poppa's workers, who were used to my speeches.

"It will take a while to usher everyone out." He stepped aside as servants brought trays of wine and finger foods. "I'll make sure you're alerted when the hallways have cleared. I'm sure you'd like to retire early."

"I would," I said. "But I'll wait here for as long as it takes Alac to find my brother."

He bowed. "As you wish."

It seemed a lifetime of minutes. I alternately sat fingering my empty goblet and pacing from one alcove to the other and back again. The faces of the dead we'd encountered along the road haunted me; Nestar could as easily have been a victim of the magic as anyone else.

Please, Holy God. Please.

And then the door opened, and Alac and Nestar stepped in.

"Nestar." I rushed into his arms and held him, grateful for the sound of his heartbeat against my ear. Then I stepped back and studied him. "You look awful."

He laughed. "I haven't slept. Or eaten." His gaze drifted to the food.

"I'll leave you alone," Alac said.

The gentleness in his voice made my heart do a funny leap. "Thank you."

After he'd gone, I gestured for Nestar to take the seat across from mine. "Eat. I'm not very hungry."

He filled a plate and sat while I poured wine into our goblets. "Fionna red," I said.

"I can smell the bouquet from here." He picked up a tiny, minced venison pie. "I've never seen food like this."

"It's easy to get spoiled."

I sipped wine while he ate, figuring I'd give him a few minutes to fill his belly. But after his third pie and a cheese bun, he set his plate on the table.

"What happened outside the gate?" he asked. "We saw them take you and Alac into custody."

"They did." And I told him everything.

He listened, cramming another pie or two into his mouth as he did so. When I'd finished, he said, "We were having trouble finding good footing for the horses Swish brought us—especially through the areas of dead trees where many had fallen over. We finally decided to stay on the road, figuring the odds of his looking over his shoulder and knowing we were following were pretty low."

"He never saw you."

Nestar took a deep swallow of wine. "When we came upon the soldiers, it took us a minute or two to realize you were in trouble. I dismounted and sneaked through the trees to catch whatever snatches of conversation I could before they led you into the city. I heard enough to understand that Ellian Milchas meant to have you both tried for treason."

"Then what did you do?"

"We rode back to tell the others. I hoped there was still a chance that you'd been successful, and when morning came, I realized there weren't any magic strands anywhere and knew you'd somehow gotten the job done. That didn't mean you weren't still in danger, though, so I gathered people together, sent out the word that we'd walk to Crownhold and declare for our queen."

"*You* brought that crowd?"

"Well, not only me. And some of those people were from Crownhold. Everyone was ready to demand your release." His eyes were bright, his voice animated. It was as though he'd come to life in a way I'd never seen.

"I want to ask you something," I said.

"As long as you keep feeding me, you can ask whatever you want." He took another cheese bun.

"Would you be happier here than at home?"

He stopped midchew. "Happier?"

"I mean . . . it's a big decision, and it would be a difficult conversation to have with Poppa, but—"

"Mara, what are you even talking about?"

"I'd like you to stay here and be on my counsel. There's nobody I trust more."

Nestar stared. "Are you serious?"

"I am."

He wiped his mouth with his thumb. "I don't know what to say."

"You can think about it."

"I don't need to think about it. I mean—I never thought I'd leave the vineyards, but . . . now that I'm here, I can't imagine going back."

I smiled. "You can think about it, Nestar. Truly."

"The only thing I have to think about is what I'll say to Father."

"That sounds like a yes."

It was his turn to smile. "It is. Though I'm not sure about living here. It's so . . . big."

"I'm pretty sure the food makes up for the wasted space."

His smile turned into a grin. "Thank you, Mara."

"You'll need a bath first, of course."

"Do you think so? Actually, I was planning to leave first thing in the morning to fetch Father to bring him here to see you. It'll be the perfect time to talk with him."

My heart sang at the thought of finally, finally relieving Poppa's heart of its sorrow. "Oh, yes! And do come right away—my coronation is in eight days."

"I can hardly wait to tell him you're alive and well," Nestar said. "And when I tell him you're queen . . ."

"I would love to see his face."

"You will, soon enough." He raised his cup. "To new beginnings." I raised mine. "And to Poppa."

His joy would make mine all the greater.

⚬∾⚬

Eight days wasn't nearly enough time to prepare for my coronation. I stood in the barely-light morning, stifling a yawn and trying not to slouch as the seamstresses completed a final fitting of the sumptuous gown I'd be wearing—pale gold damask with sleeves that trailed well past my knees. I wondered how I'd move my arms without slinging someone in the face.

"Your Grace." Zeth bowed at the entryway to the crowded chamber. "Forgive the intrusion, but your family has arrived."

My heart leaped into my throat; it was all I could do to remain still while one of the seamstresses knotted off a final stitch. "Where are they?"

"I had them brought to the solarium."

Zeth had barely departed when I began to wriggle my way from the gown, impervious to the dismayed sounds from the women around me.

"Your Grace, mind the sleeve," one of them said.

As soon as I was free from the puddle of gown, I dove into a simple dress of deep purple, waving away offers of help and tying the bodice as I hastened from the room.

"No escort required," I said to the guards at the door as I hurried past them and made my way up the corridor, anticipation swelling inside me like a thousand ripening grapes.

I saw them before they saw me—Poppa and Nestar, standing stiffly in the middle of the windowed space, Poppa with his hands behind his back, just so. Words thickened in my throat as they found their way out.

"Poppa."

I ran forward, and he caught me in his arms. I held onto him as though I were four years old and afraid of thunder. When he finally stilled, he pulled back and looked at me, his eyes wet and shining.

"I thought I'd lost you."

"I'm sorry I couldn't find a way to let you know."

Poppa shook his head. "Don't ever apologize for the actions of others, Mara." He looked me up and down. "And you! Queen of Perin Faye! I'm afraid it took your brother at least an hour to get me to believe him."

I caught Nestar's eye, asking him a silent question with my eyebrow. His slight nod told me he'd shared his plans with Poppa.

"It's a long story," I said.

Poppa squeezed my hand. "I want to hear it all. Every word."

We sat in streams of rising sunlight and feasted on soft-boiled eggs and buttery biscuits with pomegranate preserves, though I only picked at my food while I told my story, from the abduction to the moment when Alac decided to walk away from the throne. I didn't speak much of the magic—only hints and vague descriptions. Enough to let Poppa know it was real.

"How much did you know about Mother?" I asked when I'd finished.

Poppa's sigh was deep and heavy. "I knew that her husband had been executed for treason and that she feared for her life. She didn't say much about . . . magic."

"So she lied to you."

"No, Mara," Poppa said. "She came to me desperate and nearly starved to death. After we'd fallen in love, she told me the real reason why she'd run. But she also told me it was all in the past, and asked me never to bring it up again. I loved her, so I didn't."

I had to ask. "Did she use magic to make her hair go silver?"

"She did. It was the only allowance she gave herself to use the magic."

"And you never guessed that, maybe, I had the magic, too?"

"I guessed," he said. "But I didn't want to believe it."

"Well, I never guessed," Nestar said. "Though it always bothered me how much better the vines did once you started spending time in the fields."

"Mother forbade me to use the magic," I said. "But I couldn't stop. It would've been like trying to make the blood stop running through my veins."

Poppa's eyes held so much wonder. "And now you're queen."

"And now I'm queen," I whispered.

He reached across the table and curled his big hand over mine. "You never were happy in the kitchen."

I grinned, joy streaming through me in increasing waves. "But I was always happy to be with you, Poppa. Both of you."

Poppa's eyes shone. He pressed his lips together and said nothing.

"And I'm already working to dismantle the royal subsidy on Graylaern Vineyards," I said. "We'll still be the best in the kingdom, of course, but from now on it will be fair trade—for Graylaern and everyone else." I leaned forward conspiratorially. "You'll be rich, Poppa."

He laughed. "I'm already rich, with a daughter and son like this sitting before me. But thank you. No one is better suited to knowing the needs of Delthe's vintners. You'll be our champion."

"Hero, even," Nestar said.

I threw a bit of biscuit at his face.

"I'm not sure how to act at a coronation," Nestar then said. "You sure you don't want us to wait outside?"

"Don't be silly," I said. "I couldn't do this without both of you there."

And I meant it. The pieces of my world had come together again, making everything nearly perfect.

Nearly. But it was more than I might've hoped for a couple weeks ago.

"Your Grace." Nina stood just inside the solarium entrance. "It's time for you to dress."

I wrinkled my nose and leaned across the table. "It takes at least an hour to get the gown on," I whispered.

I left them smiling at the table, my heart too full to worry about the impending weight of the crown that would soon grace my head.

"After you, Nina," I said. Then I raised my chin and followed her to my chambers.

⁓∞⁓

"You're actually going to wear that thing?" Nestar gestured to the ridiculously long cape that lay draped across two seats in the small anteroom next to the king's hall.

"Not for long," I said. "It weighs as much as I do."

There was a knock, and Alac stuck his head through the door, sending heat to my face that I hoped no one else could see.

"It's time," he said.

"We'd best find our places, then." Poppa kissed me on the cheek. "I'm proud of you."

I smiled. "I know, Poppa."

My two attendants slid the ridiculous cape onto my shoulders while Alac approached, looking his part in a teal tunic with crimson trim—the colors of the house of Dallowyn.

"You look . . . stunning," he said.

"If I fall over, will you pick me up?"

"I don't know. It might be more dramatic to let you lie there."

He waited until the attendants had curtsied themselves from the room. Then he took both my hands and held them at arm's length, his gaze sweeping over me so that I felt he was drinking me with his eyes.

"Stop," I whispered.

"I'm simply admiring my queen."

"You take defeat rather lightly."

"You didn't defeat me. I let you win."

It was the lighthearted game we'd played for the past eight days, dancing around whatever real feelings we might share. We'd made a silent understanding that now wasn't the time to pursue whatever had grown between us.

"Let's get this over with," I said.

He smiled. "I'll meet you on the dais."

He held the door while I swept through with my layers of gown and miles of cape. I waited while he made his way up the aisle that cut through the pressing crowd; then I took my place in the doorway to await the sounding of the trumpets.

This wasn't a life I had imagined for myself, but it was one I was ready to embrace.

∝∽

Alac and I sat on the balcony of my quarters, where he'd visited me the morning after the Welcome Supper. It would be several more weeks before the king's chambers—now the queen's—would be fully refurbished, the chapel converted into a private library.

Alac took another sip of his Fionna white, then rolled the goblet between his hands. After the exhaustion of the coronation banquet, I'd thought that a quiet evening with him sounded perfect. Now, I wasn't sure it was such a good idea. There was a strangeness between us I couldn't account for.

"Do you remember when you caught me with the fig in my hands?" I asked.

"Of course. You looked adorably guilty."

"That's because I'd just used my magic to ripen it," I said. "I thought you'd seen me."

He shook his head. "All I could see were your eyes. And the shape of your mouth."

The hot longing I'd suppressed for days rose unbidden. I took a sip of my wine to cool it.

"I've talked with your father," Alac said. "I told him how I'd always been interested in winemaking."

"Oh?"

"Yes. And . . ." Something in the way he hesitated made my stomach turn over. "He offered to apprentice me. Said that it was good timing, since your brother won't be returning."

I looked at him, his words failing to register. "You're . . . leaving?"

"Only with your blessing," he said. "And only for a while."

"But . . ." Hadn't he promised to serve me?

He placed his goblet on the balcony rail and drew his arms around my waist. "I care about you too much to stay here and wonder if you have feelings for me because you feel sorry for me, or owe me, or are trying to make up for the complicated past that brought us where we are right now. Zeth will be here, and now Nestar, too. I can spend a season in the vineyards with your father and try my hand at something I've always longed to do. And when I come back—if you'll let me—I'll plant a vineyard right here. For you."

"I'd like that." But my voice felt like mostly air.

"So . . . will you release me? Your Grace?"

I met his eyes in the starlight and couldn't speak. Couldn't breathe. Instead, I cupped my hand around his evening-stubbled cheek.

He pulled me to him, his lips meeting mine with such intensity that everything inside me melted. We kissed until we were breathless, until I'd tipped my goblet and spilled wine down the side of his tunic, until we laughed in each other's arms before finding each other's mouths again, our kisses made richer by the taste of wine.

Poppa's wine. The prize of Perin Faye.

"Go," I said, my heart pattering against his. "And then come back to me."

"You won't marry some imbecilic nobleman? Or a power-grasping princeling from Northland?"

I smiled. "No. As long as you don't take up with some vintner's daughter."

"Hmm." He took the goblet from my hand and placed it beside his. "I think I may have already done that."

I smiled against his mouth and lost myself in his arms while the flowers and vines in the garden below sang music to my soul.

ACKNOWLEDGMENTS

Once upon a time, I believed I could never write a novel. Then I wrote one, and it was horrible. That first, terrible story was called *The Seeds of Perin Faye,* and it's what *The Stolen Kingdom* was born from. Seeing this book in print has brought me full circle—it was Maralyth and Alac and Nestar and Nelgareth who ushered me into this wondrous world of novel writing, and now I'm able to share their (different and much stronger) story with everyone. I couldn't be more thankful.

Immeasurable thanks to my agent, Danielle Burby, whose eleventh-hour editorial input truly made *The Stolen Kingdom* what it is, and without whom I wouldn't be where I am today. Thanks also to my editor, Rachel Bass, who took the reins deftly and graciously and is a delight to work with.

Special thanks to Elayne Becker, who stayed on board after she left Tor Teen, offering her editorial genius and helping to bring the vision we shared for this novel to fruition. I couldn't have done this without her!

Special thanks also to Maggie Boehme, daughter, colleague, and friend, who gave Maralyth her name and *The Stolen Kingdom* its title, and whose edits, insight, opinions, and words of encouragement are an integral part of every story I write.

I'm forever grateful for Constance Lopez, for reading, critiquing, and commiserating—her balance of empathy and keen insight is priceless. Thanks also to Nelson Literary's Angie Hodapp for her helpful critique, and to Rena Rossner for being a reader, sounding board, and friend.

To my personal cheerleaders: Jamie Soranno, my "baby" sister who continues to make me feel as though I could conquer the world; my parents, Janet and Mockie Schafer, who have the cover of *Stormrise* framed and hanging on their living room wall (with space for *The Stolen Kingdom*); Rachel Boehme, whose gift of affirmation is one of the greatest in my life; and Angela Pasquini Clifford, who probably has no idea how much she has encouraged me along the way—thank you all for *being here*.

To all the readers who celebrated *Stormrise* and have embraced *The Stolen Kingdom* with great enthusiasm—thank you! I'm honored and blessed and humbled to know that my stories are touching your lives.

To Jonathan, Maggie, Rachel, Spencer, and Molly: Regardless of my accomplishments as an author, I am always proudest to be your mom.

To my husband Eric: You first traveled to Perin Faye years ago, when I handed my wobbly, inaugural novel to you chapter by chapter. You read, though you didn't like fantasy (oh, how that has changed); you critiqued, though you knew nothing about the art of the novel (neither did I); you believed in me, though I often didn't believe in myself. Thank you for taking this journey with me, my love.

To Jesus Christ, my Lord and Savior: All that I am, all that I do, is because of you.

For there is nothing that God cannot do.—Luke 1:37

ABOUT THE AUTHOR

JILLIAN BOEHME is the author of *Stormrise* and is known to the online writing community as Authoress, hostess of *Miss Snark's First Victim,* a blog for aspiring authors. In real life, she holds a degree in music education, sings with the Nashville Symphony Chorus, and homeschools her remaining youngster-at-home. She's still crazy in love with her husband of more than thirty years and is happy to be surrounded by family and friends amid the rolling knolls of Middle Tennessee.